THE WIDOWED COUNTESS

LINDA RAE SANDE

This is a work of fiction. The events and characters described herein are imaginary and are not intended to refer to specific places or living persons. The opinions expressed in this manuscript are solely the opinions of the author and do not represent the opinions or thoughts of the publisher. The author has represented and warranted full ownership and/or legal right to publish all the materials in this book.

The Widowed Countess

ISBN: 978-0-9893973-6-0

V1.6

PRINTED IN THE UNITED STATES OF AMERICA

To Jocko, Dan, Jimmy, Sean, Nick, Alex, Ross, Joss, J.J. and all the other men who live to inspire

OTHER ROMANCES BY LINDA RAE SANDE

The Daughters of the Aristocracy

The Kiss of a Viscount

The Grace of a Duke

The Seduction of an Earl

The Sons of the Aristocracy

Tuesday Nights

The Widowed Countess

My Fair Groom

The Sisters of the Aristocracy

The Story of a Baron

The Passion of a Marquess

The Desire of a Lady

The Brothers of the Aristocracy

The Love of a Rake

The Caress of a Commander

The Epiphany of an Explorer

The Widows of the Aristocracy

The Gossip of a Earl

The Enigma of a Widow

The Secrets of a Viscount

The Widowers of the Aristocracy

The Dream of a Duchess

The Vision of a Viscountess

The Conundrum of a Clerk

The Charity of a Viscount

The Cousins of the Aristocracy

The Promise of a Gentleman

The Pride of a Gentleman

The Holidays of the Aristocracy

The Christmas of a Countess

Stella of Akrotiri

Deminon

Chapter 1

PARLOR AND PILLOW TALK

March 1817

Clarinda Fitzwilliam, Countess of Norwick, greeted her morning callers with her usual grace and happy demeanor, complimenting Lady Torrington on her gorgeous gold and blue morning gown and relaying her good wishes to Lady Pettigrew on the just-announced betrothal of her oldest niece to the eldest son of a marquess. The two women had appeared at the front door of the Park Lane mansion at exactly ten o'clock, as if they carried chronometers and timed their arrival to exactly match when it was acceptable to pay a call on a lady of the *ton*. Clarinda did not mind; she received callers nearly every morning at ten and paid her calls in the afternoons, timing her visits so they would end just as she was to make her way to Hyde Park for the fashionable hour.

She pulled the bell to summon a maid, nodding when the young girl appeared and curtsied. Asking for tea wasn't necessary. All the maids in Norwick House knew to deliver a tea cart if they were summoned to the parlor.

"I must warn you that I may have to *briefly* take my leave of you," Clarinda spoke in a lowered voice to her visitors, her slightly amused expression indicating she was letting them in on a joke. "I believe Lord Norwick is having one of his mornings." She said this last with a roll of her eyes, implying her husband might require her presence to soothe his grouchy countenance. As if on cue, the bellowing voice of David Fitzwilliam made its way into the parlor. "Porter! Where the hell is Lady Norwick?"

Despite expecting the summons, Clarinda was still a bit startled. "Oh, dear," she murmured, a hand coming up to her bosom as she watched her callers' faces suddenly turn more pale than they already were, while her own took on the blush of a chit fresh out of the schoolroom. "Adele, could you see to the tea for me, please? I'll be just a few moments," she said as she stood and made her way to the parlor door, her teal silk day gown swishing about her long legs as she moved.

"But, of course, Clarinda," Lady Torrington answered, her brow rising. "Is everything ...?"

Clarinda waved a hand through the air and turned before she made her way over the threshold. "He will be *fine*," she assured her friends, wondering for that brief moment if *she* would be fine—she was having a hard time calming the excitement she felt at her very core. "He has some important meeting with someone today, and it's his valet's day off," she added with a shake of her head before disappearing into the hallway.

Despite being married to David Fitzwilliam for nearly four years, she still responded to the man as she had that first night they'd met at the now-late Earl of Everly's ball while admiring the current Earl of Everly's tank of tropical fish. Her pulse raced, her breasts swelled, heat pooled between her thighs and she ached for his lips on hers. By the time she reached the top of the stairs, she was nearly running in anticipation. She didn't need to knock on the earl's bedchamber door; it stood wide open. She peeked in, a tooth catching her lower lip and her eyes bright as she regarded her handsome husband.

He glanced at her, his harsh expression softening as he motioned for her to enter.

Clarinda stepped into the room and shut the door behind her, driving home the lock as she kept her hands behind her back and regarded him with an elegantly arched eyebrow.

"I cannot decide between the dark blue or the scarlet," David growled as he regarded his reflection in a cheval mirror. Two topcoats were spread out on the bed's counterpane, their haphazard placement a testament to his having pulled on both of them before bellowing for his wife.

Pushing away from the door, Clarinda slowly walked up to stand in front of her husband. He was at least six inches taller than she, his dark brown hair reflecting a few golden highlights in the morning sun that made its way through the east window. Although David was nearly forty, he only looked it when he scowled, an expression he used to frighten the servants in Norwick House and the footmen at Parliament. Square-jawed, with cheekbones that could have been chiseled in stone and brown eyes under dark lashes and straight brows, he was a very handsome man. No one would expect him to be an aristocrat, for his nose was broader than a blade, and it didn't sport the hook that so many of the lords seemed to have inherited from some common ancient ancestor.

Clarinda regarded her husband with a gaze that swept slowly down his broad-shouldered body, as if she was taking stock of his crisp, white cravat, gold waistcoat, white linen shirt, and buff breeches. She barely noticed the clothing, though, remembering instead what he had looked like earlier that morning when she'd woken to find him sprawled on her bed. Naked, aroused and thoroughly male, he had her begging for his manhood even before he could strip the night rail from her body. His lips had performed their magic on her throat and breasts, his tongue tracing moist lines down her belly and his fingers expertly sliding into the swollen, honeyed folds between her thighs. He had her so aroused, she gave into the release of ecstasy and was shocked when he thrust himself into her so fast and so hard, she nearly fainted from the second wave of pleasure that tossed her body as if she were a rag doll.

Aware that her husband was watching her, she dared a glance at him through the veil of her dark lashes. From his gaze, she wondered if he was remembering the same thing she was. Reaching out, she slid the palm of her hand against the ridge of his hardening erection, the fabric of his breeches separating her hand from his skin. She heard him hiss, felt his entire body go rigid. With her free hand, she deftly undid the placket buttons of his breeches, removing her hand from the fabric only to reestablish her grip on his naked arousal. Her thumb passed over the bulbous head, already wet and throbbing from her brief ministrations.

"Clare," David forced out between clenched teeth, the word not indicating if she should stop or if she should continue.

Clarinda reached down with three fingers of her other hand and slowly lifted his balls, using her middle finger to stroke the dip between them at the same time her other hand slid down the length of his shaft, squeezing the velvety steel rod as hard as she could. Bucking suddenly, David let out a growl and grabbed her shoulders with both hands, as if to steady himself. Repeating the strokes, Clarinda could feel his body give way, knew in a moment he would be caught in ecstasy and unable to stop his release. She quickly lowered her head, bent her knees to the Aubusson carpet, and slipped her mouth over the head of his erection, feeling a great deal of satisfaction at the sound he emitted when her stroking tongue performed its magic on him.

David's sudden and rather loud curse could be heard throughout the entire household and quite possibly by some of the grooms in the carriage house behind the mansion. For a fleeting second, Clarinda wondered what the two older ladies in the parlor were thinking.

She hoped they wouldn't send a footman for a Bow Street Runner.

Running her tongue over his tip again, Clare once more

suckled him as hard as she dared with her lips. The actions incited another reflexive jerk and a curse that sounded suspiciously like a prayer of thanksgiving.

"Jesus, Clare," David breathed heavily, his entire body seeming to slump as she slowly withdrew her hands and quickly buttoned his breeches, acting as if she hadn't just had her wicked way with him. "What the ..?" he started to ask, his eyes closed. His question was stopped as her lips took purchase on his, wet and tasting like sex. Even before he could command his lips to return the kiss, Clarinda gently pulled away and regarded the two topcoats spread out on the counterpane, her manner suddenly all business.

"And what of the russet coat?" she wondered, thinking there should be a third choice that would look so much better with the breeches he wore.

David, his breaths still a bit short, got out another curse under his breath. "One of Everly's damnable fish splashed water all over it," he replied, his furrowed brows indicating a hint of disgust.

Clarinda's eyebrow arched up again, her lips barely curling. Even at a quick glance, David could tell she was trying to suppress a much larger grin of amusement. "One of his *goldfish?*" she wondered, trying to remember if any of the adventurer's tropical fish were large enough to cause a water splash capable of ruining David's best topcoat. Their glass aquarium was rather voluminous, but the fish inside were all on the small side.

"No," David replied with a shake of his head. "Something rather larger. Much larger. He called it a tiger shark. Damn thing nearly drowned me." At Clarinda's serious look of stunned surprise, he added, "I swear, those fish of Everly's will be the death of me," David claimed, not bothering to apologize for any of his frequent curses.

Clarinda rolled her eyes as she regarded her husband. "I do not understand how it is you cannot get along with his fish," she replied cheerfully. "They're in a giant tank. Swimming about in *water*," she added, one hand waving in the air as if it was a fin.

"Water!" he affirmed. "And when they see me, they start jumping about as if I plan to eat them, which I would gladly do if I was ever allowed in his house with my fishing pole. Cook could make those little beasties into quite a delectable appetizer," he vowed with a cocked eyebrow.

The thought of fish made into *anything* caused Clarinda's stomach to take a tumble just then. She forced herself to quickly swallow as she reached over to where the blue cutaway coat lay on the bed.

"Wear the dark blue, my lord," she stated as she opened it and held it out for him, brass buttons gleaming in the morning light that shone from the window. "With that waistcoat and those breeches, you'll look like you're in the army if you wear the scarlet."

Her husband blinked at her, his gaze almost doe-eyed as he took in the sight of her slightly flushed face, almond shaped aquamarine eyes, and perfectly coiffed brunette hair. One thick lock was curled and hung in front of one shoulder. And she was wearing the teal day gown he so liked, its elegant silk skirts almost revealing the shape of her bottom and the lines of her long legs when she walked. The bodice was snug enough that her breasts had to mound just a bit above the neckline. "Yes, my lady," he replied, sliding his arms into the coat, his legs still a bit unsteady beneath him. The thought of fish appetizers was long forgotten.

"Do have a good meeting," she said, her lips curling just a bit as one eyebrow arched up. Although she was curious as to where and whom he might be seeing, she did not ask. As long as he wasn't off to a brothel or a liaison with a supposedly bereft widow, Clarinda did not pay much mind to his destinations. However, if she discovered he hadn't honored his marriage vows—and, according to the investigator that occasionally sent her notes as to her husband's comings and goings, he had been faithful—she knew he would regret the poor choice. She would no longer make herself available *in that way*. Nor would she put up with his cursing or do to him the kind of wicked things like she'd just done as he struggled over what to wear.

Having not yet given him an heir, Clarinda knew she held the upper hand when it came to her husband's behavior. Knowing that was about to change, though, she feared he might return to his premarital bad boy behaviors. Prior to his announcement nearly five years ago that he intended to seek a wife, his reputation had him employing multiple mistresses, secretly owning a brothel catering to gentlemen (an establishment he was said to frequent so he might personally sample the merchandise) and, more publicly, owning a men's club that served only the very best liquors and employed only the very best courtesans in London.

David regarded her with an expression suggesting he knew exactly what she was thinking. His hand slid down to her belly, covering it protectively. "It's about estate matters, nothing more, I promise," he whispered before kissing her on the forehead.

Clarinda gave him a brilliant smile, secretly pleased she had demanded he honor his marriage vows all those years ago. She might have caused a great deal of grief among the ladies of the evening as a result, and perhaps had garnered the envy of several ladies of the *ton* who could not claim the same level of fidelity from their own husbands, but she had no regrets. As a daughter of an earl, she'd had more than her fair share of suitors from the night of her come-out; she wasn't about to accept anything less than good behavior from the man she agreed to marry. "I really must get back to the parlor. I do hope Lady Pettigrew hasn't asked Porter to call for a constable," she said with a teasing grin, one eyebrow arcing up.

His eyes widening in alarm, David straightened. "You have *callers*?" he whispered hoarsely, the look of shock replacing his normally stoic expression. "You minx!"

"It's after ten, my lord," she countered with a sly grin. She gave her husband a deep curtsy before backing up to the door and unlocking it. "Do have a good trip." And then she hurried back down the stairs and through the hall, catching her reflection in one mirror and deciding she didn't look as if she'd just had her way with her husband. At least, not quite. She rearranged the lock of hair over one shoulder as it had been done earlier by her maid.

Clarinda slowed her steps as she reached the parlor and glided to the chair she had vacated only moments before. "I do so apologize for the interruption," she murmured as she sat down and reached for the cup and saucer Lady Torrington offered her. She couldn't help but notice the look of worry on Adele Grandby's face as the older woman regarded her. When she was sure Lady Pettigrew's attention was on her teacup, she gave Adele a wink. "I really don't know what our men would do without our fashion sense," Clarinda added with a grin, hoping to put her guests at ease once more.

"We would go about looking like we're in the army instead of like the aristocrats we are," her husband suddenly announced from the parlor door, his voice not giving any hint as to whether he was teasing or serious.

All three ladies jumped at the sound of his voice, their heads quickly turning in his direction. David bowed as the ladies all stood up and gave the earl their very best curtsies. "Lady Torrington, Lady Pettigrew," he said in turn as he gave each a deep bow. "Pray excuse me for just one moment," he said as he held up a finger. He made his way to where his wife stood, and without warning, wrapped one arm behind her shoulders, another around her waist, dipped her backwards, and bestowed a rather indecorous kiss on her lips.

While neither Lady Torrington nor Lady Pettigrew fainted, they both seemed to seat themselves rather heavily into their chairs, their mouths left hanging open as David slowly raised Clarinda back up to an unsteady standing position. "I'm off to my meeting with the solicitor. I shall find you later on Rotten Row," he said with an arched eyebrow as he kissed his stunned wife once more on the temple before bowing and taking his leave of the ladies in the parlor, a huge smile on his face.

Stunned for only a moment more, all three ladies began to giggle, Clarinda more so than her two callers.

It would be the last time she did so for a very long time.

Chapter 2

DEATH TAKES DAVID

"Are you sure there isn't something else I can get for you, milady?" Missy wondered, her worried expression making her appear much older than her two-and-twenty years. "Mayhap a cup o' chocolate?" The maid had been flitting about the bedchamber for nearly a half-hour, as if she was afraid to leave Clarinda alone.

The countess had managed to keep the tears at bay for some time after the prune-faced constable appeared at the door claiming her husband had died in a traffic accident. Her first reaction had been that someone—her younger brother or one of David's rakehell friends from White's—had sent the man to make the claim as a joke. But then Milton Grandby, Earl of Torrington, appeared looking as if he'd seen a ghost, and Clarinda knew it was true—David Fitzwilliam, Earl of Norwick, was dead. A broken neck, the constable said, suffered when David was thrown from his horse in Oxford Street while on his way home from having met with his solicitor in the man's office in Bell Yard.

Remembering the overwhelming sense of loss she felt at the moment Grandby appeared, Clarinda's hand moved to rest on her belly. *At least David knew.* She hadn't even told him— she hadn't needed to say anything. The week before, he had simply placed his hand there and given her a look of profound adoration. Then he had made love to her with slow, torturous and thoroughly satisfying kisses, his manhood filling her completely while he barely moved inside her. When they both fractured, he'd captured her mouth with his so her screams would be muted and his growls would vibrate through her body as much as they did his. He had stayed in her bed that night and every night since, locking the door and insisting she sleep naked against him, either tucked up against the front of his body as he spooned her or atop him as his arms anchored her to his chest and their legs tangled together.

Tonight, she wore her night rail, the billowing fabric suddenly feeling tight around her legs and the ribbon closure feeling as if it was choking her. But she knew the constriction in her throat was due to unshed tears. She needed to be alone so she could weep in peace. "No, Missy," she finally answered the abigail. "I won't need you the rest of the night. Get some sleep," she ordered, trying not to sound cross but suddenly wanting her privacy. She nodded as Missy bobbed a curtsy before taking her leave of her mistress.

The door latch had just clicked when Clarinda felt the hot tears stream down her temples and seep into the fine bed linens. David would never share her bed again, never again hold his hand against her growing belly, never see the babe that would be born in less than six months.

Sobbing, Clarinda thought of how compassionate Grandby had been, concerned because there wasn't an heir for the Norwick earldom—at least, not yet. And if she carried a girl, then ... She sobbed again, hoping beyond hope she carried David's son.

In the meantime, Grandby saw to it a dispatch was sent by courier to Daniel Fitzwilliam, informing David's younger twin brother of the accident. A streak of fear shot through Clarinda as she thought of what would happen to Norwick House, of what would be done with the household staff, of what might become of her now that Daniel Fitzwilliam would be acting in his brother's stead.

Clarinda moved both hands to her belly, covering it protectively. She hadn't seen nor heard from Daniel in nearly two years, their last meeting so strained she was sure he hated her.

At one time, she had been fond of the man, the man who would have been the Earl of Norwick had he been born just a few minutes earlier. But David had had that honor. He'd been the heir to the earldom, assuming the role when their father had died a decade ago. Daniel had merely been the spare. And Clarinda, betrothed to the eldest, took her place as David's bride in a marriage some assumed would be a marriage of convenience that instead turned out to be a celebrated love match.

Looking back, she wondered if it would have made a difference which twin she ended up marrying—at the time, they seemed almost interchangeable. But Daniel seemed to harden as he grew older, his bitterness more noticeable and his manner more severe with the years. As far as Clarinda knew, he hadn't taken a wife, instead opting for what she assumed was a string of mistresses and immersing himself in estate work in Sussex. His brief letters to David were all about business, their content never hinting the two shared the same mother, a woman of five-and-fifty who occupied the dowager house on one of the earl's properties near the southern shore in Bognor. Nor did his letters ask about Clarinda.

She had never intended to hurt him—she didn't realize she *had* when she formally agreed to marry David. But Daniel had never looked at her quite the same way again.

And now, the spare would be the earl, if the child she carried turned out to be a girl. And if she carried David's son, Daniel would still need to assume the duties of the earldom until such time that his nephew could be properly educated, as all gentlemen were, and taught to perform those duties required of an earl, including taking his seat in Parliament.

A modiste would arrive on the morrow with a collection of hastily assembled widow's weeds. Clarinda's maid, accompanied by a footman, would be dispatched to the shops in Bond Street to secure several black bonnets and slippers. And a funeral service would take place in a few days. At some point after the service, the solicitor would come to Norwick House to read the will.

Another stab of fear shot through Clarinda, effectively ending her tears. Had David made sure his affairs were in order? Was that why he had met with his solicitor earlier that day? She shouldn't be so concerned for her own future—she might be carrying the heir to the earldom—but given the circumstances of Daniel's last visit to her, she couldn't help but wonder if he still felt anger toward her, as if she had somehow betrayed him by marrying his brother. Until that day two years ago, she hadn't known he felt affection for her, hadn't known he intended to ask for her hand when she married David.

Falling into a fitful sleep, Clarinda tried to imagine David and instead found Daniel's visage hovering in front of her, his lips, indeed, his entire face looking exactly like David's as those lips moved to cover hers. Firm and soft as silk, they touched hers briefly and then took purchase, rending her breathless as the power of the kiss took hold and consumed her. She returned the kiss as best she could, her experience so limited to David's kisses, she wasn't prepared for Daniel's tongue to stroke against hers, wasn't prepared for the sensations that coursed through her body, wasn't prepared when Daniel's hand moved from her jawline down the side of her throat and over the top of one breast until his palm captured it completely and began kneading it through her gown and chemise and corset.

The jolt through her body was so sudden, so unexpected, she jerked away and had to inhale as deeply as possible. Her eyes wide, she stared up to find David's face hovering over her.

At least, she was fairly certain it was David.

"David?" she whispered, her eyes blinking quickly.

He made a low sound in his throat that might have been a chuckle. "I should hope so, or I shall have to admonish you for cuckolding me," he said with a cocked eyebrow. One of his hands reached out to her face, his thumb outlining the bottom of her lip as his expression changed to one more serious. "I love you, Clare," he murmured, his thumb moving to caress her jaw. "I don't think I mentioned that before I left you this morning." In the darkness, his brown eyes appeared almost black, but there was adoration there, adoration and perhaps a bit of mischief.

Clare shook her head, staring at her husband in disbelief. "No. I don't believe you did," she murmured. *Did he ever, though*? The thought crossed her mind so quickly, it barely registered. "But you certainly showed it with that daring move you made in the parlor," she countered, her face suddenly lighting up in delight. "As a proper lady, I probably should have swooned." She didn't add that she thought Lady Pettigrew would have hit the floor before her—and the older woman was merely a witness.

David lifted one of her hands to his lips and kissed the back of her fingers before turning the hand over in his and kissing her palm. Clare's inhalation of breath could barely be heard in the stillness. "You never did tell me you were expecting a baby," he accused, his lips moving to kiss her wrist.

Clare smiled at that. "I didn't need to, did I?" she answered, a tooth catching her lower lip. "You just ... knew." She sucked in a breath as his kiss moved to the inside of her elbow, his lips so feather light on her skin they tickled more than tantalized. "How ... how *did* you know?" she wondered then, her whisper barely audible.

David made the low sound in his throat again, his face breaking into a grin. "You were suddenly ... more beautiful ... even more so than the day we married." He settled his elbow into the mattress, his head held up in the palm of his hand. "You looked like a Madonna the way you glowed, this halo of light surrounding you, especially at night, like you could light my way when I came into your room. In fact, I could find you no matter what room you were in." His head moved then and she felt his lips brush her forehead.

Closing her eyes, Clarinda sighed. "This is the longest I've carried a babe," she whispered. She heard David's murmur of agreement.

David had known about the first miscarriage. He'd been in the study when her anguished cries filtered from her bedchamber, her sobs so violent from the grief of her loss—their loss—David thought she would die. He stayed with her the rest of that day and the entire night, arguing with the physician over her care and ordering her maid to leave once it was clear nothing more could be done. He finally collapsed in exhaustion the following morning, wrapping his body around hers in what she remembered as a cocoon of comfort and warmth.

The second miscarriage—David wasn't at home that day — Clarinda suffered by herself. Only her maid, Missy, and the physician she had sent for knew what happened. She hadn't even known she was enceinte, so it was not nearly as frightening as the first one. Not wanting David to know, Clarinda begged the doctor and Missy to say nothing of it to anyone.

"The third time is the charm," David said, leaning down to again place a kiss on her forehead.

Gasping, Clarinda stared at her husband, a look of shock crossing her face. "You knew about the second miscarriage?" she whispered, her brow furrowing as she regarded him.

David shook his head. "No. Not until now," he commented. Sitting up straighter, he sighed. "But it doesn't matter. You'll carry this babe until it's born, and the three of you will be a happy family," he said with a wistful look. "I *want* you to be a happy family," he stated firmly, his own expression suddenly happier.

Clarinda stared at him for a very long time, believing every word he said. Smiling, she closed her eyes again, tiredness suddenly gripping her. Just as she was drifting off to sleep, something niggled at her, some little word that didn't quite make sense, didn't quite add up.

What had David said?

The three of you will be a happy family. Yes, that's what he'd said. Clarinda smiled in her sleep, feeling quite herself again.

Three?

Sitting up straight, Clarinda's eyes flew open. "What did you mean by 'three'?"

But David was no longer sitting on her bed. Nor was there any evidence that he had been there. Her eyes darting about the dark room, Clarinda wondered if she had dreamed the whole thing.

But David *had* been there, she was sure.

She glanced down at her hand, remembering the feel of his lips as he kissed the back of her fingers, her palm, her wrist, her elbow. *Was I just dreaming?* Suddenly bereft, tears once again dripped down her cheeks as she struggled to bring back the remnants of the vivid dream. "David," she whispered in a sob. She closed her eyes and fell back into the pillows, sobbing until sleep finally claimed her.

Chapter 3

THE NEW EARL OF NORWICK

Daniel Fitzwilliam brought his quizzing glass to his eye and peered through it, studying the suddenly enlarged series of numbers he'd written in the ledger. He had spent the past hour trying to make the numbers add up to the same total, even taking the time to copy them onto a piece of scratch parchment and doing the addition again, with no luck. *Drat*!

He wasn't aware he'd said anything aloud until Mr. Hildebrand cleared his throat. Daniel looked up from the ledger to see his butler in the doorway, a silver salver littered with that day's mail and a London newspaper.

"Is there a problem, my lord?" Hildebrand wondered as he gingerly stepped forward and placed the tray on the end of his master's large rosewood desk.

"My inability to add numbers, apparently," Daniel replied indignantly. "I was perfectly capable of the task yesterday ..." He allowed the sentence to trail off as he noticed one of the notes on the salver.

"A courier brought that only a moment ago," his butler spoke carefully. "I asked the man to wait in the vestibule in the event it requires a reply."

Eyeing the white folded missive, Daniel wondered at its

news. Only bad news came by courier. He lifted the paper from the tray and turned it over, one eyebrow arching when he spied the seal embossed in the red wax securing the edges together. *Torrington*. Damn! The note was from Grandby. Sliding a finger beneath the seal, the wax broke apart and the letter nearly unfolded itself. Daniel stared at the masculine hand, rereading the words twice before allowing his head to rest in one hand, an elbow keeping it propped up.

> *Dear Daniel, Your brother has died of a broken neck. He was thrown from his horse in traffic in Oxford Street. Please come at your earliest convenience. My sympathies on his death and my congratulations on your becoming the next Earl of Norwick. Yours, Grandby.*

"Do you wish to send a reply?" Hildebrand wondered, his hands clasped behind his back.

Daniel gave the question some thought. Grandby wouldn't expect one, but if a courier had been sent to his mother's house in Bognor, he would find her away from her home. "Yes. I must send word to Mother. She's at Glendale Park in Kent for a house party," he murmured, keeping his face impassive.

Hildebrand nodded."My lord, I believe the same courier was about to head her way," he intoned. "Shall I have him redirected?"

Daniel gave the question some consideration. "Yes, but let me add my own note. Could you see to a meal and some ale for the man?" he ordered, drawing a piece of the earldom's stationery from a tray.

"Of course, my lord," the butler replied. When it appeared Daniel had no other immediate need of him, the butler turned on his heel and headed back to the vestibule and the courier awaiting there.

David is dead. The words echoed in Daniel's head. Given the growing gloom outside, he wondered at when the courier had left London. How long had David been dead before

Grandby penned the note? Had David just died that morning? Or yesterday? There was much to do if he was expected in London at his earliest convenience—if his ancient valet could manage to pack everything over the course of the day remaining, he could leave on the morrow and be at his apartment in Bruton Street tomorrow night. He could then call at Norwick House the day after tomorrow.

He wondered how things were at Norwick House, how *she* might be reacting to the news of her husband's death. He imagined her tears, imagined her lower lip trembling, a tooth denting the plump flesh as she worried it back and forth. He imagined her running into his arms, relieved to have his strength, happy to have his steadfast support and love and ...

Well, *that* wasn't going to happen, he chided himself. Clarinda Ann Brotherton Fitzwilliam despised him. He rather doubted she would allow him over the threshold of Norwick House, even if he was the earl—and the de-facto owner of said house.

Sighing, he gave one last glance at the column of numbers. This puzzle would now be his secretary's to solve, he figured as he wrote a quick note to his mother. "Courage," he wrote. "See you in London." He signed his name and folded the note, sealing it with red wax and planting the Norwick earldom seal into the wet puddle. The Earl of Norwick seal. If David was dead, that meant Daniel Fitzwilliam was now the Earl of Norwick. *Courage, indeed.*

Chapter 4

LIFE AS A WIDOW

"How did you bear it?" Clarinda asked as she and Lady Torrington strolled in Hyde Park, their parasols held aloft to guard against the rare winter sunshine. Having spent the first day of widowhood trapped in Norwick House being fitted for black gowns and making arrangements for the funeral service and answering dozens of questions and ordering a hatchment be hung on the front door, Clarinda was quite relieved when Adele Grandby, Countess of Torrington, offered to accompany her on a walk in the park. Clarinda had never been so glad to see a blue sky and almost collapsed her sunshade in order to allow the sun's rays to reach her face. But now that she was almost eight-and-twenty years of age, it would do her no good to develop a sprinkling of freckles on her otherwise peaches and cream complexion. A few wisps of her brunette hair flew around her face in the breeze that reminded the women it was still late winter. At least Clarinda's hair didn't display the streaks of gray that Lady Torrington's elaborate coiffure did, although to be fair to Adele Slater Worthington Grandby, she was at least ten years older than Clarinda.

"I did because I had to," Adele replied, patting the back of Clarinda's hand as they walked arm in arm on the crushed granite path. "And, I must admit, it was easier for me because I was not in love with Worthington," she said softly, a bit of hesitancy in her words, as if she'd never voiced the admission before. She heard Clarinda's inhalation of breath and had to resist the urge to feel guilty.

"You two always seemed ... "

"Oh, I think we always felt *affection* for one another," Adele agreed with a bob of her head. "But I didn't *love* him. Not like I love Grandby." The widowed matron had been surprised when the Earl of Torrington asked to escort her to the second ball of the Season two years before. Every Season, the middle-aged, never-married earl seemed to attach himself to a young widow with whom he attended all the events. Then, when the summer came and the *ton* fled the heat of town for their country manor houses or the inns in Bath and Brighton, Grandby and his paramour would bid farewell to one another, effectively ending their liaison.

At least, that's what had always happened until two years ago, when Grandby surprised Adele first by selecting her when she wasn't as young as the widows he usually favored, and then with a diamond and sapphire ring and a proposal of marriage just before the first event of the next Season.

Never a woman prone to vapors or to fainting, she nearly did that moment when Milton Grandby took her hand in his, knelt before her in the gardens behind Worthington House, declared his undying love and asked for her hand. "My brother, Devonville, used to tell me Grandby was a bounder, but I think he's actually rather fond of him."

William Slater, the Marquess of Devonville, was quite powerful in Parliament and rather fond of his younger sister. Perhaps his initial assessment of the earl was meant to protect her from a fortune hunter—Adele had ended an earlier engagement when she discovered her intended only courted her because he had amassed a large gambling debt. Although she thought herself in love with William Weston, Adele quickly recovered from her broken engagement when Grandby showed her favor at the Harvey's annual ball. Given the earl's own vast fortune, she had no reason to fear him marrying her for the wealth that had been accumulated as a result of her first husband's involvement with the early steamships.

Clarinda gave a wan smile before her face turned quizzical. "Why is it we all call Grandby *Grandby* when we should be calling him *Torrington*?" she suddenly asked. He'd been an earl for as long as she could remember. And he'd been the favorite of his friends for the honor of godfather—many of his goddaughters had made their come-outs in the last few Seasons, and his godsons had probably finished school at Eton or Cambridge and were already beginning their careers as gamblers and rakes in the *ton*.

Adele rolled her eyes. "I have no idea. I never bothered to ask. And I have never heard anyone call him *Torrington*," she responded, apparently amused at the apparent change of topic. "He's certainly not one to flaunt his title," the countess added. "Nor has he ever called me his *countess* since we married," she said as an afterthought, her brows furrowing in what may have been a show of distress. "Perhaps my brother was right."

Clarinda gave Adele a sunny smile at the comment, glad that her friend had made such a good match. She sobered, though, suddenly remembering how she and David had been such a brilliant match. "You and the earl seem perfect for one another," Clarinda offered, struggling to keep the catch in her throat from making itself apparent. She hadn't cried over David's death for at least two hours. She was trying for a new record of three. "I rather doubt I shall ever be blessed with a loving husband again. It seemed rather amazing when David and I discovered we *loved* one another," she managed to get out, the tears pricking at the edges of her eyes. "Damnation!" she whispered hoarsely. "I promised myself I was going to last three hours without weeping, and here I am turning into a watering pot!"

Adele pulled an embroidered handkerchief from her pocket and held it out to Clarinda. "I don't know what to say," she whispered. "I don't think there's anything I can say to make you feel better." Although she had news of her own —good news, in fact—she didn't want to share it with Clarinda just yet. It would be like rubbing salt in a wound, and she dared not do that to her friend.

She would never forget the day—just two days before—when she and Lady Pettigrew called on Clarinda, the day David Fitzwilliam, Earl of Norwick, strode into the parlor and suddenly dipped and kissed his wife. A pang of jealously stabbed her just then. Grandby would probably never do anything quite that daring, but now that she gave it some consideration, she wouldn't put it past him. He was the one man on the entire planet that could render her speechless. She rather hoped her news would either render him speechless or at least leave him pleased. Or, she could always hope for the very best, imagining him as he dipped her into one of those romantic kisses like the one the earl had bestowed on Clarinda.

"Do you believe in ghosts?" Clarinda asked suddenly, reminded of her talk with David the night before last.

Adele stopped in her tracks and stared at Clarinda's retreating back. "What ... Why would you ask such a thing?" she finally got out, so stunned at the change in topic she couldn't think to simply answer the question.

Clarinda stopped and turned when she realized Adele was no longer walking beside her. "I don't. I ... I didn't," Clarinda corrected herself as she spoke softly, her head shaking from side to side. "It's just ... I had very vivid dreams these past two nights. I am sure David was right there in my bedchamber, sitting on my bed and leaning over me, telling me everything was going to be fine."

Resuming their walk, Adele gave Clarinda a nervous glance. "Perhaps ... perhaps he was," she offered carefully. "I imagine you needed to be reassured. Better by him than anyone else, don't you suppose?"

Clarinda gave Adele a sideways glance, recognizing the woman's ploy for what it was. She sighed heavily before changing the subject. "I expect Daniel will arrive tomorrow," she stated, an involuntary shudder wracking her body just then. Adele caught the movement and eyed Clarinda with furrowed brows.

"Are you ... *frightened* of the brother?" she wondered, surprised at Clarinda's reaction to her own statement. "I thought you two got along quite well," she added then, remembering back to when her first husband was still alive and Clarinda was betrothed to David Fitzwilliam. She had heard that while the twins shared similar looks—most claimed they could not tell the two apart—their personalities were quite different.

Daniel was more serious, more sober, while David had enjoyed the life of a rake. Then David began to change. The man had been an earl for a few years at that point, his devil-may-care attitude quickly changing to that of a more responsible aristocrat. Where he might have taken his seat in Parliament only on occasion, he was suddenly there for every session. The time he would have spent at Gentleman Jackson's salon was instead spent participating in hunts and practicing archery. And his evenings, rumored to feature a succession of whores, mistresses, and visits to his very own men's club for a card game, were suddenly filled with trips to the theatre and musicales. Adele believed it had more to do with his impending nuptials than anything else; the man who might have been considered a rake had quickly disappeared from the gossip columns as well as the gaming hells and brothels, preferring to be seen in the company of Clarinda at the opera and society events.

Meanwhile, Daniel Fitzwilliam moved to Norwick Park, the seat of the earldom, and began managing the properties of the Norwick earldom on his brother's behalf. His no-nonsense approach to business and his studious nature when it came to choosing suitable investments resulted in huge gains for the Norwick estate. In only four years, he had nearly quadrupled the value of the Norwick fortune. The sale of his brother's men's club and high-class brothel accounted for some of the profits, of course, but most of the coin could be directly attributed to his estate management.

"We used to get along," Clarinda agreed, although a bit reluctantly. She didn't mention Daniel's last words to her, though. Didn't mention how bitter he had been. "It will be so awkward for him," she went on. "He inherits the earldom if I carry a daughter. And if I have a son, he ..." She paused and shook her head, glancing over to see Adele's widened eyes and suddenly slack jaw. "Can you imagine being him? Knowing you missed being an earl just because your brother was born mere moments before you? And then, when your brother dies unexpectedly and far too young, you inherit, or *maybe not*, because tomorrow you find out your sister-in-law has seen fit to finally carry the child she's been trying to have for four years?"

The last sentence came tumbling out in a mix of anger and regret, as if Clarinda had somehow planned the pregnancy to occur at just this most awkward of times and was now regretting it.

Adele continued to stare at Clarinda, her eyes blinking several times as if she couldn't think of what to say in response. *A baby*?

"A bit less than six months," Clarinda spoke with a nod of her head, thinking that would be the answer to Adele's question—could she formulate one. "I haven't told anyone else, Adele," she added, her heading shaking from side to side. "I didn't even tell David, although he ... he *knew*. He was so ..." She looked up to find Adele's still regarding her in awe. "Happy," she managed to get out before tears pricked the corners of her eyes.

"Oh, Clare," Adele breathed, moving to wrap her arms around her friend's shoulders. "I had no idea!" she replied in a hoarse whisper. "And I'm usually the one that *knows* these things," she added as she pulled away and gave Clarinda's arm a gentle shove.

Clarinda smiled broadly despite the tears that limned her eyes. "I dared not say a thing until I was well past the point when I lost the last two," she whispered with a shake of her head. She resumed walking, wishing she could skip to the end of the carriageway where their coach waited. There was something very freeing about being able to talk about her pregnancy. And although Lady Torrington wasn't a gossip, news would still spread quickly, especially after Adele told her husband. The Earl of Torrington would gladly tell all the gentlemen at White's that his first goddaughter was expecting, and he would do so with the kind of fervor normally shown by the expectant father. "Will you wait to tell Grandby until the day after tomorrow? Until after I've had a chance to speak with Daniel? I would hate for him to find out from someone other than me," she reasoned, wondering how she was going to break the news to her brother-in-law. She had no idea how he would accept the news.

"Of course," Adele replied with a downward tilt of her head. "He'll be at White's tonight anyway. He's always there at seven and home for dinner at eight. And I told Lady Seward I would attend a play with her tomorrow evening," she added, knowing she could keep Clarinda's secret since Penelope Winstead Seward did most of the talking when they attended Society events together.

"Thank you," Clarinda breathed in relief. She glanced about the park, noticing how more carriages were making their way down Rotten Row. "I think I may need to return home," she said, glancing down at her widow's weeds. "Wouldn't be right for me to be seen out here after only a couple days of mourning."

Giving her friend a wan smile, Adele nodded, but then stopped and seemed to regard the handle of her parasol a bit too closely.

"What is it?" Clarinda wondered, noting Adele's look of indecision.

"I've not yet told Grandby, so you must not say anything," Adele began uncertainly. Before she could start her next sentence, Clarinda's eyes widened, her parasol fell to the crushed granite below and her arms were wrapped around Adele's shoulders.

"Yes!" Clarinda exclaimed, tears springing to her eyes. "I wondered. I thought you might say something over tea, and then, when you did not ..."

Adele regarded Clarinda with a look of shock. "How did you ..?"

"I ... I only suspected. It's that 'glow of impending motherhood' you have surrounding you," Clarinda said brightly, tears flowing down to warm her chilled cheeks. "About three months, too?"

"About that, I think. I haven't told Milton. I ..." Adele's shoulders sagged, as if the good news wasn't enough to keep her buoyed from what might be bad news to a man who had married late and never seemed concerned about siring an heir. Had he been, he certainly would have chosen a younger, more biddable wife. But it wasn't as if any of his godsons could inherit the earldom. She didn't know if there were cousins or nephews that would inherit, but Adele rather doubted he wanted the earldom to revert to the Crown upon his death.

"He'll be ... he'll be *thrilled*!" Clarinda countered. "Oh, I wish I could be there when you tell him," she murmured as she retrieved her parasol from where it had landed. She remembered David, though, and how he just *knew*. "It's possible he already *knows*," she added, with a cocked eyebrow. "Norwick did."

Adele seemed surprised by the possibility. And surprised to learn that David knew he was to be a father before his death. Certainly the man would have spread the news at White's, but since no one said a word about it in the drawing rooms and parlors she'd frequented lately, David had obviously kept the news a secret. "If Milton knew, all of London would know," Adele replied with a grin, and then she wondered if maybe he did know and was keeping it a secret like David had.

"You must let me know how it goes," Clarinda spoke as they hurried off to the waiting coach.

"You will be the first to know how he reacts from me, but if he reacts as you think he will, I cannot promise he won't head straight to White's with a large carton of cheroots, in which case this entire town will know before I have a chance to send you word," Adele responded, her mood having improved greatly with their discussion.

A footman handed them up into the town coach just as several coaches and men on horseback were about to pass. Wanting to be sure she wasn't seen, Clarinda started to pull the shade over her window. She paused, though, when she noticed one of the men remove his top hat and give her a nod.

David! she thought as she stared at the rider, his russet coat and doeskin breeches fitted to perfection, the Hessians he wore polished to a gleaming shine. But before she could catch another glance, the man's hat was back on his head and he seemed to blend in with the other riders. His back was to the Norwick coach as they turned the corner to make their way out of the park.

David's ghost, Clarinda amended with a slight shake of her head. While others might have felt frightened by the thought of seeing their deceased husband as a ghost, Clarinda found herself hoping he would appear often. The comforting thought settled over her as the coach made its way back to Norwick House.

Chapter 5

THE DOWAGER COUNTESS ARRIVES

A dusty coach-and-four was parked in the semi-circular drive in front of Norwick House when Clarinda's coach pulled up in front. The unmarked equipage looked as if it had arrived only moments before, a pair of footman appearing from the house to unload a trunk from the back while a stable boy held the horses. One of the Norwick House footmen had jumped from the box of Clarinda's coach and was about to open her door when Clarinda realized the other coach must belong to the dowager countess.

Surprised at its appearance so soon after David's death, Clarinda wondered how the woman would have been able to reach London so quickly. Dorothea Fitzwilliam made her home near the southern coast, and Clarinda was sure the courier wouldn't have reached the dowager's house until early yesterday. If Lady Norwick was already here, it meant she would have traveled through the night, changing horses several times along the way. Or, she might have just arrived with the intention of paying a visit. This last thought had Clarinda panicked.

Allowing the coachman to hand her down, Clarinda gave him a nod and made her way to the front of the house, mindful of the footmen behind her who labored under the weight of the trunk they had just unloaded. Porter, the house's majordomo, held the door for her and took her pelisse and bonnet. "Her ladyship has been shown to the Blue Room," he said with a raised bushy eyebrow, as if he wondered about the suitability of that particular bedchamber.

"Thank you, Porter. It *is* the best room in the house," Clarinda assured him as she dared a glance in a looking glass mounted near the front door, wincing at the sight of her hair. "I never imagined she would get here so quickly."

Porter lifted his head a fraction. "I do not believe her ladyship was in residence in Bognor when the courier delivered the news of the earl's death to his lordship," he whispered.

Clarinda pushed a few stray hairs behind her ear and gave Porter a sharp glance. "Why not?" she wondered, nervously smoothing her bombazine skirts. "Was she at Norwick Park?"

The majordomo seemed suddenly embarrassed and did not respond. He was already aware of the dowager countess descending the main stairs. Clarinda took a deep breath and nodded in his direction, acknowledging his expert use of his eyebrows to warn her of Dorothea's impending entrance. She made her way to the foot of the stairs. Sure enough, from the swish of silk skirts and petticoats, she could hear that Dorothea Wright Fitzwilliam was nearly down to the first staircase landing. Not wanting to have to look up at the formidable woman as she made her way down the second set of stairs, Clarinda gathered up her skirts and hurried up the steps to meet the woman on the lower landing. Her timing proved perfect as she reached the broad carpeted landing just as the Dowager Countess of Norwick was about to step onto the same landing.

"My lady," Clarinda managed to get out before noticing her mother-in-law looked positively resplendent in a fashionable scarlet carriage gown. *Why isn't she wearing black?* was the countess' first thought, although she saw that Lady Norwick did at least have a black armband secured around the sleeve of her gown. She immediately sealed her lips, realizing she should have waited for the older woman to speak first. Performing a perfect curtsy, Clarinda waited for the dowager countess to make her greeting.

"Oh, Clare," the woman said with a shake of her head. "You needn't be so damned formal with me," Dorothea claimed, moving to wrap her arms around the younger woman's shoulders. "I am so very sorry for the both of us," she murmured before she pulled away and stepped back, leaving her hands on Clarinda's shoulders. Her gaze swept down her daughter-in-law's dress, making a 'tsk' sound as she did so. "I promised myself after spending a year in mourning for Norwick that I would never again wear black. Or black and white. Makes me look like the living dead, and I fear it almost does the same to you. Although ..." She moved her gaze to Clarinda's face. "You look ..." Her eyes suddenly widened. "You look ..."

"Like I'm with child?" Clarinda offered in a very quiet voice, hoping it was the sentiment the dowager countess was trying to vocalize.

"Oh!" Dorothea said as she stepped back, a hand pressed against her bosom as her face changed from shock to joy. "Oh, Clare. This is ... this is ..."

"Complicating, I know," Clarinda said, not quite sure if it was what Dorothea was trying to say.

"That wasn't *quite* what I was going to say," Dorothea protested with an arched eyebrow. "But ... Oh, Clare!" She pulled Clarinda into a heartfelt hug. "How long?" There was a hint of a hiss, as if her mother-in-law suddenly clenched her teeth before asking. Clarinda wondered if David had mentioned her previous miscarriage to his mother.

"More than three months," Clarinda whispered, remembering how many times she had consulted a calendar in the eleven weeks since she'd missed her monthly courses. The hug got a bit harder.

"That's a relief, then," Dorothea said as she pulled away

again. "Or not," she suddenly said as her face lost its joy. She took Clarinda's arm in hers and steered them to the stairs.

Clarinda rolled her eyes. "I don't know *how* I'm going to tell Daniel," she said as she descended the steps with Dorothea. They made their way to the parlor and Clarinda rang for tea. "I fear he already despises me, and I cannot imagine how this news will help his opinion of me."

Dorothea regarded Clarinda with another arched eyebrow before taking a seat in the chair her son usually used. "When do you suppose you lost his good opinion? I ask only because ..." She paused for a moment and regarded her daughter-in-law with furrowed brows. "I have not heard an unkind word of you from his lips." She thought for a moment and bounced her head back and forth a bit. "Of course, that's probably because he knows I would box his ears if he ever said an unkind word of you," she added with a hint of humor.

How can she be so damned flippant at a time like this? Clarinda wondered. But the woman's words surprised her. "We have not spoken to one another for two years, my lady," she said as she remembered the last time she'd ever even *seen* Daniel Fitzwilliam. At Christmastime in Bognor. He was there for a dinner party, but avoided Clarinda the entire evening, his seating at the table preventing them from conversing. And then he had departed before the men had finished their port and cheroots and joined the ladies in the drawing room. It was as if Daniel had deliberately avoided her that evening.

Dorothea huffed, holding back her retort until the maid had set the tea tray on the low table between them. Once the girl bobbed a curtsy and left, the dowager countess leaned forward. "*Why* haven't you two spoken?" she asked, taking over the tea pouring before Clarinda could reach over to do it. "And where's the brandy? I do think something a bit stronger is called for, don't you?"

Stunned at the woman's comment, Clarinda hardly knew what to say. She stood up and hurried to a cart set off to one side of the room. Grabbing a crystal decanter of amber liquid, she returned to her chair and set it down, a bit harder than she intended. "Your younger son thinks me a fortune hunter. He accused me of marrying David for his money and title." At Dorothea's surprised expression, Clarinda added, "I would have thought he knew I had some fortune of my own coming to me on my twenty-fifth birthday," the comment suddenly reminding her that David had actually never claimed the money due her when she reached her majority. "And I could have afforded to live a very comfortable life as a spinster if I wished."

This last was delivered with enough venom that Dorothea arched that elegant eyebrow again. Clarinda thought that eyebrow a rather effective weapon. She imagined if it were made of iron, the woman could detach it and throw it like a boomerang, its pointed ends knocking out an opponent with one fell swoop before she would calmly reclaim it and reattach it above her eye.

Clarinda closed her eyes and shook her head. "I apologize, my lady," she said in a quiet voice. "I married David because ... because our fathers practically arranged a betrothal ..."

"Which could have easily been broken," Dorothea interrupted.

"And because he *asked* me, and I ... I *wanted* to marry him," Clarinda finished, ignoring Dorothea's comment about the worthlessness of marriage contracts.

The dowager countess regarded her daughter-in-law for a very long time before pouring brandy into a teacup and lifting it toward Clarinda. The younger woman shook her head, so Dorothea brought the cup to her lips and sipped delicately. When she set the cup down onto a saucer, she tilted her head to one side. "Even though you were in love with Daniel," she said with a kind of certainty that wasn't to be questioned. She leaned over to pour a cup of tea for Clarinda. The statement was almost a rhetorical question, but it caught Clarinda completely off-guard.

"What? Yes. No. *No*!" Clarinda claimed as she shook her head, her jaw slack. "I was never in love with *Daniel*," she claimed, her head shaking back and forth. She regarded the decanter of brandy for a moment, thinking perhaps she *should* add a dollop or two to her tea.

Not looking the least bit convinced, Dorothea took another sip of brandy. "Could you be, do you suppose?" she wondered then, her manner quite matter-of-fact. "In love with Daniel, I mean."

Clarinda blinked. And blinked again. "Wh ... What?"

Shaking her head, Dorothea set down her cup and saucer on the table and leaned back in the chair, looking every bit the aristocrat she was. "Really, Clare. It would make this whole situation so much easier if you and Daniel would settle whatever differences you have and marry. He'll have to provide protection for you anyway, and should you carry a son, it will still be heir to the title," she explained with a wave of her hand. "I can speak with him about it if you'd like ..."

"*No*!" Clarinda countered, her mouth now wide open. "My lady," she added on seeing Dorothea's look of shock. "No. I cannot marry a man who ... who *despises* me," she spoke in a much softer voice. "And I do not think you could compel him to consider such an arrangement." *David must be spinning in his grave!* she thought in horror, his mother's discussion of marriage quite improper considering a year was the proper amount of time for mourning a dead husband.

And then she realized why this talk was *really* improper. David couldn't be spinning in his grave. *He wasn't even buried yet!*

Dorothea drained her brandy, arching her eyebrow as if Clarinda had dropped a gauntlet at her feet. But the older woman's countenance suddenly softened. She leaned back into the chair, as if her backbone was suddenly gone. Tears welled in her eyes. "I apologize. I ... You carry my grandchild. I want to be sure I am allowed to spoil it," she whispered sadly.

Clarinda dipped her head, wondering if Dorothea's tears

were real or if they were meant to elicit sympathy from her. "And you shall, of course, my lady. I promise. And I would offer a hanky, but mine are quite drenched," she added as she pulled one out of the pocket of her gown and held up the damp linen.

"Mine, too," Dorothea replied, holding up her own damp hanky. She gave her daughter-in-law a wan smile before sighing. "We're a pair, aren't we?" she murmured with a sigh.

Clarinda offered a wan smile in reply. Then her brows furrowed. "How is it you were able to get to London so quickly?" she wondered, thinking the dowager countess and Daniel would be arriving together the following day.

Catching her lower lip with a tooth, Dorothea sighed again. "I was attending a house party in Kent. Daniel had a courier sent up with the news moments after it reached him. I expect he'll be here on the morrow." Her gaze settled on Clarinda again. "Do afford him all the courtesy you would your earl," she said in a quiet voice. At Clarinda's surprised expression, she added, "Well, except for the conjugal visits, I suppose."

Clarinda's eyes widened even more. "You mean, have him move into the earl's apartments?" she asked in surprise. David had only been dead a couple of days. She was sure his belongings were still where he'd left them, although she intended to spend some time with his valet determining what should be done with some of his more personal things that probably wouldn't be included in his will. There were paintings meant for David's eyes only. And the bed. Well, David hadn't slept in *that* bed for some time, she realized, remembering how wonderful it had been to have him sleep with her in her bed this past week.

"Yes. Even if you carry David's heir, Daniel will still have to run the earldom until the little bastard is old enough to take over." At the sound of Clarinda's audible gasp at her motherin-law's use of the word 'bastard,' Dorothea shook her head. "I meant that in the most *loving* way, I assure you," she stated with a nod, not even bothering to apologize. When Clarinda's eyebrows didn't come down from their record heights, though, she added, "I almost called him a 'little bugger,' my dear," she claimed, as if that would have been worse.

Somehow, the comment, or perhaps just the tone of voice in which it was made, was absurd enough that Clarinda had to allow a smile. "I can hear you now, calling your grandson, 'Bugger'," she replied, her smile of amusement genuine. The smile slowly faded as tears began dripping down her cheeks. Before long, Dorothea's cheeks were just as wet.

Later that night, after a casual dinner with her mother-in-law and an evening in the parlor reviewing plans for David's funeral service, Clarinda dismissed her maid and climbed into bed. Settling herself into one of the pillows, she was struck by the scent of David that suddenly wafted over her. She closed her eyes and breathed in the familiar fragrances; sandalwood and citrus, and the musk he gave off when they had just finished making love.

"I always wondered if you liked that particular scent," David said in a whisper. "I still can't decide if I do."

Smiling, Clarinda reached up as if to cup her hand along his jaw, sure she could feel the rough texture of his unshaven face. "I do like it, David. I always have," she answered in a whisper. "In fact, I'm thinking of forbidding the maid to ever wash these pillow coverings," she said with a grin.

"Ewww," David replied with a frown. "There's a bottle of cologne in my room. If you like it that much, simply sprinkle it on your linens ..."

"I like it on *you*, silly man," Clarinda interrupted him. They shared several moments of silence. "I saw you in the park today," she said then, her voice quieter. The hand against his face moved up so her fingers could slide through his dark, silken hair.

"Hmm. It was a nice day for a ride," he said, leaning over to kiss her on the forehead. Clarinda closed her eyes and relished the sensation.

"Your mother is here."

David nodded. "I saw." After a time, he said, "She lacks subtlety, but she means well, Clare. If Daniel is stubborn, as I expect he may be, you may have to apply some … feminine encouragement."

Clarinda blinked, her brows furrowing. "What? What do you mean?"

David leaned over and kissed her on the nose. "I love you, Clare," he said in a whisper.

Clarinda's eyes closed as his lips took purchase on hers, the kiss so gentle it was almost ethereal. When her eyes opened again, David was gone.

Chapter 6

IMPENDING FATHERHOOD MAKES FOR A FOOL IN LOVE

Milton Grandby, Earl of Torrington, entered White's at precisely seven o'clock. His arrival each night was so precisely timed, other gentlemen set their chronometers based on when he stepped into the men's club. One of the club's butlers was even spied resetting a mantle clock above a fireplace a moment after the earl took his usual seat.

Grandby's visits, usually finished in forty-five minutes so that he might arrive home at precisely eight o'clock for dinner with his wife, afforded him an opportunity to enjoy a pre-dinner drink and a cheroot. He spent the time conferring with other members of the peerage, taking a peek at the betting books, and listening to the day's gossip. Ensconced in his favorite overstuffed chair, he sipped a brandy as he surreptitiously listened to the conversation of some gentlemen at a card table. Although Grandby wasn't a gossip monger, he still rather enjoyed hearing it whenever he had the chance.

"I have rather momentous news to share this evening," Viscount Barrings was saying proudly as he finished shuffling a new deck of cards.

"Did your horse finally win a race?" Jeffrey Althorpe, a baron, asked, his elevated eyebrow suggesting his comment was made in jest. Lord Barrings frowned. He dealt the cards as if he'd been doing it since he was in leading strings.

Lord Everly leaned in to pick up his cards, his lit cheroot sending tendrils of smoke in its wake. "Now, now, Jeffrey. Don't be making fun of Barrings' bay. That nag came in second last week," the earl scolded. The adventurer had been in London only a fortnight, his most recent trip having been to the southernmost tip of Africa in search of tropical fish. His avocation—the study of natural sciences—had him traveling around the globe more often than he was home in London. The man could be forgiven his frequent explorations except he hadn't yet seen to arranging a suitable marriage for his younger sister, Lady Evangeline. He promised himself he would see her settled before he took off on another trip. Grandby was quite certain a marriage was in the cards—as the girl's godfather, he had made it clear to Everly that further delays would not be tolerated. If Everly didn't have someone in mind soon and see to it a courtship was in the cards, Grandby would deck him.

Everly took a look at his cards and was about to scold Barrings for his bad deal when he decided he might be able to bluff his way through this hand.

"Thank you, Everly," Barrings acknowledged the mention of his race horse's recent success with a nod. "No, gentleman, my wife has seen to it I will be a father. Probably before Parliament reconvenes in the fall," he stated proudly. He picked up his own cards, giving them a quick glance before looking up to accept congratulations from around the table.

"Mary will be relieved to hear of it," Sir Richard commented, his attention on his cards. "Only last week, she claimed your wife looked as if she was eating a few too many cakes at tea."

Grandby had to stifle a chuckle at the comment lest he be discovered listening. Just last week, he'd made a similar comment to Adele, although he was careful to add that he rather liked her with a bit more meat on her bones. She'd been far too thin when they married.

Barrings gave Sir Richard a nod. "Well, she is, at that, but she is eating for two now," he commented, his proud grin never leaving his face, even as he was forced to fold.

"She'll be in good company," Sommers commented as he considered his hand and the growing pile of chips in the center of the table. "Seems there will be a crop of heirs born this fall."

Everly looked up from his hand, deciding he might not be able to bluff his way through this hand. "That would be due to that nasty snowstorm we had last December, just after Christmas," he stated with some authority.

Barrings made a sound that could best be described as a snort. "As I understand these matters, Everly, snow had nothing to do with it."

The other three gentlemen guffawed in response. "Oh, yes it does. What else are you going to do when you're trapped in your country estate for three straight days?" Sommers asked, making a rude gesture with his hands.

"And your wife complains of boredom and the cold?" Sir Richard added rhetorically, his eyebrows waggling suggestively.

"I daresay, I remember wishing I was married during that long week," Sommers murmured as he pretended to study his cards, thinking he still wished he was married. All his friends were. And now they were about to become fathers.

In the middle to taking a sip of brandy, Grandby stilled his movements. *Sommers wishes he was married. Lady Evangeline Everly needs a husband.*

And there was that snowstorm.

He held the brandy on his tongue for a very long time, finally swallowing when the alcohol threatened to burn a hole in his mouth. He remembered that snowstorm quite clearly. Remembered where he was during the second and third days of it. Remembered where Adele had been—usually under him, although there had been those rather delightful times when she was on top of him—and he suddenly realized why it was she looked as if she'd been eating a few too many cakes at tea.

Lord Everly, having taken a sudden interest in Jeffrey Althorpe's quiet declaration that he wished he was married, decided his bluff definitely wouldn't work and folded. He turned to the baron and lowered his voice. "If I might have a word with you when we're done here tonight?" When Sommers gave him a noncommittal shrug in response, Everly piped up and said, "Be prepared to bed your wife more frequently, Barrings. Her appetite for your favors will be insatiable. At least, it is for most of the females of our species when they are breeding." A hearty round of laughter erupted from the table as Barrings' back was slapped and pounded.

Grandby's heart pounded in his chest. His pulse pounded in his head. *How did Everly know such things?* He wasn't married. Grandby's breaths came a bit too quickly. He stared at his cheroot as if he didn't recognize it. *I'm going to be a father.* The words, barely formed in his mind, repeated themselves with a bit more certainty.

Downing the rest of his brandy as if he'd spent a week in the desert, he stubbed out his cheroot and quickly made his way to his coach, his early exit from the club causing one of the butlers to pick up and study a mantle clock to ensure it still worked. The footman on the back of his coach did a double-take. "My lord?" he managed to get out as he moved to open the door and set down the steps.

"Stedman and Vardon in Bond Street, and make it fast," Grandby ordered, stepping into his coach. He was barely seated when the coach lurched forward to make its way up St. James Street. He took the opportunity to breathe, feeling rather proud that he had enough sense to stop at a jewelers to secure a rather expensive bauble before heading home for dinner. *I'm going to be a father*, he thought again. For a man of his age—he was in his forties—to marry a widow—who, as near as he could tell was in her thirties—to discover he was going to be a father, was, well, it wasn't exactly a miracle, he knew. Lord Seward had fathered his fourth son when he was in his seventies, and although some claimed he'd had a bit of help in that regard (there had been rumors he'd been cuckolded by his wife), the boy was the spitting image of him. *Poor child.*

But for Grandby to think of himself as a father was ... unthinkable. He was the godfather to the *ton's* sons and daughters, not a *father*.

Adele, bless her heart.

Why hadn't she said anything? Was she afraid he didn't want a child? She must have known he needed an heir. Was she waiting for the right time to tell him? Perhaps she intended to tell him tonight during dinner. She'd said something about arranging for his favorite meal to be served that evening. Or did she even know she was expecting?

That last thought had him pausing suddenly. There was something different, he was sure now. It wasn't just that she had put on a few pounds. She was ... more beautiful, to be sure, her smile more radiant. And she was certainly more willing to be bedded. Christ, she'd been in his bed as much as he'd been in hers this past month or so!

What had Everly said?

Be prepared to bed your wife more frequently. Her appetite for your favors will be insatiable.

He was still ruminating on insatiable appetites when the coach came to a stop in front of the goldsmith's shop. He was out of the coach before the footman could even move to get the door open, hurrying into the shop at Number 36. Scanning one of the display cases, he wondered what would be appropriate. He'd never bought jewelry for a an expectant wife before. Necklace? Bracelet? Ear bobs? Brooch? All of the above? And with what gemstone?

"May I be of assistance, my lord?" Mr. Stedman wondered, stepping up to the counter where Grandby's attention was directed at a collection of necklaces displayed on black velvet.

When Grandby looked up, a panicked expression on his face, one of Stedman's eyebrows lifted. "Have you forgotten a special occasion, perhaps?" he asked *sotto voce*. The jeweler noted Grandby's nervousness. "Or, is there one about to occur?"

"Yes," Grandby replied with a quick nod of his head. Not knowing if Stedman could be trusted to keep a secret, Grandby was trying to decide how to broach the subject of an appropriate gift.

"Does it involve your ... wife?" Stedman ventured. He had to be careful—too many men of the *ton* purchased baubles for their mistresses—usually of better quality than the ones they purchased for their wives.

"Yes."

Stedman nodded, pulling a tray of necklaces from another drawer. "Does she look better in blue or red?" he asked then, showing him a display of sapphire and ruby necklaces featuring his signature gold filigree chains and settings. He pulled out another tray, this one showing two rather ornate diamond necklaces. "Or white?"

Grandby pondered the questions, thinking she looked her very best when she was wearing nothing at all. Was there any reason he had to *choose* a color? Why not all of them? "I'll take one of each," he announced, pointing in turn at one of each that he supposed would look especially lovely on his naked, expectant wife.

Mr. Stedman's eyebrows lifted so they nearly joined his hairline. "Very good, my lord," he answered with a nod, secretly wondering what momentous occasion could induce a gentleman to purchase *three* necklaces for his wife. Had he been caught with another woman? "Should I have them ... delivered?"

His own brows furrowing, as if they had to even out Stedman's still mighty high brows, Grandby shook his head.

"Heavens, no. I wish to give them to her tonight."

"*All* of them, my lord?" the jeweler replied, obviously astonished by Grandby's proclamation.

"Yes. Of course. After dinner. Or maybe one during dinner and one during dessert and the other one after dinner." He checked his Breguet. "Which is scheduled to start in fifteen minutes," he said in a voice filled with enough warning that Mr. Stedman was motivated to move the selected necklaces into black velvet-lined boxes with great speed.

"Thank you," the earl stated as he collected the three necklace boxes and headed for the door. "Wish me luck."

Rather happy to have made such a large sale, and to such an esteemed gentleman as the Earl of Torrington, the jeweler stared at the door to his shop for a long time after the earl had departed. "I might have wished him luck if he had *paid* for his purchases," Stedman grumbled to the now empty shop. He took out a large sheet of parchment and prepared to complete a bill of sale to have sent to Grandby's home.

Adele Grandby descended the central stairs in Worthington House, her shoulders pulled back and her head held as high as she dared. Glancing down, she was a bit dismayed to discover she couldn't see the next step down. At least her lack of vision wasn't due to her swelling abdomen, which wasn't really that swollen.

Yet.

Her ample bosom was the culprit. Tonight, thanks to her maid having tugged on her corset strings a bit more than usual, the swells of her breasts were mounded well above the neckline of her low-cut gown. The deep sapphire blue silk brought out the violet of her eyes and contrasted beautifully with her golden blonde hair, its streaks of gray indicating just the barest hint of her age. Her hair was caught up in an elegant coiffure featuring a series of curls across the front and a chignon in the back. Tiny sapphire ear bobs hung from her ears, bouncing against her neck as she took each step.

At the sound of the front door opening, she paused, hoping her husband had finally returned from White's. He was late tonight—not especially so, but enough so that the flutterbies in Adele's stomach had more time to fly about. After her walk with Clarinda, she had decided tonight was the night she would tell him her news. She still hadn't quite figured out *how* she would tell him, but she would.

Maybe during the soup course.

No, that wouldn't do. If he was too stunned or upset at the news, he might leave the dining room and order the rest of his dinner be taken to his apartment.

Perhaps during the fish course. Her stomach roiled at the thought of fish, and she remembered her instructions to the cook that no fish be served that evening.

Dessert, she decided. She would tell him over dessert.

Holding her pose on the steps, Adele waited patiently as she heard the butler welcome the earl. She heard her husband ask about dinner. She imagined Milton removing his great coat, imagined him giving Bernard his top hat and cane. She imagined him looking slightly tousled and ever so confident and calm and collected ...

She blinked as she realized she was suddenly staring down at him. Grandby had come from the vestibule —no, he had *shot* out of the vestibule, as if from a canon, his eyes wild, his hair even more so, his hands filled with small black boxes. He had been running, and when he was halfway to the dining room, he had attempted to stop, his Hessians sliding on the marble floors and leaving black streaks in their wake until he could turn around and retrace his steps. He had finally come to a dead stop at the bottom of the stairs.

"Hallo," he managed to say as he stared up at her, his mouth hanging wide open, his arms dropped to his sides, the flat boxes barely held by his long, tapered fingers. When he closed his mouth, his cheeks puffed out a bit, and then he opened his mouth again, as if he couldn't believe what he was seeing. Adele had to stifle a giggle when she was reminded of one of Lord Everly's tropical fish.

"Good evening, Milton," she answered, resuming her regal descent down the stairs. When she reached the last one, she curtsied.

Moving all the boxes he held to the crook of one arm, Grandby bowed and brought her hand to his lips, kissing the knuckles. "Are you ... are you going somewhere?" he wondered, his voice very quiet.

Adele arched an elegant eyebrow. "I am." She motioned toward the dining room. "Would you care to join me?"

Grandby swallowed, his gaze taking her in from the tips of her satin slippers to the top of her curls, pausing briefly on her décolletage. Adele found herself wondering if he had misinterpreted her invitation and intended to join her *there* by planting his face between her breasts. "I would, my lady," he replied, his casual and confident demeanor having just then returned. He held out his available arm and Adele placed a hand on it, giving him a tentative smile as they followed his black streak marks to the dining room.

"I bought you a gift," Grandby stated as he indicated the boxes barely held in the crook of his arm.

Adele angled her head, intrigued by the way he said the words. "*A* gift?" she repeated, giving the slim boxes a pointed glance. Adele knew from experience what they contained. "Is assembly required?"

Grandby placed the slim boxes on the table between where they would be sitting that evening. "A bit," he answered, his mischievous grin appearing. He lifted one of the boxes and peeked inside, quickly shutting it and setting it aside. "Wrong color," he murmured before lifting another box. He barely opened it and his eyebrows cocked. He glanced in her direction, shaking his head before closing that box. He set it atop the other one. Without looking inside, he gave the last box to her.

Drawing her long fingers along the top edges, Adele knew what hid inside boxes of this shape and size. She'd received enough gemstones during her time with Worthington to recognize a jeweler's velvet covered pasteboard box. Gifts such as these were bestowed for a reason, though, and since there were no special occasions scheduled anytime soon ... and there were *three* boxes ... "Have you gone and done something naughty?" she asked then, a flush of color rising to her face. "Several times?"

Stunned at her question, and knowing her use of the word 'naughty' really did mean 'naughty,' as in, he'd been guilty of participating in some kind of bad behavior that involved Cyprians or courtesans, Grandby's eyes widened. "No!" he claimed, his head shaking back and forth. "Well, only with you," he amended, looking ever so contrite. "The result of which is why I bought this ..," he motioned toward the box, "... for you." One hand lifted to cover his eyes a moment when he realized he hadn't actually *bought* the necklaces—he'd managed to leave Stedman and Vardon without having *paid*, or at least arranging for the bill to be sent to him! It was a wonder a constable hadn't shown up at the front door.

At the sound of the front door being opened by the butler, Grandby nearly panicked and then realized it was probably just the bill being delivered. Certainly Stedman would know to have the bill sent to him at home.

"What is it?" Adele asked, seeing the flash of distress cross his face.

"Well, open it," he replied, surprised she hadn't behaved like every other mistress he had ever employed by tearing the lid off the box before it was even out of his hands.

"I will. When you tell me *why*," Adele countered, rising up to regard him, her expression once more severe.

Grandby blew air out from between his lips and shrugged. He remembered the discussion at the card table at White's.

"Remember last Christmas? When we were snowed in at Torrington Park? And we spent all that time ... being bad? And since then, you've continued to be rather bad? Insatiable, in fact." At Adele's suddenly arched eyebrow and startled expression, he hurried on. "Which I don't mind a bit. I rather adore it, really. I do," he was saying as his head bobbed up and down. "And now you look as if you've eaten a few too many tea cakes and ..." His hand had suddenly moved to her belly and protectively rested there. He let out a sigh.

"Milton!" Adele whispered. Her arms wrapped around

his neck, one hand still clutching the box and her lips finding his to kiss him as thoroughly as she could. When a maid suddenly entered from the butler's pantry, she gasped and quickly retreated from the room.

Grandby stifled his chuckle and instead nuzzled Adele's neck with his nose and lips. "Did I get it right?" he asked then, suddenly wondering what he would do if he had misjudged the whole scenario.

"Oh, yes," Adele whispered, kissing his jaw and his neck. "I was going to tell you tonight. During the dessert course."

Taking a step back, Grandby ran his gaze down the front of Adele again. "And I was going to give you that during the dessert course," he countered, his head nodding toward the black velvet box Adele still held. "But I rather doubt we'll make it to the dessert course, my love," he added. "Unless we take it up in my bedchamber," he suggested, an eyebrow waggling.

Adele smiled, her cheeks flushing pink. "You are incorrigible," she murmured. She held the box up between them. "Some assembly, hum?"

"I'll help you put it on," he offered as he took the box from her and opened it. The sapphires sparkled with blue-violet light, the gold glinting from the flames in the chandelier overhead.

"Oh, it's beautiful," Adele breathed, reaching out with a fingertip to gently nudge the necklace around the raised circle in the middle of the box. "I do hope it's a boy," she said then, her attention returning to him.

Grandby shrugged. "I was thinking a girl, but if it's a boy, we can always be bad and have another," he suggested hopefully. *In for a penny, in for a pound.* Lifting the necklace from the velvet bed, he opened it around her neck and secured the clasp. He noticed Adele's attention on the other two boxes.

"Did you try to guess what color gown I would be wearing tonight?" she wondered, her fingers barely touching the gold filigree and sapphires that encircled her neck. She couldn't imagine what stones might be featured in the other necklaces.

"I didn't actually buy them to go with any particular gown," Grandby countered, his lips curling up as he regarded the sapphires, deciding they looked especially regal with the gown and ear bobs she was wearing at the moment. He tried to imagine her in just the necklace and ear bobs, and he found he rather liked that image even better. He glanced back at the table. "Now that I think on it, I was rather patriotic when I made by selections," he added, the mischief back in his eyes. "And a bit naughty, too," he added.

"Oh?" Adele replied, one eyebrow arching up. "Do tell."

Shrugging in that way he had of making himself seem cavalier and confident at the same time, Grandby leaned closer and whispered in her ear.

Adele regarded her husband for several moments and cocked her head to one side. "Indeed?" she commented. "Then what were you imagining me wearing..?" Her eyes suddenly widened. "Milton!" she admonished him.

"You can wear them with gowns, of course," the earl assured her quickly, hoping she hadn't just thought the very worst of him at that moment. "But, if you would be so accommodating, I would love to see these on you while you're ... wearing nothing but my bed linens, so to speak. Perhaps, later tonight?" he hinted hopefully.

Although her face kept its slightly flushed coloring, Adele gave him a teasing smile. "Milton Grandby, if I wasn't so damned hungry, I'd let you undress me and have your way with me right now. On this table," she whispered, leaning in to capture his lips with another kiss.

Grandby's arms wrapped around her waist, pulling her hard against his body just as the maid reappeared with the soup course. Letting out a gasp, the servant immediately turned around and started to go back into the butler's pantry.

"Hold it right there," Grandby ordered, pulling away from the kiss. He waved toward the maid. "We're ready for dinner. Truly." He placed Adele's hand on his arm and led her to a place to his right. “However, my lady will be eating here instead of way down there,” he said, pulling the chair out from the table. A footman, who had apparently appeared from almost nowhere, hurried to reset the table so that Adele’s place setting was in front of her before she’d even taken her seat. “And we’ll be having the dessert course in my apartment,” he added to the second footman who appeared with wine.

“Very good, my lord,” the footman murmured as he poured the wine. Within seconds, the servants had disappeared and the two lovebirds were left enjoying their dinner.

They enjoyed the dessert far more.

Chapter 7

DANIEL ARRIVES

Daniel Fitzwilliam, the second son of the ninth Earl of Norwick, reined in his horse as he approached the semi-circular drive in front of Norwick House. The fashionable mansion in Park Lane featured the *de rigueur* Palladian style architecture that had become so popular at the turn of the century. Grecian columns acted as sentries on either side of a set of large double-doors and held up a portico above the landing at the top of the deep, shallow steps. A pair of topiary trees flanked the columns. Rows of arched windows were lined out on either side the front of the house, various plantings at their base trimmed so as not to hinder the view from inside. The effect was stately and elegant, a London-based home suitable for an earl and his wife in which to live and entertain. A home suitable for Daniel's older brother, the tenth Earl of Norwick.

At one time, Daniel railed against his fate as the second son. Born only minutes after David Alexander George Fitzwilliam, Daniel Jonathan Andrew Fitzwilliam was identical to his older brother in every respect. They had both grown to just a bit over six feet in height, had broad shoulders and torsos that featured muscular chests, flat stomachs and thin hips. The dental gods had bestowed them with straight teeth and saw to it none were missing. Their facial features were so much the same, they were frequently mistaken for one another, making it possible for them to play practical jokes on their governess, tutors, teachers, friends and even some family members. The Fitzwilliam men were both expert horsemen, good marksmen, adequate fencers and abysmal boxers. Their taste in clothing was even similar—they employed tailors who used the best cloth and could fashion coats and breeches that suited their larger than normal bodies. And their taste in women ... well, it was this trait of their sameness that led to their falling out four years ago.

They had both fallen in love with the same woman.

Because David was due to inherit, their father encouraged a betrothal to the daughter of another earl. David would marry Lady Clarinda Anne Brotherton no later than her twenty-second birthday. Despite the fact that betrothals were no longer the binding contracts they had been at one time, David had every intention of honoring his father's arrangement. He'd had a fondness for Lady Clarinda from the time he'd danced with her at her come-out ball, a lavish affair given in her honor by her parents on the eve of her eighteenth birthday. Trouble was, Daniel already felt affection for the girl, having met her in Hyde Park while she and her chaperone rode horses in the afternoons. By the time Clarinda married his brother, nearly five years after Daniel and Clarinda had been introduced to one another, Daniel was hopelessly in love with the chit. As he stood with his brother during the wedding, he only had eyes for the brunette-haired beauty, her aquamarine eyes occasionally glancing in his direction as she blushed and repeated her vows. Vows to his brother.

For the next two years, Daniel lived in town, attending Society events and occasionally visiting Boodles for drinks and a hand of cards. At some point, he was sure a debutante might catch his eye and help him forget his lovely sister-inlaw. But none did. And after the horrible row he'd had with

Clarinda, he escaped to Norwick Park, the earldom's country estate in southern Sussex. He took up residence there, his somber moods finally driving his mother to the dowager house in Bognor. Left to run the estate in a manner he thought best, and given free rein to do so by his older brother, Daniel settled into life as the spare heir.

Life in Sussex was pleasant. The estate proved profitable for the earldom, and, until he received word from the courier that David had died of a broken neck, Daniel thought to remain at Norwick Park for rest of his days. The news had nudged him from a kind of waking dream, though, his days so much the same he hardly noticed the passage of time.

Suddenly, he had a mission in life beyond seeing to the day-to-day operations of the earldom. The spare was now the heir. He was now the earl.

His valet packed his trunks, his secretary took over the books, and he made the trip, part by horseback and part in a coach, to London. He'd spent the night at his apartment in Bruton Street, but given the lack of servants there, he decided to move into Norwick House this morning. At least breakfast would be served there.

Two years, he thought, staring up at the house, wondering if Lady Norwick had her rooms looking over this side of the house. *It's too early for a lady of the ton to be out of bed, though,* he thought as he regarded his new home.

Two years. What had he done to make Clarinda so angry she would react as she did that day two years ago? At the moment, he couldn't even remember. And he didn't much care. He had only seen her once since that day two years ago — at a dinner party—but he'd made his excuses and left before it would have been necessary for him to exchange at least a bit of small talk with his sister-in-law. Now he might have the opportunity to see her everyday for the rest of his life.

I can only hope.

And then he wondered if she would even look the same as she had back then. Perhaps she'd grown old being married to his older brother. Perhaps her hair was thin and white, her cheeks hollow and sunken, her skin wrinkled and sallow, her hands covered with liver spots, her teeth crooked with some missing, the skin on her neck sagging.

He shook his head. *No, that's what Great Aunt Mildred looks like*, he realized. Clarinda would never look like that, not even when she was a hundred-and-ten.

Dismounting, Daniel handed the reins to a stableboy who appeared from the mews behind the house. At the same time, the carriage with his trunks pulled into the drive. He took a deep breath and mounted the steps, nodding to the butler as the doors opened to admit him.

After a fitful night of weird dreams featuring her late husband and his mother trying to make her wed Daniel at the very moment she was going into labor, Clarinda awoke at dawn feeling exhausted. Her night rail was so twisted, the neckline nearly choked her. While she tried to smooth out the fine lawn fabric, the scent of David reached her again. She inhaled the calming scent and let out a long sigh.

She remembered her last conversation with him. It had been about what he was going to wear when meeting with his solicitor. *Wear the dark blue or you'll look like you're in the army*. Which was ridiculous, because David would *never* look like he was in the militia, no matter what he wore, she thought, remembering how dashing he appeared when he stood on the threshold of the parlor before striding in and dipping her into that delicious kiss. And then he had bid her farewell. She sighed happily as she recalled that last bit, her hand moving to slide over her abdomen.

Wait. That hadn't been their last conversation, she reasoned. They'd last spoken of his cologne and something about Daniel being stubborn. *What had he said?* she wondered as she tried to remember. The tendril of a memory disappeared before she could capture it fully.

Deciding she wouldn't be able to fall back to sleep, Clarinda rang for her maid and ordered a bath. Her night-dress clung to her damp skin as she slowly emerged from the bed. She sighed as the scent of David was left behind. With that realization came another.

Daniel was due to arrive today.

Damnation! She still hadn't decided how to broach the subject of her pregnancy. Daniel's mother had agreed to say nothing of it until Clarinda had had a chance to break the news to him. The funeral service was scheduled for the following day at St. George's, and shortly after, the solicitor would arrive with David's last will and his final instructions.

"Mourning must be making you hungry, milady," Missy commented as she held out a linen. Clarinda was half out of the copper tub, rivulets of water streaming down her body as she caught her reflection in the cheval mirror near the doorway. She didn't think she appeared any heavier, and she certainly didn't feel *different*. Except for when the odor of fish assaulted her nostrils, she'd managed to avoid morning sickness. Other than making sure the dinner menus rarely included fish, she hadn't changed anything in how the household was run since the day she was sure she was with child.

"Why do you say that?" she wondered, giving Missy a quizzical look.

"You look like you've been eating a few too many cakes at tea, my lady," Missy replied, a smile on her face. "If I may say, it's a relief to know your appetite hasn't suffered with his lordship's passing," she said in a lowered voice, her face taking on a suitable expression of sadness.

Clarinda caught her bottom lip with a tooth. At some point, she would have to tell Missy about the baby. In the meantime, she would let the maid continue to think she was a glutton at tea time. "Food is good for the soul," Clarinda commented as she dried herself off and stepped into her bedchamber. As Missy helped her into a chemise and corset, she thought of the look on David's face when he'd run his hand over the front of her body, gently rubbing her belly and leaning over to kiss her *just there*. She had to fight back the smile she felt coming on as she remembered how he had placed an ear against her belly then, as if he thought he could already hear his future offspring.

She fought back the sudden catch in her throat at the thought of David. A mortician was seeing to his remains and would deliver his coffin to St. George's for the funeral and then see to its transportation to Norwick Park for burial. A small graveside service would take place—only a few family members would attend, Clarinda thought—and then life would go on. In six months, she would have a baby to keep her company, to love and cherish and spoil rotten until it was time to send it off to school or marriage.

And that would be that.

She frowned. Perhaps she could become a merry widow (after the requisite year of mourning, of course). Lady Winslow had done that, although she'd only made merry with the Marquess of Devonville for a month before agreeing to marry him. Going from a position as a baroness to the Marchioness of Devonville had to offer benefits beyond longer trips to New Bond Street and a larger jewelry box. Clarinda often wondered what Adele Slater Worthington Grandby thought of her new sister-in-law.

The sudden thought of not being bedded for an entire year had Clarinda raising her face to stare at herself in the oval dressing table mirror. Missy stood behind her, pinning a series of curls across the front of a rather ornate hairstyle. "Am I going somewhere?" Clarinda asked in wonderment. Her maid had never done her hair with quite as many pins before. Of course, David would have had them all out in a few flicks of his wrist when he escorted her to her bedchamber at bedtime. They would scatter about the Aubusson carpet, acting as little land mines when he sneaked back into her room later that night, his bare feet managing to step on enough so he exhaled exclamations of pain and curses as they impaled him. Clarinda smiled at the thought, her eyes suddenly filling with tears as she realized he would never be doing that again.

"The new earl is due to arrive today," Missy replied, her

face falling at the sight of her mistress on the verge of tears. "Oh, my lady, don't cry!" the abigail ordered, reaching over Clarinda's shoulder to fetch a hanky from the tabletop. "I hear he is a very pleasant man, and a handsome one, at that."

Clarinda took a deep breath and willed away the tears that pricked the corners of her eyes. "Well, he ought to be. He's Norwick's identical twin brother," she replied with just a hint of derision, realizing talk of David's brother had her tears dried up faster than the hanky would.

Missy caught the annoyance in Clarinda's comment and regarded her mistress' reflection in the looking glass. "You two do not get along?" she wondered, placing another curl in the coiffure she was creating.

Realizing her maid might speak of the rift between her and Daniel with the other servants, Clarinda quickly waved a hand as if it was nothing. "Oh, we get along fine," she lied, surprised her voice didn't give her away. "I only mean that he's so good looking because he is the epitome of his late brother."

Truth be told, she didn't know if Daniel still looked anything like David. She couldn't imagine him having changed much in two years, though. Although, if she gave it some more thought, she could imagine his hair thin on top and turning gray, the crinkles around his eyes becoming deep wrinkles, age spots covering his face and hands, his eyebrows turning into a bushy white unibrow looking something like an albino caterpillar, all his teeth but one or two missing, his cheeks sunken, dark circles beneath his eyes ... trouble was, David would have looked like that, too, if he had lived to be a hundred-and-ten.

Clarinda shivered, pushing the image out of her mind as Missy announced she was almost done with her hair. "Finally. I'm *starving*," Clarinda said as she got up from the dressing table and made her way to the door. "I'm off to indulge my appetite, Missy," she claimed happily. "After all, I can let my figure go for an entire year!"

Daniel Fitzwilliam followed Porter as the majordomo

preceded him to the earl's bedchamber, his boot heels clicking on the glossy marble floor of the vestibule and hall. Before his arrival at Norwick House just moments before, Daniel had thought to insist on a guest suite, unsure as to the length of his stay and not wanting to disrupt a household already reeling from an untimely death. But Porter seemed to expect his arrival and commented that the earl's suite was in readiness.

"Already?" he'd asked, masking his surprise by keeping his face impassive. Daniel had managed to become quite good at the expression of blandness—it was the only one he allowed to show these days.

"Yes, my lord," Porter responded with a nod.

"And what of my brother's ... effects?" Daniel asked this last with a bit of trepidation. Although he had on occasion employed an adequate tailor in the village near Norwick Park, he did not have the quantity of clothing he would require for formal dinners and *ton* events in London. The last thing he wanted to have to deal with at this point was an appointment with a London-based tailor and the wait for suitable clothes to be made.

"The countess was quite insistent they be kept for you or your valet's review," Porter offered in reply. "Her thought was that everything would fit you, but she wasn't sure if the styles would be to your liking."

Daniel considered this comment, wondering why it would bother him. He wasn't *that* different from his brother—in *anything*. If a suit of clothing suited David, it would no doubt suit him. "Very generous of her ladyship," Daniel offered, pausing as Porter opened the door to the earl's bedchamber. He stepped over the threshold as the major-domo stepped aside, pausing for only a moment as his gaze swept the room.

The deep navy blue fabrics that draped the windows and formed the bed curtains and counterpane were an elegant contrast with the rich golds that made up the fringe trims, pillows and chair coverings. The two large dressers, matching nightstands, and four-poster bed were all made from rosewood, their lines rather more masculine than Daniel would expect for such furnishings. A couple of paintings graced the walls, although, with his quick perusal, he didn't take the time to determine their artists or their subjects. An Aubusson patterned carpet covered the entire floor.

"This will do fine," Daniel said as he strode toward the nearest paneled door. Pangs of hunger reminded him he hadn't yet eaten that morning. "I could do with some breakfast, Porter."

The majordomo nodded from where he stood. "I'll see to it the breakfast parlor is set up immediately. Do you have a preference as to your morning meal, my lord?"

Daniel almost allowed a smile. He was definitely in civilization again if he could actually request a specific food and expect it to be served. "Eggs, toast, kippers, chocolate and coffee," he listed without having to think about it.

"Very good, my lord. I'll see to it." Porter bowed from his place at the door and disappeared down the hall.

Daniel considered the dressing room door, curious as to what lay beyond. Did her ladyship's clothing hang in the same room? Or did she have a separate dressing room? The doors would no doubt connect even if there were two rooms, he considered. The thought had his heart racing even before he opened the door.

The scent of apple blossoms drifted past his nose. He closed his eyes as he inhaled. *Clarinda*! Just the thought of her, probably still asleep on the other side of the wall of the dressing room, made him aroused. Suddenly aware of the bulge behind the placket of his buckskin breeches, Daniel forced himself to think of something else. *Clothes*. He should be thinking about clothes.

Although the dressing room wasn't lit by its own window, he could see from the light that filtered in from the open door that his brother had been a clothes horse. A series of shelves held stacks of breeches, pantaloons, waistcoats, and perfectly folded cravats in both black and white. Coats of every conceivable color were hung on carved forms lining the long wall. If his valet was fifty years younger, he would be ecstatic. Several pairs of boots and buckled shoes stood at attention, their gleaming surfaces a testament to the excellent job David's own valet had been doing. Daniel wondered if the man was still employed at Norwick House or if he'd been let go due to the death of his master. He made a mental note to ask about him as he moved back into the bedchamber. His own valet hadn't seemed too keen on the move to London. Perhaps the older man would be willing to accept a stipend and retire in the country.

Daniel scanned the room and noted another paneled door. Striding toward it, he suddenly felt overwhelmed by the sense that he wasn't alone. Pausing, he glanced around. When he was sure there was no one else in the room, he continued to the door and peeked in. The huge bath featured its own fireplace and a device in which water could be heated for bathing. The tap at the bottom hung over the edge of the largest copper tub Daniel had ever seen.

"Two can bathe in there," a familiar voice said as Daniel stared at the bathing tub. "Never tried it myself, but I recommend you do."

Startled, Daniel glanced around, sure no one was physically in the room and yet ... "Who's there?" he asked, thinking a footman must have arrived with the first of his trunks.

"Who do you think?" David's voice replied, a bit indignant.

Damnation! Daniel spun around to find his brother leaning against the wall, his arms crossed in front of his body in the stance he used when he was in casual conversation. "David?" Daniel whispered, blinking a few times to be sure he was indeed seeing and hearing his brother.

"Aye," his twin replied. "Thought I would welcome you to my old world before I left for my new one."

Daniel wondered if perhaps his gnawing hunger was playing tricks on his mind. He could swear his brother stood against the wall and was regarding him with that mischievous look he used when he was playing a trick on him. Deciding David *couldn't* be standing in front of him, Daniel gave the room another quick glance and strode into the bedchamber. He nearly tripped over David's outstretched boot.

"God in heaven," Daniel breathed as he backed away from this twin brother.

"I couldn't tell you if He is or He isn't," David murmured with a shrug. "As you can see, I haven't made it there yet," he added, uncrossing his arms and walking toward Daniel as if he intended to join him in the bedchamber. "How was your trip?"

Staring at his brother as if he couldn't believe what he was seeing, Daniel shook his head.

"That bad?" David offered, his hands moving to clasp together behind his back. "You made it here in record time. I was going to visit you at your apartments, but I thought you should get a good night's sleep before I ... paid a call," he added uncertainly. Perhaps it was nervousness that made him shift his weight from one leg to the other.

"How thoughtful of you," Daniel managed to get out before he gave his head a quick shake and turned away from what he had decided was a figment of his imagination.

David's chuckle filled the room. "I don't think you've ever accused me of being thoughtful before," he said with a wide grin.

Turning to face David again, Daniel regarded his smiling brother. "Aren't you supposed to be ... dead?" he managed to get out, his impassive expression threatening to be replaced with something darker, as if he thought he was the brunt of a rather cruel joke.

"I am dead," David countered, the grin disappearing. "I'm just not ... *gone* yet," he added in a quieter voice. "Before I go, there are two things I need to be sure are ... sorted first."

Daniel regarded his brother for a long moment, his brows furrowing. Still not believing what, nay, *who* he was seeing, he took a deep breath and decided to simply listen to what his brother had to say. He'd challenge the jokester to a duel with pistols at dawn if it turned out his brother was really alive and well—and still the Earl of Norwick. "Go on," Daniel encouraged. He turned his attention to the dressers, where he knew several small boxes held cravat pins, rings and other jewelry passed down from their father. Hearing David's audible sigh, he couldn't help but glance back in his brother's direction. "What is it?"

David shrugged, a mannerism matching his own so closely Daniel wondered if he was merely seeing himself in a mirror. Then he glanced down at what he wore and realized David's attire was entirely different.

"It's about Clare."

The mention of the love of his life had Daniel ignoring the box of cravat pins and giving his full attention to his twin brother. "And what about Clare?" he asked with a noticeable degree of concern.

"She's fine," David replied quickly, as if he could tell his brother had jumped to the wrong conclusion. "She's better than fine, in fact. She's ... expecting!" he blurted out, his smile displaying his perfect teeth. He poked Daniel in the arm as he made the claim.

A sense of shock settled over Daniel, caused his eyes to glaze over and his heart to stop for a moment. *Clarinda. With child. With his brother's child.* "Congratulations," he managed to get out. "You must be very proud." It took a good deal of effort, but he managed to make it sound as if he was happy.

The late brother didn't seem to notice Daniel's effort, but his own enthusiasm waned just a bit. "She lost the last two babies she was expecting," he said quietly, a good deal of sadness sounding in his simple words.

Daniel's heart clenched at his brother's comment. "She was with child before?" he whispered, a sudden need to go to her nearly sending him through the connecting door in the dressing room. *The poor woman!*

Nodding, David reached out and touched Daniel's sleeve. "She was devastated. I didn't even find out about the second miscarriage until .. well, until just a couple of days ago. It's amazing what you find out when you die," he added with that familiar shrug.

Daniel's gasp was audible. "*Two* miscarriages?" he managed to get out in a hoarse whisper. *Christ*! Why hadn't he known? Why hadn't someone told him? He turned on his heel and headed for the dressing room door, determined to go to Clarinda, to pull her into his arms and hold her, comfort her, tell her everything would be all right. The loss of one babe was sad enough, but two? She must have been so heartbroken. His hand reached for the door knob, but David's hand covered it before he could turn it.

"Those miscarriages happened a couple of years ago, Danny."

Daniel stepped back, his look of annoyance falling on his older twin. "If she's suffered the loss of a babe in the past, what makes you believe she'll carry this one to birth?" he asked, his chin shoved out in defiance. Had it been he who Clarinda married instead of his rake of a brother, he was sure she would have carried a babe to full term and given birth to a healthy heir.

David waved a hand in the air, as if there was no reason to be concerned. "She's past the point where she miscarried the last two times ... she's almost four months gone," he said softly. He poked Daniel in the shoulder. "With twins," he added proudly. He poked Daniel once more to make his point.

Daniel blinked. Twice. "Good grief, Davy," he managed to get out. "Does she *know?*"

This last seemed to catch his older brother off guard. "Well, she knows she's expecting, of course. But ... I haven't told her the rest. Yet."

Raising a hand to the side of his head, Daniel wondered if he felt a headache coming on. His stomach growled just then, a sound that even David heard from where he stood.

"So, what? You're just going to show up, *dead*, and just tell her she's having twins?" Daniel asked, his mouth left open by the thought. "The sight of you alone is going to be enough of a shock to cause a miscarriage!"

David regarded his younger twin for a moment before he hung his head. "Not if I do it in the middle of the night. When she's asleep. She'll just think it's a dream ..."

"Nightmare, more like it," Daniel countered.

"... And when she wakes up, she'll remember everything I tell her." David crossed his arms in front of his chest again, apparently satisfied with himself. "I've already done it. Twice," he added, an eyebrow wiggling to indicate his mischievousness.

Daniel shook his head as he regarded David. "When you showed up, you implied you had to get something sorted before you left for good. What were you talking about?"

Rolling his eyes, as if he'd completely forgotten why he'd shown up in his old bedchamber, David nodded. "I want you to marry Clare," he stated quite firmly. "The sooner, the better." His lips pressed together in a line, as if he was asking his brother to grant a huge favor and doubted he would accommodate him.

Daniel blinked and shook his head, not quite sure he'd heard his brother correctly. "You *want* me to marry Clare?" he repeated. *What the hell?* "She can't. She's in mourning. For a year, if she follows custom," he replied in disbelief.

"But you *want* to," David answered, as if he'd heard his brother's reasoning and agreed.

Shocked by David's insight, Daniel stared at him for several moments. Of course, he wanted to marry Clarinda! He'd wanted to kiss her the first time he laid eyes on her. He'd wanted to dance with her the very first time they attended the same ball. He wanted to marry her even before David had *met* her. Wanted her in his bed, wanted her in his life, wanted her in every way a man could want a woman. And despite having courted her and kissed her and asked for her hand in marriage, she still ended up married to his brother.

The bitterness of that time came back to haunt him just then, the anger and disbelief filling him as it had four years ago. "Of course, I want her. I never stopped *wanting* her, damn it!" he got out between gritted teeth. "But she despises me, David. She probably hates me."

David smiled, a huge smile that split his face and made him look years younger than his almost four decades. "Thank you, Danny," he said as he wrapped his arms around Daniel's shoulders and hugged his brother to him. "I knew I could count on you. Take care of her, will you?" he said in a quieter voice. "I beg you."

Stunned at his brother's response, Daniel nodded as he felt David's arms fall away. He couldn't remember a time they had embraced like that, other than when they were fighting. Or wrestling.

David wanted him to marry Clare. Wanted him to take care of her. "I will," he stated with a nod. "Of course, I will." He sighed, remembering his brother's earlier words. "Now, what was the second thing you wanted ..?" When he looked up, David was gone.

Chapter 8

DANIEL AND CLARINDA GET REACQUAINTED

"You cannot go to breakfast dressed like that, my lady," Missy announced just as the perfectly coiffed Clarinda was about to open her bedchamber door. Wondering what Missy meant by the proclamation, Lady Norwick looked down and realized she only wore her chemise and corset under a silk dressing gown. A black kerseymere gown was spread out on the bed. Black silk stockings dribbled over the edge of the mattress, and a pair of black slippers were on the floor beneath. Black would be the extent of her wardrobe for a long time to come, she realized.

"Oh," Clarinda managed to get out before her shoulders slumped. *Good grief*! Had she really almost left her bedchamber wearing nothing more than a dressing grown? Well, so what if she had? No one would even notice what she was wearing given the elaborate hair style Missy had managed to create!

She thought of Adele Grandby and decided she could do with a walk in the park. When she finished her breakfast, she would send a footman with a note asking if Adele could meet her at their usual spot in Hyde Park.

Once Missy had her dressed, Clarinda once again

announced she had every intention of *eating* and then made her way downstairs to the breakfast room. Moving through the doorway, she smelled the kippers long before she realized they were on the sideboard.

And on the plate in front of Daniel Fitzwilliam.

Her stomach suddenly roiling, Clarinda gasped and hurried through the room, passing her startled brother-in-law and holding a hand against her belly as she mumbled an, "Excuse me," and disappeared into the butler's pantry. She found a chamber pot underneath the silver cabinet just in time. Well, it wasn't really a chamber pot, she realized too late. The rather large and elaborately decorated soup tureen worked just as well, though.

"My lady! Are you all right?"

Clarinda whirled around to find Rosie, one of the main floor servants, carrying a stack of dishes through the butler's pantry. The sudden motion did little to settle her stomach, but at least the smell of fish didn't reach her here. "I'll be quite fine, thank you," Clarinda answered as she finished wiping her lips with her hanky.

But Rosie's eyes widened. "My lady! You look like you've seen a ghost!"

Gasping, Clarinda's own eyes widened. *Damnation! Was it that apparent she'd been visited by David?* she wondered as she straightened and put one hand up to her face. "Oh?" she ventured as calmly as she could manage, wondering what gave it away.

"You're quite pale, my lady," Rosie said as she put down the dishes. "Should I have Porter send for the physician?"

Swallowing hard, Clarinda considered the offer. There really was no need to have Dr. Collins come over when she already knew *why* she felt sick. All he would do is confirm her state of impending motherhood and probably attach a few leeches to her. She shuddered at the image of the slimy things on her skin, deciding the thought alone made her sicker than the smell of kippers in the next room. "No, Rosie, that won't be necessary," she managed to get out before she inhaled a deep, cleansing breath. "I'm feeling better already, although I do think I'll just make my way back to the hallway using a different route," she said as she left the butler's pantry from the direction the maid had come.

"Yes, my lady," Rosie reluctantly replied as she bobbed a curtsy. "May I say, my lady, your hair looks very nice today."

Clarinda fought the urge to look up. "Thank you, Rosie." Once again very hungry, Clarinda wanted nothing more than to have breakfast, but the thought of going back into the breakfast parlor was rather unappetizing. Not only did it smell like kippers, but *Daniel* was in there. She thought he'd been reading *The Times*—at least, he'd been holding up a newspaper as he ate, she remembered—so perhaps he hadn't even noticed her quick trip through the room. To him, she probably just looked like a black whirling dervish, although she was sure her skirts created a breeze that probably ruffled his dark, silky, wavy hair. She was quite sure he hadn't taken his attention away from the newspaper, though. But from the very brief glimpse she'd had of him, he was still the epitome of David in appearance. So handsome, so fit, so very much a *man*.

"So the mere sight of me makes you *ill*, does it?"

Clarinda had just come around the corner from the servant's hall into the main hall, nearly colliding with Daniel as she did so. As tall as David and just as developed across the shoulders and chest, he made for an imposing figure. And, at the moment, a rather frightening one.

"Daniel!" she gasped, stopping suddenly, one hand pressed to her bosom. After another loud heartbeat, she took another breath. "No," she added with a shake of her head when she realized what he'd said. She could feel ... was that *anger* emanating from his body? "I just cannot bear the odor of..."

"Oh, so now I smell bad?" he countered, his eye blazing with barely contained fury.

Taking an involuntary step backward, Clarinda dropped her hands to her sides, allowing her fists to clench. "You don't. Truly. But the *kippers* do," she managed to get out in a voice that belied the sudden embarrassment that colored her face.

There was a very long pause as the two regarded one another. Clarinda's hands unclenched and Daniel's stance seem to relax just a bit.

"Kippers?" he replied, one eyebrow cocking into an expression that suggested disbelief.

"Kippers, yes," Clarinda acknowledged with a nod, her face still red with embarrassment. Of all the things to happen when she was faced with the prospect of seeing Daniel for the first time in nearly two years, she never would have expected to feel nauseous and have to cast up her accounts, especially in front of a servant.

Daniel blinked, a mannerism Clarinda found very similar to the way David would sometimes react when she said something that befuddled him. Which, now that she thought about it, was quite frequently.

"Not because you find the sight of me somehow ... repugnant?" This last was delivered in a voice that suggested Daniel Fitzwilliam still didn't believe her.

It was Clarinda's turn to blink. "No! Of course not," she replied with a bit too much emphasis.

Daniel seemed to take a step backward, even though his feet did not move an inch. "You do not find the sight of me to be ... repugnant?"

Clarinda's mouth opened in astonishment. *How can this man be so thick?* she wondered, fighting to keep her annoyance from showing on her face. She took a deep breath as she gazed at David's identical twin, looking for any sign of *something* that was different from her late husband. "Since you look *exactly* like the man I married, and since I found that man to be quite handsome, I have to admit I could never find the sight of you repugnant," she said in a careful, measured tone, thoroughly explaining her reasoning in the hopes her brother-in-law would understand. Then she found herself hoping she wasn't going to have to deal with Daniel's newly inflated ego, which had probably grown several times larger given her adamant assurance that he was handsome.

Damnation, though. He *was* handsome. There were a few differences between him and David, she now was coming to realize, although none of them were differences a casual acquaintance would notice. The little scar near his eye, the one he'd suffered at the point of a bayonet during one of the wars in France, gave him a rakish air. And given his hair was just a shade darker and held just a bit more wave than David's did— probably because David spent more time out of doors—she would have to admit that Daniel was just a bit more handsome than David. *Damn, damn, double damn!* she thought, not able to tear her eyes away from David's twin.

Daniel's mouth began opening and then closing, over and over, as if he was about to say something and then suddenly thought better of it. Clarinda thought he looked somewhat like the tropical fish Lord Everly kept in the large glass tank in his library. "But ... I thought you ... despised me," he finally managed to get out.

Clarinda's brows furrowed, a little wrinkle developing between them. "Only because ... because you despise *me*," she countered, rather surprised he would voice the sentiment and she would bother to reply.

"I do not!" Daniel exclaimed, his protest a bit too loud. He reached out with a finger and poked her right between her brows, as if he was curious about the little wrinkle that had appeared there and thought he could simply press it away with a push of his fingertip. Pulling his finger away, he stared at the spot, mesmerized. "You really need to stop doing whatever it is that creates that little ..." He pointed at the fold between her brows using the same finger he'd poked her with before, adding, "Or you'll find it will be permanent," he stated with a finality that suggested he was an expert on such abnormalities. "At least, that's what Mother is always telling me about mine."

The feel of his finger touching her sent a shock wave through Clarinda. She might have found it rather pleasant, except something akin to a volcano had began to build deep inside of her, with its molten lava heat and steam churning and rumbling. Although the rumbling was probably due to her hunger pangs, Clarinda realized the rest—the suppressed anger and outrage over his impertinent comment, the sudden desire to see him uncomfortable, to see him suffer for poking her—was about to erupt all over Daniel Fitzwilliam. *Pity the man who witnesses a volcanic eruption in the home he is expected to occupy for the next several years*, Clarinda found herself thinking, knowing just then she would have to gain the upper hand on this poor excuse for a man *right now*.

But then Daniel's last comment and the denial made just before it tamped down the volcano. She felt the steam inside her suddenly dissipate. *He doesn't despise me?* she wondered in awe.

"You're doing it again," Daniel murmured as he kept his eye on the furrow between her brows. "It's rather ... cute when *you* do it, though," he added, his words sounding as if he were in awe rather than pointing out an ugly feature on her otherwise beautiful face.

She is still so beautiful, he thought as his gaze took in her oval face with the perfect complexion, the high cheekbones, pert nose and aquamarine eyes that seemed to see right into his soul. The lashes that surrounded those eyes were dark like her hair, and curved so they seemed to sweep through the air as they fell over the light blue-green of her eyes. And when they lifted, it was like a curtain rising to reveal the aquamarine jewels of her countenance.

Her maid had obviously become adept at dressing her hair. The elaborate coiffure would have been suitable for a ball at Carleton House. He noticed how she had a tooth caught in her lower lip, the plump flesh bent in just a bit where it made contact. And she was watching him as if she was trying to solve a puzzle. *She is more beautiful than she was when we cursed one another all those years ago.* At the moment, he couldn't even remember *why* they had cursed one another. Couldn't remember what had brought on the accusations that caused her face to redden and her anger to erupt so forcefully. *Like a volcano*, he thought, *all steam and molten lava roiling out of her*. And then she'd slapped him. Even today, he could feel the sting of that open-handed hit. *Like a steam burn*, he remembered. He could feel the force behind it as her arm swung hard and impacted him like shrapnel from an explosion. He was sure it had hurt her more than it did him, but if it did, he never saw Clarinda flinch.

The target of Daniel's never-ending gaze continued to regard him warily. *Why is he looking at me like that?* she wondered, making sure to keep continuous eye contact. Clarinda didn't want to be the first to look away, thinking it would be some sort of surrender or admission of guilt if she did so. And he'd just said the wrinkle between her brows was *cute*. At the same time, his brown eyes had taken on the look of a lovesick puppy. *Look who's calling the kettle black!*

It was the same look David had given her that day in Kensington Gardens when he'd taken her to the area surrounded by pink roses and lowered himself on one knee and asked for her hand in marriage. She'd accepted the ring he gave her, of course, and told him pink roses were her favorite flower and would be for the rest of her days. The simple gold band with a square-cut emerald had been his paternal grandmother's, he'd said back then. And then David went on to explain that he'd wanted to give her his maternal grandmother's instead, but his mother was still wearing it.

Clarinda knew very well why Dorothea Fitzwilliam still wore that ring—the sapphire was huge, and the diamonds that surrounded it weren't too shabby, either. But Clarinda was quite happy with her engagement ring and told him so.

It was quite a surprise then, when two years later, David was off on a hunting trip with friends when Daniel related the story of how *he* had asked for her hand in marriage. How he knew from asking her friends that she favored pink roses, so he took her to Kensington Gardens and asked for her hand amongst the pink roses. He explained how surprised and disappointed, nay, heartbroken he was when Clarinda married David instead of him, the tone of his voice suggesting he had never forgiven her for choosing his older brother over him.

Even if she was betrothed to David.

Stunned that he would claim *he* had been the one to ask for her hand—not David, as Clarinda believed all this time — Clarinda had allowed her anger to build in the ensuing argument, the steam and molten lava causing such pressure that when the volcano finally erupted and she vented the steam, she did so by slapping Daniel so hard her hand, indeed, her entire arm, had hurt for nearly two weeks afterward. She often wondered if she had done permanent damage to his facial bones, for she was sure she had at least cracked some bones in her hand or wrist or arm. But she'd never had the chance to ask him, for he disappeared that day, apparently to take up residence at Norwick Park, and he never returned to Norwick House.

At least, not until today.

"I'll have a footman deliver your breakfast to the parlor, my lady," Daniel said in a very quiet voice, his eyes finally looking away as his face displayed a slight flush. "In the future, should I desire kippers for breakfast, I shall be sure to take my morning meal in my bedchamber."

With this last comment, Daniel bowed to a rather stunned Clarinda and turned to make his way back into the breakfast parlor. Clarinda stayed rooted to the same spot for several minutes, lost in thought as she remembered more of the details of that day in Kensington Gardens. Could Daniel really have been the one who asked for her hand? She struggled to remember, but the dowager countess interrupted her thoughts when she appeared at the bottom of the stairs.

"Does everyone get up *early* in this household?" Dorothea asked with a hint of annoyance. She was already dressed in a dark green silk gown, her hair caught up in an elegant chignon and adorned with a wide green ribbon. A black armband was the only hint the woman knew someone who had died.

"I apologize if you were disturbed, my lady," Clarinda offered contritely. "Your son arrived this morning. He's in the breakfast room," she added as she pointed in the general direction.

Dorothea glanced at the door to the breakfast parlor and then turned her attention back to her daughter-in-law. "Aren't you eating, darling?" she asked, one elegant eyebrow arched up, as if she was looking forward to the spectacle of seeing Clarinda and Daniel sitting together at the breakfast table.

"In the parlor," Clarinda acknowledged with a nod. "Far away from the odor of kippers, my lady," she added with a wan smile, hoping the dowager countess wouldn't think she was deliberately avoiding Daniel. Which she *was* doing, but she didn't want Dorothea to know. She gave a curtsy before she turned and made her way to the parlor. A footman carried in a tray covered with a silver dome just as Clarinda settled into a chair at the card table. "Thank you, Nichols," she said as he removed the dome to reveal her usual morning meal of coddled eggs, toast, and chocolate. As she took the steaming cup of chocolate to her lips, Dorothea appeared in the doorway.

"Before I join my son for breakfast, Clare, I thought I should ask if you'd had a chance to share your good news with him?" she wondered with a mischievous grin.

Clarinda fought the urge to roll her eyes and instead shook her head. Surely Daniel would not find the news of her pregnancy *good*. But she had no idea how the man would react once she told him. She would have to tell him before tomorrow afternoon, though, before the solicitor read David's will. "No, my lady. Our entire conversation consisted of me trying to convince him that the sight of him was not repugnant, and that he didn't smell bad, while he informed me the furrow between my brows was cute but no doubt permanent."

Dorothea seemed to consider Clarinda's words for several moments before her face suddenly brightened. "Oh, well now you two *are* getting somewhere," she announced happily before she disappeared from the doorway, the retreating swish of her skirts suggesting she was on her way to the breakfast parlor.

Wondering if anyone would notice, Clarinda toyed with the idea of adding a dollop of brandy to her chocolate before she sighed and ate her breakfast alone, sans brandy. Penning a note to Adele, she mentioned she would be taking a walk in the park at eleven and wondered if Adele might want to join her. She almost tacked on the words, 'Save me,' along with a drawing of her neck-deep in water made up of the name 'Daniel', but thought better of it. It would be eleven o'clock before she'd have the note ready for the footman. The footman hurried off with her note, leaving Clarinda to finish her second helping of coddled eggs and toast.

Chapter 9

PARLOR TALK

Daniel stood in the parlor doorway, not quite sure if he should step over the threshold. Clarinda sat facing the fire, her profile suggesting she was deep in thought and hadn't noticed his presence. He was surprised, then, when she took a deep breath and stood. Turning to face him, she afforded him a deep curtsy."My lord. Forgive me for not properly welcoming you to Norwick House," she said in what sounded like a truly repentant voice, her eyes downcast.

Unsure of how to respond, Daniel bowed and entered the room, stopping just in front of Clarinda so he could reach for her hand and lift it to his lips. Brushing them over the backs of her fingers, Daniel continued to hold onto her hand as he regarded her. "Thank you, my lady. I am ... sorry for your loss."

Raising her eyes to meet his, Clarinda realized he meant the sentiment. "And I am sorry for yours, my lord," she answered formally. *God, he looks just like David!*

Daniel nodded, his eyes closing briefly.

"Did you have a good trip from Sussex?" she asked then, wondering if now would be a good time to tell him the news of the baby she expected in five months, three weeks and one day.

Daniel shrugged, glancing toward one of the chairs. "As good as could be expected, I suppose," he murmured. "May we sit?" he asked, one brow furrowing as if he thought she might deny him the hospitality.

Clarinda's eyes widened. "Oh, of course," she replied with a nod. "Please," she motioned toward the chair David would normally take. Daniel eyed it with a frown and instead took an adjacent chair after Clarinda took her place on the settee. She was careful to sit up straight as possible, as if she was preparing for a verbal battle.

"As mistress of this house, I suspect you are best equipped to tell me what I need to know," he stated, not waiting for her to comment on the weather or the funeral scheduled for the following day. "We should start with the staff. As a result of my brother's untimely passing, has anyone resigned their post or given notice they intend to leave their employment?"

Clarinda stared at Daniel in surprise. "No," she replied with a shake of her head, wondering why he would think they would. Most of the household staff had been with the house since before David moved in, and those who were newer servants all seemed satisfied with their posts.

Daniel blinked at her response. "Oh," he responded, his quizzical expression suggesting he thought the entire staff would have given their notice. "And those who work in the stables? In the carriage house?"

"No," Clarinda answered carefully.

Frowning, Daniel leaned forward and clasped his hand together, his elbows supported on his knees. "And the house? Any ... overlooked maintenance? Leaky roof? Drafty windows?"

"No," Clarinda shook her head, joining her own hands together on her lap. Then, thinking she should make some comment other than 'no,' she added, "The kitchen was recently remodeled and now has a newer stove. And we acquired an ice box." She was rather glad for this last addition since it allowed her to serve her guests cold lemonade instead of the lukewarm lemon water that reminded her of the dreck they served at Almack's.

"Oh," Daniel answered with a nod that seemed to suggest he was impressed. "And the gardens?"

Clarinda smiled then. "Mr. Foster does a wonderful job keeping the grounds trimmed and the gardens looking neat and tidy," she offered with a nod. Of all the staff at Norwick House, she liked Mr. Foster the best because he did such a good job in the only position that was the most evident to anyone who drove up to Norwick House and parked in the semi-circular drive in front. As for the gardens in the back, she frequently walked through them with her visiting friends when the weather permitted.

"I take it he can grow roses," Daniel stated, a slight smile finally touching his lips.

Clarinda nearly sucked in a breath at the sight of his changed expression. It was the first hint he'd shown of not being angry. Her face changed to a slight frown, though, when she realized what he had said. "We actually don't have any roses in the gardens, nor out front," she murmured, a look of puzzlement crossing her face.

"No roses?" Daniel repeated, his brows furrowing as if she'd said there was no brandy in the library.

Thinking of brandy, Clarinda remembered she hadn't rung for tea. Nor had she offered Daniel anything stronger. "Would you like a glass of brandy, my lord?"

Daniel blinked. "It's not even ten o'clock in the morning, my lady."

Clarinda regarded him for a moment, wondering as to the significance of his statement. She was quite sure David imbibed anytime of the day or night. "Tea, then?" she suggested, reaching over to shake the silver bell that she'd left on the edge of the settee the morning when David had swept her into the dip and kissed her senseless. She almost imagined Daniel doing the same and had to shake her head to rid herself of the almost-formed picture in her mind.

"Fine," Daniel responded with a wave of his hand. "No

pink roses?" he asked then, apparently not willing to give up the conversation about the gardens.

Clarinda turned to him from having nodded at Rosie, who had appeared in the doorway as if she had been camped out in the hallway. "No pink roses, my lord," she affirmed, "Although the maid's name is Rosie," she added as she waved a hand toward the doorway. She wondered if she needed to direct Mr. Foster to plant a huge rose garden before the day was done. There was certainly room in the back, near the edge of the parkland that bordered the property line.

Daniel stared at her for a very long time. "I thought ... I thought they were your favorite flower," he stammered, a muscle in his jaw working overtime.

Clarinda leaned her head to one side and regarded her brother-in-law for a very long time. "They are," she acknowledged with a nod, wondering how Daniel knew such a thing. Had David mentioned it to him? She could hardly imagine the brothers discussing her love of pink roses. "How ... how did you know?" she asked quietly, deciding she wanted to know.

His lips thinning to a straight line, David ducked his head a bit. "Your friends did," he replied quietly. "They told me. The day before I took you to Kensington Gardens and asked for your hand in marriage."

There.

Despite what had happened the last time he mentioned his proposal, the words were out again. He wondered if the volcano that was Clarinda Ann Brotherton Fitzwilliam's anger would suddenly erupt and leave him awash in molten lava.

Clarinda held her breath, remembering where this conversation had taken them the last time they'd had it two years ago. "I wasn't aware my friends had shared that information with *you*," she replied, her voice barely a whisper.

Porter appeared in the doorway, clearing his throat to make his presence known. "Yes, Porter?" Clarinda and Daniel replied in unison.

"My lady, a floral delivery for you. Where shall I put the bouquets?" the butler asked as his eyes shifted nervously to his right.

Clarinda realized almost immediately that since David's death notice had appeared in *The Times*, flowers would start arriving. Gladioli, no doubt, most from the hot houses just outside of London. "You can put them here on the table," she offered, waving to the tea table in front of the settee. She noticed one of Daniel's eyebrows arch up, but he said nothing.

Meanwhile, Porter gave his mistress an uncertain look. "My lady, all of these bouquets are ... far *larger* than that small table will allow, I should think," he replied uncertainly.

"Oh?" Clarinda answered, coming to her feet. Caught by surprise at his sister-in-law's quick rise, Daniel moved to stand and instead stayed seated, heaving a sigh. Clarinda made her way to the doorway and peeked around the corner. Several liveried delivery men stood in the vestibule and hallway, all burdened with large bouquets of pink flowers. "Oh!" she said, her hands coming up to clasp together in front of her waist.

There were at least seven very large vases of roses—pink roses—being hefted by the gloved servants. The scent of them filled the hallway, intoxicating her instantly. "Oh!" She stole a glance back at Daniel, but his attention was elsewhere, one leg crossed over the other and bobbing up and down. *This cannot be a coincidence*, Clarinda thought as she turned back to consider the huge rose garden that had suddenly appeared in her hall. "Um. One on that table over there," she pointed toward the round table near the base of the stairs, "One in my bedchamber, one in here on the card table, one in the dining room, one in the breakfast room, one in the dowager countess' bedchamber and one in the library," she counted off as she pointed at each footman in turn. "Was there, perhaps, a card?" she asked in a whisper, leaning toward Porter as she made the query.

"If there is one, we haven't yet found it, my lady," the butler replied in an equally quiet voice.

Clarinda realized that looking for a pasteboard card in this mass of roses would be like looking for a needle in a haystack. "If you do find one, be sure to bring it to me straightaway," Clarinda said, more of a suggestion than an order. *Damn thing was probably pink to match the flowers*, she thought as she stole another glance in Daniel's direction.

"Very good, my lady," Porter replied as he saw to the disbursement of the floral bounty.

Clarinda watched as the roses paraded past, one of them moving into the parlor, its carrier completely hidden by the display. The last time roses had been delivered to Norwick House, they had been red roses, roses ordered by her husband in honor of her birthday. And every birthday for the past four years, she remembered. Always red. Never pink.

She turned to re-enter the parlor at the same time Rosie appeared with the tea tray. "Thank you, Rosie," she said as she returned to the settee. Spreading her black kerseymere skirt, she seated herself and regarded Daniel with a raised eyebrow, daring him to deny his involvement in the floral delivery.

Daniel returned her gaze and finally gave her a shrug. "I despise gladioli," he stated with a frown.

"That's hardly grounds to buy out every hot house within a fifty mile radius of their entire stock of pink roses," Clarinda chided him with a mischievous grin.

"It was only three greenhouses, and they were all in Chiswick," he countered stubbornly. A slight flush had colored his face, making Clarinda wonder when he had managed to order so many roses. At least Chiswick was on the way from Sussex, given the road he would have traveled to get to Norwick House.

"Where did you stay last night?" Clarinda asked quietly, realizing he had to have arrived in London sometime the day before.

Daniel seemed surprised by the question, but shrugged.

"I have an apartment in Bruton Street," he stated in a manner that suggested every bachelor had such a thing.

Leaning over to pour tea, Clarinda wondered why he would have waited until this morning to move into Norwick House. "You were welcome to stay here," she countered, handing him a cup and saucer. He seemed for a moment to be lost in thought. "This is your home now, after all," she added, wondering if now would be a good time to tell him about the baby. She poured a cup for herself and stirred in a several spoonfuls of sugar.

Daniel took a deep breath, glad to hear her make the offer and amused at the amount of sugar she was adding to her tea. *She's nervous*, he realized, *but ever the gracious hostess.* He would never have asked if he could move into Norwick House, even if it was now his right to take up residence in the beautiful home David had made into the family's London seat. "Thank you," he said with a nod. "I do hope you are planning on remaining in residence, my lady," he added, his eyes downcast as he made the statement.

Clarinda relaxed a bit and settled against the hard back of the settee. As she took a sip of her overly sweetened tea, she realized she hadn't given much thought to where she would live. There had been too many other details to consider. "I had hoped to be able to stay," she answered carefully. "I will take another bedchamber, of course," she added, remembering that it was his right to take David's bedchamber. The room and hers shared a closet and dressing room; it wouldn't suit to live in adjoining chambers.

"You shall do no such thing, my lady," Daniel replied with a shake of his head.

Stunned at his insistent tone, Clarinda blinked at his statement. "But, won't you want that bedchamber for your future wife?" she asked in surprise, leaning forward to place her cup and saucer on the tea table.

Daniel lowered his eyes and did not give his reply for some time. Clarinda waited patiently, wondering what he was about to say. "Yes," he finally acknowledged. "But I expect it will be some time before I can convince the lady to be my wife," he stated carefully. "Probably a year or more."

"Oh?" Clarinda replied, instantly wondering who he had in mind for the position as his countess. *I'm a dowager countess now*, she suddenly realized, the thought so appalling she actually shuddered.

No wonder Dorothea didn't wear black.

"Are you cold?" Daniel wondered, leaning forward again, his look of concern surprising Clarinda.

"No, I ... I just thought of my new title, and I find I don't particularly like it," she murmured, her brows furrowing so the little wrinkle between them appeared again.

Daniel angled his head, a look of consternation on his face. "Dowager Countess, you mean?" he offered, wishing he could lean over and poke the little wrinkle into submission. *God, she's beautiful.* She was more beautiful now than that day he'd asked for her hand in Kensington Gardens. There would be no dowager countess title for her if he could help it.

Clarinda shuddered again, giving him a quelling look at his slightly amused expression. "Yes. I hadn't expected to be such a thing for many years to come."

Daniel regarded the love of his life for a very long time. "My lady ..."

"You should call me 'Clarinda'," she interrupted suddenly. "Or 'Clare'. We're family. It hardly seems proper for you to call me anything else."

Daniel could think of many monikers he would like to call her, some not appropriate for anywhere but the marriage bed. "Clare," he amended, "I have every intention ..."

"I am with child," Clarinda blurted suddenly, surprised at herself that she would simply announce it out loud like that.

But the time seemed right, and she was afraid she would lose her nerve if she didn't say something right then.

"I am well aware of your condition," Daniel replied, his lower lip suddenly trembling.

Clarinda regarded him in surprise, the little furrow

between her brows reappearing. "You are?" She remembered Daniel's mother and immediately thought the woman must have said something. "I told her *I* would tell you," she said, her indignant tone clearly evoking her sense of outrage.

Holding up his hand as if it alone could stave off a volcanic eruption, Daniel said, "Mother didn't tell me," with a small shake of his head. He swallowed, just then realizing that he would have to tell her how he knew. "David did."

Clarinda's jaw slackened, stunned that her husband would have sent word to his brother when they hadn't told anyone else. She hadn't even told her best friends! Well, she'd told *one*. "When did he do that?" was all she could get out.

His eyes suddenly darting to one side, Daniel straightened in his chair. He couldn't exactly tell her he'd learned of her pregnancy from David that *morning*. What would she think if he told her that David had visited him in his old bedchamber? Had repeatedly poked him, reminiscent of the way he did when they were young boys? And then proceeded to brag about the fact that he'd managed to get his wife with child, nay *with twins*, apparently for the third time?

Daniel had furrowed his brows at this bit of news, remembering what had happened the other two times. *Good, God! Poor Clare*, he remembered suddenly, his response at the time so visceral he nearly left his apartment and headed for Norwick House that very moment. But David must have realized that was his immediate plan, for his twin brother shook his head quickly. "Not necessary," he'd said. "Happened a long time ago. But the third time is the charm," he'd said proudly, his grin doubling when he'd whispered the word, "Twins," and given Daniel another two pokes to emphasize his accomplishment.

Although Daniel was happy for this brother, he had to admit a sense of disappointment at the news, and not for the reason Clarinda would assume. She probably thought he wanted the earldom for himself and would be jealous if she gave birth to a son. Daniel was the spare in the old "heir and a spare" scenario, after all, his mother having completed the heir and spare bearing all in one fell swoop (although, to hear her tell it, she would have preferred to do it the more traditional method. Apparently, carrying twins made her twice as sick, caused her to gain four times as much weight, and ended up causing eight times as many stretch marks. *Whatever those were.*) But Daniel had never begrudged his older brother's right to sire an heir. He simply wished he would have done so with a different wife. Daniel still wanted Clarinda for himself. He still intended Clarinda to be the mother of his own children.

Well, all in good time. He had plenty of that.

"Not too long ago," Daniel finally answered carefully to her question of when David had told him her news. "You must be thrilled." He almost added, "To be expecting twins," but managed to stop himself when he remembered David saying he hadn't yet told her. When Clarinda's eyes widened in shock, Daniel immediately regretted saying anything about her condition.

He wondered how she'd feel when she discovered she was carrying *twins*.

What had David said? That he would just visit her in the middle of the night and tell her she was carrying twins? Damn! *Double damn, in this case.*

"He told you I was with *child*?" Clarinda stared at Daniel for a very long time, her mouth hanging open in shock.

Daniel reached over and placed his hand beneath her chin, pushing it up so her mouth was forced to close while resisting the urge to tell her she was carrying twins. Although he wanted to see her reaction at the news, she would forever wonder how he knew unless he admitted David had told him that, too. What would she think then? She would probably think she had a Bedlamite on her hands. "Congratulations, Clare," he said with a mischievous grin. "You'll make a wonderful mother." He decided now was not the time to inform her he would do his best as their father, even if he was really just their uncle.

Clarinda studied her brother-in-law for a very long time,

wondering just when David had sent word to his brother about her condition. And she couldn't exactly tell Daniel how David came to her in the middle of the night. He'd think she was a Bedlamite!

"Thank you," she murmured, very aware of Daniel's hand still touching her chin, although now his fingers moved ever so lightly along her jaw until his hand cupped it. She was sure he was considering kissing her, the way his eyes kept glancing toward her lips and then back to her eyes, as if he was seeking her permission. And Clarinda was quite sure she hadn't given him permission when she realized his head was moving toward hers. And try as she might, she couldn't pull away. She might have even leaned forward a bit. She should really pull away. She despised him. She should admonish him for his impertinence. Scold him for thinking he could simply kiss her in the parlor. She was in mourning!

"There you are!" Dorothea announced happily from the doorway.

Clarinda had never seen David move as fast as Daniel did just then, his hand suddenly gone from her face and his body settled back into his chair as if he had just been motioning nonchalantly at something over her shoulder. Then he stood up with the air of a gentleman, turning to bow to his mother.

Dorothea swept into the room as if she owned the place. In a way, she sort of did, Clarinda had to admit as she rose to meet her mother-in-law. "Good morning, Clare. You're looking especially lovely this morning," Dorothea claimed as she moved to the chair opposite Clarinda, acting as if they hadn't already had two conversations that morning before breakfast.

"Thank you, my lady," Clarinda acknowledged the compliment, realizing almost immediately her face was displaying a bit more color than usual because she'd almost been caught kissing her impertinent brother-in-law in the parlor! *The despicable man*! "Would you like tea?" she asked as she reached for a cup and saucer and the tea pot.

"Of course. I just had the most delicious breakfast, even

if my son neglected me for half of it and then disappeared for the other half," she stated in a manner suggesting her son wasn't in the room just then even though she was angling her head in his direction. "But he's forgiven since he's here and not already locked away in the study doing God-knows-what with the estate papers."

Daniel cocked an eyebrow and nodded in his mother's direction. "Thank you, Mother," he murmured. If he made the comment facetiously, he didn't let on with either the tone of his voice or with his impassive expression.

"I will let Cook know of your sentiments," Clarinda responded with a smile, handing the teacup to Dorothea. "And the reason Daniel disappeared from the breakfast room was so I could share some good news he apparently already knew."

At this, Dorothea's eyes widened. "*I* didn't tell him!" she claimed rather defensively. She turned her attention to Daniel, her eyes widening even more. "You already *knew*?" she questioned, her face taking on a look of confusion. And then it changed to something approaching offense, as if she thought he should have shared the news with *her* just as soon as he learned of it.

Daniel sighed in a manner suggesting he was a dead man. "My brother informed me," he said simply, hoping he wasn't going to be pressed for more details. At least with his mother, he could have told her the entire truth of it, David's ghost and all, and she would scoff and admonish him for telling fibs. He was pretty sure Clarinda would take him at his word.

Dorothea huffed. "You men are worse gossips than we ladies," she stated before helping herself to a cake. After a bite, she smiled. "If you haven't already, Clare, you really must have one of these," she said before discreetly wiping a crumb from her lips. "I just adore lemon cakes."

Clarinda didn't have to be encouraged to try one; despite having just finished breakfast a half-hour ago, she was hungry again. She held the plate of cakes for Daniel and then took one after he did. *I am eating for two now*, she thought to herself. And so what if she'd already gained half a stone in the past couple of months? It wasn't as if she had to keep a trim figure for her husband.

"Now, Clare, what do you plan to wear to the funeral service?" Dorothea asked suddenly.

Suddenly self-conscious, Clarinda put the remaining bite of her cake on her saucer and considered her limited choices. "I believe a black silk carriage gown was included in the dresses the modiste brought yesterday," she answered uncertainly. "And there was a black hat with a veil."

Dorothea nodded, looking suitably somber. "That sounds lovely, darling," she replied, her voice quite at odds with her comment. She turned to regard her son. "And you, Daniel?"

Daniel gave her an uncertain look, as if he'd been ignoring her comments and was suddenly caught not having heard the original question. "A suit of clothes," he replied with a shrug.

"Daniel!" she admonished him. "Details, please," she encouraged before finishing off her tea cake.

Giving his mother a quelling glance, Daniel sighed. He wasn't really sure what the valet would choose, but given the circumstances, he could at least guess. "Black swallowtail coat, silver waistcoat, black breeches, black boots, black cravat ..."

"Ooh!" Dorothea interrupted with a wave of her hand. "You will look quite dashing as you escort Clare," she said with an air of appreciation.

Daniel dared a glance at Clarinda, his first since his aborted attempt at a kiss. He hadn't intended to kiss her, at least, not today. And not for several months, truth be told. She was in mourning. *He* was in mourning. But she'd looked so beautiful, so willing, so much like she had that day in Kensington Gardens when he'd asked for her hand in marriage amongst the pink roses. "I shall escort both of you," he countered, realizing he had paused too long in his response.

"Oh, that won't be necessary, Daniel," Dorothea replied,

one eyebrow arching suggestively. “Lord Wallingham will see to me,” she explained with a mischievous grin.

Clarinda’s gasp was barely audible, but her mother-in-law turned to regard her with a smile. “Wallingham and I have renewed our acquaintance this past week in Kent. He insisted he escort me tomorrow,” she said with a slight shake of her head. “And I am not about to deny him his pleasure.” She said this last with an elegantly arched eyebrow, daring anyone to guess what she really meant by the comment.

Daniel regarded her with a not so elegantly arched eyebrow of his own. “Am I to expect he will be my step-father soon?” he wondered, no amusement evident in the question. Although he held no particular dislike for the viscount, he didn’t really like the man, either. *Oily*, he thought as he remembered the man’s card play at the last ball Daniel had attended.

Dorothea’s eyes widened. “Goodness, no,” she replied, almost as if she was horrified by the thought of being married to Thurston Wallingham. Although Viscount Wallingham was a tall, dark-haired aristocrat, the son of an earl and a countess who was a daughter of a viscount, he was a rake and a gambler. But he was exceptional between the sheets. And given his propensity for bedding widows—and not necessarily young widows, as most rakes did—Dorothea Fitzwilliam thought to take her place among his conquests before she saw her sixth decade. “I’ve no intention of giving up my freedom to marry *anyone*,” she announced happily. She followed her proclamation with a sigh. “You, of course, will need to marry again,” Dorothea stated as she suddenly regarded her daughter-in-law. “The sooner, the better.”

Clarinda blinked. And blinked again. “I believe I have a year of mourning before I should even consider the idea of marriage, my lady,” she countered, daring a glance in Daniel’s direction and hoping he might admonish his mother more forcefully than she could.

Catching Clarinda’s expression of surprise, Daniel straightened in his chair. “Mother, really,” he said in a tone that clearly sounded admonishing. "David isn't even in his grave yet. And had he heard your comment, he would be spinning in it."

Clarinda's mother-in-law was about to defend her comment, but closed her mouth and looked suitably saddened. "I just meant that Clare won't have the freedom in her widowhood that I have in mine," she said with a nod. "She'll have a baby ..."

Or two, Daniel amended to himself, realizing just then that Clarinda really wouldn't be able to adopt the lifestyle of most young widows. Having twins would certainly put a damper on being a merry widow.

His mood improved considerably.

"A baby I intend to spend a good deal of time with," Clarinda interrupted as she glanced at the mantle clock. "If you two will excuse me, I'm scheduled to meet Lady Torrington in the park at eleven. I need to leave now so she doesn't wonder as to my whereabouts."

Dorothea's eyes widened. "You're going *outside*?" she nearly shouted. "You'll catch your death!"

"Mother," Daniel spoke firmly, his voice held low as he stood to bow. "You will take a footman for protection, I hope?" he asked carefully, not wanting to offend Clarinda. He knew she could take care of herself, but if he was going to let her out of his sight, he wanted to be sure someone was looking after her.

"Of course, Daniel," she answered, curtsying. She hurried from the room, feeling an immense sense of relief as she left her in-laws behind. And relief that Daniel hadn't offered himself as her escort. Clarinda was quite convinced that if he had been her escort, he would complete the kiss he had almost started in the parlor.

So much for protection.

Chapter 10

A WALK IN THE PARK

"Oh, Adele, you must tell me every bit of gossip you can manage," Clarinda insisted as she hurried up to meet her friend. The late morning fog was just then lifting from the secluded area of Hyde Park where Adele Grandby had agreed to meet her for a walk. "I cannot imagine having to give up all social engagements for the next few months. I'll go mad!"

The other countess gave her an understanding smile. "The time will pass far faster than you can imagine," she assured her as she linked arms with Clarinda. "Especially since we're both with child. We'll pay a visit to the Temple of the Muses when you return from Norwick Park. I expect there are a good deal of books to read on the topic of being with child." She gave her friend a long look. "I admit I was a bit surprised to get your note this morning," she said, changing the subject suddenly. "Wasn't Daniel supposed to arrive today?"

Rolling her eyes, Clarinda nodded. "Oh, he did," she said with a sigh. "First thing this morning, in fact."

Patting Clarinda's arm where it was linked with hers, Adele gave her friend a sideways glance. "And?" she prompted, expecting Clarinda to say something on the topic of Daniel Fitzwilliam.

"What is there to say? As usual, we had a bit of a row ..."

"Tsk," Adele sounded with a shake of her head.

"Then we spoke civilly for nearly a half-hour ..."

"There is hope!"

"But he still despises me ..."

"He does not," Adele countered, her rebuttal suggesting she actually knew the man personally and had spoken with him only moments before. Actually, she couldn't recall ever having been introduced to Daniel Fitzwilliam, but then, he hadn't been to London in several years.

Clarinda turned to regard Adele. "How do you know he does not?"

Smiling in her all-knowing, older, wiser woman sort of way, Adele shrugged. "Perhaps you should tell me just why it is you think he despises you," she suggested, one eyebrow arching up. "What happened, Clare?"

Inhaling deeply, Clarinda gave Adele a look of resignation. "When I was about to marry David, Daniel called on me, rather incensed to have learned that David and I were betrothed. He wondered how I could agree to marry David when I had already agreed to marry him."

The words surprised Adele. She stopped walking and turned to stare at Clarinda. "And, had you? Agreed to marry Daniel, I mean?"

Clarinda rolled her eyes again. "Of course not!"

Adele's brows furrowed. "Why would he claim that you had?" she countered. At Clarinda's quick shrug, Adele thought a moment. "I hear he looks exactly like his brother," she commented, keeping a wary eye on Clarinda.

"He does. They're twins. Almost identical in appearance," Clarinda agreed. "But they could not be more different in temperament. Where David is ... was ... carefree and agreeable, Daniel is ... morose and serious."

Adele's eyebrow arched again. She had never thought the Earl of Norwick to be carefree, nor particularly agreeable—

the sound of him bellowing to Clarinda the morning he died immediately coming to mind—but then, she hadn't lived with the man. Adele held her tongue until Clarinda didn't elaborate. "Is it possible there was a case of mistaken identity? Perhaps Daniel really had asked for your hand, and you only thought him to be David."

Clarinda smiled at that. "Daniel accused me of the same thing two years ago."

Sighing, Adele shook her head. "But, I take it, he was unable to convince you?"

Clarinda resumed walking. "I know I have never displayed my anger in your presence, Adele, but David claims I am like a volcano. I hiss, and I spit, and steam comes out of my ears until I finally erupt and leave boiling hot lava dripping over the victims of my rage," she described, her arms waving about her head to further illustrate her point. "Not very ladylike, I know, but it is my only vice." This last was said with a great deal of humor.

"Oh, my, I would not expect such behavior from you, Clare," the countess claimed, her merriment quite at odds with the stern sound of her voice. "It must take a great deal to set you off, though."

Dipping her head slightly, Clarinda allowed a wan smile. "I was never so bad as the day Daniel cornered me in my salon. He was truly hurt, I think, wondering how I could have thrown him over for David. He accused me of marrying David so I would be a *countess*. I could not believe his impertinence. I ... I blew up. I erupted ... I was so rude, Adele, you would not have recognized me. And then I slapped him very hard across his face and told him never to speak to me again."

Adele stopped walking again, her mouth agape at Clarinda's admission. "You *didn't*," she whispered.

"I did. Which is why he despises me."

Staring at Clarinda for several seconds before she actually believed the younger woman's claims, Adele sighed and shook her head. "How long has it been? Since you last erupted on him, I mean?" Adele wondered.

Clarinda sighed, suddenly embarrassed about her behavior. "Two years. And it was just the one time. I remember because David and I had been out for our two-year wedding anniversary at the Clarendon Hotel. Daniel was there with some friends, so David invited him to Norwick House for drinks. That's when he found me and ..." She shrugged, not sure what else to say. She sighed and resumed walking, her shoulders sagging a bit.

Adele shook her head and hurried to catch up with the younger countess. "And you apologized."

Clarinda's face displayed a sour look. "I did not. As I said, he despises me." She closed her eyes, shaking her head as if to clear it. "It would not be so bad if he didn't *look* so much like David."

"He still does?" Adele queried, thinking that a few years would have changed the two men enough so their features were no longer so identical.

"I thought I saw a ghost when I went into the breakfast room this morning," Clarinda claimed, not adding that she had actually seen—and spoken with—a ghost in the middle of the night.

Adele gave her a knowing look. "Perhaps you two will get on now that David has departed," she said, a bit too hopefully.

Clarinda wasn't about to tell her friend that David hadn't exactly departed. "Perhaps I will encourage a truce. He'll have to take on the earldom until this baby is born and old enough to take on the responsibilities. He'll probably wish to remain in London, at least for the time being," she reasoned, glad she had Adele as a sounding board just then. Everything seemed far less overwhelming when she spoke of her future out loud. "I will learn to deal with him, I suppose." She was quiet a few moments, apparently relieved to be done speaking of Daniel. "Since I have provided you with an interesting tale, could you at least provide some gossip?" she wondered, hoping to change the subject.

"Oh, I do have news, thanks to Grandby," Adele

responded, her suddenly happy expression seeming to cause the fog to clear and the sun to finally make an appearance.

Clarinda opened her parasol and regarded Adele with an appreciative glance. "Oh, good. I think it's rather fun to hear the news the men bring home. I do believe they're the better gossip mongers," she claimed, remembering Dorothea's earlier comment. David had been quite decent about sharing the news he heard at White's every day.

Adele grinned. "It would seem we'll need to secure the services of a midwife well in advance. Apparently you and I aren't the only ones who are in the family way and due to deliver about the same time."

Her face brightening, Clarinda was about to ask who else was expecting when Adele added, "Lord Barrings told his contingent of card players that Mary is expecting." Her arched eyebrow suggested there might be some scandal associated with the pregnancy.

"And, why is that so hard to believe?" Clarinda wondered. She barely knew Lord Barrings, although she had met his wife in various drawing rooms when she called on others.

Adele's lips thinned. "She is at least as old as me!" she claimed. "And she has been heard to claim she dislikes what happens in a marriage bed. One can only surmise that Lord Barrings' mistress must have taught him some skills he could employ to convince her otherwise." This last was spoken in a whisper, as if they might be overheard despite being the only people in the area of the park where they were walking.

"Or that she was as bored as everyone else at Christmastime," Clarinda countered, her eyebrows cocked mischievously.

Adele paused mid-step. "What did you say?"

Clarinda inexplicably blushed. "Well, what else are married couples supposed to do when they're stuck indoors for days on end because of a snowstorm?"

It was Adele Grandby's turn to blush. "Oh, my. I'd quite

forgotten about that. Grandby and I were at his house in the country ..." She suddenly clammed up, her eyes widening.

"What is it?" Clarinda wondered, not sure if she should remain amused or be concerned for her friend.

"Last night, when Grandby came home for dinner, he ... he was quite ... excited. He figured it out, Clare," she said in a quiet voice. "From what was said at White's, I think, and something he remembered telling me, about how I looked—as if I'd had too many cakes at teatime—and that snowstorm ... he knows I'm with child and he's ... beside himself with excitement. He bought me the most exquisite necklace, Clare." She reached up to undo the top button of her pelisse, opening the neckline so the gold and sapphire necklace shown over her morning gown. "I haven't taken it off since Grandby gave it to me last night during dinner."

"Adele! It's gorgeous!" Clarinda exclaimed, one gloved hand going to her lips. "It has to be from Stedman and Vardon. The gold filigree is exquisite," she murmured in awe.

"And there are two more, although I haven't yet opened them," Adele confided. "He must have spent a fortune or two."

"Or three." Clarinda was shaking her head, suddenly wondering why David hadn't bestowed a piece of jewelry on her person when he figured out she was carrying his child. "And, of course, Grandby is excited. The godfather will finally be a real father," she added with a grin. "How long has he known then?" she wondered.

Adele shook her head. "He only figured it out while he was at White's last night. He left there earlier than usual—which must have caused quite a stir among the regulars—so that he could stop at the jewelers on his way home." She rebuttoned her mantle, another blush coloring her face.

Clarinda noticed. "Adele! You're blushing!" She gasped. "You haven't taken it off since he gave it to you, which means you wore it to bed." Her eyes widened. Before she could even wonder if Adele had worn anything else when she went to bed, Adele arched an elegant eyebrow.

"Have you ever worn a piece of jewelry and nothing else to bed?" the older countess asked conspiratorially. "It's divine, I tell you." She sighed.

Clarinda moaned, as much from jealousy as from the thought that she would never again experience what Adele had only the night before. "I have not. But I will be sure that when this mourning period is over, and I have the opportunity to be a merry widow—should I wish—that wearing a divine necklace to bed will be my first order of business."

Adele giggled, thinking there were still two more such necklaces for her to wear to bed at some point in the future — as well as several others in her jewelry box. "You won't regret it," she murmured with a sideways glance at Clarinda. "You won't regret it at all."

Chapter 11

PILLOW TALK

Clarinda inhaled deeply, reveling in the familiar scent of David as she settled into the pillows. *I should have worn a necklace*, she thought. A smile spread over her lips. "I was wondering when you would visit me again," she said, opening her eyes slowly to find David leaning over her. "I missed you this morning," she murmured, her hand reaching up to cup his cheek. She pulled his head down to brush her lips over his. The kiss was brief, but it was enough to satisfy her just then.

"I apologize for not paying you my usual visit this morning, my love," David replied before he seemed to take his own deep breath. "But Daniel arrived unexpectedly early, and I thought perhaps it would be best if I made myself scarce." He reached out with a finger and drew Clarinda's profile in the air next to her where she lay, deciding not to admit he'd spent the morning with his brother instead of her.

Some things were just more important.

Rolling her eyes, Clarinda sighed. "What an impossible man," she said with a huff. "How could you two grow up in the same house?" she wondered then, her brow suddenly furrowing so the little wrinkle appeared between her eyebrows. "How did your *mother* put up with you?"

David moved his finger from the side of her face to the wrinkle, pushing on it much as Daniel had done earlier. His attention was on the little wrinkle as Clarinda's eyes tracked his hand and nearly crossed as he pressed his finger against her brow. "She complained bitterly, I assure you," David murmured absently. "Do you know, this little spot here quite made me fall in love with you," he said quietly, his finger gentling the wrinkle until Clarinda relaxed her brows and the fold disappeared.

Clarinda stared at him for a long moment. Hadn't Daniel said something about her wrinkle this morning? He seemed quite fascinated by the annoying fold in her forehead. "Your brother said something to that effect," she commented, trying to remember Daniel's exact words.

"I stole you from him, you know," David said suddenly, pulling his finger away now that the wrinkle was gone.

It nearly reappeared as Clarinda regarded him in surprise. "What did you say?" she countered, remembering Daniel's earlier accusation about his brother having stole her from him.

"I stole you from him. I knew you cared for him, but I wanted you for myself, so I took you away from him," David explained, the tone of his voice suggesting he might have felt regret over what he had done to his brother.

Clarinda couldn't help but notice he wasn't apologizing, though. "And how could you steal me from him if I only wanted *you*?" she countered, her smile returning as if she'd outmaneuvered him.

"You wanted *him*, actually," David accused as he straightened on the bed, his shoulders slumping in a way Clarinda had never seen him do before.

Shocked at the statement and his suddenly sagging self, Clarinda raised herself on her elbows. The wrinkle between her brows had returned, deeper than before. "What makes you say that?"

Her late husband shrugged. "You really couldn't tell the

two of us apart, so it was rather easy for me to sweep you off your feet."

Clarinda's face split into a huge grin. "I can, too, tell the two of you apart, you bounder," she claimed. "Daniel's hair is darker than yours. He has a scar by his eye. And he has that little ..." She reached up and pointed a finger between David's eyebrows. "Fold between his brows," she finished.

David reached up and captured her wrist in one hand so he could kiss the finger that had been poking him. "You recognize the differences *now*, but you couldn't back then," he accused in a teasing voice. "And, no, I am not sorry I stole you from him. But it's his turn to have a happy life, Clare. So, I do hope you two can settle your differences so the four of you can make a life together."

Clarinda's eyes widened. "Are you claiming you pretended to be him when you were courting me? Or was he courting me and you just pretended to be him?"

David cocked his head to one side as if he was trying to figure out which way things had been all those years ago. "No. You were betrothed to me, but I think you truly loved him first," he answered as he lay a hand over her belly, giving it a gentle pat. "Remember, we supposedly didn't love each other when we married. We barely knew each other, in fact," he added, as if he was just then realizing how lucky they had been to have their betrothal turn into a celebrated love match. He wasn't about to admit he had felt affection for her long before their wedding day.

Lowering herself back into the pillows, Clarinda regarded David for a very long time, her hands clasping together over the top of his. There was something very comforting about having his hand right there, but his words were at odds with his behavior. "That was, what? Four years ago?" she countered. "We certainly know each other *now*." She sighed again, suddenly feeling very sleepy. "I miss you so much," she whispered. "I don't know how I could ever love another as much as I do you."

David leaned over and kissed her on the forehead. "You already do, silly goose," he whispered. "Now, go to sleep."

Clarinda's eyelashes slowly lowered as she decided David wasn't making any sense. How could he expect she would ever love another—that she already *did* love someone else? And how could he expect she would ever make a life with his insufferable brother? So the four of them could make a life together? She couldn't imagine ...

Four?!

Sure she could hear David's deep chuckle as she sat up straight, Clarinda was stunned to find Missy opening the drapes to let in the weak March morning light.

"Four, my lady?" her maid replied with a quizzical look as she turned to regard her mistress. A pair of black stockings hung over one of her arms along with a chemise.

Clarinda glanced around the room, at once wanting to burst into tears and laugh at the very same time. *Four*? How could she explain herself? *Four of spades, four pounds, four stone, four-thousand, four buns, four friends, four peas in a pod? Well, there are just two peas in this pod*, she thought as she realized her hands were still clasped together over her belly. "The solicitor. Is he coming at four o'clock?" she hedged, hoping her query would steer Missy away from any notion that she looked as if she'd been eating too many cakes at tea time because she was carrying *twins*.

Missy shrugged. "I haven't heard anything mentioned, my lady," the younger woman replied as she went about opening the other set of drapes. "The funeral service is to be at eleven, though," she murmured. "Do you suppose I might be allowed to attend?"

Clarinda combed her fingers through her mussed hair, realizing she hadn't braided it the night before. At least it would be hidden under a black hat during the service. "Of course, Missy," she replied, wondering if all the servants planned to attend their late master's service.

A rich black crepe day gown, far nicer than the mourning clothes Clarinda had worn the past few days, lay spread out on the coverlet. She wondered how many times she'd be able to wear it before she would be too large with child. *With children*, she amended, a glimmer of happiness, absent for too long, enveloping her.

Oh, David, you bounder, she thought with a grin. Despite having to dress for his funeral, Clarinda's mood was lighter than it had been in days. *Twins*!

Chapter 12

GHOST TALK

"Oh, good, you're awake," David said as he walked into the master suite by way of the dressing room.

Daniel started from where he stood at the end of the bed looking up at the painting that hung above the four poster. How could he not have noticed it yesterday when he toured the room? How could he have ignored it twice more during the course of yesterday's visits to this room, the one time to confer with David's valet as to whether or not the man would remain in his employ, and then again to change into dinner clothes? It hadn't been until he was about to climb into bed when he finally glanced up and noticed the painting, really realized for the first time *who* it featured—and how *much* of her was featured. "You're back again, I see," Daniel answered, pretending he hadn't been caught staring.

"Gorgeous, isn't she?" David remarked, turning to glance up at the painting above the bed. "She posed for it. And that one, too," David added motioning up to the other painting across the room and above the escritoire.

Daniel couldn't help but glance at the other painting, stunned that he hadn't noticed *that* one either. But given that less of *her* was featured and what was featured was merely a naked back, well, Daniel decided he could be forgiven the oversight. “Yes, well, unlike you, I’ve always known she was beautiful,” Daniel replied curtly.

“Now, now. I’ve given you permission ...” David paused in his comment. “Nay, I have *ordered* you to marry her, so there’s no need to be curt with me.”

Cocking a mischievous grin in his brother’s direction, Daniel countered with, “I wasn’t being ‘Kurt’, I was being myself. Something you were guilty of doing too much of.”

David chuckled, the deep sound of humor causing Daniel to give him a quelling glance. “What is it?” he asked, wanting his dead brother gone from the room. “Have you come to let me know about the other topic you needed to get sorted before you see fit to depart for good?”

Holding up a finger while his face took on an expression of feigned offense, David nodded. “Indeed,” he answered finally. “I left too soon yesterday to bring it up.” He seemed to ponder how he was going to bring it up when he finally just shrugged and blurted, “It’s about my death.”

The words were simple but said in a way that had Daniel giving his brother his entire attention. He probably would have anyway, given he still found the idea of David’s ghost haunting him a bit ridiculous. He had been wondering if the death was some sort of ruse—that perhaps David was truly alive and well and playing some kind of cruel joke on Daniel and his family. When he’d considered the possibility the night before, it seemed to make more sense than David actually being dead and coming back as a ghost. But seeing David like this, as if he was there but not completely, had him questioning his late-night conclusion. “What about it?” Daniel asked then, his breath held in anticipation of David’s next words.

“I was shot.”

Daniel’s eyebrows furrowed, causing the skin between them to appear as a folded wrinkle.

“If you keep doing that, it will be permanent,” David said, poking his finger into the wrinkle.

Sighing, Daniel pulled his face away from David's finger. "Damn it, what did you say?"

"I was shot," David said again, his expression indicating he was as bothered by the thought as Daniel was at seeing him as a ghost. "I know my neck broke when I was thrown from Thunder—he's my horse—he's a good horse, by the way. I think you'll like him," he commented then, not seeming to realize he had strayed off topic again.

"Who shot you?" Daniel asked, suddenly impatient with his dead brother. And just what was the fascination with the name 'Thunder' for a horse? Every man in the *ton* seemed to have a horse named Thunder.

David shrugged. "If I knew, well I ... well, I wouldn't be here. I think that's why I haven't yet ... departed." He said the last part carefully, his face displaying a wince before showing a kind of seriousness Daniel hadn't seen David display since his appearance as a ghost.

"You're telling me someone shot you, and that's why your horse reared and you broke your neck?"

David was nodding as Daniel verbalized his understanding of the situation. "Well, my neck broke because I hit the pavement head first. But I'm pretty sure I was already dead when I hit the cobbles."

Daniel sat down on the bed. Hard. "Where did the bullet enter?" he asked, his brows still furrowing, the resulting fold of skin probably now a permanent feature of his face. Certainly the constable would have noticed a bullet hole in his brother. Or the mortician who was seeing to preparing his body for burial.

"Just below the back of my neck," David said, turning to show Daniel exactly where as he pushed the bottom edge of his hair aside with a couple of fingers. "It took me awhile to find it, especially since I can't see myself in a mirror," he murmured quietly.

Daniel stared at the small hole that was revealed by his brother's fingers. No blood appeared there, but the hole was black and was centered in the nape of his neck. "Good

God, David. You've been shot!" Daniel breathed. He resisted the urge to poke his finger into the small hole, thinking perhaps his brother was playing a trick on him and the hole was merely a smear of charcoal. One of David's fingers gingerly rubbed around the spot, though, and dipped in a bit.

Startled when he saw the end of David's finger disappear into the hole, Daniel jumped away. As he did so, he caught his reflection in the cheval mirror in the corner, and just as quickly confirmed what David had just said about mirrors—only Daniel's own reflection appeared, his face showing what could only be described as shock and horror. "Who would want you dead?" he asked then, tearing his gaze from the mirror and turning it onto his brother.

There had been a brief moment when Daniel was about to chalk up David's wound to an errant bullet, fired perhaps to bring order in the street or meant for someone else. But David's death had occurred on a busy street. Certainly someone would have heard the shot, noticed the shooter.

David turned around, his hand coming away from hole in his head. "Well, there's the question. I have no idea."

Staring in disbelief at his older, dead brother, Daniel had reason to think his simple claim was bogus. "No idea?" he repeated. "You used to own a brothel. You used to own a gaming hell. Your were a *rake*. As far as I know, you still are," he accused, his voice rising a bit until David put up a finger in front of his lips to remind him that Clarinda was in the next room. Daniel lowered his voice. "Who did you offend?"

Given that option, David's look of innocence was suddenly one of contrition. "When you put it like that ... almost everyone."

Daniel huffed and rolled his eyes. Perhaps his brother had gotten what he deserved, but he had barely formed the thought when he realized his brother truly hadn't deserved to die, unless he was guilty of murder or rape or some other heinous crime. "Did you ever commit a heinous crime?" Daniel asked, crossing his arms.

David's brows furrowed in thought for a moment. "No," he replied with a slight shake of his head.

"What is the worst thing you did to someone?" Daniel pressed, thinking his brother would eventually come up with some offense that warranted his death. He wouldn't have been shot unless he'd done *something*.

Resting a hand on the side of his chin and his elbow in his other palm, David thought for a moment. "I stole Clarinda from you," he sighed. "Did *you* shoot me?"

His mouth dropping open, Daniel shook his head. *Did the dead truly suffer from a distorted sense of reality?* "I was at Norwick Park," he replied, almost not giving his brother the satisfaction of an answer. "Try again."

Scrubbing his face with his hand, David thought for another moment. "I beat Sommers at cards last week. First time that's happened."

"How much did the baron lose?" Daniel wondered, thinking a huge loss at a gaming table might be a motive for murder.

"About five pounds."

Daniel blinked. *Five pounds?* Most card games at White's required a buy-in higher than ten pounds. "Try again," Daniel sighed, wondering how long it might take for David to think of someone who had a good reason to see him dead. "What about courtesans or ... mistresses?"

"Don't have one." At Daniel's surprised expression, David gave him a quelling glance. "I had to give up all my vices to marry Clare," he said defensively. At Daniel's continued look of disbelief, he added, "I had to, Danny. For Clare. It was a ... condition ... of our marriage. I promised to forsake all others," he stammered. "She even had investigators following me to be sure I was staying faithful."

Daniel had to suppress the sudden urge to chuckle. No one could accuse Clarinda of being a milk-and-water miss when it came to her marriage, but the fact that she'd been able to convince a rake to give up his mistresses as well his ownership of a brothel and a gaming hell was a testament to how much David must have wanted her as his wife. Perhaps the man had really loved Clarinda, Daniel realized.

The thought was more sobering than he wanted to admit.

"She would have taken me out to the stables and castrated me if I bedded another woman," David whispered, a distinct wince appearing as he said the words.

Daniel couldn't help himself, and he winced in sympathy.

Deciding David no longer had enemies from his days as a bachelor, Daniel tried a different tact. "Did anything happen in Parliament?"

David gave him a sideways glance and then seemed to give the question a good deal of thought. "Well, you probably heard about last year's Corn Law. That hasn't been very popular ..."

"You voted against it, if I remember correctly," Daniel sighed.

"Right," David agreed, his face displaying deep concentration. "And I rather doubt Liverpool would have me killed over it," he murmured.

"Have you had an argument with a servant or a tradesman or a ... or a merchant?" Daniel persisted, beginning to understand why someone would want to shoot his brother. At the moment, he was pretty sure he could. If he had a gun at his disposal.

David was obviously considering possible suspects, but his shaking head indicated his inability to come up with a name.

"Christ, Davy, can't you think of *anyone* who would want you dead?" Daniel asked in exasperation. "If you didn't anger someone, is there someone that benefits from your death? Someone who gains something? Some who inherits ..?" Daniel stopped mid-sentence, realizing he was describing himself.

"Besides me, of course."

David's eyebrow arched up. "And why shouldn't I consider you a suspect?" he countered, moving so he stood closer to Daniel as he crossed his arms over his chest. "You're a good marksman, an excellent horseman. You could have made that shot if you were behind me."

Daniel rolled his eyes and crossed his own arms defensively. "I wasn't *in* London the day your were shot. I was at Norwick Park, remember?"

"Oh," David replied, his teeth sinking into his lower lip. "Actually, I didn't think we were done considering Parliament," he added. "We should be thinking about my enemies in the House of Lords."

"What enemies?"

The question had David's face contorting a bit as he tried to think of a duke or a marquess or an earl or a viscount or a baron who might want him dead. "I impugned Wallingham's honor," he stated with a nod, "I questioned Lord Sommers' sanity when he agreed with Prinny on not just one, but *two* matters before the Lords, and I accused Lord Barrings of cheating at cards."

Daniel shook his head from side to side, and then stopped. "Wallingham? How did you 'impugn' his honor?" Daniel at one time thought of the viscount as a bit of a dandy, best known for his frequent affairs with older widows. But the man was well-liked. Those older widows had obviously enjoyed their time with the man for, according to the gossip in the Society pages of the newspapers Daniel read, Wallingham continued to enjoy a steady stream of willing widows.

"I overheard him saying he was looking forward to our mother's next visit to London," David stated, crossing his arms over his chest.

"So?"

"Because, and I quote, 'I have always wished to plow that delectable creature's pussy'," he continued, as if Daniel hadn't interrupted him.

Daniel's eyebrows shot up. "Ewww!"

"I slapped a glove in his face and said, 'Over my dead

body', to which he said, 'Choose your seconds for pistols at dawn'."

Daniel's jaw had dropped open and now hung that way. "You challenged Wallingham to a *duel?* Did you ... *shoot* him?" he whispered.

"Of course not. I didn't show up for the duel."

Daniel shut his mouth. "Why not?"

David shrugged. "Well, for one thing, he didn't say *where* to meet him, and I had a full schedule and never had a chance to choose my seconds. Truth be told, I sort of forgot about it. Until the following afternoon when I heard my absence at Wimbledon Commons had been noted. I was in bed at the time when any common duel would have taken place."

He didn't add that he was in Clarinda's bed.

"What did Wallingham say when next you saw him?" Daniel countered, wondering if the viscount really had shot David, or had, perhaps, hired someone to do the dirty deed on his behalf.

David shrugged. "Challenged me to a game of piquet," he replied quickly.

"Piquet? To settle a duel?"

His brows furrowing at the odd question, David's hands spread out. "No, no. Turns out, Wallingham forgot about the challenge, too. He'd had entirely too much to drink when he made the comment about our mother's pussy, and he forgot all about the duel."

Daniel gave him an uncertain glance. "So, who made the trip to Wimbledon Commons to witness the duel when the duelists didn't even show up?" he wondered, his eyebrow arching.

David shrugged again. "I don't know."

Sighing loudly, Daniel crossed his arms over his chest and regarded his brother with derision. The man couldn't even defend their mother's honor! Perhaps he should force Lord Wallingham to marry her, he considered. That would teach the viscount to keep his comments about ladies' nether regions to himself. On top of that, Daniel rather doubted his mother would put up with a philandering husband, which meant Wallingham would be unable to continue making all those other merry widows merrier.

"If you were truly shot, I haven't any idea who I should approach with questions. But, in the meantime, I shall pay a visit to the constable who was on the scene of your death as well as to the mortician who is seeing to your body. I'll let you know if I discover anything," Daniel offered, wondering how he would summon David or if his brother's ghost would just appear when Daniel had news.

"Oh, I'll just show up when it's convenient," David assured him, before Daniel had a chance to ask. "In the meantime, take care of Clare and the babies, won't you?"

Before Daniel could even respond, David disappeared from the room.

Chapter 13

THE FUNERAL

Clarinda donned the black satin hat and lowered the veil from its wide brim so her face was kept in shadow. Two hankies were stuffed into the pockets of her gown, and she held one in a black kid-gloved hand. Although she had thought she might like to cry all morning and most of the day before—ever since the incident with the kippers—she had held her tears at bay, deciding they were better shed at the service if at all.

When the Norwick town coach pulled into the drive, she noticed the crest of the earldom painted on the door. She was sure it had always been there, but for some reason, it seemed especially bright, as if it had been newly repainted. And then it dawned on her that the coach was new—David had mentioned ordering it from Tillbury's several months ago. She supposed it shouldn't surprise her. Her husband had always taken great pride in his conveyances, buying new and different equipment about as often as he bought horses at Tattersall's.

Daniel bowed to her when he found her in the vestibule, offering to escort her to the coach by holding his elbow for her. He looked stunning in his black mourning clothes, the worsted wool of his swallow tail coat fitting his shoulders to perfection, a silver waistcoat barely showing above the top button of this top coat, and his impeccably cut breeches tucked into black Hessians. A black cravat, folded, wrapped and tied in a flawless mail coach knot, completed his suit of clothes. The only color displayed on his person was provided by the emerald pin in his cravat.

Clarinda was so taken with his resemblance to David, she had to turn from his questioning gaze. Speechless, she merely allowed her brother-in-law to escort her and then hand her up into the coach, the smell of new leather filling the immaculate interior. When Daniel started to excuse himself, Clarinda gave him a questioning look. "I thought Lord Wallingham was going to escort your mother," she said quietly.

"I did, too, but he's not yet arrived," Daniel replied with cocked eyebrow, suggesting Lord Wallingham would be begging forgiveness from Dorothea Norwick before long. The dowager countess would no doubt grant it with some conditions that involved a tumble or two.

Daniel went back to the house for his mother. He found Dorothea in the parlor and gave her a sideways glance, wondering how he might bring up the topic of Lord Wallingham in the few moments they had. If the gentleman was in Kent at the same house party as she'd been attending, then the viscount couldn't have shot David—but that didn't mean he hadn't arranged for someone else to do the shooting. "Tell me, Mother. How did you find Lady MacAllister's house party?" he wondered, hoping to keep his voice conversational. He figured once he got her going, she would divulge all the information he needed.

Dorothea gave her son a look that suggested he'd sprouted horns and a trident tail. "Why, Daniel, I am surprised you would even be the least bit interested in what happened at a house party," she commented as she pulled on a pair of black kid leather gloves. At his cocked eyebrow and look of disappointment, provided to show his feigned interest and offense at her comment, the dowager countess smiled. “The weather was abysmal, of course. It rained nearly every day of the five days I was there. But the company was most scintillating. And Georgette always has such diverting activities when the weather doesn't cooperate.”

Numerous ideas crossed Daniel's mind as he considered what those activities might have been, but he thought he should have her clarify. Before he could do so, though, she continued. “We played whist, put on a production of one of the Bard's comedies, had a small soirée, and we played charades—Wallingham and I were partners for that.” She flung a shawl around her shoulders, watching how it fell in the reflection from a mirror on the parlor wall.

Both of Daniel's eyebrow cocked up. “Really. Was the viscount there for the entire house party?” he wondered, hoping his question implied he was expected somewhere else during the week.

Dorothea regarded him, one finger going to the side of her mouth. “Why, I believe so. I saw him everyday I was there except at luncheon on Wednesday, but that's because most of the men went fishing. The lake at Glendale Park is stocked with the very best trout, they say,” she murmured. “So, of course, we had trout for the fish course that evening.” She paused and gave her son a quelling glance. “You seemed surprised he was there for the entire party.”

Shrugging in an attempt to seem nonchalant, Daniel paused before responding. “I had heard David challenged him to a duel and then apparently forgot to show up. Lord Wallingham was no doubt incensed at my brother's apparent cowardice.”

Dorothea's mouth dropped open in shock. “He was not! In fact, he told me he did not show up, either. He thought the entire episode a mere folly on David's part.”

“Did he now?” Daniel replied, his brows furrowing. What else would Wallingham say, though? It wasn't as if he could tell Dorothea what the viscount had said about his intent to bed her.

"Well, of course. When David's seconds didn't contact Wally's seconds to confirm the details, Wally left for Kent."

Wally? Daniel struggled to keep his face as impassive as possible.

"I know because we arrived at Glendale Park within moments of one another," his mother continued, her lashes seeming to flutter as if a speck of dirt had landed in her eye. "He was ever so pleased to see me, I thought."

No doubt, Daniel thought as he realized Wallingham's reason for attending the house party was probably for the sole purpose of plowing Dorothea.

"And although I wasn't supposed to discover the reason behind how Lady MacAllister assigned the rooms, I was quite pleased to learn Wally's room was right next to mine. He was ever the gentlemen, seeing fit to escort me to every activity," she claimed as she beamed happily, a pink blush suddenly suffusing her face.

Especially the carnal ones, Daniel thought when he saw her blush. "That was very sporting of him. Did he happen to mention what caused the disagreement with David then?" he asked, offering his arm.

Dorothea laid a hand on his arm. "It was nothing, truly," she replied, allowing him to lead the way to the vestibule. "He merely voiced his intent to plow me," she added with a shrug.

Somehow, and it took a great deal of effort, Daniel managed to keep his face impassive and his feet from stumbling as he escorted his mother to the coach.

Clarinda was beginning to wonder as to the whereabouts of Daniel and Dorothea when the two finally approached the coach. Dorothea surprised Clarinda when she appeared wearing a black silk de Naples gown and black fringed shawl.

"Will Lord Wallingham be meeting you at St. George's?" Clarinda asked as mother and son took the seat opposite Clarinda. From what Dorothea had said in the parlor the day before, Clarinda expected the viscount would appear that morning to take the dowager countess in his equipage. A high-perch phaeton, no doubt, probably in bright yellow or red.

Dorothea waved a hand in the air. "I expect he'll show up here in a few minutes. Porter knows what to tell him," she said coyly.

There would be no funeral reception at Norwick House — Clarinda hadn't even considered hosting such an event— but Adele and Milton Grandby had insisted they would do so at Worthington House. That meant her afternoon would be spent hearing condolences from any number of mourners and endless anecdotes featuring David.

"Which reminds me," Dorothea suddenly said in a tone of voice that had Clarinda and Daniel turning their attention to her. "I'm thinking word of your condition should probably be made public today," she claimed as she directed her gaze on Clarinda. "You'll want to elicit as much sympathy as possible, and to be a widow with child will certainly do the trick."

Clarinda stared at her mother-in-law, wondering if the woman was serious. A glance in David's direction proved he found the suggestion a bit questionable as well. When neither of them gave Dorothea a verbal response she said, "So it's settled. We'll just drop the hint that your carrying a child ..."

"Two," both Daniel and Clarinda interrupted at the same time. Realizing she'd heard an echo of the word, she dared at a glance in Daniel's direction. *What*?

Dorothea's eyes widened again as her gaze went from Clarinda to her son and back again. "Two?" she countered, not quite sure at first what they meant.

"Two babies," Clarinda said with a nod, wondering how it was that Daniel knew. She dared another glance in his direction and couldn't help but notice he avoided making eye contact with her. Unconsciously, one of her hands moved to rest against her belly. How could Daniel know she carried twins?

But, come to think of it, how could David even know?

she found herself wondering. A shiver coursed through her body just then, a pleasant sensation that happened so quickly she nearly let out a gasp of surprise.

"Twins," Daniel put in, as if that would help his mother more easily process the information. The woman could be quite dense at times.

There was a hint of a gasp as the dowager countess processed the information. "Twins?" Momentarily speechless, her head continued to glance back and forth between Daniel and Clarinda, as if she were watching a lawn tennis match despite there being no ball.

It was during this momentary silence that Clarinda caught Daniel's gaze on her, saw his brown eyes darken while his expression seemed to soften. And then, just as quickly, his eyes turned to his mother and his face hardened again. Clarinda felt something tighten inside her. She wondered if her breakfast was offended at the ride in the coach and had decided it wanted out. But a second later she realized that wasn't it at all.

Daring another glance in Daniel's direction, she felt the same reaction, the same tightening deep inside, the awareness her body had of *him*—the man that could cause shivers of pleasure to course through her with the slightest touch, that could cause her breath to catch with a simple grin, her breath to cease with his smoldering gaze, her heart to pound if he touched his lips to hers.

Not *him*, though. Not Daniel. *David*. David was the one who did those things to her.

"Well, how can you even know you're carrying twins?" Dorothea asked in a huff, as if her plan to announce Clarinda's condition had to be revisited because expecting twins was abominable compared to expecting a single bundle of joy. Although the woman should know—she had borne a set of twins, after all. "I didn't discover I was carrying twins until my seventh month! Good God, Clarinda. You'll be miserable," she added, her mouth screwing up into an expression that made it very clear she'd had a rather hard time of it and remembered the experience quite clearly.

"Mother," Daniel said in that low, warning tone that seemed to put Dorothea in her place for at least a few moments. "If Clare wishes the *ton* know she is with ... children, then she will be the one to make the announcement."

Suitably chastised, Dorothea nodded her head from side to side. "Very well. But you must know, it's become quite the thing to be with child right now. I hear tell there are over a dozen ladies in your condition," she announced, news she'd no doubt been keeping in reserve in the hopes she could convince Clarinda it was time to add her name to those of the pregnant *ton*. "According to Wallingham, there was a huge snowstorm at Christmastime." She made this last comment as if the *snowstorm* had impregnated the dozen ladies that shared Clarinda's affliction.

Clarinda watched as Daniel's brows furrowed, the little fold of skin appearing between them to show he was truly vexed by his mother's comment. Covering her mouth to hide her amusement, Clarinda was forced to think more somber thoughts, or she would be left in tears of laughter.

Just one day, Clarinda thought, determined not to cry as she half-listened to her mother-in-law's continuing ramblings. And then she could begin her year of mourning. She would have to acquire a large number of books and renew her acquaintance with needle and thread. But with babies due in five months and three weeks, she would manage.

Despite arriving more than a half-hour before the funeral service was to begin, Clarinda was surprised to find a large number of mourners outside St. George's. The rosewood coffin containing David's body, its polished surface gleaming in the pale morning light, lay near the entrance. Two men were draping it with a blanket of red roses. Roses had to be his favorite flower, Clarinda considered, remembering how often he had them delivered to the house. Always red. Never pink. She started to dwell on this bit when Adele and Milton

Grandby stepped up. Clarinda was about to give her godfather a smile when she noted the expressions on the couple's faces. The shock on Adele's face was quickly masked, but Grandby didn't bother hiding his.

"Norwick! Damn!" Grandby cursed under his breath, his gaze squarely on Daniel as he obviously forgot he was in front of a church. "You really are Norwick's identical twin," he breathed.

"Grandby," Daniel acknowledged with a nod, his own expression showing some surprise. He angled his head toward Lady Torrington, expecting Grandby to take the hint that they should be introduced. He was fairly sure she was Lady Worthington, but he wondered if she had recently become Lady Torrington. Had the confirmed bachelor taken a wife?

"Daniel Fitzwilliam, Lady Norwick," Grandby added suddenly, just then noticing the dowager countess on Daniel's other arm. "I'd like you to meet my countess, Adele Grandby," the earl finally spoke, only doing so because Adele had shoved a rather sharp elbow into his ribs.

"Lady Torrington," Daniel replied, lifting her gloved hand to his lips and kissing the backs of her knuckles. "'Tis a pleasure. And a pleasant surprise to know that there is a woman on this planet brave enough to tame this beast of a man," he added with a twinkle. "My sympathies."

Clarinda's eyes widened nearly as much as Adele's did, although Clarinda realized why Adele still seemed so shocked. She had never met Daniel. At least, Clarinda didn't think she had met him. Perhaps she had and merely assumed he was David. To see David's younger brother standing next to her, looking all the world like David, had to be disconcerting. But Daniel's comment was obviously meant to either tease the earl or compliment the countess. Perhaps both.

"You were once Lady Worthington, weren't you?" Dorothea wondered as she reached out to grasp hands with Adele.

"Yes, my lady," Adele afforded Daniel's mother the courtesy of a deep nod. "I am very sorry for your loss, Lady

Norwick. I do hope you'll be staying in London for a time," she murmured quietly.

The bishop suddenly appeared in the large doorway of the church, obviously informed when the Norwick town coach pulled up and disgorged the family of the deceased. Seeing the Norwicks on the pavement in front of the church, the bishop nodded. Several pall bearers moved to lift the coffin and carry it into the sanctuary, the bishop's tenor voice ringing out, "Blessed are those who mourn, for they will be comforted."

As members of Clarinda's party made their way up the steps and into the church, several nattily dressed men passed them, turning to frown or show expressions of surprise at the sight of Daniel. Despite his having been gone from London for most of the last four years, it was obvious many people were unaware of Daniel's uncanny resemblance to David.

Clarinda couldn't help but notice that several pews in St. George's were already occupied. Those who followed them down the center aisle peeled off and quietly took seats, the swish of silks and the rustle of taffeta and a few murmurs the only sounds in evidence.

Daring a surreptitious glance, Clarinda could see that most in attendance were David's fellow members of Parliament and their ladies. Some were acquaintances, like one of the lawyers from Hammond's office, although Clarinda wasn't sure which Hammond it was who sat in the third pew from the front. Several servants from their household were clustered together in the back, their black shawls and coats adding to the somber mood in the sanctuary. And, having been settled in place by the pall bearers at the very front in the middle of the aisle, was David's coffin.

Once they reached the front pew, Grandby leaned over toward Clarinda, lifting the veil of her hat with one hand. He kissed Clarinda on the cheek. "Courage," he whispered.

Clarinda nodded, realizing she had managed to make it this far without shedding a tear. She doubted she would make it through the entire service dry-eyed, though.

Dorothea, who had kept close to Adele as they made their way to the front of the church, seemed to remember Adele's query as to how long she would stay in London. "As soon as I see my son settled into his new roles, I expect I'll be returning to my home in Bognor," Dorothea replied airily, careful to keep her voice low.

Roles? Clarinda wondered after a second. She felt Daniel's arm flinch beneath hers and realized he'd had the same reaction. She dared not say anything. Lady Norwick had made the comment expecting someone would want an explanation, though.

The Earl of Torrington took the bait. "What roles can the new earl expect to fill besides that of earl?" he wondered as he turned his attention to the dowager countess.

Trapped!

Dorothea leaned her head to one side, her lips curling up at the edges. "Uncle, husband, father, favorite son," she spoke wistfully. "Not necessarily in that order, of course."

A rather stunned silence followed this comment as all eyes seemed to gaze at Daniel. *Of course, not necessarily in that order,* Clarinda thought, nearly rolling her eyes.

And then she found herself wondering what order Dorothea had in mind.

Grandby gave Clarinda a pointed glance, but he seemed to sense the growing unease first and made the motion to move the group into their seats in the front pew.

Clarinda had been quite aware of the quiet murmurings that followed their trek up the center aisle. Relieved to have the cover of the veil, she was able to allow her eyes to seek out and identify several people in attendance. Lady Pettigrew and her niece were suitably gowned in black bombazine. Lord Attenborough looked bored in his black mourning clothes, his wife gazing about the church as if she was looking for someone she knew. David's London estate manager was staring into space, perhaps wondering if he would still have a position now that Daniel would be overseeing the earldom.

At the rate people were pouring into the church behind them, it was quite evident the place would be full even before the bishop welcomed them to the service.

Grandby managed to sit next to Clarinda, leaving Daniel to sit on her left and his mother on his other side. Once they were all settled, Clarinda felt Grandby turn in her direction. "'Uncle' implies a niece or nephew. Unless the dowager countess had other children I am not aware of, that leaves you and David as the likely sources. What say you?" he asked in a whisper so quiet she almost couldn't make out his words.

Clarinda sighed and turned to her right, her chin almost resting on her shoulder. She waved a finger for Grandby to face front so she had access to his ear. "About six months," she whispered. She turned and faced front, having a devil of a time keeping a straight face as Grandby's face turned hard left. A huge grin lit up his face. "Me, too!"

And then he did something Clarinda would not forget for a very long time.

Milton Grandby, Earl of Torrington, stood up and, grabbing one of her hands, hauled her up, as well, embracing her in front of the entire assembly with so much enthusiasm, her feet left the floor.

"Milton!" Clarinda heard Adele hiss from behind her. She caught sight of the bishop staring down at the spectacle, his brows furrowing before his eyes flitted between the coffin and her. A murmur rose up from those who had their heads raised up; the murmur grew as others lifted their heads to see what the commotion was about.

Grandby let go his hold on Clarinda, making sure her feet were firmly under her before turning to the bishop. "Forgive me, Your Grace," he called up to the bishop, *sotto voce*. "I have just been told my prayers were answered," he stated in a lowered voice, his bushy eyebrows dancing in delight. He rather hoped the bishop wouldn't request his immediate departure from the church.

Clarinda quickly took her seat, wanting to disappear into the floor. Daniel was quick to clasp her hand onto his arm;

Clarinda wondered why he hadn't been holding on a moment ago. Perhaps he could have anchored her to the pew and saved her from her unwilling participation in Grandby's display of joy. Now she would be the *on dit* for at least a week.

Before the start of the funeral service of David Fitzwilliam, the Earl of Norwick's widow was seen being twirled by her godfather in front of her husband's mourners at St. George's ...

"What was *that* all about?" Daniel hissed, obviously angered at the earl's indiscretion. His eyes were following the earl's subsequent movements with suspicion.

Something about the tone of his voice put Clarinda on the defensive. Grandby's reaction had been so heartfelt, so full of joy, she could hardly find fault with the man. "Your mother's reference to you becoming an *uncle*," she whispered back, her breathing still labored from the excitement of being swept up and spun in a circle in front of the entire church. *St. George is probably spinning in his grave*, she thought. *Hell, the dragon is probably spinning, too. And belching fire, no doubt.* At least her stomach wasn't; it seemed to have survived the joy ride just fine.

Clarinda had to admit it was rather fun to be picked up like a child and spun around like that, but the black satin gown was certainly not the proper attire for such an activity. At least her skirts had been suitably shook out from the carriage ride.

From the corner of her eye, she could see that Dorothea was quite amused at Grandby's behavior, hiding her smile behind a fan she had suddenly flipped open. At some point, Lord Wallingham had appeared on Dorothea's left, taking the seat next to her before she even realized he had arrived. And when she did, her lashes sprung into action and Clarinda could hear the man apologize for not having arrived at Norwick House in time to bring her to St. George's in his new sporty phaeton. Dorothea would no doubt go home in the phaeton, although Clarinda wasn't too sure *whose* home it would go to.

"My goddaughter is with child," Grandby was saying to the bishop. "Lord Norwick's wife," he amended, pointing back at Clarinda.

Aware she'd just been pointed out to the bishop, Clarinda slumped as far down in the pew as she could, which wasn't very far given the nature of the straight back and shallow bench. Besides, the bishop could see her quite clearly; she was in the front pew.

The bishop's brows furrowed, and then they lifted so they nearly touched the rim of his mitre. The frown he'd displayed since noticing the earl's escapade changed to one of amusement, and he gave Clarinda a nod. The general din in the sanctuary died down to silence as the bishop held up a hand and welcomed the mourners.

There was a prayer followed by a hymn, but Clarinda hardly noticed the proceedings. She felt as if she was somehow disconnected from her body, and at the same time, very aware of so much around her—Grandby's lime cologne, the swish of silks when Adele suddenly straightened in the pew, Dorothea's almost silent sniffle as tears pricked her eyes, and her own sense of being at odds with what the bishop was saying only a few feet in front of her.

But what assaulted her senses the most was Daniel. His proximity was suddenly noticeable, as if he had just that very moment sat down next to her, when, in fact, he had been sitting so close the entire time. *David!* she thought, her sense of loss so profound she could barely breathe. And yet, when she did, she smelled David. Smelled the worsted wool of his topcoat, the slight citrus of the laundry soap used to wash his cravat, his amber cologne and the slight scent of musk he gave off early in the day. *He is here!* she thought, tears spilling from the corners of her eyes. She had to resist the urge to glance about in search of him. *Is he somewhere in the back?* It would be just like him to take a seat directly behind her, just so she would not be able to spot him if she turned slightly to the left or right to look. She did turn her head then, so her gaze was mere inches from Daniel's profile, tears dripping from her cheeks with her sudden movement. The scents of amber cologne and citrus laundry soap and musk surrounded her, blanketing her with comfort. She breathed in deeply, stifling a sob as she did so.

Daniel turned his head ever so slightly to find Clarinda staring at him. He realized, a bit belatedly, that tears were streaming down her cheeks. He fished his handkerchief out of his pocket and held it out to her. When Clarinda didn't move to take it, probably because she already had one stuffed in her other hand, he noticed, he lifted a corner of his own and slipped it beneath the netting, dabbing the fine linen against her cheek. "Shh," he whispered, his own resolve to remain steadfast crumbling. *She is so beautiful*, he thought, the back of one finger accidentally brushing against her soft skin.

The touch set off a shock of *something* through his entire body, an awareness that sizzled along every fiber of his being. Struggling to remain in control, Daniel tried to concentrate on the square of fabric he held in his hand. One corner was already damp with her tears. And then, as more fell from her eyes, he watched Clarinda raise her hanky to take over the task of catching the tears before they slid off her face and onto the black silk of her gown.

Daniel thought for a second to reach out with his tongue and catch the tear drops, as if their salty wetness could quench the thirst he suddenly felt for her.

Reluctantly, he tore his gaze away from Clarinda and faced front. He thought of how pale she looked in black, how vulnerable and small and delicate. Daniel wanted nothing more than to take her into his arms and comfort her right then and there. He wanted to kiss away her tears, assure her everything would be all right. He wanted to strip her of the ugly widow's weeds and kiss her breasts and suckle her taut nipples and stroke his fingers along the length of her naked body and make love to her with slow, gentle strokes of his manhood tucked tightly inside her warm, wet ...

Jesus! Daniel took a deep breath, surreptitiously giving his crotch a glance. *St. George must be spinning in his grave*, he thought. And the dragon ... *ah, to hell with the dragon*, he almost said aloud. The tightness of his black breeches seemed to ease a bit. He dared not look over at Clarinda, afraid if he did, she would notice his erection and wonder how a man could get aroused in the middle of a funeral service.

The minx. Did she have any idea the effect she had on him? Any idea that he'd spent last night tossing and turning with thoughts of what he could be doing to her if she was in his bed? Of how he imagined removing her night rail so the fabric would barely skim over her silken skin? Of how his hands would follow the fabric to continue the caress, their gentle touch tickling the back of her thighs, sliding around the swells of her bottom until his fingertips could dance around the small of her back? And then barely touch every bump along her spine to the nape of her neck? Then to move ever so lightly across her shoulders and down along her collarbones and up to the hollow of her throat? His lips would take over at the point to suckle and kiss ... *Christ*! Daniel swallowed the growl he'd nearly allowed to escape his throat. His breeches were about to rend from the pressure of his erection. *Think of the dragon! Think of Mother!* The pressure subsided as quickly as it had built.

He'd promised himself he wouldn't think of her *that way*, the way he'd thought of her for the entire year she was betrothed to his brother and those first two years of their marriage, when he believed she would realize at any moment that it was *he* who had courted her, and *he* who she had kissed in the garden behind Norwick House, and *he* who had asked for her hand in marriage amongst the roses in Kensington Gardens.

Not David.

But David Fitzwilliam was the beneficiary of all Daniel's work to make Clarinda Anne Brotherton his wife. The heir to the Norwick earldom was betrothed to her, but he had never courted her, never kissed her, never even asked for her hand before their wedding in front of a magistrate. Daniel knew he resembled his older twin brother, but it wasn't until he watched Clarinda marry the bounder that he realized just what it meant to be David's Fitzwilliam identical twin.

Well, his brother was dead, damn it. It was his turn. His turn to make Clarinda his wife. And to hell with a year of mourning. He wouldn't last that long, and he rather hoped Clarinda wouldn't be able to, either. If it was the last thing he did before he died, Daniel vowed, he would make Clarinda his wife.

Chapter 14

LAST WILL

Feeling exhausted, Clarinda climbed the steps to Norwick House, very aware of Daniel as he escorted her home. His mother had left Worthington House on the arm of Lord Wallingham, her eyes suitably wet and a hanky clutched in one fist while her other hand rested on the viscount's beautifully dressed arm. Wallingham assured Daniel he would see the dowager countess to Norwick House in time for the meeting with the solicitor, but Clarinda wondered if the viscount knew the meeting was later that afternoon and not some day the following week.

"It was a splendid service," Daniel said in a solemn voice. "I was quite impressed with the bishop's sermon."

Clarinda dared a sideways glance. She wondered at first if Daniel was being facetious. She'd listened to every word the bishop had said and could hardly find his sermon of any comfort, nor his prayers the least bit affirming. And the gathering at Worthington House had been more of a garden party than a post-funeral soirée. It hadn't been the fault of their hosts, of course. Adele and Milton Grandby had been gracious hosts, their home suitably solemn, the small sandwiches and cut fruits unlike the more festive fare served at a ball. The guests, however, behaved as if it was just another gathering of the *ton*. Clarinda heard at least two mothers attempt to gain advantageous marriages for their daughters and three arrangements for illicit assignations later that evening. "I fear I cannot share your praise," she murmured as Porter opened the front door and stepped aside, his head lowering.

Daniel allowed Clarinda to proceed him and then followed until they were well inside the vestibule before he responded. "You're right, of course. It was all a load of horse manure," he groused, handing his great coat to Porter as he made the proclamation. The majordomo struggled to keep his face impassive.

Clarinda wondered if Porter wanted to laugh or to punch Daniel for the impertinent comment. Not able to help herself, she gave Daniel a brilliant smile, an expression she hadn't made since the morning of David's death. "If you hadn't said it, I would have," she whispered as she allowed Porter to help her out of the carriage gown's pelisse. "Thank you for escorting me, by the way. I rather liked that people seemed to forget it was David we were mourning. They all thought he was right there on my arm the entire time." She made the comment as she rolled her eyes, hoping Daniel would understand her meaning. It had been positively amazing to watch how some of those in attendance had simply assumed he was David, addressing him as Lord Norwick (which he probably would be, actually, although not until after her babies were born), and then helping themselves to the funeral food and drinks as if they had no clue as to whom they were supposed to be mourning.

Clarinda might have been horrified except for the fact that she'd had no idea whose funerals she'd attended the last two times she'd been to funerals. That thought alone had her staring into space for several seconds, forcing Daniel to wave a hand in front of her face and ask as to her welfare.

"Are you up to this, Clare?" he asked softly. "Because, if you're not, I can have Mr. Hammond return another day," he offered, one of his hands cupping her elbow.

Clarinda regarded him for a long moment. "I'm fine, Daniel. Really," she assured him. "I just want this all to be over," she said with a wave of her hand. She didn't add that she wanted it to be over because she was looking forward to climbing into bed and spending the night with David. He might be dead, but he wasn't buried yet, and she expected he, or his ghost, rather, would pay a visit to her bedchamber at some point during the night.

"I expect mother will be here shortly," Daniel said as he led her to the study. "In the meantime, would you like a glass of sherry? Or a brandy, perhaps?"

Clarinda considered the offer and shook her head. "I'm thinking I would like some tea," she said with a shake of her head, not adding that the thought of alcohol of any kind would have her casting up her accounts in a matter of moments. Porter overheard her comment about tea and said he would see to its delivery to the study.

Even before Clarinda and Daniel made their way into the dark paneled study, Dorothea Fitzwilliam appeared in the vestibule looking every bit the merry widow, her face flushed and her manner suggesting she'd been tumbled at least a couple of times in the last hour. "Thank you, Porter," she said brightly as the majordomo took her pelisse and reticule. "If Lady Seward dares to show her prune face visage, I am not in residence. But, if Viscount Wallingham pays a call, please let me know immediately." With that last order, the dowager countess made her way to the study.

"So glad you could join us, Mother," Daniel said, his derision barely concealed.

Dorothea regarded him with an arched brow. "Why, thank you, favorite son," she countered, her head held high as she made her way to the sideboard and poured herself a brandy. "I learned long ago how to handle my grief. Perhaps, in time, you will learn how to handle yours."

Clarinda had to suppress the gasp she almost made audible. She had never heard her mother-in-law sound so bitter, so angry with one of her sons. But then, she had never heard one of the woman's sons sound so judgmental, either.

Daniel almost countered his mother's statement with a scathing retort of his own, but he had to still his response when he realized how he planned to behave later that night. He, too, would be seeking solace in the arms of another, although he could argue he was merely staking a claim that had been unjustly taken from him so many years before. "I apologize," he whispered, his hand coming to rest on his mother's back as he moved to stand next to her. "I have allowed by opinion of Lord Wallingham to come between us, and your association with him is none of my concern," he said quietly.

Lady Norwick raised her eyes to her son's gaze, surprised he would apologize. "You're forgiven, of course," she replied with a nod, her eyes suddenly limned with tears. Apparently embarrassed, she turned away and caught Clarinda's gaze. "Now, who is this solicitor we're waiting for? One of the Hammonds, perhaps?" she wondered, her manner suggesting she was annoyed. She swirled the brandy in the crystal balloon she held, her tears gone as quickly as they appeared.

Clarinda glanced at the mantle clock. Had they been at Worthington House for only two hours? The afternoon had seemed to go on forever. "Yes. Mr. Hammond should be here shortly," she said with a nod. As if on queue, Porter appeared in the doorway to announce the arrival of the solicitor.

"Send him in," Daniel stated. He moved to position three chairs in a semi-circle in front of the massive mahogany desk that sat in the middle of the room, intending for the solicitor to sit behind it as he read David Fitzwilliam's last will and testament. Daniel motioned for Clarinda to take a seat, and she did so just as Mr. Hammond entered the room. The man bowed to them all, apologizing for his tardiness.

"I have just come from the office. I wanted to be sure I had all the final papers," Mr. Hammond explained. Daniel motioned him to the desk, carefully pushing aside David's papers to make way for the solicitor's stack of papers and a briefcase that seemed overstuffed with documents. As he did so, Mr. Hammond gave Daniel an odd glance.

When he caught the solicitor staring at him, Daniel raised an eyebrow. “I am David’s brother, Daniel Fitzwilliam,” he said as he held out his right hand.

“Oh, forgive me, Mr. Fitzwilliam,” the solicitor said with a sudden exhalation of breath. “For a moment there, I thought I was seeing a *ghost*,” he said in awe as he shook Daniel’s hand. He returned his attention to the documents he was arranging on the desk. “Given Lord Norwick’s visit to our office just moments before his untimely death, I have had to pull together his last wishes at the last minute.” The man’s comment caught everyone by surprise.

“Excuse me, but what did you just say?” Clarinda managed to get out, her face displaying her shock. “When he said he was off to see his solicitor, I didn’t realize he meant you,” she whispered, remembering what David had told her the morning he’d come to the parlor and bid her farewell with his elaborate dip and kiss.

Mr. Hammond frowned. “If he visited another solicitor, he did not make it known to anyone in our office,” the balding man replied. He settled himself into the overstuffed leather chair behind the desk and went to a good deal of trouble to put on a pair of spectacles, wrapping the gold wires around each ear and then settling the arched wire between the thick lenses on the end of his nose. He regarded the three family members seated before him. “Shall I begin?”

Daniel, seated between his mother and Clarinda, shrugged. “Please do.”

The solicitor took a deep breath and picked up the first piece of parchment he had laid before him. “Lord Norwick’s last will and testament is dated four days ago. From the comments he made during our meeting, he knew he was destined to die and wanted to be sure arrangements were in place for his loved ones.”

This time, Clarinda’s gasp was very audible, as were Daniel’s and Dorothea’s. “Destined to die?” Clarinda repeated in a hoarse whisper. "How could he know he was going to die of a broken neck in a traffic accident?" she breathed, her thoughts spinning out of control.

Mr. Hammond merely shrugged. "I do not believe he knew he was going to die that afternoon, Lady Norwick. He just knew he would eventually. As we all do," he added with a cocked eyebrow, his manner suggesting he had accepted his own fate as a man who would die at some point.

"Oh," Clarinda managed to get out, somewhat embarrassed at her outburst. "Please, go on," she said, hoping her mother-in-law wasn't sending her dagger-filled stares.

"Just because death is inevitable does not mean you need to take such a tone with my daughter-in-law," Dorothea countered, her rebuke so surprising that Clarinda made another audible gasp. *What had happened to upset Lady Norwick so?*

"Pardon me, Lady Norwick," the solicitor said, holding a flat hand against his chest as he seemed to bow in his seat. "I tend to indifference in these proceedings as a means to keep the tone professional and not .. emotional," he explained. "I will endeavor to be more sympathetic to the widow's situation."

Daniel sighed. "Please proceed, Mr. Hammond," he encouraged, placing one hand over one of his mother's and another over one of Clarinda's.

"Of course, Mr. Fitzwilliam." The man took a deep breath. "As there is no heir apparent, the earldom would normally pass to the heir presumptive, Daniel Jonathan Andrew Fitzwilliam, however, Lord Norwick stated that Lady Norwick was with child at the time of his visit to our offices. Is this still the case?" he wondered, pulling his spectacles down a bit so he could peer over the top of them.

"Yes, it is," Clarinda replied, leaning forward a bit, wondering how quickly the news was spreading across London given Grandby's earlier comment to the bishop.

She didn't add that she was carrying twins.

"Then Daniel Alexander George Fitzwilliam may or may

not be the next Earl of Norwick. We shall have to wait until you've given birth. At such time, the earldom will either pass to your son, should you have one, or, if not, to Daniel Jonathan Andrew Fitzwilliam. Entailed properties will remain with the earldom," the solicitor stated, apparently reading from the parchment he held up. "These include Norwick Park and all of its lands and tenant cottages, a house and various other support buildings on said property; Norwick House along with its carriage house and stables; and a dowager cottage in Bognor. The unentailed properties having belonged to David Alexander George Fitzwilliam pass to Daniel Jonathan Andrew Fitzwilliam and include a townhouse in Mayfair currently under lease to Lord Pettigrew for use by his mistress ..."

The solicitor didn't seem the least bit embarrassed by the mention of a townhouse leased for use by a mistress, but Clarinda had to suppress a shudder. She wondered if Lady Pettigrew knew of her husband's arrangement with a mistress and then wondered if perhaps Lady Pettigrew had urged her husband to take a mistress. Some women in the *ton* didn't like sharing a bed with their husbands—ever –, she remembered, feeling gratified that she and David's love match had probably started in the marriage bed. Clarinda had to shake herself from her reverie as she realized Mr. Hammond was continuing his recitation. "...Several additional tenant cottages and two other properties in south Sussex." He looked up at the two women before him. "The widow is to continue living at Norwick House, the mother is to continue residing in the cottage in Bognor, and it is recommended Mr. Fitzwilliam give up his apartments in Bruton Street and make his primary residence at Norwick House to better facilitate attendance at Parliament and Society events," the solicitor said before moving to a new sheet of parchment.

Daniel struggled to keep his face impassive. David really had intended him to live at Norwick House, even before the man had died and become a ghost! But to direct Clarinda to live there, too? Didn't the man know she despised him? *Of course, he did.* What had he said about giving Clarinda to Daniel? Because he'd stolen her from him? Daniel felt a sudden appreciation for what his brother had been up to—what he was up to—the man was playing matchmaker! *Bless his heart!*

Clarinda found herself wondering what David could be thinking by having her live under the same roof as Daniel. What could the man have been thinking just four days ago? He'd never made mention of his intention to have his brother and her live under the same roof! They could barely tolerate each other's company!

Trying to keep her attention on the solicitor, Clarinda dared a glance over at Daniel and found him doing the same in her direction. They both turned their heads toward the solicitor as if they'd been caught doing something illegal, guilty looks quickly replaced by bland expressions.

"All clothing and personal items such cravat pins, cuff links, shoes and sundries, including the sandalwood and amber colognes, are bequeathed to Daniel." The man's face seem to scrunch up as he read the scrawls on the page. "It says here you're to wear the colognes whenever you are expected to be in the company of Lady Norwick as she is especially fond of the scent," he said, his face suddenly turning a dark shade of scarlet. "Can't say I've ever had that mentioned in a will before," he commented.

Clarinda stared at the solicitor and slowly turned to Daniel, her gaze quickly returning to Mr. Hammond when she realized Daniel's gaze was on her again. *I never said anything about his cologne before he died,* Clarinda thought frantically.

What must Daniel think? *That I had David add the request to the will? He'll probably think of it as some kind of punishment.*

Mr. Hammond had moved to the next page of the will, holding it up as he squinted at the words. "This next section has to do with the livestock now belonging to Daniel Fitzwilliam. It appears, my lord, that you are the owner of all the animals in the stables at three properties, except," he said this last with a good deal of emphasis on the word 'except', "There is a bay gelding used by the dowager countess that's to become her property, but all costs of care will be borne by the Norwick earldom," he said as he glanced in Dorothea's direction, "And a black that is a particular favorite of the countess," he paused and nodded to Clarinda,"That is to remain her property until its death. In both cases, replacement horses are to be provided upon request by the ladies."

Dorothea leaned back in her chair and regarded Mr. Hammond through narrowed eyes. "Am I to believe, Mr. Hammond, that my late son actually had you write these instructions into his will?" she asked, somewhat incredulous. "I only just acquired my high stepper from Over the Hill Farms last month! I can hardly believe David knew anything about Mr. Popper Over the Hill."

Clarinda and Daniel both turned in unison to regard the dowager countess, their mouths suddenly hanging open in a most unbecoming manner.

"Mr. Popper Over the Hill?" Daniel repeated, his eyebrow arching up nearly into his hairline.

Her shoulders suddenly pulled back, Dorothea turned her head to regard her son. "He was named based on his lineage, of course," she stated quite firmly. "The sire was Mr. Peeper and the mare was Popover." Clarinda found herself struggling to maintain an impassive expression, while Daniel's eyebrows continued to attempt a merger with his hairline.

"A peeper and a popover gets a popper, then?" Daniel managed to get out with a perfectly straight face. Even after another couple of seconds, he showed no signs of being amused by his own deduction.

How does he do that? Clarinda wondered in amazement. The man obviously had no sense of humor, no sense of the absurd. She was forced to use her hanky to cover her mouth, sure her amusement would make itself apparent at a rather awkward moment. At any moment, in fact.

"Of course. The more likely moniker was already taken by the colt born the year before," Dorothea said defensively, one hand waving in the air.

Clarinda hoped Daniel wouldn't take the bait. She was sure she would be reduced to giggles should he ask as to the older colt's name. Tears had already pricked the edges of her eyes, ready to break forth with the least provocation.

Unfortunately, Daniel straightened in his chair and regarded his mother with a stern look. "And what, pray tell, is the yearling's name?" he asked.

"Why, Mr. Peep Over the Hill, of course," his mother responded, as if the name should have been apparent to her son.

No longer able to contain her giggles, Clarinda tried to make them sound as if she was sobbing. And, in a way, she was. Could a reading of a will be any more unusual than this one? She rather doubted it. When she pulled the hanky from her eyes, she found Daniel watching her, not with a look of sympathy, but with a gleam in his eye that suggested he knew perfectly well she found the proceedings absurd. "I apologize," Clarinda said as she turned to regard her mother-in-law. "I don't know what came over me," she said lamely.

Dorothea rolled her eyes. "Just be glad the second foal was a colt," she said with an arched eyebrow. Not giving Daniel the opportunity to ask after that horse's possible moniker had it been a filly, Dorothea straightened. "Had it been a filly, I would be riding Miss Popper Over the Hill, which makes it sound as if she would be ready for a tumble at every opportunity," she murmured, returning her attention to the rather startled solicitor. "Do continue, Mr. Hammond," she encouraged as she waved her hand again.

The solicitor stared at her for a moment too long before he said, "As to your question about Lord Norwick knowing about your recent purchase of Mr. Popper Over the Hill—I can assure you he was quite aware of your acquisition of the horse since he paid for said horse the week prior to his meeting at our offices."

Dorothea's eyes widened. "Indeed? I'm surprised he would even notice the invoice," she murmured, lifting one shoulder in a small shrug.

Mr. Hammond's white eyebrows lifted quite a bit. "I believe his comment was 'Mr. Popper Over the Hill had better not, or I shall pop him off to a glue factory'."

Clarinda didn't dare glance in her mother-in-law's direction, knowing the woman would take umbrage at David's comment. "Oh!" Dorothea gasped, one hand moving to cover the cleavage that showed above the neckline of her gown. "How dare he?" she uttered, clearly incensed that her son would threaten her new high-stepper in such a manner.

Suddenly nervous, Mr. Hammond returned his attention to the pages he held. He dared a glance at the other Lady Norwick, who was still wiping tears from the corners of her eyes while Mr. Fitzwilliam was doing a damned good job of keeping a straight face. *How does he do that?* he wondered as he moved to the next page of the will. *This has to be the most unusual reading of a will I've ever presided over*. He cleared his throat. "Moving on. The Earl of Norwick was in possession of several collections. First and foremost, of course, are the paintings."

At Dorothea's sudden gasp, Clarinda and Daniel turned to regard her while Mr. Hammond simply continued. "The paintings of the past earls and all the family portraits are to remain where they currently hang in this residence as well as in the portrait gallery at Norwick Park. The nudes are to be sold, if desired, by the next earl, and the proceeds donated to a worthy charity of his choice."

Daniel's eyebrow cocked. *If desired?* And what paintings of nudes could David have been referring to? "Excuse me," he spoke, holding up a hand and looking to Clarinda. "My lady, are you aware of any nudes in this residence?" he asked, his brow furrowing as if he were truly befuddled.

Clarinda's face took on a decidedly pinkish cast. She knew of several nudes hanging in her late husband's library and here in the study. There was one hanging on the wall directly to their left! Hadn't Daniel noticed? He had certainly been in both rooms since his arrival. Hadn't he?

But it was the nude above the massive four poster and a partial nude above the long dresser—both in David's bedchamber—that had her blushing profusely. She had posed for the French artiste Jean-Claude Lamorette for the paintings, her likeness and her unclothed body quite faithfully rendered for both works of art. Surely David did not intend to have Daniel sell those? She would be mortified! She would certainly be recognized if the buyer lived in London! *And, oh my, Daniel has no doubt seen those paintings*—he had been ensconced in David's old bedchamber just last night!

Mr. Hammond suddenly straightened in the chair, a move that seemed almost impossible for a man with his protruding belly. "The exceptions to this are the two paintings that hang in the earl's bedchamber. They are to remain *in situ*. Lord Norwick writes here that his brother should find those paintings pleasing to the eye, and if not, he will, and I quote, *Haunt the man until his dying day.* Unquote." He looked up to regard Daniel, his gaze suggesting the younger brother had better find the paintings pleasing to the eye. And perhaps some other body parts, as well.

Daniel suddenly colored up, his attention suddenly no longer on Clarinda. "If there are such paintings in Lord Norwick's bedchamber, I assure you, I have not noticed," he stated emphatically, his face suddenly turning to stone.

Clarinda's mortification eased a bit, only to be replaced by indignation. *He hadn't noticed?* How could that be? The paintings were huge! Almost life-size! And quite well-lit during the day. She was about to call him out on the topic—she was rather well depicted in both paintings, her poses somewhat provocative but no more so than those shown in paintings done by the Masters! *How dare Daniel?* Why, the one over the bed showed her at her very best, one breast quite pert and one hip and a very long leg very much on display while she lounged in David's bed with an artistically draped satin throw covering her nether regions. Her one arched eyebrow suggested … well, it was the reason David claimed he made his way to her bedchamber so often after the painting was hung!

As for the one above the dresser, well, she'd been much younger then, and the large vase of strategically placed flowers and the silk drape barely covering her derriere made it more titillating than truly provocative.

"How could you not have noticed?" Clarinda demanded suddenly, the words out of her mouth before she realized she'd even said them. She was about to mention the paintings had been birthday presents for her husband when she realized both Dorothea and Daniel were both staring at her. She sat up straighter, her bosom thrusting out. *Damn the mourning clothes*, she thought as she realized the effect of her still pert bosom was lost on her audience when it was shrouded in black.

Daniel gave a quick glance toward the solicitor before turning his attention back to Clarinda. "I assure you, my lady, I have not seen said paintings since I have not frequented my brother's bedchamber since my arrival at Norwick House," he lied quite convincingly.

He, of course, knew *exactly* which paintings featured Clarinda as their subject; the sight of the arched eyebrow alone nearly had him visiting her bedchamber a few moments after he stood staring at the painting. And then he'd had trouble sleeping when his cock kept reminding him of what, nay, *who* lay in the adjoining bedchamber, presumedly with one pert breast and a rather long leg on display with a counterpane barely a covering the rest of Lady Norwick. Knowing how one of each of those body parts looked meant he could be fairly certain how the other one of each would look. The sight of the pair of each in his mind's eye, along with the image of her long, naked back all the way from her shoulders to just above the satin drape featured in the other painting had him quite aroused that very morning as he stood in the middle of the bedchamber and attempted to pull his breeches over his manhood. The task proved next to impossible as there simply wasn't room; he was forced to imagine Great Aunt Mildred's face, and by extension, what her body looked like before his manhood lost its pertness.

Even now, as he thought of the provocative paintings, he was aware that his cock was aware, and he had to quickly imagine something entirely different. Such as Great Aunt Mildred's face. His groan was nearly audible, but the dowager countess, bless her heart, was voicing her own complaint.

"And what of the nude at the house in Bognor?" she huffed, her arms crossing in indignation, their placement beneath her own still-pert breasts merely enhancing their pertness. "I have no intention of allowing *that* to be sold," she announced, her dagger stare pointed directly at her son.

The solicitor removed his spectacles and gave Daniel his own pointed look, but Daniel had a vision of his mother in a pose much like Clarinda's in his favorite above the bed, and he frowned. "Did Jean-Claude Lamorette paint one of you, too?" he asked, directing his gaze at his mother, just then realizing he'd said entirely too much by mentioning the artist by name. *Oh, horrors!*

Dorothea Norwick glared at her son while Clarinda's eyes widened in horror. "I paid Monsieur Beaulieau to paint that nude of Wally, and I'll not allow it to be sold!" Dorothea announced with a fair bit of indignation.

"Wally?" Daniel repeated. He'd intended to tease his mother by wriggling his eyebrows, but he suddenly realized who Wally was. The thought of a painting of a nude Lord Wallingham didn't exactly incite humor at that moment. He managed to avoid acknowledging Clarinda's glare even though he was quite sure a volcano might be building behind those livid eyes.

Upon hearing her mother-in-law's protest, Clarinda stilled herself, knowing right away that 'Wally' had to be Lord Wallingham. Had her mother-in-law really commissioned a French artist to paint her lover? And Lord Wallingham of all people? *Eww!*

Dorothea thrust her own bosom out, her mourning

clothes covering far less than Clarinda's so that the effect was quite convincing. "I find it very ... soothing," Dorothea countered, not about to tell her son just who Wally was. He could figure it out if he gave it one iota of thought, she realized. She huffed and turned her attention back to Mr. Hammond. "My nude is *not* for sale," she stated quite firmly.

Clarinda was amazed that the older woman didn't blush. At all. *How does she do that?* she wondered as she regarded Dorothea with new-found respect. But *soothing*? *Lord Wallingham?*

Mr. Hammond was waving his hands in front of him, his expression looking quite pained just then. "Ladies and ... Mr. Fitzwilliam, a moment, please," he begged as he lifted the papers once again. "Lord Norwick was referring specifically to the nude paintings he has collected in a vault in the cellar of Norwick House," he clarified. He returned his spectacles to the end of his nose.

"Cellar?" Clarinda repeated, her voice barely audible.

Good grief, what has David been doing these past few years?

She would have to make a trip downstairs just as soon as Mr.

Hammond took his leave. And she had a feeling she was going to have company. The mere thought of looking at paintings of nudes with Daniel at her side brought a spot of color back to her cheeks. Despite his assurances he hadn't noticed the paintings that hung in David's old bedchamber, Clarinda knew from his having mentioned the artist that he had, indeed, noticed the paintings. And noticed them enough that he would study the artist's signature. *And probably all the other details, too.* Well, she had nothing to be ashamed of, she decided. Her husband had owned a brothel and a gaming hell. There were certain conditions he'd had to meet in order for her to agree to be his wife, such as selling said brothel and gaming hell, so the least she could do was provide him with a daily reminder of what he'd gained in the process.

"Cellar, yes," the solicitor repeated with a nod. "Again,

they can be sold or kept according to the new earl's discretion. Now, moving on to the next collection," he said, hoping no one would interrupt. He paused, expecting someone to say something. When no one did, he struggled to find his place in the will. "Ah," he said. "Vehicles."

The urge to sigh audibly had to be tamped down. Clarinda considered all the conveyances that crowded the carriage house out back as well as the additional carriage house that had to be built to accommodate David's collection of every kind of cart, carriage, chaise, barouche, phaeton, and coach known to England. *Boys and their toys.*

"Daniel Fitzwilliam may use his discretion to determine what is kept and what is sold. The former earl notes here that the yellow phaeton is especially sporty and easy to drive and the new, larger town coach has deeper seats and more comfortable squabs than the smaller version. He goes on to write that the barouche is a piece of ..." Mr. Hammond suddenly stopped and took a deep breath, removing his spectacles to rub his eyes and give an audible sigh. "As there are ladies present, I shall not read what Lord Norwick said in regard to said barouche, but it seems he is recommending it be sold," he said as diplomatically as he dared.

Daniel waved his hand, wondering when he would ever have a chance to drive any of the conveyances mentioned.

"Is there more, Mr. Hammond?" Daniel wondered when it sounded as if the solicitor would be sidetracked once again. It was bad enough that Clarinda was reminded that paintings of her still decorated the master suite—he didn't want another surprise to reveal anything else untoward. *No pun intended*, he thought to himself.

Mr. Hammond looked up and over his spectacles, still hung precariously on the edge of his hooked nose. "Oh, yes, my lord," he said with a nod. The tone of his voice seemed sad, almost as if no one in the law office had wanted to do this reading and he'd been the one to draw the short straw. He lifted several hand-written pages from the desk as if to illustrate his point.

"Carry on," Daniel said with a sigh, hoping Clarinda was holding up all right. Although she wasn't crying at the moment, he thought she might erupt in tears at any moment. *Like a volcano*, he thought just then. One moment she would be calm and collected and ever so ladylike, and with the just right provocation, she could erupt in anger or sadness or righteousness. The thought of all that passion and how she might behave in bed had his cock hardening so fast, he was forced to consider his mother and Lord Wallingham. He breathed a sigh of relief as his manhood diminished as quickly as it had grown.

"Now, the late earl's desire was that a small collection of books be given to Lord Everly," Mr. Hammond went on, pulling out the next page of David's will. "These are apparently in the library here at Norwick House."

Clarinda's brows furrowed at the mention of the eccentric explorer. She found herself wondering if the man would ever see to finding a suitable husband for his younger sister. "Did he list the titles?" she wondered.

The solicitor gave her a glance over the top of his spectacles. "He did. They are all on the topic of *fish*, especially those species found in tropical waters," he murmured as he consulted the writing on the page he held. "Seems Lord Everly lost the books to Lord Norwick in a game of piquet, and it is Lord Norwick's wish the books be returned to their original owner because, and I quote, *The damn books have been nothing but trouble, their weight having contributed to at least one broken toe and a sprained wrist, and their illustrations so frightening I have been left with nightmares. I swear those fish will be the death of me.* Unquote." The solicitor looked up to find three pairs of rather startled eyes regarding him.

"He has never been particularly fond of Lord Everly's fish," Clarinda commented with a shake of her head. "I, on the other hand, recall it was when I was looking through the glass of his rather large fish tank that I first set eyes on my late husband."

Dorothea let out a long sigh. "How romantic," she purred. "I never knew."

Daniel merely rolled his eyes, thinking his brother must have looked rather odd when viewed through a fish tank filled with water. And tropical fish.

When none of his audience asked for further information about the offending books or the fish, Mr. Hammond set the page down atop the others he had read and picked up another.

"Servants are to receive bequests commensurate with their time in service to the Norwick households. Mr. Fitzwilliam," the solicitor raised his gaze from the parchment he held, "You are to use your discretion in determining the amounts, but none are to be less than fifty pounds and none are to exceed five-hundred pounds." He glanced back down again before adding, "The earl wrote, 'And do try to be generous as these are the people who will be doing your bidding for the next forty years'."

Although Daniel merely nodded at hearing his brother's instructions, the words 'forty years' repeating themselves in his head, his mother let out a huff that was probably heard by any servants listening outside the closed study door. "Five-hundred pounds? To a servant?" she questioned with another huff.

Mr. Hammond lifted one shoulder. "As a maximum. The earl mentioned a butler at Norwick Park that he thought should be, and I quote, *Put out to pasture with a padded purse*, unquote. It is up to Mr. Fitzwilliam to determine the final amounts, although I might recommend he seek input from you and the countess as to the worth of the servants in your employ."

Clarinda struggled to keep from giggling at her late husband's reference to the ancient butler that had served at Norwick Park since before David and Daniel had been born. She straightened and turned to regard her brother-in-law. "Porter and I can help you with those who are in service to Norwick House, of course," she murmured.

"Thank you," Daniel replied with a nod. He turned to his mother. "Will you assist with those employed at your house?"

Dorothea let out a huff again. "Yes," she responded, none to happy with the idea of giving any servant such a large amount of money.

"Now comes the topic of the late earl's jewelry," Mr. Hammond intoned, as if it was the most important part of the will.

"Oh, thank goodness," Dorothea breathed. "I was afraid he would have forgotten."

Clarinda and Daniel both turned to look at the dowager countess. "Forgotten what?" Daniel asked.

His mother gave him a slight shrug. "The disposition of the family jewels, of course," she replied. All the distress and anger she'd displayed when she'd arrived for the reading, as well as her displeasure at giving money to servants, seemed to melt away, as if the mere mention of jewelry acted as a kind of calming balm.

Daniel's eyebrows cocked in a manner suggesting he was about to inform his mother her phrasing wasn't suitable for mixed company and then thought better of it. He stole a glance at Clarinda and realized she thought his mother's phrasing was exactly as she intended it to be. Resisting the urge to cover his crotch with his hands (his were the last of the family jewels, after all), Daniel gave a nod in the solicitor's direction. "Please, go on," he stated, hoping it didn't sound too much like he was begging.

"Gladly," Mr. Hammond intoned. He cleared his throat.

"Upon his inheriting the earldom, Lord Norwick came into possession of several pieces of jewelry. Since they belong to the earldom, they are considered entailed and must remain so. These pieces include a wreath tiara made of emeralds and diamonds, a matching necklace, earbobs, brooch, bracelet and a ring." Mr. Hammond paused and removed his spectacles. "At this point, Lord Norwick made a comment implying he did not know the whereabouts of these pieces, but it was his opinion they were 'somewhere'."

Leaning forward, Dorothea gasped. "They had better be in the vault at Norwick Park," she stated in a manner that suggested a theft had occurred if they were not. "I planned to wear some of those pieces when I'm in London for the Season!"

"They are in the vault, Mother," Daniel assured her as he reached out to pat the back of her hand with his own hand, his eyes rolling at her apparent hysteria. He had rather hoped to bestow Clarinda with a piece or two to help smooth the waters before he made his intentions clear as to their future together. He was now reconsidering that thought. Although Clarinda would look stunning in emeralds and diamonds (and probably nothing else), he was leaning toward finding her a necklace with a combination of emeralds and sapphires. The combination of the blue and green would be stunning with her brunette hair and aquamarine eyes.

"Well! That's a relief," Dorothea said with a wave of her hand. "And what of the diamond set?" she wondered, directing her query to the solicitor.

Mr. Hammond returned his glasses to his face, adjusting them so they were perched on the very end of his nose. "The remaining jewelry, which Lord Norwick supposes is in the vault at Norwick Park as well as some he mentioned would be in his jewelry box or in his wife's jewelry box, is to be distributed as follows." At his point, the solicitor took a deep breath, sure that whatever he said would be unfavorable according to the dowager countess. "The diamond set, which includes a necklace, earrings, bracelet and ..." He looked up. "I quote, *a damned huge diamond ring,* unquote, are bequeathed to my mother, Dorothea Fitzwilliam."

At this, the dowager countess let out a long sigh. "David was always my favorite son," she murmured, a comment that had Clarinda glancing over at her in stunned surprise. The woman's face positively glowed, as if just the thought of diamonds was enough to bring her happiness. She didn't dare look at Daniel. *Poor man!* Just a few moments ago, Dorothea had referred to him as 'favorite son', although she'd done so when she was in a snit.

The solicitor cleared his throat. "The pearl set, consisting of a necklace, earbobs, bracelet, *obscenely expensive coronet* ..." Mr. Hammond sighed and added, "His words, not mine," before continuing, "Three rings, two brooches and two hair combs are bequeathed to my beautiful wife, Clarinda. A garnet pendant and a sapphire pendant along with a gold chain are also hers."

Clarinda raised a hand to her mouth, stifling the sound she might have made at her surprise. *Pearl coronet?* When had David acquired a pearl coronet? *And why?*

The solicitor picked up the last page and continued. "Any jewelry in the earl's bedchamber, including the miniature of Clarinda Fitzwilliam, an emerald signet ring, and the, and I quote, *monstrously large and very green emerald cravat pin and matching cuff links*, unquote, are bequeathed to my brother, Daniel Fitzwilliam. All other possessions belonging to me may be distributed according to his direction." Mr. Hammond lifted his head and regarded the three people before him. "Those are David Norwick's final wishes," he stated, a hint of relief sounding in his voice. "Are there any questions?" he asked, almost afraid of what might be asked.

The solicitor had warned the earl that some of his assumptions might cause problems, that some of his language might be inappropriate for such a document as a last will, but the man seemed quite sure of himself as he dictated his wishes.

"Was anything mentioned as to the size of the allowances that should be provided for my mother and my sister-in-law?" Daniel asked, his brow furrowing so that the little fold of skin between them appeared. He wanted to be sure to ask the question before Dorothea had a chance to do so.

Mr. Hammond shuffled back through the sheets of parchment, finally lifting the very first one so he could peruse it in detail. "According to your discretion, it seems," he replied, feeling a bit sorry for the brother.

Daniel cursed to himself, annoyed at David for not having been specific as to an allowance for their mother. He would see to Clarinda, of course. "I will be sure they are at least as much as they are used to receiving," he said carefully, making sure to watch his mother's expression. When she didn't show disappointment, he felt relief. "Thank you for your time today, Mr. Hammond," he said as he stood up. "I'll escort you to the door."

The solicitor nodded, gathering his documents into a single pile and shoving them into his leather case. "Thank you, Mr. Fitzwilliam. I'll see to it you're provided with copies as soon as they're made." He bowed to the ladies and took his leave of the study, his exit causing several maids and one footman to suddenly scatter through the hallway and disappear into adjoining rooms.

Turning to Dorothea, Clarinda heaved a sigh of relief. "That's that, I suppose," she said, taking her time to stand up. She had to resist the urge to stretch her arms and yawn.

Dorothea sighed as well, a grin of satisfaction showing on her face. "Yes. I'll instruct my maid to pack for the trip tomorrow," she said, getting up and moving to the door. "I do hope you'll honor David's wishes," she added in a quiet voice.

Before Dorothea could step over the threshold, Clarinda furrowed her brows. *What wishes?* "What wishes might those be?" she wondered. The will hadn't provided any specific instructions for her, other than to ask for a new horse when it became necessary.

Dorothea sighed while placing a hand on her bosom. "Why, to marry my other son, of course," she replied, as if the will had contained those very instructions. She departed the room in a swish of silks, leaving Clarinda staring into the hall and feeling every bit as stunned as she must have looked.

Chapter 15

THE NUDES IN THE CELLAR

Daniel returned to the study just as Clarinda was about to take her leave of it. "My lady," he said with a nod, his eyes not quite making contact with hers. "I was about to make my way to the cellar and wondered if ..." He allowed the sentence to trail off, not sure how he should ask Clarinda if she intended to join him.

Since David had never mentioned being a patron of the arts, Daniel had no idea his brother had a collection of paintings. Daniel had been keeping track of the expenses associated with the earldom for several years, and if the paintings had been done by any of the Old World masters, he rather doubted David could have easily hidden their purchase. Perhaps David had acquired them with his winnings from gambling—David had always been quite lucky when it came to card games. Or, more likely, the paintings could have been his winnings. Daniel had no idea what to expect.

Clarinda ducked her head, knowing red splotches were probably developing on her cheeks. "Although I must admit I was not aware that David collected paintings, I can assure you none of the ones in the cellar are depictions of me," she said in a lowered voice.

Tempted to express sadness at this news, Daniel straightened. He was thinking how memorable his next birthday would be should Clarinda bestow him with a painting in which she was depicted as the goddess Venus. He could just imagine her standing in an open clam shell, her wavy brunette hair flowing over one shoulder and curving around a breast tipped with a succulent nipple. He had only a faint idea of what that nipple might look like, indeed, of how her entire naked body might look like, but he intended to find out that very night. He intended to wait until the household was asleep, make his way to her room, crawl into her bed, and pull her into his arms. And then he intended to hold her body against his until dawn. Perhaps, if she was willing, he would even kiss her. He wanted to this very minute, but she was gazing at him with a look of expectation.

Paintings. They were talking about *paintings*.

"Of course not. If there were such paintings, David would have built a private wing onto the house for the sole purpose of displaying them. And he would have the only key to that part of the house," Daniel replied, keeping his face from showing the desire he felt for her.

Stunned at his words, Clarinda's eyes widened, the high color in her cheeks blooming to include her entire face. "What makes you think that?" she wondered, her voice sounding more curious than angry. The flutterbies had begun to flutter, and somewhere deep inside, something seemed to melt, to liquefy. Her breasts, suddenly heavy, ached to be touched. For the first time that day, she was glad the mourning gown covered her from neck to ankles.

"It's what I would have done," Daniel responded with a slight shrug. He held out his arm. "Shall we?"

Clarinda dared to take a breath, wondering if he was teasing her. But there was no humor in his manner, no light in his eye to suggest that what he had said was a joke. His words suggested he found her pleasing to the eye. She remembered the solicitor reading David's words—his directive that Daniel had better find the paintings in his bedchamber pleasing to the eye or he would—what had the will said? *Haunt him until his dying day.* She had to suppress a grin at the memory now. She should be mortified by the thought that Daniel had seen those paintings, mortified that he had seen parts of her completely uncovered. But she found she could not summon the emotion.

From Daniel's last comment, she realized she instead felt a bit of pride—a man she was sure despised her was able to admit he found her pleasing in at least one sense. Never mind that he was her brother-in-law. Never mind that he had at one time declared he loved her and claimed he had courted her and asked for her hand in marriage.

Ever since their uncomfortable meeting the morning before, Daniel's manner toward her had been most civil. Had he forgiven her then? Did he no longer despise her? Or was this his attempt to form a sort of détente? An alliance that was neither adversarial nor friendly?

Suddenly conscious of Daniel's gaze on her, she remembered that he had asked if she wanted to join him for a trip to the cellar. "Yes, let's," she replied, placing her hand on his arm. The tingle set off by that simple touch seemed to shoot along her arm, reminding her of the sensations she'd felt only moments before. Stilling herself, Clarinda allowed Daniel to escort her, although she had to direct him to the doorway that led to the cellar stairs. She took great care in how she negotiated the steps, knowing that, although they were solidly built, they were steep.

A series of small gas torches lit the well worn path to the wine cellar, while the other path disappeared into the darkness beyond the pool of light in which they stood. Daniel took one of the torches from the wall and handed it to Clarinda. He took another for himself and stepped in front of her, his boot heels thudding on the flat stones that led into another part of the cellar.

"Have you been down here before?" he wondered, his voice nearly swallowed up by the dead air.

"Never," Clarinda replied, her gaze taking in the wisps of cobwebs and other evidence that no one else had been in this part of the house for some time. A set of large wooden doors, arched where they met at the top, opened once Daniel was able to turn the stiff handle. The hinges creaked and groaned as he pushed the doors, their weight evident from how he had to use his shoulder to get them to open. Beyond the entry to this part of the cellar, Holland cloths covered what appeared to be small tables and a few chairs. Against the far wall, more cloths covered what Clarinda realized had to be more than a dozen paintings. From their outlines silhouetted in the fabric, the frames were ornate and all about three feet wide and at least two feet tall. Several rows were evident from the way the Holland cloths draped over their tops. "Over there," she said as she pointed to the far wall.

Daniel swung his torch around and let out a low whistle. From the depth of the rows, he figured there had to be well over a dozen paintings—perhaps more than twenty. Clarinda reached down and pulled up a cloth from one row, giving her wrist another flick to force the cloth to unfurl from all the paintings it covered behind the front painting. The top edges of at least five gilt frames appeared as did the image in the front painting.

"Oh!" she breathed, holding her torch to one side of the painting. Daniel moved to stand next to her, his torch adding to the light on the painting from the other side. A naked woman lounged on what a appeared to be large, colorful pillows, reminiscent of those found in a desert caravan tent. The woman's long, blonde hair splayed out to one side, draping over one pillow so the ends disappeared over the edge. One hand was held out with a finger that seemed to beckon the viewer. The painting, rendered in rich colors and tiny brush strokes, was obviously the work of an accomplished portrait artist, although the style didn't suggest an Old World master had painted it.

"Who is she?" Clarinda wondered, not recognizing the woman. She'd had a passing thought that perhaps a lady of the *ton* had commissioned the work for her husband, much like Clarinda had done with the paintings in the earl's bedchamber.

Daniel had to stifle a snort. "How should I know?" he retorted. He was about to mention that it was a mistake for Clarinda to even be looking at the paintings—that he should have done this by himself. She was a lady. To see such a wanton display rendered so life-like in a painting was not appropriate for any woman to see. But Clarinda's reaction had been unexpected—she seemed almost in awe, as if she was viewing real art.

He pulled the painting forward to expose the one behind it, lifting his torch to illuminate the canvas. Done by the same artist, it featured a younger brunette woman seated at an escritoire. Her breasts, although not large, were uncovered despite the sleeveless short gown she wore. Long legs and bare feet were evident beneath the furniture. She held a quill as if it were a cheroot.

Clarinda regarded the image for a moment. "I rather doubt she even knows how to write," she murmured, her eyebrow cocked up.

"Probably didn't need to know for her line of work," Daniel replied with a sigh, leaning over to pull the frame forward and expose the next one behind it. A flame-haired beauty, lying on a bed with the front of her body pressed into a green velvet counterpane, appeared ever so coy as one knee was bent up so her foot was in the air and almost touching her well-rounded and very naked bottom. The woman's arms were bent, one hand cradling her head and the other clutching the velvet. The tops of her breasts showed above the counterpane, the way they mounded suggesting they were quite large. Daniel blinked and angled his head, his brows furrowing so the fold of skin appeared between them.

"You recognize her," Clarinda accused, her attention suddenly on Daniel.

Daniel's mouth did an imitation of the mouths on several of Lord Everly's tropical fish. "Not because of ... not how *you're* thinking," he stammered, his head shaking. "She's ...

her name was Ann. She was one ... she was one of the ladies of the evening that worked at David's brothel," he finally managed to get out, glad he was able to think of another term to describe the prostitutes that plied their trade at the high-end brothel his brother had established when he was in his twenties.

The Elegant Courtesan had featured women who were a step above the typical brothel harlot, their services sold to gentlemen who expected far more than a simple tumble and who paid dearly to spend the entire evening with the same woman. Daniel knew at least three of the women had gone on to become celebrated mistresses, their favorite customers having bought their contracts from David so they could have exclusive rights. "In fact, I think these are all from that establishment." He leaned over and lifted the next painting from behind the one of Ann, setting it down in front.

Clarinda angled her head to the left and then to the right, trying to make sense of what she saw in the painting he had just exposed.

"Boo," Daniel said with a sigh.

Clarinda nudged him with her elbow, but took a quick glance around the storage room. "Trying to scare me?" she wondered, thinking he was pretending to be a ghost.

"What?" he responded, pulling his attention away from the painting of a lithe blonde who was posed in a provocative position that seemed to suggest she didn't possess normal joints.

"Boo?" she repeated, glancing around the room again. *Did he think David's ghost was with them?*

"Boo," he affirmed, pointing to the painting. The woman's exotic eyes and upturned breasts were rendered so realistically, he could swear the woman was alive and looking right at him.

Clarinda followed his line of sight and angled her head again. "What, pray tell, is she *doing?*" she whispered, not sure she could be any more shocked by what David's painting collection contained. "And why do you keep saying, 'Boo'?"

Daniel sighed, not quite sure himself. "Everyone called her that because they couldn't pronounce her real name," he explained, angling his head again. "Specialized in positions featured in an East Indian book called *The Kuma Sutra*," he went on with a shrug. "All sixty-four of them. She was Lord Boomerant's favorite, as I recall."

"Lord Boomerant?" Clarinda repeated with surprise, wondering if 'Boo' got her moniker from her client.

"'Boomer', we called him," Daniel said with a chuckle, just then realizing that, of course, Boo's name was probably Lord Boomerant's nickname for his favorite lady of the evening. "Man spent four nights a week with her. Always came out of the room limping, but he had a huge grin on his face when he did," Daniel added with a shake of his head. "She was ... flexible."

Giving Daniel an arched eyebrow, Clarinda was about to say something when he held up his free hand. "Having never spent time with *any* of these doves myself, I am only repeating what our patrons said," he was quick to add, leaning over to pull Boo's painting forward.

"Oh, now I really have seen everything," Clarinda murmured, taking in the sight of another naked blonde with dark, almond eyes. This one's fair-skinned body was wrapped quite snugly by some kind of large snake, her curves made more obvious by the way the snake conformed to her reclined body. *Or perhaps she is wrapped around the snake*, Clarinda considered, shivering in disgust.

"Ah, Debra," Daniel said with a bit too much appreciation. "Snake charmer, she was," he murmured. "Always had at least a few in a big wicker basket. We never had problems with mice in the brothel."

Gasping, Clarinda leaned down to get a better look. "Why ever would Debra allow a snake to coil itself around her breasts like that?" she whispered in wonderment. *Or any place else on her body?* Indeed, this snake seemed to not have an end, although perhaps its tail was somewhere near her well-turned ankle. "Her toes are painted!" she murmured as she admired the courtesan's feet.

Daniel straightened and surreptitiously glanced at Clarinda's bottom, the fabric of her mourning gown hugging her shape to his advantage. "As I recall, if you could get the snake off of her, you could put your snake ..." He stopped mid-sentence, realizing too late what he was about to say, a truly inappropriate comment given his audience was Clarinda. At her suddenly arched eyebrow, Daniel shook his head. "Forgive me. I ..."

"Oh, please, Daniel. I appreciate your candidness. It was my choice to see these, after all." After a pause, she lifted her eyebrow again. "And, if they couldn't get the snake *off* of her?" she asked, straightening so she could see his reaction to her question.

Taking a deep breath, Daniel could feel color suffusing his face. "Well, I guess you didn't have to get the snake *completely* off of her. You just had to ... to be willing to ... to work ... with the snake there," he stammered.

"And whose favorite was she?" Clarinda asked with a hint of mischief.

Daniel started to shake his head, as if he didn't want to admit he knew exactly who could not only remove the snake, but get the damned thing to wrap itself around the both of them as they enjoyed rather loud and frantic intercourse. "Harry Tennison had that honor," Daniel whispered, one finger held to his lips in the hope that Clarinda would realize she could saying nothing of what he was divulging.

"Lord Everly?" Clarinda repeated with a shocked expression. Her eyes were suddenly wide, but then she closed her mouth and shrugged. "Well, of course, he would be the one to appreciate a snake, I suppose. He's always off on those adventures to the jungles of Africa," she commented as she crossed her arms. "I hope he's not expecting his future wife to bring a snake to their marriage bed," she added with an expression of distaste. "I cannot imagine there is a woman in

London besides ..." She waved at the painting of Debra ... "Who would be *willing*."

"Indeed," Daniel agreed with a nod. Hoping he wouldn't have to answer any more questions about Debra, he pulled her painting forward to expose the next one.

Clarinda had to suppress a gasp—this one had a raven-haired beauty posed exactly as Clarinda was posed in the painting above David's bed, but there was no strategically placed throw covering any of her nether regions. In fact, there wasn't anything of the olive-skinned woman that was covered.

"Angelika," Daniel spoke quietly. "She was Italian," he added, as if it was necessary to mention what was obvious. He didn't add that she had been one to become a mistress. Lord Pettigrew's mistress, in fact. Daniel wondered if she was still employed by the old geezer, for if she was, then she was the mistress living in the townhouse Mr. Hammond had mentioned during the reading of the will.

"Your favorite?" Clarinda wondered, a streak of jealousy making the words sound more bitter than she intended. She didn't have a chance to realize how she sounded, didn't have a chance to recognize the emotion that had her feeling suddenly angry and just a bit ... lacking.

"No!' Daniel replied, forcing his attention back on Clarinda. "No, of course not. I would never ..." He stopped and lowered the painting to the floor so it leaned against the others. Taking a deep breath, he found a hook on the wall on which to hang his torch. "Lord Pettigrew's, actually." In the dim light, he didn't see Clarinda flinch the same way she had when the solicitor had mentioned the unentailed property let to Lord Pettigrew for use by his mistress. "I did the books for David. For his brothel, and for his gaming hell. I would never ... sample the wares," he struggled to get out. "This was his business," he explained, one hand waving over the paintings, "Before he inherited the earldom and had to sell it. Besides, I ..." He lowered his head and directed his gaze back down to the painting of Angelika. "I was in love with another," he whispered, his attention slowly moving back to Clarinda's face.

Clarinda wondered at his whispered words, but she had other concerns she wanted addressed. "Well, why ... why would David even have these paintings in his possession? Did he ... *commission* them?" she asked, a feeling not unlike morning sickness churning in her stomach. If David sold the brothel, as he claimed to have done, why would he keep the paintings? Wouldn't they have been sold with the brothel?

Daniel sighed. "They're like ... menu boards. They were hung in the brothel's parlor so gentlemen could look and choose which ... which lady of the evening they wanted to spend their time with." He threw up his hands. "I shouldn't be telling you this," he said suddenly. "Christ, Clare! I shouldn't have brought you down here!"

"I brought *myself* down here," Clarinda responded, her growing ire evident in her voice. "I was hoping David had amassed a collection of valuable paintings, and instead I find he has a collection of *harlots!*" This last came out a bit too loud, the hurt in her voice more evident than she intended.

Daniel knew from the moment she'd ignored his comment about being in love that Clarinda's volcano was close to erupting. Besides it being wholly inappropriate for a gently bred lady to be viewing paintings of prostitutes, Daniel cursed himself for having said too much about the brothel in which they had once hung.

Clarinda knew about the businesses David owned prior to his inheriting the Norwick earldom. If he hadn't sold them upon inheriting the title, she would have demanded he sell them if he truly wanted her as his wife. As the heir apparent, David knew he couldn't keep an interest in such businesses once he became an earl—it would appear as if he was working to earn his living—an unacceptable situation for a gentleman of the *ton*. So he had directed Daniel to sell off the businesses and use the proceeds for investments of a more appropriate nature. Daniel had done just that, ensuring the earldom was flush with ready blunt and enjoying annual incomes from all the properties on which tenants were living and working.

David had inherited ten years ago, so it was a surprise to Daniel to find evidence of David's former business in the cellar of Norwick House. *What was David thinking to keep the paintings?* Daniel wondered. *Nostalgia?* Daniel rather doubted any of the prostitutes featured in these paintings were favorites of David's—the man preferred a string of mistresses he kept in their own homes. Besides the three harlots he knew to have gone onto become mistresses, he wondered if any of the other women had gone on to become famous. He didn't think so, although he wouldn't know for sure unless he went through every painting, and he wasn't about to do that—especially in Clarinda's presence. So why keep the paintings?

Daniel shook his head. "I do not know why he kept these. I am sorry you saw them," he apologized, reaching out to take one of Clarinda's hands. "I shall see to it they are ... sold. Discreetly, of course," he added. *And I'll take the matter up with David, next time he pays me a visit,* he considered. *The rake.*

Clarinda regarded Daniel for a very long time, her eyes limned with tears. She believed what Daniel said, but she couldn't help but feel betrayed by David. *Damn him!*

Without another word, she pulled her hand from Daniel's and made her way out of the vault, out of the cellar and out of Norwick House.

Chapter 16

THE EARLS ON MARRIAGE

Despite having attended the funeral of a fellow earl, making a spectacle of himself by twirling the widow in front of a crowded church, and co-hosting the post-funeral reception at Worthington House, Milton Grandby, Earl of Torrington, strode into White's at precisely seven o'clock for his usual evening visit. The butler nodded as he passed, surreptitiously checking the time on the clock in the entry to see that it was, indeed, seven o'clock.

A footman saw to his usual drink as he took his seat in a wingback chair near one of the card tables. Although the usual foursome wasn't in place, Grandby knew at least two of them would be arriving shortly. He hoped one of them was Lord Everly. If the explorer hadn't yet made arrangements for his sister, Lady Evangeline, to be married, Grandby intended to inform Everly he would be taking matters into his own hands. At three-and-twenty, it was high time the comely blonde was settled. And Grandby knew who would do the settling if it was up to him.

"Has Lord Everly arrived yet?" he asked the footman as the young man set his brandy on the small table next to his chair.

"He has, my lord. I believe he's in the large card room."

Grandby considered what to do. He pulled a crown from his coat pocket. "Could you let him know I would like to see him for a meeting of a private nature?" He held out the coin.

"Of course, my lord," the footman replied as he took the crown and disappeared from the room.

A newly ironed copy of that day's *The Times* lay on the table next to his drink. Although Grandby had read most of it that morning before the funeral, he picked it up and turned to the pages at the back. Having barely begun reading about some actress who was scheduled to begin a run in a Drury Lane production the following month, he was surprised when he heard the sound of a throat clearing. Lowering the paper, he found Lord Everly staring down at him.

"I believe I was summoned?" the explorer stated, his manner suggesting he was none too pleased at being interrupted during his game of whist.

"I simply requested to meet with you," Grandby replied, setting the newspaper aside and indicating the chair adjacent to his own. "It's about my goddaughter."

Lord Everly's eyes widened behind the gold wire spectacles he wore. "Which one?" he wondered as he took the chair to Grandby's right. "Don't you have ... some twenty or more?"

Grandby sighed, not wanting to admit he had no idea how many there were. He'd been deep in his cups when agreeing to be a godfather to the first four or five, and after that, it was almost expected that he would accept the honor even if the father hadn't asked directly. "Your sister, of course," he countered with a raised eyebrow. "I know of a possible suitor for your sister, and I hope you will give him your blessing—and encouragement—to court her."

The explorer's mouth opened and closed, not unlike the mouths of the fish he kept in the large tank in his library. "And what if I find this ... possible suitor ... lacking?"

His eyebrows arching up in surprise, Grandby regarded the younger man with a hint of derision. "Do you honestly think I would allow a less than suitable suitor to court your sister?"

Lord Everly shrugged and appeared suitably set down. "Well, I suppose not. But what makes you think my sister wants to be settled?"

The simple question caught Grandby off-guard. "She's almost on the shelf, she's lonely when she's left behind at Everly Park when you're off globe-trotting, and she told me so at the last ball," he replied, his tone a bit impatient.

"Oh," was all Everly could manage in response. He suddenly looked uncomfortable. He had to admit he knew his sister wanted to get married. She'd wanted to for the past two Seasons. But his trips to the ends of the earth hadn't been conducive to her attending Society events. She needed a chaperone, and if her brother wasn't in attendance, then neither was she.

"Have you someone in mind for her?" Grandby wondered. Perhaps the explorer had the perfect mate in mind but hadn't yet made the necessary introductions. Or perhaps the mate wasn't yet back in London for the Season.

Looking even more uncomfortable, Lord Everly seemed to squirm in his chair. "Yes, but I would be much obliged if you could give voice to your choice first. In case mine is ... less than suitable."

Grandby nearly said the word, "Coward," but managed to suppress the urge. "Lord Sommers, of course," he stated, as if there could be no other choice for Lady Evangeline.

The sigh of relief that came from Lord Everly could almost be heard into the next room. "Of course. He was my choice as well. And I shall speak to him upon our next meeting," he assured the Earl of Torrington.

Nearly draining his brandy in one gulp, Grandby nodded at the younger man. "See to it. If Lord Sommers hasn't paid a call on Lady Evangeline by this time two days hence, I shall take matters into my own hands." With that declaration, Grandby stood and bowed to Lord Everly before taking his leave of the men's club. A footman near the entry double-checked the time on the clock, sighing with relief when he saw it displayed seven-forty-five.

Lord Everly watched as the older earl left the club, shaking his head ever so slightly. How had Grandby guessed Sommers was Everly's first choice for his sister? Everly hadn't discussed the matter with anyone. Not even his sister. Evangeline had attempted to raise the issue at least a couple of times in the last week, knowing that Everly wouldn't leave on his next expedition until she was suitably settled with a suitable gentleman of the *ton*. But the idea of arranging his sister's marriage was such a source of consternation, Everly had avoided the issue at every turn. What if his choice proved a poor choice? He'd never be able to forgive himself if Evangeline was left unhappy. Or if her husband turned out to be deep in debt or deep in his cups or deeply disturbed, Everly would end up deeply depressed.

No, it was far better that someone else—someone of Grandby's choosing—be his sister's husband. Then Everly could head off for the islands of the Caribbean for his next adventure knowing Grandby had the situation well in hand. And if Grandby would see to encouraging Lord Sommers to court his sister, then there really was no reason for Everly to discuss the matter with his friend—especially if he wasn't going to be meeting the man in the next two days.

He could easily avoid Jeffrey Althorpe for two days.

After three, Grandby would have spoken with the man. The baron and his sister might be betrothed in four.

And, with any luck, his sister would be married by this time next week, and he could be on his way to the Caribbean! Everly made his way back to his game of whist, a knowing smile the only evidence of his logical thought process.

Chapter 17

ADELE GIVES HER ADVICE

"Thank you so much for not turning me away," Clarinda said when Adele swept into the Worthington House parlor at seven o'clock in the evening. Although the funeral and reception had gone well, the reading of the will had raised more questions than it had answered. Why had David kept the paintings from his brothel? Why hadn't David been more specific about the monetary arrangements? Why had he left so much to Daniel's discretion?

And from where (or whom) had Dorothea been left with the impression that David wanted her to marry Daniel?

Clarinda felt exhaustion overwhelm her. Given the oddities revealed during the solicitor's visit, she didn't look forward to that night's dinner with Dorothea and Daniel. In a display of true cowardice, and with several cobwebs still attached to her skirts, she had taken leave of Norwick House with not so much as a word to anyone but Porter, who had arranged the town coach and the driver who now waited out in the drive in front of Worthington House.

Adele gave her friend a heartfelt hug. "Clare! I could no more turn you away than my own husband. Even if he was three sheets to the wind," she claimed, stepping back to regard Clarinda. Tendrils of cobwebs clung to the silk of Clarinda's gown, the light gray contrasting so much with the black fabric that they were hard to ignore. "What has happened?" She started to allow Clarinda to answer and then said, "Besides my husband having embarrassed himself in front of the entire church with his pronouncement to the bishop of your condition?" she added, *sotto voce*, not letting on that she had noticed the cobwebs.

Clarinda's eyebrows cocked up as she grinned. "And yet, I couldn't help but notice he didn't say anything about *your* condition," she accused, her manner almost breathless.

Adele rolled her eyes and tried hard to suppress her surprise at Clarinda's manner. "Believe me, he made sure the bishop knew long before we left St. George's," she claimed, shaking her head in disbelief. "I nearly died of embarrassment!"

Clarinda regarded her friend with furrowed brows. "Why? Why would you think it so hard for people to believe you to be with child?" she wondered.

The older woman shook her head but finally allowed her shoulders to drop. "I never imagined *me* to be with child, Clare. Never in my life did I think I would ever have a baby. And now Grandby is talking about having two!"

Clarinda giggled, imagining her godfather's enthusiasm for fatherhood. "Let me guess –he wants a girl first and then a boy," she offered, grinning mischievously.

Adele's eye widened in surprise. "How did you know?" she asked, her hands going out to her sides.

"You could have twins and get it over with in one pregnancy," Clarinda offered, the humor gone from her voice.

Her eyes widening even more, Adele stared at her. "No!" she replied in alarm. "Is that ..." Her eyes turned to slits as she regarded her friend. "Is that what you're doing?" She asked the question as if Clarinda had some say in the matter.

"I ..." Clarinda paused, not sure how she should tell her

friend how she knew she was carrying twins. "I have reason to believe I carry twins," she acknowledged with a hesitant nod.

Adele stepped back, her eyes now blinking. "Oh!" she replied. "You might carry a boy and a girl. Or one of each!"

Clarinda's eyebrows furrowed as she considered Adele's phrasing, deciding she wouldn't correct the countess. *I'd better not have two of each*, she thought. *At least, not all at once.* "Exactly," she replied. "But that's not my immediate problem," she added, remembering why she'd taken the trip to Worthington House at a time she knew Grandby would be at White's. Adele's inhalation of breath had Clarinda pausing. "What is it?" she wondered.

"Was there something ... in Norwick's will?" Adele asked, her expression indicating alarm. She remembered Clarinda saying the funeral reception would need to be kept short as the solicitor was expected at Norwick House at four o'clock that afternoon.

Rolling her eyes, Clarinda shrugged and shook her head. She hadn't even thought to tell Adele about the comedy of errors that had only concluded two hours earlier. "Too much," she finally answered. "Not the least of which was the revelation that my husband has a collection of paintings in the cellar." She still didn't know what to think of those paintings. Why would David have kept them? For his own titillation? Or did they have some other value?

"Nudes?" Adele half-questioned, her eyebrow arching up in amusement.

Clarinda fought hard to hide her surprise. Leave it to Adele to correctly guess the nature of the paintings. "How did you guess?" Clarinda replied with a wiggle of her own eyebrows. "They're from ... the brothel he used to own," she whispered. "There must be twenty of them. Daniel said they were like menu boards—to show what a harlot looked like so a gentleman could choose which one he wanted."

Adele mouth opened a bit, but not in alarm. "Really?"

she murmured slowly. "The Elegant Courtesans. Did you ... look at them?"

Clarinda's own mouth dropped open. Adele knew of the brothel? Clarinda was about to deny having seen their subjects but decided to tell the truth. "A few of them. Ann and Angelika, a brunette with a quill and some buxom blonde. I was so angry, so hurt—I had to leave."

Adele's head dipped a bit. "Samuel's favorite was a woman named Meg. She had dark red hair and could do somersaults in bed," Adele claimed, her delivery so calm Clarinda had to blink a couple of times.

"Somersaults?" Clarinda repeated, doing her best to keep her mouth closed.

Adele gave her a shrug in return. "So he said. I only know because he used to tell me everything when he was drunk. Meg was just one of the reasons I didn't mourn him," she whispered with a shake of her head.

Clarinda inhaled slowly, realizing just then that she should be grateful David hadn't bedded anyone else since their wedding. "I'm so sorry," she murmured, her head shaking a bit. "I knew of David's businesses, of course," she said with a sigh. "I know I probably shouldn't have known, but ... I wasn't about to be wedded to someone only to find out he was a rake, not like Lady Brockhold did," she explained, remembering how the petite milk water miss, a perfect gently bred daughter of an earl, had married a viscount who not only kept a string of mistresses but also had at least four illegitimate children and was deeply in debt. "So, when our fathers arranged the marriage, I used my allowance to pay a former Bow Street Runner to find out everything about David. And then I used what I discovered to demand his fidelity. He had already sold the businesses, of course, but I thought it best to be certain he wasn't bedding a mistress or two."

Adele pursed her lips, as if she had to hide a smile. "I did the same before I married Milton," she whispered.

Clarinda nodded, not surprised by the admission. Adele's

first marriage might have left her a wealthy woman, but she deserved every pence she inherited. To use some of that money to pay for an investigator before marrying another rake made a good deal of sense. "Why do you suppose David kept the paintings?" she asked, obviously still annoyed with her late husband.

Shrugging, Adele crossed her arms. "Because he could? Because he liked them? Because the artist might one day be famous, and they'll be worth buckets of blunt?" she countered, a wan smile appearing. "What's to become of them in the meantime?"

Clarinda sighed. "It's up to Daniel. He assured me he would see to it they disappeared."

Smiling, Adele cocked her head to one side. "That's not all that's got you upset, though," she accused, realizing Clarinda harbored more troubling news.

Clarinda started to object until she remembered the part of the will where David claimed she should continue to live at Norwick House and that David should take up residence there. She told Adele about David's wishes, all the while wondering about David's motives. What could her husband have been thinking? The arrangement was practically scandalous! "Adele, what do I do tomorrow? In the coach? On the way to Sussex?"

Adele took Clarinda's hand and led her to the nearest chair, indicating she should sit down. "Will Daniel's mother be with you?" she asked carefully, an eyebrow cocked to add weight to her question.

"Yes," Clarinda replied carefully.

"Then your problem is solved. Dorothea will talk the entire trip—you won't need to say a word," she claimed, shaking her head.

Although there was wisdom to Adele's words, Clarinda shook her head. "She'll run out of talk eventually," she countered.

The older countess regarded her with sympathy. "Clare, if it was up to me, I would apologize to Mr. Fitzwilliam ..."

"Apologize?" Clarinda interrupted, astonished at her friend's comment.

"Apologize. The man adores you. Even Grandby noticed. In fact, Norwick looked just like Milton did when he was about to ask for my hand," she said as she took Clarinda's hands in hers. "And when Norwick does offer—Milton is quite sure the man will do so because he would be a fool not to—accept him," she finished, holding her breath as she watched the volcano building right before her eyes. "Clare, please, think about it. He loves you. He needs you. You're expecting ... twins, perhaps ... and they'll need a father," she said in a voice that was as soft as a sigh.

"Adele ..." Clarinda paused, realizing the fight had gone out of her. She was too tired to argue. Too tired to think straight. "I'll think about it, of course," she finally managed, her shoulders dropping.

"How can you not? He looks just like David! I admit I was surprised," Adele spoke in a tone suggesting she was awestruck, "I cannot tell you how surprised I was that he really does look just like David. No one would know you hadn't mourned a full year if you marry him tomorrow. People will see him on the street and call him 'Norwick' without even knowing," she claimed. "They won't even realize his brother has died," she added quietly.

"Ewww!" Clarinda countered, her look of distress replacing the visage of the volcano that was about to erupt.

"Well, you don't have to marry him *tomorrow*," Adele assured her with a shake of her head. "Next month, or the month after," she suggested, as if she was being helpful.

"What about tomorrow?" Clarinda insisted, the entire reason she'd come to Adele for help.

Adele's eyes widened. "Well, tomorrow might be a bit too soon to get married," she countered, thinking Clarinda was replying to her comment about getting married.

"No!" Clarinda whined. "Tomorrow. In the coach. What do I do tomorrow?"

Adele took a deep breath and let it out slowly. "Sleep. Or pretend to. You're entitled, after all."

Sleep. Blessed sleep. Maybe David would pay her a visit in her dreams. "I can do that," Clarinda replied with a nod, her head bouncing up and down. "I can sleep." She allowed Adele to embrace her, returning the hug with a satisfied sigh. "Thank you for hosting the reception this afternoon. It was a lovely party. David would be quite pleased to know his death was noticed by so many." She didn't add that David had been there; she'd seen his ghost wandering amongst the guests, occasionally stopping to eavesdrop on conversations.

"It was my pleasure," Adele replied with a wan smile. "I do not think I shall ever forgive Lady Wingate for using it as an opportunity to find a husband for her youngest daughter, though."

Clarinda allowed her own small smile. "I do think Lady Morris was a bit worse. She was trying to find husbands for *two* daughters," she countered. "And I do wish Lord Sommers would make a play for Lady Evangeline. I watched him watching her for most of the afternoon. And when he wasn't watching her, she was watching him. If her future is left to her brother, the poor girl will never be settled."

Adele's smile had widened at the mention of the Everly girl. "Grandby is working on that very match, probably at this very moment," she replied, her arched eyebrow indicating she approved.

Clarinda allowed a brilliant smile. "Then it shall happen. He is the very best godfather a girl could have, you must know," she added. "Now, I really must take my leave of you. Dinner will be served at eight, and I still have to change into a dinner gown." She glanced down as she swept her hand across the front of her skirts, dislodging a string of clinging cobwebs with her gloved hands. She allowed a sound of disgust. "I believe a cleaning of the cellar is called for, but I sure wouldn't want to be the one to direct a servant to do it," she murmured.

Nodding, Adele led her guest to the vestibule and gave

her another hug. "Good luck, Clare," she whispered. "Do take care of your little ones. And think about what I said," she added.

"I will," Clarinda nodded. *Probably the entire time I'm pretending to sleep tomorrow.*

Clarinda hurried out to her coach, determined to make it home in time to change gowns before eight.

Chapter 18

DANIEL STAKES HIS CLAIM

When the sounds of the house faded to the occasional creaks and groans of a structure the size of Norwick House, when he was sure no servants were still about, Daniel stared at the ceiling above his newly adopted bed and made a decision. Climbing out of the bed, he stripped himself of his night clothes, wrapped himself in his chenille robe, and made his way to the dressing room. He was almost all the way through the thin room and to the connecting door to Clarinda's room when he stopped and thought about turning back. *This is madness,* he thought, wondering what had possessed him to think he could simply walk into the countess' bedchamber and join her in her bed.

When he'd considered it earlier that day, it made perfect sense. He intended to take solace in the arms of the woman he loved. Or provide comforting arms for the woman who mourned her late husband. Once Daniel had climbed into bed, though, he started having second thoughts. But then the image of her sleeping alone came to him. Something had woken him, something had urged him to seek her company, to lie next to her and provide a warm body against which she could sleep and feel protected. Before he realized he had even turned the knob on the door, he was in her room, his bare feet padding softly on the Aubusson carpet.

In the dim moonlight that filtered through the closed drapes, he stood next to her bed and simply watched her for a very long time. Half on her side, half on her back, Clarinda lay sleeping soundly, her chest rising and falling with each breath. Her dark hair lay spread out to one side of the pillow. The gleam from wetness on one cheek was a testament to her earlier weeping; Daniel had overheard her crying shortly after her maid had left her chambers. That was about the time David had appeared in his bedchamber.

"You need to be with her," he'd said, his voice a bit harsher than Daniel expected. But before Daniel could offer his agreement—he'd spent most of the day thinking he would go to her, to spend the night holding her, offering her what comfort he could, despite the fact that Clarinda was in mourning, and it was scandalous to simply show up in her bedchamber and crawl into her bed—David added, "To hell with propriety. If you don't get in there *tonight*, I'll haunt you for the rest of your *life*." And after a short pause, he added. "Don't forget to lock the door."

Normally Daniel Fitzwilliam would ignore David's threats. His older brother had made plenty of them over the years, able to do so simply because he was older, even if he was only a few minutes older. But tonight, Daniel decided to heed his brother's threat. The last thing he wanted was to be haunted by his dead brother for the rest of his life. He'd had quite enough of him when he was alive.

Remembering David's comment about locking the door, he moved with stealth to do so, driving home the bolt until it made the small snick that told him it was engaged. He stepped on something that poked his toe, causing him to wince and almost sound a curse. Reaching down, he plucked a hairpin from between his toes, shaking his head as he did so. David probably planned for him to step on the pin, he realized.

Annoyed, he slipped it into one of the large pockets of his robe and continued to make his way back to the four-poster that held Clarinda.

So, here he was, standing by the side of the bed of the only woman he had ever loved, watching her as she slept. The top edge of her night rail appeared ghostly white against the dark velvet of the counterpane. *At least she is wearing a night-gown*, he thought, for he was quite sure if he found she was naked beneath the covers, his intentions toward her would change instantly. He had no intention of bedding her this night; he simply wanted to sleep next to her soft, lush body.

Daniel removed his robe, the cool air of the room rushing around him so that his heated body shivered slightly. Lifting the edge of the bed covers closest to him, he paused one more time before sliding onto the bed. He wasn't even settled into the soft mattress and bed linens before Clarinda rolled over. Her head, followed by all her glorious brunette hair, settled into the small of his shoulder at the same time her arm snaked over his chest and one of her legs slid over one of his. Stunned, he'd wrapped one arm around her shoulders in response, wondering if she was awake. But her even breathing continued, her heart beat thumped softly against his ribs, and soon he was sound asleep.

"I wondered when you might pay a visit."

Daniel allowed a half-smile at the sound of Clarinda's voice, but he dared not give up the wonderful dream he was having. Clarinda in his arms, her soft breaths warming his chest, the weight of her body pressed against his side a source of comfort, the scent of her filling his nostrils. *Apple blossoms*, he thought. He kept his eyes closed, but when her fingers started stroking his ribs and moved up to barely skim over a nipple, sending a jolt of pleasure through his upper body, Daniel gasped and woke up completely.

Given the level of darkness—the moon had obviously set—he thought it was well past midnight. "I could not stay away," he whispered, wrapping his other arm around her waist and giving her a kiss on the top of her head. If she dared touch him again like she just had, he wouldn't be able to go back to sleep. His body was becoming very aware of the woman he held, and he'd been living the life of a monk for too long to ignore the desire he felt.

Her finger stroked his nipple again, harder this time, and his entire body jerked in response. "You minx," he murmured, giving up on his idea of simply sleeping next to Clarinda. A giggle sounded from somewhere below and her hand very lightly skimmed over his skin from his chest to the top of his thigh, sending shivers through his entire body. His cock hardened instantly. Daniel sucked in a breath between clenched teeth. Is this how Clarinda was with David? Was her touch always so erotic, so arousing, so ...wanton?

"If you keep this up, my lady, I shall be forced to do something similar to you," he whispered, thinking she would still her fingers at the sound of his threat. Those fingers were stroking up the back of his manhood, setting the vein there pulsing and creating a tent pole for the bed covers out of his hardening cock.

"Mmm," she purred in response.

Not exactly the reaction he was expecting, Daniel sucked in another breath. "You have been warned, my lady," he whispered. The arm that was wrapped around her waist moved lower so his hand could grasp the hem of her night rail and lift it slightly. His hand settled on the side of her bent knee, one finger drawing circles on the warm skin. He heard her slight gasp, the sound urging him to continue. Barely touching her, he slid his hand up her long leg, his palm skimming her silken skin while the fabric of her night rail bunched up against his wrist. When his hand reached her hip, he shifted her so she lay atop him, his other hand continuing to pull on the fabric until it would come up no further. He tried to ignore the feel of his erection pressed into her soft belly, but Clarinda was wriggling a bit, making his already warm skin hot with desire. Moving quickly, he flipped them both over. Once he was on his hands and knees, he used his teeth to made quick work of the bow that held the top edges of the night rail closed and then used his stubbled chin to part the fabric from in front of her breasts.

Clarinda's back arched in response, her breasts rising from the bed to meet his mouth while she seemed to have trouble catching her breath. His lips barely touched the top swells as they traveled over the delicate skin. Once they reached the rosy skin of her nipples, his lips took purchase and gently nibbled. Spurred on by her quiet moans and occasional cries, Daniel continued suckling one ruched nipple until it was peaked before moving to the other. His beard scratched Clarinda's skin as he did so, eliciting more breathy sounds from her. He was suddenly aware of her fingers in his hair, parting the waves and raking his scalp with fingernails that sent pleasure skittering through his head.

He slid his tongue up through the valley between her breasts to the hollow of her throat. Clarinda's head angled back in response. Daniel took the opportunity to lift her from the bed, to grasp the night rail and pull it slowly from her arms and over her head. When it was free of her thick hair, he lowered her to the bed and followed her down, his lips and tongue leaving moist trails on her heated skin as he moved down the front of her body. He dipped his tongue into her navel and then down and over the swell of her belly, leaving urgent kisses as he went.

When his chin abraded the soft skin of her thighs, he heard her hiss. He allowed himself a smile before using first one knee and then the other to separate her legs. Reveling in hearing her soft whimpers as he slid his hands beneath the globes of her bottom, he lifted them slightly. Clarinda's legs spread wide, as if she had no strength or simply no desire to keep them closed. Daniel reached out with his tongue to part the moist folds hiding her womanhood. At the slight touch, her body flinched.

He heard her squeak of surprise, but held her hips firmly in place as he flicked his tongue across her most private place.

He felt her fingers rake into his hair. If she meant to push him away, he would have none of it. His tongue circled between the folds, finding its prey and licking it gently as Clarinda's soft moans filled the quiet room. When he was sure the bud of her womanhood was as swollen and as sensitive as it could be, his lips took purchase and gently suckled it.

Clarinda's sudden cry was stifled as one of her hands suddenly left his head to cover her mouth. Her hips jerked in response to the wave of pleasure he'd set in motion, the hand on his head clenching onto a fistful of hair. He kissed the swollen bud again, ready this time to hold her down with his splayed hands covering her belly. When the wave of pleasure crested in her, he pulled his head away so he could watch her chest lift from the bed, watch her swollen breasts rise, watch her chin lift up before her head turned on the pillow and her whimpers turned to stifled cries.

When he saw she was nearly replete, he lowered his head once more and lathed his tongue across her womanhood. She might have screamed from the sensation that was so powerful, it was almost painful, but if she did, Daniel did not hear it. Her legs had folded up to close about his head, enveloping him in the soft flesh of her thighs, the scent of her sex intoxicating him.

He considered he should have shaved; his stubble would leave her bare thighs red from where they rubbed against his cheeks. Clarinda didn't seem to mind, though, as she kept him trapped there for several seconds, her hips lifting and lowering slightly while her ankles rested on his back.

"Take me." The plea came out as a whisper, the words as much an invitation as a betrayal of her desperation.

Daniel froze, wondering for only a second what to do. He hadn't intended to do this with Clarinda, at least, not yet. But his body wanted it, nay, demanded it, he realized as he noticed his hardened manhood dripping in anticipation. His erection actually hurt, a sensation he hadn't experienced for a very long time.

Lifting himself onto his arms, he slid up the front of

Clarinda's body, barely aware of her legs remaining wrapped around his body as he did so. When his face hovered over hers, he lowered his lips onto her lips, barely touching them in a kiss that was almost a caress. His turgid manhood slid into her wet folds, finding the opening to her tight, moist sheath. Very slowly, he pushed himself in, ignoring his body's desire to simply thrust himself hard and allow the release his body had begged for since the first time he'd stared at the damned painting over his bed.

Clarinda's lips captured his, her arms wrapping around his neck to pull him down closer. When he pulled out just a bit, he felt her clench on him, forcing him to inhale and push back into her. Her hips lifted to meet his thrust, and then relaxed back into the mattress, allowing him to nearly slide all of the way out of her cocoon. But before he could, her hips rose up to meet his thrust, forcing his manhood all the way into her slick, hot depths. From there, they rocked against one another as if they had made love like this every night of their lives.

Stunned by her body's grasp on him, Daniel found he couldn't hold himself back much longer. "Clare!" he managed to get out, the word almost a prayer. He wanted to see to her ecstasy, though, before he allowed his own release. Lowering his head to one of her breasts, he pulled the nipple into his mouth with his tongue and nipped it. Clarinda's entire body seemed to clench as she arced up and cried out. He quickly moved his mouth to cover hers, absorbing the moan of her orgasm with his own before his body spasmed with untold pleasure. A growl unlike any sound he'd ever made was forced from his throat, his lips lifting from hers as his own back stiffened and the sensations took hold of his body.

It was a very long time before he was aware of Clarinda's gentle fingers caressing his back, of her soft lips kissing his shoulders. He had collapsed onto her body, squishing her into the mattress, his head tucked into the space between her neck and head.

Oh, God, what have I done? Daniel wondered, feeling so replete he could barely move. With Clarinda's soft caresses in his hair, he knew she was still conscious. And there was the sound of a purr and the sensation of a kiss on his head.

Gathering the necessary strength, Daniel rolled off of Clarinda and onto his back. He wondered if he would ever be able to walk again. After a moment thinking about it, he decided he never wanted to walk again. He only wanted to stay right there in the four poster bed with Clarinda nestled up next to him. Daniel sighed as he allowed a small smile to form on his lips.

A sound of disappointment came from Clarinda's throat. "You were welcome to stay there for as long as you wished," she murmured sleepily.

Daniel dared a sideways glance. "And I was thinking of staying there for the rest of my life, but you were quite thoroughly squished into the mattress," he replied in a hoarse whisper. He turned onto his side facing her. "If my lady would allow it, I should like to sleep here for the rest of the night," he whispered, knowing there was no way he was getting out of the bed anytime soon.

Clarinda's lips curled up. "My lady?" she repeated, her eyebrows arching in a teasing sort of manner.

Daniel stiffened. He was supposed to call her 'Clare.' How many times during their lovemaking had he called her 'My lady'? He regarded her for a very long time before leaning forward to kiss her on the nose. "I love you, Clare," he said quietly. "I will love you always."

Clarinda's inhalation of breath suggested she was surprised by the declaration. "You are always welcome to sleep in my bed," she finally spoke, a slight catch in her throat.

Daniel leaned forward again and captured her lips with his own, his tongue finding hers as he deepened the kiss. Sleep once again overpowering him, Daniel ended the kiss and then pulled Clarinda's body closer, tucking her back against his chest and bending his legs so his knees were tucked behind hers. "Good night, my love," he whispered. Even before sleep took him, he could tell she was asleep, her breathing deep and even. Yes, he decided, this was how he wanted to spend the rest of his life. He had to hope Clarinda felt the same way.

Chapter 19

A SEND-OFF OF SORTS

When Clarinda woke at nine o'clock, she rolled back and expected to collide with a large, male body. Instead, she landed on her back and discovered she was alone. The scents of sandalwood and musk permeated the pillows, though, and she inhaled deeply. When her eyes opened again, she found David hovering over her. She smiled.

"You are very beautiful," he said as he cocked his head to one side. "Especially after you've been tumbled so thoroughly." There was a good deal of humor in his comment, and his grin let her know she was being teased.

Color suffused her face as her smile widened. She'd had the most wonderful dream of being held and kissed, fondled and, yes, even tumbled. Her lips seemed swollen. The space between her thighs was moist. Her skin felt sensitive, especially her nipples, as if the silk of her night rail was almost abrading her them.

And then she realized she wasn't *wearing* her night rail.

She glanced at where it lay on the edge of the bed, neatly flattened and spread out as if she'd never put it on the night before. "I cannot imagine not being able to make love for an entire year," she whispered, wanting to be sure no one overheard her talking to what she decided had to be her husband's ghost. He was so real, so solid, so ... David. And so clean shaven. *When had he shaved?*

"Then you shan't," David replied with a shrug. At Clarinda's arched eyebrow, he shrugged again. "I'll see to it you are kept quite thoroughly satisfied until the day you give birth," he said confidently.

Clarinda pushed herself up on her elbows. "I'll be as big as a horse! How would we even ..?" She allowed her question to trail off as she considered how a woman who was almost nine months into breeding could possibly have sexual intercourse.

"When suitably challenged, we men can come up with a myriad of ways to pleasure our women, no matter what might be in the way," he boasted happily, his hand patting her belly.

Clarinda considered the way she'd been pleasured just a few hours ago. "I have no doubt you could," she agreed, wondering if he really would continue to visit her like this.

How long could a ghost haunt their loved ones? For some reason the question reminded her she was supposed to be miffed at him. "Why did you keep the paintings from the brothel?" she demanded, her good mood sobering a bit.

David cocked an eyebrow, his own good mood turning more serious. "Have you looked at them?" he asked, as if that was answer enough.

Clarinda let out a huff. "A few of them. Ann, Boo, Debra and Angelika," she said in a manner suggesting she might have been a bit jealous of one or both of them. An idea struck her. "Did you store them in alphabetical order?" she wondered then, her mouth left open in surprise by her sudden deduction.

Shrugging one shoulder, David sat on the edge of the bed. "I tried. I thought if I ever had a query regarding one of the girls—someone wanting to buy their painting—I would have an easier time finding it," he remarked casually as he leaned over and used one finger to lift her jaw up. When her mouth closed, he continued. "They were quite popular, those girls.

Many are still in the business as mistresses." This last was said with a hint of pride, as if he'd been the one responsible for their success.

Clarinda thought for a moment, her anger at him from the day before now just a feeling of disappointment—that he had somehow betrayed her by keeping something from his days of being a rake. "Do you ... do *you* look at them? Now and again?" she wondered, her lower lip quivering.

David regarded her for a long time, his attention suddenly on the night rail where it lay over the edge of the bed. "Actually, no," he answered with a shake of his head. "I thought you had when you gave me that one of you that hangs above the bed, though. If I remember correctly, there's a very similar one in that collection."

Stifling a gasp, Clarinda sat up in the bed, the bed linens sliding down to reveal her bare breasts. She certainly hadn't seen the paintings before, but David obviously remembered them well enough. "So, why did you keep them?"

Looking as if he was swallowing—hard—David directed his gaze at her bosom. "God, you're beautiful," he breathed.

Stunned at his comment, Clarinda pulled the bed linens up to cover herself. "Don't change the subject!"

David sighed, his eyes rolling. "I forgot about them until I was at the solicitor's office last week. Old Hammond reminded me to list any art I thought might be worth something," he explained, another sigh escaping. "And I remembered thinking the painter who did those portraits might one day be famous," not adding that he also thought some of the Elegant Courtesans featured in the paintings might also someday be famous. He shrugged again. "I'm sorry if you were offended. I didn't intend for you to see them. I just figured Daniel would see to their sale and enrich the earldom a bit more. He's going to need some blunt for the dowries for those girls you're carrying."

"That's it?" Clarinda asked in disbelief, ignoring the comment about the dowries.

Looking rather melancholy, David nodded. "That's it," he answered.

Clarinda regarded him for a moment, her head cocked to one side. "Do you ... did you ... miss your life as a rake?" she wondered suddenly. "Miss being able to bed any woman you wanted after you married me?"

Shaking his head from side to side, David leaned forward and kissed her forehead. "God, no," he replied simply. At Clarinda's wide-eyed expression, he shrugged. "My life as a rakehell was almost over when I first laid eyes on you," he explained, his voice barely louder than a whisper.

"Liar," Clarinda countered, her arms crossing over her barely covered breasts. "I saw how you behaved with women at balls. You were shameless!"

David allowed a grin. "I said, 'almost over'," he countered. "Truth was, I was growing tired of the life. I was bored with the women ..."

"Liar."

"... Bored with the gambling ..."

"Liar."

"... Bored with the late nights and the dreadful balls and the insufferable soirées." David waited for Clarinda to interrupt him, and when she did not, he cocked his head to match hers. "You were a Godsend," he said quietly.

He heard Clarinda's slight inhalation of breath. "I love that sound," he whispered.

"What sound?" she wondered, unaware she had made any sound and quite sure the room was quiet.

"The sound you make when you have a catch in your breath," he explained, leaning over so his lips nearly touched her face. His tongue reached out and barely touched her ear, the sensation causing Clarinda to react with a small gasp. "There. That sound," he whispered. "Ever since the first time I heard you make that sound, I have lived every day just to hear it," he claimed quietly.

She made the sound again, staring at him in wonderment. "Every day?" she squeaked, stunned at his claims.

David nodded. "It's your sound of wonder and awe. The sound you make when I've just done something to pleasure you. The sound you make to let me know I'm welcome in your bed and in your body." He moved his head to one side, his lips nearly touching hers. "And the sound that lets me know you're about to drown in waves of pleasure so I can allow my own release." He kissed her then, his lips finally pulling away but still held close as he added, "The sound you make when I leave your body."

Clarinda's breath caught again at the simple statement. David smiled then and rested his forehead against hers. "That little sound makes me want to pull you against me and keep you close always. And," he added with a sigh, "It's why I had no desire to continue my rakehell life after I married you.

"I stayed true to you," he added then, the claim spoken with a fervency that surprised Clarinda.

"I know," she replied, her head nodding against his. When her nodding stopped, she pulled away to regard him. "So, why did you keep the paintings?"

David suppressed the urge to laugh out loud. "I don't know," he responded with a shrug. "I certainly didn't give them any mind after their placement in the cellar. Until Hammond mentioned the need to include any unentailed artwork in the will, I had quite forgotten about them."

Clarinda took a deep breath, a sense of profound relief settling over her. Perhaps she had overreacted to the paintings. Daniel would see to their sale, and they would be out of the cellar and out of the house.

But not before she had a chance to look at every last one of them.

Clarinda thought of what lay ahead. "Are you ready for the trip today?" she wondered, suddenly wishing she could spend the entire day in bed. Instead, she would be in the coach with Daniel and his mother for the trip to Sussex and David's burial in the Norwick Park's small cemetery.

Despite Adele Grandby's recommendation that she simply spend the trip asleep, she still dreaded the ride in the coach.

"You do not have to go, Clare," David said with a shake of his head. "I do not want to think of you being jostled about for six or seven hours in your delicate condition."

Clare waved a hand through the air, dismissing his concern. She was suddenly wondering again how he would know how to pleasure a very pregnant woman. "I'll be quite fine. We're taking the good coach—the one with the deep squabs." She resisted saying, "Instead of the one that's a piece of ..." and instead said, "Your mother will keep us entertained with stories of her last house party, and we'll make her tell us all about Lord Wallingham," she claimed, her eyebrows wiggling in delight. "Wally."

There was a knock at the door.

When Clare turned to bid David farewell, she found he was already gone. "Come!" she called out, sure it was Missy come to dress her for the day. But when the door opened, she was instead surprised to find Lady Torrington peeking around the door frame.

"Good morning, Clare," the countess offered, immediately noticing Clare's night rail neatly draped on the edge of the bed. She glanced about the room, half expecting to find someone else in the room. She was sure she'd heard Clarinda's speaking aloud.

Clarinda sat up, remembering to clutch the bed covers to her neck as she did so. "Adele! Is something wrong?" she asked, her happy response suddenly turning wary, for why else would Adele Grandby find it necessary to pay her a call this early in the morning? Especially when they'd said their 'goodbyes' only the night before?

"Nothing, except that you'll be leaving for Sussex, and I won't see you for at least a few days or five or ten," she countered with a wry smile. "I wanted to wish you well and beg of you to pay me a call when you return," she said, her gaze still darting about the room. The drapes weren't moving, and she didn't hear anyone else breathing, but she was sure Clarinda had been talking to *someone.*

"I doubt we'll be gone that long," Clarinda countered with a shake of her head. "Daniel has to wrap up a few things at Norwick Park, but he thought it would only take a few days. I'll send word when I return, of course," she assured the older woman. "And pay a call, of course."

Adele angled her head. "I do believe we'll have news concerning Lord Sommers any day now," she spoke in quiet tones. "When Milton returned from White's last night, he told me he has decided to speak with Lord Sommers about Lady Evangeline. It turns out, Lord Everly had already requested to speak with Lord Sommers on the matter, but the two haven't yet had the necessary conversation."

Clarinda grinned. "It won't be long before Lady Evangeline is settled, then," she murmured. She wondered if it would be acceptable for a widow to attend a wedding should the two decide to marry in London.

Nodding, Adele bit her lip. "I wanted to let you know that I've decided I will have two ... or even three babies should Milton want more than this first one," she whispered. "I figure if Lady Seward could have children well into her forties ..."

"I heard she was five-and-fifty when she had her last," Clarinda interrupted.

Her eyes widening, Adele's hand went to her belly. "I think early forties is quite late enough for breeding," she replied with a firm nod. "Anyway," she glanced about again, but when she saw that the connecting door to the earl's suite was closed, she shrugged. "I will miss you. Stay well."

"Adele," Clarinda spoke, a bit of hesitancy in her voice. Lady Torrington paused in her retreat from the room, glancing at Clarinda with a raised eyebrow.

"What is it, Clare?" the countess wondered.

Clarinda regarded her visitor for a moment. "When Worthington died, did you ... did you *miss* him?" she asked carefully, feeling a flush of embarrassment suffuse her face.

Adele arched her eyebrow farther up and moved back into the room, closing the door firmly. "That depends on how you mean," she answered, her lips curling at the edges. She moved to the bed and sat on the edge of it, making sure not to sit on the night rail that still lay spread out over the edge.

"At night," Clarinda responded, her face blushing even more.

Adele's gaze softened. "I did. For a time," she admitted. She lay her reticule on the bed and reached over to take one of Clarinda's hands in hers. "I found the nights too lonely to mourn as I should have, though," she whispered hoarsely. Her eyes brightened, as if she was about to cry.

Clarinda's own eyes widened. "Did you take a lover?" she wondered, straightening from the pillows.

Adele shrugged and gave a quick glance toward the window. "Worthington's brother," she replied finally. "I discovered very quickly that Samuel's younger brother was more skilled in bed, but then, rakes usually are," she said with a wave of her hand. "I was so flattered—Stephen is at least five years younger than I am—so I was under the impression he was taken with me. That is, until he admitted he'd promised Samuel he would look after me if something should happen." The light that had come to her face faded a bit, and her eyes were downcast. "Then I was never sure if he bedded me because of his promise to Samuel or because he truly found me desirable."

Clarinda gave a small gasp. "Of course, he found you desirable! And he must have been extremely discrete—I never heard a bit of gossip about you!" she insisted, awestruck at the idea that her friend had been carrying on with her younger brother-in-law when she was in mourning.

"It would have been as much an embarrassment for him as for me," Adele commented lightly. "I was essentially his mistress for those seven or eight months." Her eyes lifted to Clarinda's. "I was so relieved to hear Weston wanted to court me, and I was so certain I wanted to marry again, I accepted his offer without even knowing enough about him," she went on, her eyes clearing. "And then Lady Ellsworth informed me she'd overheard her husband say something about Weston's gambling debts—I was so stunned, Clare, I thought I would die of embarrassment. I ended the engagement that very night. Gave back the ring Weston had given me. It was probably paste," she hissed in disgust. "Madame Suzanne had already made my wedding gown. Thank goodness it suited Cunningham's wife. She wore it to the Harvey ball. It was at that ball when Grandby told Cunningham he was looking for a widow for the season. Olivia Cunningham informed him I was available, bless her heart. She knew it, of course, because she was wearing my gown."

Clarinda gasped again. "That's how you came to be with *Grandby*?" she asked in surprise. She gave a gasp again. "I had no idea!"

"I haven't exactly told many people," Adele countered. "It's not as if I wanted everyone to know I was Grandby's rich widow for the Season," she said with a shake of her head. "But I could not have asked for a better husband. He has been everything a woman could want in a man. I love him dearly. And I tell him so every day."

Clarinda brought her knees to her chest and wrapped her arms around them. "So, you're telling me I could take a lover if I am extremely discrete," she said with a cocked eyebrow. She sighed and shook her head. "I do not know where I could find such a man," she whispered. "Last night ..." She allowed her voice to trail off before shaking her head.

At Adele's arched eyebrow and gentle, "Go on," Clarinda bobbed her head from side to side.

"I had the most ... erotic dream. David came to me in the middle of the night and made love to me. And not like he usually did. This David was ... more passionate and slow and tender and ..." She shook her head, trying to ignore how her body remembered when it sent a shiver of pleasure coursing through her.

"And?" Adele urged her, a look of amusement crossing her face. "Do tell, Lady Norwick!"

Clarinda blushed, her face reddening so quickly, Adele put a hand to her bosom as if she was prepared to be shocked. "He called me 'my lady' a few times. David never did that in bed! But the most amazing thing was afterwards, when he pulled me against his body and held me. It was like he was really *here*, Adele. Telling me he loved me and whispering my name like it was a ... like it was a *prayer*." With this last word, her eyes filled with tears. "Oh, Adele! I miss him terribly!" she managed to get out before a sob wracked her body.

Adele cocked her head to one side and reached out to grasp Clarinda's hand again. "Clare," she said in a soothing tone. "Pull yourself together *right now*. The traveling coach is already in the drive. You need to ring for your maid and get dressed and head to Sussex. *Now*," she encouraged her friend. "And if you find yourself missing David, then simply set your gaze on Daniel," she said with a wave of her other hand. "He is the spitting image of David, after all."

Clarinda stared at Adele for a very long time. "He is," she agreed with a nod, not about to remind Adele how at odds she was with the younger brother. She sighed, a sob interrupting her breath. She reached over and grabbed the bell pull. "Thank you, Adele," she said, wiping a tear from her cheek. "I'll call on you when I return. It seems Norwick House is to be my home for some time. According to David's will, I am supposed to live here as long as I wish no matter who becomes the next Earl of Norwick," she explained, fighting the urge to roll her eyes. *What could David have been thinking when he added that tidbit into his will?*

"Well, at least you won't be stuck in some dowager cottage on the southern coast of England," Adele countered with a giggle, one eyebrow cocked suggestively. She moved to the door and opened it, giving Clarinda one last nod of farewell.

"There is that," Clarinda responded with a nod,

wondering how Dorothea managed to live her days near Bognor. Perhaps there was enough Society present during the summer months to stave off boredom, but what did the woman do with herself during the winter months? A fleeting thought of men like Lord Wallingham made her reconsider the question. "Thank you," she added with an uneasy nod, realizing just then that Adele must have overheard part of her conversation with David. "Adele," she called out, hoping the countess was still within earshot. When Adele reappeared with an expectant look on her face, Clarinda said, "I will miss you, too." She moved a hand over her belly. "But I find talking to the babies helps," she whispered. The look of relief on Adele's face made her wonder if the woman had been worrying for her sanity.

"Are you truly going to name the boy 'Wally'?" Adele asked then, her brows furrowing in concern. "I just ask because ... well, *Wallace* just doesn't seem a suitable name for your son."

Clarinda blinked, just then realizing Adele really *had* overheard her talking to David. "I was merely trying out names when you arrived," she said with a wave of her hand. "I assure you, I will not name David's son 'Wallace'."

Adele gave a sigh of relief. "All right. But please don't even think to name him *Milton*, for my husband's ego doesn't need any more reinforcement," she said with a wicked grin. "No matter what you intend to name him, keep him well fed," the countess ordered with a wink. And then she was gone.

Daniel took a deep breath, the solidity of the dressing room door at his back the only thing anchoring him at that moment. He'd woken much later than he intended, sunlight already peeking around the edges of the drapes in Clarinda's room. Leaving Clarinda's bed was one of the hardest things he had ever done in his life. He'd wanted to continue holding her against his body, he wanted to kiss her awake and make love to her slowly, gentling her to the idea of him as her lover. But he'd heard the coach pull into the drive out front and realized they needed to get on the road to Norwick Park. So he'd left her bed, pulled on his robe, and, halfway to the connecting door, remembered to unlock the bedchamber door. *Thank the gods he had!* For he heard Clarinda's voice, speaking as if someone else was in the room. He could only hear most of her side of the conversation, though, and he wondered as to the identity of her early morning caller. That is, until she'd said, "Your mother will keep us entertained with stories of her last house party, and we'll make her tell us all about Lord Wallingham."

She could only be referring to his mother, the Dowager Countess of Norwick. And the only other child of Dorothea Fitzwilliam was David. *So, was David's ghost visiting Clarinda, too?* Talking to her? Comforting her or guiding her or ... *haunting her?* Daniel hadn't even had a chance to think on this revelation when he heard the knock on her bedchamber door.

Lady Torrington's arrival was as unexpected as it was an opportunity for Daniel to learn more about Clarinda and what she thought of the night before. She spoke of it as if it was all a dream! *And, damn it! She thought I was David!* Although he'd listened closely and heard her as she described the differences between David and the man that had shared her bed. He caught the sound of longing in her voice, as if she wanted the night to happen again. And apparently she had favored the way he had held her against his body as they slept, and the way he'd said her name. He could do that all again. Every night.

They would reach Norwick Park in time for dinner. He would see to it she was assigned to the room adjoining his. And once he was sure the household was asleep, he would join her in her bed and repeat what he had done last night.

At some point, Clarinda would have to realize *he* was the one who made love to her and not David—or his ghost.

And when she did, Daniel could only hope she wouldn't hate him for it.

Chapter 20

A TRIP TO SUSSEX

After her maid helped her dress in record time and had her hair pinned up in a simple bun, Clarinda hurried down to the breakfast parlor. She was surprised when she found Dorothea nearly finished with her breakfast but no sign of Daniel. Her mother-in-law explained that Daniel's valet had been there to request that a plate be taken up to his master's bedchamber. Clarinda wondered what might induce the future earl to forgo eating in the breakfast parlor and instead eat in his room. A vision of the painting above his bed came to mind, and she blushed before dismissing the idea of Daniel eating breakfast while gazing at her scantily clad likeness.

"Was that the Countess of Torrington I saw leaving your room this morning?" Dorothea wondered as she added cream to her tea. Although the question was innocent enough, there seemed a hint of mischief in the tone of her voice.

Clarinda regarded the plate of ham and toast that a footman had just placed in front of her. "Yes. Adele wanted to say a farewell, I suppose," she responded, remembering the countess' comments. Had that been the real reason for the woman's visit, though? Her behavior had been somewhat unusual, but her reticence in expressing her concerns was completely out of character for a woman who was always quite honest with Clarinda. And there had been a mention of her decision to have more children beyond the babe she carried.

What was the countess thinking?

And then the older woman had the gall to suggest Clarinda should accept Daniel's suit should he offer for her hand! Adele had mentioned it the night before, too, as if she thought Clarinda should remarry as soon as possible, despite her mourning period having barely begun! And for Adele to recommend Daniel seemed rather odd given Adele had only met the man at the funeral the day before. "She's expecting a babe about the same time as this one is due," Clarinda added, realizing the news was no longer secret—the Earl of Torrington had announced his wife's pregnancy shortly after the funeral and guaranteed most of London knew when he told those in attendance at White's later that night.

"Poor woman," Dorothea replied with a shake of her head. "I do not think I could have survived being with child at that age," she added in an effort to make herself understood when Clarinda's eyebrow arched up. "Which is why I insisted Daniel's father bring French letters with him when he came to my room. Since I'd already provided him with an heir and a spare, I wasn't about to breed again."

The blush that suffused Clarinda's face gave away her embarrassment immediately. How could her mother-in-law talk about prophylactics over breakfast? Or at all? Clarinda was saved from further reproductive discussion when the butler entered the breakfast parlor and announced the traveling coach was loaded and ready to depart. She excused herself and hurried upstairs to pull on her pelisse and bonnet and to retrieve her reticule. As she turned to leave the room, she was suddenly face to face with ... *David?* Before she could utter a greeting, his hands were on her shoulders and his lips were covering hers. The scents of sandalwood and amber surrounded her as the soft kiss deepened. Oh, how she would miss this! Before she could even finish the thought, though, he ended the kiss and pressed his forehead to hers. "Courage," he said and then disappeared through the door to the dressing room.

It was half past ten before the dowager countess, the countess, and the future Earl of Norwick stepped into the traveling coach and began the trip to Sussex. Given the way Dorothea arranged her carriage gown across the width of the seat, Clarinda opted to take the opposite seat. She quickly scooted to one end of it as Daniel stepped in, realizing it was Dorothea's intention that she and Daniel sit together. At least she wouldn't have to face him during the long trip. She was afraid that by seeing him for an extended period of time, she would be reminded of what happened in her bedchamber the night before, when she dreamed that David had made slow, languorous love to her and then held her as she slept. Just thinking of it made her blush, and she rather Daniel not wonder why her color was so high.

As the Countess of Torrington had predicted the night before, Dorothea Norwick did offer enough one-sided conversation so that it was unnecessary for Clarinda to say much during the trip. Before the coach had made it past Chiswick on its way south, Clarinda's eyes grew heavy and her head fell to one side. The familiar scent of amber and sandalwood surrounded her, reminding her of David's delicious kiss. Soon, she was sound asleep.

Daniel regarded his mother as a mischievous grin spread over her face. She'd just completed a tale of how Lady Margaret and Lady Annabeth, both older spinsters and daughters of earls, had entertained the house party contingent with their brilliant acting abilities during the production of "A Midsummer's Night Dream". Now Dorothea was quiet as her head cocked to one side.

"Given the stories you've been sharing, I rather doubt you find this the least bit scandalous," Daniel commented dryly.

His mother was apparently finding his seating arrangement with Clarinda a source of amusement. The side of Clarinda's head had come to rest against Daniel's shoulder. In an effort to ensure she stayed nestled in the squabs and didn't topple forward, he had angled his body a bit in her direction, one hand resting on his thigh just in case the coach should shift or stop suddenly and he would need to prevent her from pitching forward. For a moment, he rather wished it would just so he could capture her body in his arms and pull her more securely against his own.

His entire body still thrummed with the memory of what he and Clarinda had done in her bed only hours ago. He wanted to be doing it now, wanted to be sliding the palms of his hands over the silken skin of her breasts and belly and bottom, down the length of her legs and back up along the tender skin of her inner thighs. He wanted to bury himself inside her, pleasure her until she cried out and then take his own blessed release in a shower of bright stars and heavenly sensations. The mere thought of it had his manhood straining against the fall of his breeches. If not for his cape coat, the evidence of his arousal would be apparent to his mother, who continued to regard him with that mischievous grin.

"I think it's rather sweet. And chivalrous of you," Dorothea responded quietly. She straightened and let out an audible sigh. "I do hope you two marry soon," she added, her tone suggesting it wasn't a desire as much as a directive to her son. "A small, private ceremony would suffice."

Daniel arched an eyebrow, stunned at his mother's comment. "Indeed?" he replied, not sure what else to say.

Dorothea lifted one shoulder in a quick shrug. "You still love her. Don't you?" The last part was said in a suddenly doubtful voice that could barely be heard over the noise of the horses and spinning wheels.

Streaks of red appeared on Daniel's cheekbones. "I hardly think that matters," he countered, not meaning to sound as defensive as he did with his response. His mother's quelling glance had him heaving a sigh. "Oh, if you must know, I do … I feel affection for her. I have since the first time I danced with her," he admitted, his chin coming up defiantly. He wasn't about to admit to his mother that he loved Clarinda—that she had been the only woman for whom he had ever felt affection for as long as he'd lived.

"She needs a husband, Daniel. She cannot have this baby as a widow …"

"Society expects her to," Daniel interrupted, his voice a bit louder than he intended. Clarinda, apparently briefly awakened from her nap, readjusted her position against Daniel so that her head nestled into the small of his shoulder. Stunned when she settled back to sleep so quickly, Daniel carefully wrapped his arm around her back and slowly settled his hand on the side of her hip. When he dared a glance in his mother's direction, he found her face alight with a brilliant smile. "For propriety's sake, she really should wait and have the child before marrying again," he added *sotto voce.*

Dorothea waved a gloved hand in a dismissive gesture. "Society will have forgotten all about David once you two are wed," she argued. "And speaking of my eldest, just where *is* he?" she asked suddenly.

Daniel resisted the urge to say something like, "In hell," and instead said, "The dray with his coffin left for Norwick Park yesterday after the funeral. I expect he's next to a rather deep hole in the cemetery there."

Suddenly somber, Dorothea nodded and turned her attention to the window, apparently to take in the passing scenery. When she didn't offer any other conversation, Daniel stifled a yawn. His eyelids grew heavy. His chin soon brushed against the top of Clarinda's head. At some point, she'd had the foresight to remove her hat so it's short brim and tall crown wouldn't get crushed as she slept. When he inhaled, the scent of apple blossoms filled his nostrils. *Had she planned to fall asleep against his arm?* Daniel wondered, hoping she had. Before he could think more on the subject, he was asleep.

Dorothea Norwick pulled her gaze from the window and regarded her son and daughter-in-law with a shake of her head. Pulling her black kid glove from her left hand, she studied the new gold and sapphire ring at the base of her fourth finger.

What had Lord Wallingham been thinking to ask for her hand? And in the middle of the night, no less, when he had seen to her pleasure a second time and seemed quite sated and settled for the night?

The proposal had been most unexpected, and yet more welcome than Dorothea could admit even to herself. Had he been sincere in his assertion that he was finally ready to settle down and marry? That he had seen first-hand what marriage had done for a man like Grandby and wanted that life for himself?

When Dorothea countered with a question about his lack of an heir, he shrugged and said his eldest nephew would do quite well in the role.

And what of fidelity? How could she expect a man with his reputation for bedding widows to give up his frequent and apparently very satisfying assignations? He already had, he claimed, swearing he had bedded no other woman but her since their meeting.

So, she had accepted his offer of marriage with the caveat that he had to repeat the proposal when they were both fully clothed and in their right minds. It was a coward's reaction, she knew, and she would be the first to admit it. But she also knew she would give Wally the same answer if he asked her again. And he had, the following morning when he met her in the breakfast parlor and slid the gold and sapphire ring on her finger.

She smiled as she studied the gemstone. There was something to be said for having a person to converse with during dinner, a companion for long walks along the sea, an escort for the occasional soirée and a warm body close by at night.

The man was not perfect, but he would do.

Now, as Dorothea regarded her son and daughter-in-law and thought of their concern for propriety and *Society* over their concern for their own lives and well-being, over the welfare of her grandchild, she couldn't help but feel a bit incensed. She heaved a sigh. "Stubborn children," she whispered, finally closing her own eyes to take a nap.

Chapter 21

POST FUNERAL

A southerly breeze caught the lock of hair that had escaped from Clarinda's elegant coiffure, momentarily blinding her as she stood at the end of the broken ground where the coffin had been buried earlier that afternoon. The faint hint of salt in the air reminded her of how close she was to the southern shores of Sussex. The mason hadn't yet completed the headstone, so a simple cross marked the place of David's burial. Clarinda hadn't cried since that moment when the coffin had been lowered, hadn't felt anything since leaving the graveside service with Daniel and Dorothea and the small band of mourners who had joined them for the brief service earlier that day. *I should feel something*, she thought, a pang of guilt clutching at her.

"You needn't feel guilty, my love," she heard from behind her. She whirled to find David regarding her with an expression that suggested he was sad.

"David," she breathed, a rush of relief coursing through her, the sensation so welcome she almost smiled. Instead she moved to join him, lifting her face to look up at him. "I was afraid ... I was afraid I'd never see you again," she managed to get out.

Her late husband regarded her with a wan smile. "You

can always summon me," he replied, using a finger to tap her forehead. "You have a vivid memory of what I look like." He didn't need to add that the memory was so vivid because she saw Daniel everyday.

"I'd hoped you would ... be here ... during the service," she stammered, briefly glancing toward the gravesite. A collection of headstones were neatly lined up beneath a live oak tree, some several centuries old, their north sides covered in moss. Some were as new as the one that marked her fatherin-law's grave. She'd been present for that burial, too, although she wasn't yet David's wife.

"As I seem to recall, I *was* here," David countered, a brow cocking mischievously as he glanced at the broken ground. "Can't be two places at once," he added, ducking his head suddenly.

Clarinda sighed and shook her head. "I suppose not," she murmured, not the least bit humored by his poor attempt to make her smile again. Closing her eyes, she found herself wondering if he would still be standing in front of her when she opened them again. *Please be here*, she prayed, a tear forming beneath her eyelid and escaping when she opened her eyes and found David still standing before her, his expression one of concern.

"Are you ... feeling faint?" he wondered, reaching out to cup her cheek with this hand, the touch so ethereal Clarinda wasn't quite sure she felt it. But, like everything else in the moment, she couldn't seem to feel anything. The numbness was at once comforting and a source of concern. Certainly she should feel *something*. Agony, loss, anger, relief, grief, panic ... something.

"I miss you so much," she managed to get out before a sob took her breath. *I'm feeling hurt*, she realized, the unfamiliar sensation overcoming her ability to feel anything else.

"Oh, God," David said as he wrapped his arms around her shoulders and pulled her against him. "You really have to stop this perfect imitation of a watering pot," he chided her, his chin nearly colliding with the brim of her black hat.

"I cannot ... help ... help it," she replied, the tears now flowing freely. Despite the hanky she held in one fist, she allowed the tears to fall onto her pelisse. "I love you. I miss you. My heart ... hurts."

David tightened his hold on her, whispering softly as one hand rubbed her back. He pulled away briefly and slid the other between them, laying his palm across her belly. "You have the twins all in a twitter," he whispered, his stern expression more effective at seizing her attention than the gentle scolding.

Clarinda's eyes widened as one of her hands covered his. "Oh, dear," she managed to get out before she hiccuped and worked hard to arrest her sobs. She wiped away her tears with the hanky. "Are they ... are they well?" she asked then, moving his hand away so that her own was pressed against the wool of her pelisse.

"They're fine. They're probably just hungry," he replied, his manner suddenly as nonchalant as he'd been before her outburst. "Go on. Get something to eat," he urged her, waving his hand toward the country manor home atop the nearby hill.

"I will," Clarinda replied with a nod, reluctantly moving in that direction. "Come with me?" she invited, hoping he would at least escort her to the front doors.

David gave a glance toward the Portland stone monstrosity that was the center of Norwick Park. "No," he replied with a shake of his head. "It's such a nice day, I think I'll stay out here."

Clarinda regarded him uncertainly before nodding. "If you're sure. I'll see you ... the next time I summon you," she said, her voice sounding brighter than she felt. She turned and began hurrying up the faint walking path toward the house. She looked back, comforted to see that David still stood there, the bottom of one boot and his back resting against the tree while his arms were crossed in front of his chest. But when she was about to reach the first step of the stairs leading into the front doors of the house, she looked back again.

David was gone.

Daniel stood in the second floor parlor window overlooking the front of Norwick Park. Off in the distance he could see Clarinda, still dressed in the mourning clothes she'd worn for the burial, standing near where his brother had been buried earlier that day. He wondered if she was weeping, wondered what she might be thinking, wondered if David was somewhere nearby or if he was gone now that he was buried.

As if he was conjured up by Daniel's thoughts, David suddenly appeared behind Clarinda, striking a pose that seemed almost carefree. Stunned, Daniel stared at the pair as they seemed to converse with one another. *He really is haunting her, too*! he realized with a start. *Damn him*!

Wishing for a pair of opera glasses, Daniel glanced around the room, looking for something that might act in their stead. A small telescope stood mounted on a tripod, aimed out the north window from his last attempt to discover a comet. He quickly lifted and moved the instrument to the east window, lowering the tube and training the sight on the tree in the graveyard. Peering through the scope's lens, he readjusted the focus and position until he could clearly see Clarinda and David. Even though she was in profile, he could see she was crying, and for a moment, his heart clenched on her behalf. He hated to see her like this, hated to see her so bereft—perhaps because he knew she mourned for David, but more likely that he never wanted her to be in so much pain. He was sure he could make out the words she was saying. "My heart ... hurts."

Daniel pulled his face away from the lens, suddenly ashamed that he would eavesdrop like this, spy on the woman he was determined to make his own. Curiosity pulled him back, though, and he resumed his watch. David was waving toward the house, apparently telling her to leave the gravesite. Clarinda was no longer crying, but she held one hand against her pelisse as if she was cradling her belly. Remembering his brother's mention of her earlier miscarriages, Daniel felt alarm slam into his gut.

Afraid something was wrong with the babies she carried, Daniel rushed from the parlor and down the main staircase, his boot heels clicking on the marble as he descended. He was through the hall and vestibule and out the front door just as Clarinda was about to take the first step up to the house.

"I've got you!" Daniel called out, rushing down the stairs to scoop her into his arms. Suddenly airborne, Clarinda's half-boots kicked into the air, the edge of her white petticoats appearing from beneath her black gown and pelisse just as she let out a squeak of surprise. Her hat, crushed against Daniel's chest, hid her face from view.

Daniel hurried back up the steps, a bit surprised at how heavy Clarinda seemed. *Of course, she is carrying twins*, he reminded himself. And lately, she had been eating as if she carried quadruplets.

"What are you *doing*?" Clarinda screeched, her legs kicking up and down as Daniel barely managed to get her up the steps. "Put me *down*!" Clarinda shouted, kicking her legs so that her skirts hiked up to reveal her black stocking-clad shins and half-booted feet, and tossing her head so that she could get the damned hat out of the way. She had managed to get one arm behind Daniel's back so that she could pound on it with her fist while she used the other hand to clutch his lapel. In the event he really did put her down, she didn't want to tumble to the steps below.

"My darling Clare, I shall get you settled and send for the physician immediately," Daniel was saying as calmly as he could, his heart racing with the fear he felt for her and the babes she carried.

The ancient butler, Hildebrand, appeared at the door. His face, usually a model of impassivity, took on a look of alarm as he eyes rounded and one hand went to his mouth. He stepped back to open both doors as Daniel struggled to get his bucking burden through the opening and into the vestibule.

"Daniel Jonathan Andrew Fitzwilliam, you put me down this *instant*!" Clarinda cried out, her volcanic emotions seething. Having divested herself of the crushed silk-covered hat somewhere near the top step, she had a clear view of Daniel's face, of the look of determination and ... was that *fear* she saw in his eyes? His heart hammered beneath where her hand still clutched his lapel. The fight, and the pent up steam and pressure, went out of Clarinda in an instant.

Not ready for Clarinda's sudden lack of movement, Daniel nearly dropped her on the black and white marble tiled floor. "Confound it, woman, I am trying to *help* you," he whispered hoarsely. Glancing about, Daniel realized there was nothing cushioned on which to place Clarinda, so he merely hurried into the salon just off the vestibule. "This would be much easier if my lady would calm herself," Daniel said, keeping his tone as even as possible. His heart was racing. Fear was threatening to overcome his calm façade. And something niggled at his brain, something that warned him to heed her ladyship's words.

Given she was as calm as she'd been since he'd collected her at the bottom of the stairs, and given Daniel's repeated pleas to calm down, Clarinda's temper flared back to life. "I would be far more *calm* if you would just put me down!" Clarinda insisted again, this time punctuating her words with a punch to his shoulder. The volcano had returned, ready to erupt in a massive explosion that would no doubt leave Daniel with purple bruises and blistered ears.

"Ow!" Stopping in the middle of the room, Daniel looked down and regarded his burden for several seconds. *Beware the volcano*, he remembered. Her face was flushed, her anger making her aquamarine eyes turn a stormy green. Under his scrutiny, she seemed to settle a bit, her body no longer fighting his hold. Her eyes met his, and for a moment, they simply stared at one another. *Dormant for the moment, but its power can be unleashed without warning*, he remembered reading about some volcano that had taken out an entire ancient civilization.

Clarinda fought the urge to gasp, stunned at what she saw when she finally *looked* at Daniel. His concern for her was evident in his face. Drawn and pale, he appeared every bit as fearful as he must have felt. *Worried*, she realized. *For me.* She thought to remind him once again that he should put her down, but she thought better of it, thinking he really would drop her on the floor. There was Axminster carpeting below, but Clarinda doubted it would absorb much of the shock of her solidly landing on it. And, at that moment, she found she rather liked being in Daniel's arms. He was certainly stronger than she would have imagined, given he seemed to be able to hold her up when she was already a stone heavier than usual. In fact, she could feel the muscles of his upper arm bunched behind her back, the muscles of his lower arm bunched under her knees—even through the fabric of her gown and coat. The thought of it caused her breath to hitch, and a pleasant sensation rippled through her belly.

"Are you ... well?" Daniel asked then, his words so quiet she had to read his lips to be sure she heard them correctly.

"I am fine, really," she replied with a nod, opening her fist so her palm rested on the front of his coat. She felt his racing heartbeat beneath the fabric, wondered at his fear for her. Her other arm snaked up his back so she could grip his shoulder from behind. "What were you ... thinking?" she whispered then, noting how very much like David he looked just then. His hair was only a shade darker, probably because he's spent far too much time indoors working on estate matters when he could have been out riding or fishing or hunting. The golden highlights were just then glinting in the late afternoon sun that filtered through the salon windows. The scar next to his eye was barely visible; perhaps in a few years, it would be completely gone, and then he really would look exactly like David. He was certainly stronger than David; she rather doubted her husband would have been able to hold her like this as long as Daniel had. And he had even carried her up the steps with her fighting him every step of the way.

"I thought you were ... in distress. You looked as if ... as if something was ... *wrong*," he stammered, never taking his eyes from hers.

Clarinda shook her head. "I ..." She had only ever seen that look of fear one other time, seen it on the face of her husband when he'd been summoned to her room as she lay bleeding from her first miscarriage. Something clutched at her chest just then, a sensation she probably would have recognized if her present situation wasn't so otherwise unexplainable. "What do you think is wrong?" she whispered then, just then realizing she hadn't let go of him so that he could put her down.

Daniel frowned. "You had your hand ... you looked as if you were ... in pain," in managed to get out. He took a deep breath and let it out in a whoosh.

"Pain?" she repeated, her brows furrowing as she tried to reason how he would have come to that conclusion. "I am hungry," she complained, her breaths finally coming in even bursts.

"Oh," Daniel exhaled, nodding his head as if he finally understood. He glanced about the room, deciding Clarinda was truly growing heavier by the moment. Noticing the Greek lounge near the north window, he moved there and settled her down onto it, keeping an arm around Clarinda as he sat next to her.

Her energy spent, Clarinda removed her hand from his lapel and loosened her arm from around his back. Without the weight of her hanging onto him, Daniel nearly lost his balance. He righted himself, noticing his thigh brushed hers as he did so.

"I was speaking with David," she blurted out then, not intending to actually admit she saw her late husband down by his grave.

"I know. I was ... I was watching," Daniel admitted,

wincing when he realized his words made it sound as if he'd been spying on them. When one of her eyebrows shot up, he added quickly, "I didn't intend to, I promise, Clare."

"You *saw* him?" Clarinda whispered, stunned at his comment. If Daniel saw David's ghost, did others as well?

"Yes. Unfortunately," Daniel answered with a nod. "He has been haunting me since my arrival at Norwick House." The air seemed to go out of him all at once as his gaze settled on Clarinda. Several pins were missing from her hair. A long, thick lock of brunette silk lay across her throat while another trailed over one shoulder. Her skirts and petticoats were left barely covering her knees, leaving her black stockings exposed. They enhanced her shapely calves, which curved down to dainty ankles that barely showed above her black half-boots. Despite her state of dishabille, she was beautiful. More beautiful than he could have imagined. And he was about to put voice to the sentiment when he remembered they were discussing how David had been haunting them.

"When you said David had told you things, I didn't realize he was *haunting* you, too," he stated, using his now-free hand to unfasten the buttons of her coat. He straightened her so he could help remove the garment. Her bonnet fell from her lap in the process, but she ignored it as it rolled away from them.

"I would not say he was *haunting* me," she countered, her eyebrows indicating she took a bit of umbrage at his comment. "Just ... visiting and ... checking on me and the babies," she explained, her face suddenly flushing when she realized she could not tell him he had kissed her. Even made love to her the night before last and held her close just last night. That had been heaven, to be held and caressed and pleasured as if she was made of bone china, much like Daniel's fingers were caressing her face and throat right now.

Daniel frowned. "Does he ... visit you in your bedchamber?" he asked, remembering her words to Lady Torrington when she had mistaken him for David.

Clarinda's face suddenly reddened with embarrassment.

"A few times, although it was usually to tell me ..." She stopped. She couldn't tell Daniel what David had said. She couldn't tell him that David insisted she marry Daniel! "To tell me about the babies," she managed to get out.

Daniel was about to ask about her feelings on the subject when his mother appeared in the doorway.

"What, pray tell, is going on here?" Dorothea Fitzwilliam demanded as her fists took purchase on her hips. Somehow her face managed to display an expression that made her appear both scandalized and extremely satisfied by what she was witnessing.

How does she do that? Clarinda wondered, suddenly realizing her thigh was pressed rather solidly against Daniel's thigh while the edges of her petticoats and most of her calves were on display. She decided to leave her thigh exactly where it was. *Let my mother-in-law think what she will.* Reaching over her knee, she shook out her skirts so they would settle back down to her half-boots. At least she could display some sense of propriety.

How does she do that? Daniel wondered at seeing his mother's expression. He considered moving his thigh a bit to the right, but decided his thigh rather liked where it was. He made no move to move it. He felt a bit of satisfaction when he realized Clarinda didn't mean to move her thigh, either. "Is everything all right, Mother?" Daniel wondered, realizing just then that his thigh had to move—a lady had just entered the room. He stood, reluctantly, and gave a bow in his mother's direction. Clarinda, bless her heart, remained exactly where she was.

"Well, obviously," Dorothea responded, her arms spreading out to her sides. "Why, this is the best news I've had since Wally said he was paying a visit to Rundell and Bridge!"

"Wally?" Clarinda repeated in a whisper, remembering when she'd last said the name. Adele had overheard it when she came to see her off the day before.

"Wallingham," Daniel clarified, his own voice barely a

whisper. He had to suppress a shudder at the realization that the viscount might soon be his step-father. The man may have been responsible for the shot that killed his brother.

"What news is that, my lady?" Clarinda called out, her brows furrowing in confusion.

Dorothea frowned as she gave her son one of those Meaningful Looks. She had obviously jumped to an incorrect conclusion. Although, Daniel realized later, if he thought about it just a bit more, he could have used the opportunity to inform Clarinda she would be marrying him. He was rather glad that he didn't inform her of the fact just then, though—she would have been incensed at being *informed* she was to marry him. No, it was far better that they have the opportunity to discuss the issue in private, perhaps when they were naked in bed, when she was replete with having been pleasured within an inch of her life and was unable to argue convincingly. Of course, that would require that he be of sound mind, and he rather doubted he could ever be accused of having a sound mind and certainly not a sound body when he had just made love to her. He wasn't sure he was recovered from their last encounter. Since Clarinda seemed to believe David had been the one to visit her in her bedchamber, Daniel thought he could just consider that last encounter a practice session.

Dorothea realized she needed to come up with some answer to Clarinda's query. "I meant, I have good news, of course," she hedged. "Lord Wallingham visited his favorite jeweler because I have accepted his offer of marriage," she announced with a slight curtsy.

Clarinda stood up just then and hurried to embrace her mother-in-law. "Best wishes!" she exclaimed as she hugged the older woman. "My goodness, when did this happen?" she asked then, thinking the viscount hadn't yet made an appearance at Norwick Park. That meant he had to have proposed the day of the funeral. *Ewww*. Or maybe he had paid her a call prior to their departure from London. *Or perhaps he had sneaked into Norwick House and spent the night in Dorothea's bedchamber.* The last possibility was the most likely, Clarinda realized. She was pondering these possibilities as she returned to her seat on the Greek lounge.

Dorothea's eyes widened just a bit, seeking Daniel's for help. He shrugged, not about to guess what she was about. But he was rather happy that Clarinda had returned to sit exactly as she had been doing so that his thigh would once again be pressed against hers just as soon as his mother either saw fit to be seated or, preferably, left the room entirely. "Why, early yesterday morning, before we left to come here, of course," she replied carefully, not wanting to admit it had been so early, it was essentially the middle of the night. Given the location of the Blue Room in Norwick House, it had been quite easy to sneak Lord Wallingham into the house and up to her bedchamber. "Although, he has been hinting he would do so for some time," she added with a flutter of her eyelashes and a wave of one hand—the hand that clearly displayed a sapphire of some considerable size.

"He probably needs her funds to pay gambling debts," Daniel murmured under his breath, hoping Clarinda would hear him and his mother would not. The quelling look his mother gave him was the only indication his words carried too far.

"Have you set a date?" Clarinda asked, hoping to cover Daniel's gaff. She wondered how Dorothea had managed to keep news of her engagement a secret during the entire trip to Norwick Park.

Dorothea finally moved into the room and took a seat in the chair nearest them. Daniel sat down, making sure his thigh ended up right against Clarinda's. Although her eyes closed for an instant, as if she was either very excited by his improper move or very offended by it, Clarinda made no move to move her thigh away from his.

"I think he'll just get a special license so we can wed wherever and whenever we wish," Dorothea replied, her hands settling onto her lap.

"Do you expect that will be somewhere near here?"

Daniel wondered. "I ask only because we really should be getting back to London," he added, waving his hand to indicate Clarinda and himself.

A jolt of excitement shot through Clarinda. The thought of Daniel sleeping in the chamber next to hers had her thinking of how often their thighs might be pressed against one another. He must know how her thigh looked—a painting featuring one of her bare thighs hung right above where he slept. She wondered what he thought of that painting, wondered if he found it pleasing to the eye.

"Already?" Dorothea questioned, surprised her son would be anxious to return to London so soon."We only just got here yesterday."

Daniel nodded. He'd spent the past two years, and several months of the two years before that, sequestered at Norwick Park working on the earldom's books and overseeing the estate. He could do that just as well if he was in London, and even enjoy doing it knowing Clarinda was under the same roof. They could always return to Norwick Park for the summers. "And, yet, we've already stayed too long," Daniel countered, one hand seeking Clarinda's. When he had it securely wrapped around hers, he lifted her hand to his lips and kissed the back of it.

Stunned at the intimacy of his kiss, Clarinda's eyes widened. "I suppose I can be ready to leave ... the day after tomorrow, let's say," she offered, wondering what Daniel had in mind.

"Well! I cannot be ready so soon," Dorothea countered, her hands going to her hips. Since she was sitting down, the action didn't hold as much menace as it would have if she'd been standing. "Besides, Wally is due here tomorrow. You were supposed to escort me home sometime next week." From the glare she directed in her son's direction, Clarinda knew Dorothea to be incensed.

"Perhaps Lord Wallingham would allow you to join him for the trip to Bognor in his carriage?" Clarinda suggested. "You could enjoy a bit of privacy before you two have to return to London. Once you're back there, you won't have the opportunity to spend much time together since there will no doubt be balls and soirées in honor of your betrothal," she added, making her words sound ever so innocent.

Daniel could have kissed her just then. Almost did, in fact, but remembered where they were and who else was in the room with them. "Clare's idea holds merit, Mother," Daniel affirmed. "And, if Lord Wallingham arrives on horseback, or in a gig that doesn't afford room for all those trunks of gowns you brought from London, you can always take one of the conveyances in the carriage house here. Mr. Hammond mentioned there are several." He was imagining the barouche, the one his brother had described as a piece of …

"Why, what a splendid idea!" his mother agreed, her face brightening. "Oh," she stood up suddenly, as if she'd just remembered something. "I just remembered something!" she announced. "I really must get back to my room. I have so much to do before Wally arrives," she said over her shoulder as she hurried out of the parlor.

Daniel barely had a chance to stand as his mother took her leave. He seated himself just as quickly, making sure his thigh returned to what he had decided was its rightful place against Clarinda's.

"What do you suppose she meant by that?" Clarinda wondered absently, suddenly overcome by exhaustion.

Taking her hand in his again, Daniel shook his head. "I can only imagine," he murmured, "Not that I really want to, mind you. In fact, I'd rather not think of what she does with the manacles and rope she brings along on these trips." Clarinda's eyes widened, then blinked. "I'm teasing," Daniel said, his deadpan manner making Clarinda wonder if he really was teasing. For some reason, it seemed perfectly reasonable that Dorothea would tie up her lovers or handcuff them to bed posts and have her wicked way with them. "And don't even imagine it," Daniel added, suddenly afraid he was too late with his directive.

"Too late," Clarinda countered, her head tipped back and her eyes closing to try and erase the image from her memory. She sat like that for a very long time, suddenly wondering if her husband had engaged in such activities prior to their marriage. It would have been legendary if David had engaged in that kind of hedonism, she thought. His string of mistresses would have been rather daring women who thought nothing of being tied up or handcuffed or tumbled every which way. *However had he reformed to marry me?* she wondered. He'd had to sell his brothel and gaming hell, give up all his mistresses, and swear off whores in favor of marriage to her. And he had done so, quite completely. For she knew he had been faithful to her; the two investigators she'd hired over the past four years had reported on his every move. And lack thereof.

"He loved you," Daniel stated suddenly, as if he'd overheard her every thought.

Clarinda's slight inhalation of breath suggested he had guessed correctly as to her line of thinking. *Like mother, like son,* he thought, secretly glad he hadn't been the older brother. Sometimes, there was something to be said for being second.

"He must have. I had investigators following his every move," she replied in a quiet voice.

Daniel's eyebrows nearly climbed into his hairline. "What?" he responded suddenly. "You didn't ... you didn't *trust* him?"

Sighing, Clarinda considered how to respond. "Would you? Had you been me?" she asked instead.

Daniel started to answer but then stilled himself. *Clarinda agreed to marry me. I was the one who courted her.* And yet, all that time, she thought she was being courted by his brother. She knew what a rake his brother had been, and yet she still agreed to marry *him*. "Why did you marry him, then?" he asked, struggling to rein in his temper, a temper definitely directed at her instead of his brother.

"We've been over this Daniel," she warned, her own

indignation suddenly apparent. Her anger dissipated quickly, though, as if the volcano that had threatened to erupt suddenly settled into dormancy. In its place, there was a sad visage and tears limning her eyes.

Daniel covered her hand with one of his. "Well, there's no need to cry about it," he managed to get out before he gathered her into his arms, holding her on his lap and burying his head into the space between her head and her shoulder. "David doesn't deserve your tears."

"I can't help it," Clarinda whispered, tears suddenly flowing down her cheeks. "I'm with child ... with children," she amended, causing the tears to flow faster. "I just buried my bastard of a husband. I'm a widow with a year of mourning to endure. And I'm *hungry*. So, I think I'm entitled to cry," she managed to get out between sobs.

Chuckling softly, Daniel grinned as he held Clarinda's body against his own. "Dinner will be served in just a few minutes," he murmured, noticing the mantle clock was about to strike seven. Once it did, their moment of privacy would be gone. Daniel suddenly dropped to the floor, one knee down and the other supporting an elbow as he reached for her hand. "Marry me, Clare," he whispered, his hold on her suddenly firmer. "Say you'll be my wife."

Clarinda pulled her hand from Daniel's grip, stunned at his words. "I cannot marry you," she countered, shaking her head as she struggled to back away.

Daniel let her go, his face displaying his surprise at her refusal. "And why not?" he countered, stunned that she would give him an answer so quickly. And not the answer he was expecting.

"You despise me. You probably hate me ..."

"I do not hate you, Clare," Daniel managed to get out. "In fact, I'm ..."

"... And I'm supposed to be in *mourning*," she went on, apparently not hearing his rebuttal. "For a year!"

"I'm sure we can work around that if you'll just hear me

out," he responded, rising to face her. He took her hands in his again. "Please, Clare," he whispered.

The dinner gong sounded. Clare shook her head as she pulled one hand from his and placed it over her belly. "I have to get something to eat," she stated. "Right now," she added. Then she turned and practically ran from the room.

Bereft and just a bit angry, Daniel cursed as he stood in the middle of the salon and pondered what to do next. *Damn you, David Fitzwilliam! Damn you to hell!* He half expected his brother to reply with "I'm already there," or "I'm on my way," but there was only silence surrounding him as Daniel made his way to the dining room.

Chapter 22

POST PROPOSAL PROGNOSTICATIONS

"I heard my brother asked for your hand in marriage," David murmured, his lips curving up. He didn't add that he'd also heard his curses. "When will you say your vows?"

Clarinda sat up in bed, her eyes wide, her thoughts still in the dream where she was ten months pregnant and Daniel was quite thoroughly pleasuring her. Or was that David? She shook her head. *Where am I?* This wasn't her bedchamber. This wasn't Norwick House.

The cobwebs of sleep slowly cleared from her mind as she tried to think. "Vows?" she repeated, still surprised that *David* was perched on the edge of her bed. "What vows?"

"Marriage vows," David repeated, one of his hands reaching out for hers. It settled over the top of the one that wasn't clutched to her abdomen.

Clarinda realized she'd been doing that a lot lately, as if she had to in order to remind herself that she was carrying twins. Not that she really needed much reminding; she'd gained a few more pounds in the past week and was ravenously hungry. *Norwick Park*, she remembered suddenly. She was at Norwick Park with Daniel and his mother. "If you're referring to Daniel's proposal of marriage, I can assure you I told him 'no'," she finally spoke, her shoulders slumping. She had been tempted, albeit for only seconds, to accept his offer, there was no doubt about it. The way Daniel had looked at her, the way he'd held her hand—it was exactly the same as when David had asked for her hand in Kensington Gardens amongst the pink roses. And for the babies to have a father—that alone would have been enough for most women to say 'yes' to such a proposal.

But how could she agree to marry a man who she was sure despised her? Wouldn't he always remember how she slapped him that day? Remember her stinging rebuke? Remember how she could behave like a volcano erupting whenever her anger was provoked? No, Daniel Jonathan Andrew Fitzwilliam was far safer keeping his distance from her.

"You *have* to marry him, Clare," David whispered, one hand reaching out to caress her cheek. "It's his turn, after all."

Gasping, Clarinda regarded her dead husband with a look of disbelief. "His *turn*? What? And I have no say in the matter?"

David shrugged and seemed suddenly a bit confused by her response. "No," he answered simply. "You were supposed to marry him in the first place."

Silence filled the space between them for several heartbeats. Clarinda's mouth opened in shock. She shut it about the time David's hand reached over to push up her lower jaw. "What are you saying, David?" she asked, a surge of anger building inside. Molten lava, or at least the remains of her late night snack, threatened to erupt if she didn't control the sudden urge to throttle her dead husband to death. *What, indeed, was he saying*? Had Daniel been telling the truth when he claimed to have been the one to ask for her hand that day in Kensington Gardens?

David noted the sudden wash of red that colored Clarinda's face and thought of a volcano's eruption. He took a step back, not even thinking that she could do him no harm. He was dead already, after all. "I admit, I ... I sort of ... usurped

Daniel's place in your heart. In your life. Actually, in all of life, truth be told," he stammered, not sounding the least bit like the earl he had been when he was alive. Death had taken his confidence, it seemed, along with his sense of entitlement and his apparent dislike of his younger brother.

He had to admit to himself, 'dislike' wasn't quite the right word to describe his feelings toward Daniel. It was jealousy. Simple, green jealousy. For Daniel was always right there on his heels, from the time they were born. And then, when it really counted, Daniel had somehow stepped ahead of David and managed to secure the love of a woman David realized he wanted for himself. How could he live with himself if he allowed his wife to believe his lie any longer? Especially now that he was dead?

The irony of that last thought went unnoticed by the late David Fitzwilliam as he pondered his fate and those of his wife and his brother. He had been a rotten brother, a scoundrel and a rake, and yet his brother had forsaken a care-free life as one of London's young bucks and willingly taken over the responsibility of the earldom's business affairs, had overseen the management of Norwick Park and seen to its tenants in David's stead. All David had done was attend sessions of Parliament, listening intently when something was of interest to him and spending the rest of the time daydreaming of what he might be doing if he was at White's or in Hyde Park or at home with Clarinda.

Sighing, Clarinda regarded David for a very long time. He was lost in thought, an activity she knew him to engage in at some of the most inopportune times. "Explain yourself," she demanded, suddenly wary.

Crossing his arms, David cocked his head first to one side and then to the other. "It's tough being a twin, you know." When the statement didn't elicit the sympathy he was looking for from Clarinda, he sighed. "Danny and I fought constantly. From the time we were in the womb ..."

"The *womb*?!" Clarinda countered, her eyebrows indicating her growing impatience with the only man she thought she had loved for the past four years. The man with whom she was currently quite miffed. The man who was now making no sense. But then, for a moment she had to remind herself that he had been dead for several days and was now finally buried. It was a miracle he was even here talking at all.

"Aye," he answered with a nod. "Ask Mother. She'll tell you. It's a wonder my brother and I are so poor at pugilism," he added as his attention seemed to stray for a moment. "Horses and guns, no problem, but swords and fists ... I'd die in a duel if I had to fight with a rapier. Or my fists."

"David," Clarinda sighed in exasperation. "You're dead already," she whispered, no longer caring if she offended him. What was he going to do? Haunt her? He was doing that quite effectively at the moment.

"It's true!" David insisted, ignoring her comment about him being dead. "Ask the dowager countess," he said in a voice that suggested he was daring to bring up the matter with Dorothea. "I'd kick Daniel, and then he would hit me with an uppercut to the jaw, so I'd counter with my left hook, and then he'd kick me," he pantomimed as one leg seemed to intersect the edge of the bed. The contact made no sound, nor did the bed seem to move. "It's a wonder we were both born with *balls*. It's a bigger wonder we didn't kill each other. There's not a lot of room in there," he added as he pointed toward her slightly rounded belly.

Clarinda simply shook her head from side to side, not quite believing the scenario her dead husband was describing. "How do you even *remember* that far back?" was all she could think to ask in response.

David straightened. "Trust me, sweeting. When you're dead, you can remember *everything*," he claimed with a raised eyebrow. "Makes me a bit ashamed, in fact," he added, a hand going through his hair so it was left in unruly spikes atop his head.

"What are you saying?" Clarinda wondered suddenly, becoming alarmed at her husband's strange words.

"Daniel was supposed to have been born first," he

replied, his matter-of-fact tone making the statement sound not quite as ridiculous as Clarinda was imagining. There was a sort of *whoosh* sound just as he finished the admission, as if he'd been harboring the truth for all his almost forty years and was relieved to finally be able to speak the truth.

"Really?" Clarinda managed to reply, keeping her expression in check. "And ... how do you know that?"

David uncrossed his arms and let out a 'huff '. "When mother's water broke, Daniel was asleep, so I took his place," he said with the sort of nonchalant attitude he'd adopted for most of the conversation.

Clarinda blinked. And blinked again. "The way you just said that ... are you *sorry* for having been born first?" she wondered, not quite sure what she should say.

Good grief, when had David lost his mind?

Probably when he died, a part of her brain argued. The other part was telling her she had lost *her* mind.

David shook his head. "No, Clare, I'm not," he said suddenly, his face brightening. "I probably even managed to get in the last kick as I was on my way out." He said this last with a hint of pride.

Her mouth open once more, Clarinda regarded David with a scowl. "So, why are you telling me this now?" she countered. Was he telling her so his conscious would be clear? Burdening her with the truth of his existence, of his having stolen his brother's birthright so he could, what? *Rest in peace*?

David sighed, his shoulders suddenly slumping. "Don't you see, Clare? You were always supposed to end up with Daniel. He was supposed to be born first. He was supposed to be the earl. He was the one who courted you and asked for your hand in marriage. I just ... took his place in every step of our lives," he admitted with a shrug. "Now that I'm dead, I want to set things to right."

Shaking her head in disbelief, Clarinda wondered when she might wake up. Because David's claims were starting to make sense, and she was suddenly questioning everything she'd been led to believe by the man who stood before her. *And when did he stand up?* she found herself wondering. She was sure he was sitting on her bed just a moment ago.

"I love you, Clare. Truly. The hardest thing I ever had to do was ... *die*, since I knew I would have to give you up. And I can't even do that very well," he added with a mischievous grin as he motioned with his hands to indicate the body that stood before her. "But now that I am—*dead*, that is—it's Daniel's time to take his rightful place as earl."

Clarinda's eyes narrowed. "What about the twins I carry? What if one is a boy?" Clarinda quickly countered. Daniel wouldn't be the earl if she gave birth to a male heir.

Taken aback at the reminder of the impending birth of her twins, David took an uneven breath. "Well, since they're both girls, they won't inherit, of course," he answered in that matter-of-fact tone he was so good at using. "I absolutely adore that my daughters will look just like their mother, by the way," he managed to get in before leaning over to lift Clarinda's suddenly slack jaw back into place with his forefinger. "But your next set of twins will be Daniel's, and they'll both be boys." He paused for a moment as he watched Clarinda's face take on a second look of shock. "Don't faint on me, sweeting. They won't come for almost two years," he commented with a wave of his hand.

"Twins. *Again*?" Clarinda whispered, her hand moving again to rest on her belly.

"And just wait until *they* start fighting with one another. Then you'll know I was telling the truth about Danny and me," David seemed to brag. He sat still for a moment, deep in thought.

When had he taken a seat back on the bed? Clarinda wondered suddenly.

"As I was saying," he spoke with a finger in the air. "It's Daniel's time to take his rightful place as earl, and time for you to be his countess. Think about it. You won't even have to change your name!" He said this last as if he had just then realized the coincidence of he and his brother sharing the same last name and the same title.

Clarinda regarded him for a very long time, shaking her head, as much in disbelief as in astonishment. When she didn't make any attempt to reply, David moved so he was sitting next to her and took one of her hands in his. "He loves you, Clare. He always has. Longer than I have, in fact."

Clarinda's head seemed to loll to one side. "So, you weren't the one who asked for my hand in marriage in Kensington Park?" she managed to get out, her eyes suddenly limned with tears. *Oh my, the awful things I said to Daniel! The awful way I treated him!*

David sighed. "No." He was quiet for a moment. "I wanted to, though."

"And you weren't the one who courted me?"

David closed his eyes and shook his head. "No. Daniel did all of that."

"And you weren't the one who came into my bedchamber every night and made love to me?"

David's eyes widened with alarm. "That most certainly *was* me!" he countered, his face displaying a look of stunned surprise.

Clarinda bit her lip to suppress the smile that threatened.

"Well, except for that one time," David added with a shake of his head.

It was Clarinda's turn to look stunned. "*What*? When?" Her eyes were wide with disbelief. A frisson shot through her entire body, as if *it* remembered perfectly well when such an event had occurred. She shifted slightly on the bed, as if she was trying to shake off the troublesome memory.

But David was smiling, shaking his head and *smiling* while he regarded her. "He's even a better lover than me," David murmured. "Isn't he?"

Ignoring his question and struggling to keep her embarrassment from showing on her cheeks, Clarinda held her breath for a very long time before letting it out. "Oh." How else was she supposed to respond to her dead husband's comment? "David, you're barely dead and buried. I hardly think I can even consider marrying anyone until ..."

David waved a hand dismissively in the air. "No one will notice if you mourn me for an entire year or not. They won't even remember I died when they see you on his arm. They'll just think he is me. All will be fine. You'll see."

Making a sound that could best be described as an unladylike snort, Clarinda leaned forward and buried her face in the counterpane that covered her knees. How could David be so cavalier? How could he expect she would ignore the dictates of polite society and simply remarry before at least six months of mourning had passed? And how could he have been so cruel to Daniel?

Daniel!

She should go to him. Apologize. Beg forgiveness. Yes, that's what she'd do.

Later, though.

She was hungry again.

Chapter 23

A MARRIAGE IS ARRANGED IN HASTE

Jeffrey Althorpe regarded his image in the looking glass in his bedchamber. *Happy birthday,* he thought, his mood somber and perhaps even morose. The past years hadn't been kind to his visage. There were tiny lines on either side of his eyes and mouth, his nose appeared to have extended at least an eighth of an inch, and there were what could only be described as worry lines across his forehead.

When did this happen? he wondered. The late nights at White's had probably taken their toll to some degree, and he found the days spent in Parliament didn't help when issues important to him weighed heavily long after their fate had been decided.

Indeed, the only light in his life had been Lady Evangeline. Had it just been eight days since the two had argued over who would take possession of *The Story of a Baron?*

Eight days.

And now that they had finished reading it, he no longer had an excuse to see her every day.

God, how he missed her!

For a reason he had yet to discover, Harry Tennison had been rather effective at avoiding him. Until he secured permission from the earl, he dared not court Evangeline, nor could he formerly propose to the lady.

To the love of his life.

He let out a heavy sigh, turning when the bedchamber door opened to admit his valet. "Ah, Timmons," he murmured. He watched as the young man hurried about, retrieving breeches, a waistcoat and a topcoat from the clothes press to present to him for his approval. "Fine," he nodded at the valet's choices. "I'm thinking I'll ride later, perhaps during the fashionable hour," he added. He was feeling restless.

A knock at the door preceded his butler's unexpected appearance. "A note just arrived for you, my lord," the older man intoned, his voice several octaves deeper than one would expect from such a small man.

Jeffrey nodded as he took the note from the silver salver, turning it over to see the Earl of Torrington's seal in the dark red wax. "Thank you," he murmured, breaking the seal and unfolding the white parchment. The handwriting was obviously masculine, and knowing the earl as he did, he figured the man had penned it himself rather than have his secretary write it.

I am paying you a call at precisely eleven o'clock this morning. Be dressed and ready. Torrington.

"Faith," Jeffrey whispered. Grandby never called on him! In fact, Jeffrey was rather surprised the earl even knew who he was, although he had been invited to the man's house that one time for dinner. "What time is it?" he asked, not addressing his question to either the butler or his valet.

Timmons glanced at the mantle clock above the fireplace. "Ten-forty, my lord," he answered.

"No bath today. But I need a shave," Sommers ordered, moving to take a seat before the mirror in his bathing chamber. "And make it quick. I must be in my study at ten-fifty-five," he added, his stomach churning. *The one morning I don't get up early and this happens.* Indeed, had he arranged to read another book with Evangeline, he would already be on his way to meet her, which made him wonder what Lord Torrington would have done when he found him already gone from Sommers Place.

True to his short missive, Milton Grandby, Earl of Torrington, appeared on the doorstep of Sommers Place at exactly eleven o'clock. He was led directly to Jeffrey's study, where he found the baron at his desk, looking as if he'd been there for several hours reviewing the books for his estate.

Milton knew better, though.

"Sommers," he said by way of a greeting, acknowledging the baron's short bow with one of his own. "I see thirty minutes was enough to get you ready this morning."

The baron regarded the earl with a frown. "It usually is," he replied. There was no reason to admit he had been abed until ten-thirty, although it was a bit later than he usually slept. *Another effect of aging*, he thought. "Would you like coffee? Or tea, perhaps?" he asked, remembering his mother's lessons in hospitality.

"Coffee, please," Milton answered with a slow grin, settling into the chair across from the desk.

Jeffrey made a motion with his hand, apparently to a servant who had followed the earl into the study. "And to what do I owe the honor of a visit from you? Did you come to wish me happy?"

The earl cocked a dark eyebrow. "Did you already ask for her hand?" Milton asked, his grin turning to a frown.

The question had Jeffrey blinking. *Ask for her hand?*

Faith!

Torrington wasn't here about his birthday. "No," he replied carefully. "It's my birthday," he said after a pause.

Milton took a quick look at the ceiling before returning his attention to the baron. "And how many years have you been on this damned planet?" he asked, the question tinged with anger. From the looks of the man who sat before him, he would guess Jeffrey Althorpe was in his early to-mid thirties. If he ever left White's at an earlier hour of the morning, he might actually look younger than he was.

"Thirty," Jeffrey replied hesitantly.

Grandby gave a noncommittal grunt. "It's time you were married," he stated firmly.

"I agree," Sommers replied with a firm nod.

"Time you gave up your bachelor ways, and your late nights, and your whoring, and…" He paused a moment, one bushy eyebrow cocked up. "Wait. What did you say?"

Jeffrey sighed. He supposed he should have taken offense at the earl for making his state of matrimony his business, but he found he couldn't. He'd had the vague idea of marriage on his mind since late December. Since the weekend after Christmas, when the massive snowstorm had buried most of England in the cold, white stuff. While most men of the *ton* were ensconced in their bedchambers with their wives, seeing to the creation of the next generation of the peerage, Jeffrey had been holed up at his country estate with several friends—all bachelors—and a deck of cards.

It was the worst holiday of his life.

"I agree," he repeated. "And, as for the whoring, I haven't indulged in quite some time. I've an aversion to venereal disease," he added. *And a lack of funds to pay for a mistress.* But he didn't put voice to his thoughts, thinking his financial state was really none of the earl's business.

Milton regarded the baron for a long moment. "Do you have someone in mind for your baroness?" he asked then, the one already arched eyebrow lifting nearly into his hairline.

Jeffrey took a deep breath and finally nodded. "I do."

When he didn't offer a name, Grandby's other eyebrow joined the first in elevation. "Does the future Lady Sommers have a *name?*" he finally asked, his eyebrows finally settling into their normal location.

Jeffrey was tempted to put voice to his annoyance, but he decided the earl could be of some help. "Lady Evangeline," Jeffrey offered, his voice barely audible. "I believe she'll have me," he added, dipping his head before meeting Milton's gaze. She had said she would. Promised him she would. But they both knew it wouldn't matter if her brother didn't agree to the betrothal.

"*Have* you?" Milton repeated. "Of course, she'll *have* you. I'll tell her to *have* you. She's three-and-twenty and not getting any younger," he claimed, one hand waving as if to reinforce his point.

The door opened and a maid appeared with the coffee service. She set the tray on the corner of the desk before pouring two cups for the gentlemen.

Glad for the interruption, Jeffrey swallowed and considered Grandby's words. He was curious as to why the earl had taken such an interest in Lord Everly's sister. Lord knew, Lord Everly certainly didn't. The two times Jeffrey had tried to bring up the topic of courting Lady Evangeline had left him frustrated and impatient with the explorer. The man might be a genius when it came to some scientific topics, but he was a dunce when it came to the matter of marriage for his sister.

The maid curtsied and left the study. Milton continued to regard Jeffrey with an expression that required some kind of response.

"I kissed her," Jeffrey stated, straightening in his chair as he made the claim. He thought it better not to mention how many times. Or that she had initiated a few herself.

"Proud of yourself for that?" Milton asked rhetorically, and then wondered why the baron would admit to having kissed Evangeline Tennison if not to reinforce some kind of claim on the young lady.

Jeffrey shrugged. "Not proud, exactly," he replied. After a pause, he added, "It was necessary. I... I was about to take my leave of her, and I knew it might be some time before I could see her again, and... I did not wish to part as mere... friends."

Milton regarded Lord Sommers for a few moments. "Did she... *welcome* your advance?" he asked, thinking Lady Evangeline might have put up a fight if she didn't. *And if she didn't, the fish in that damned glass aquarium would.*

"Of course she did. Do you think me capable of forcing

my advances on an unwilling lady?" Jeffrey answered, obviously annoyed.

Angling his head to one side, Milton gave a huff. "What are your plans for her?"

Jeffrey was about to respond with something along the lines of, "It's none of your concern," but thought better of it. The Earl of Torrington was a powerful man and well-liked among his colleagues. "I shall send a note and ask if she'll join me on a drive in the park this afternoon," Jeffrey suggested, hoping that would be enough to get Torrington out of his study and on his way.

"Agreed," Milton stated before taking a drink of his coffee. "Given her age, I think you can forgo a chaperone, but if she insists, recommend she bring her lady's maid," he suggested quickly. "They're more willing to go if they don't have to walk. By the end of the drive in the park, ask if you can court her, and then, when you get back to Everly's house, ask for her hand."

Jeffrey blinked once. He blinked again. "All in... all in one *day*?"

Milton's eyes widened. "Yes, in one day! Today!" he responded, his patience at an end. "Get a special license and marry her next week. You're thirty, for God's sake. It's time you were leg-shackled," the earl nearly shouted. "With luck, she'll be with child by the end of the month, and you'll have an heir at Christmas."

Jeffrey Althorpe regarded the earl for several moments. "You're quite serious," he finally responded. "Will you... will *you* be explaining all this to Lord Everly? Despite my requests for an audience with Lord Everly, the man hasn't made time to meet with me."

Milton regarded the baron for a moment, somewhat surprised to learn that Sommers really had been considering Lady Evangeline for his baroness. "Leave it to me," the earl replied with a nod. "Never let it be said I don't see to my goddaughters' welfare—"

"Goddaughter?" Jeffrey repeated in shock. *No wonder he's so concerned!*

"Since she was born," Milton said with some pride. He rose from his chair. "By the way, Lady Torrington is expecting, you might have heard."

The baron gave a start. "Congratulations," he said with as much reverence as he could muster. "You must be—"

"Scared to death. Thrilled. Happy. Humbled. Excited," Milton interrupted with several nods. "I am. Stedman is thrilled, too. I've made him a very rich man," he added, his head still bobbing up and down. "Bought three necklaces for my wife last night."

Sommers didn't know just then who the Stedman was that Milton Grandby referred to in his discussion that morning, but by that evening, he knew. Knew the man personally, in fact. For after Grandby had taken his leave of Sommers, the younger man had dispatched one of his footmen to Lord Everly's house with a note to Lady Evangeline asking for the pleasure of her company for a drive in the park that afternoon. And his footman had returned with a note written in a beautiful, feminine hand with the simple words, "I await your arrival, Eva."

Eva.

Jeffrey Althorpe closed his eyes for a moment after reading the simple missive. *To hell with waiting until the fashionable hour.* Eva was waiting for him.

Lady Evangeline sat by herself drinking a cup of tea in the parlor of her brother's house. Harry Tennison, Earl of Everly, had left some time ago, shortly after asking that his carriage be brought around. Curious, Evangeline thought to ask if she might join him on his errand, intending to use the time to tell him she had accepted Lord Sommers' offer of a ride in the park. But Harry's attention was entirely on a book he had open and was apparently reading as he made his way to the vestibule. Sighing audibly in the hopes he might hear her, Evangeline resigned herself to another early afternoon spent alone at Rosemount House.

She was about to pour herself another cup of tea when Jones, the butler, cleared his throat. "Do I have a caller?" Evangeline asked before Jones could announce anything. She was nearly to her feet, hoping some lady of the *ton* had remembered she was sequestered in her brother's house for the Season and had taken pity on her by paying a call.

Jones held his hands together behind his back, his discomfort apparent. "Lord Sommers has asked if he might have a word," he intoned, obviously bothered by the impropriety of a gentleman calling on an unmarried woman without there being a companion or chaperone present.

Evangeline was sure her suddenly thundering heartbeats could be heard from across the room. *He was here. Already.* She dared a glance at the mantel clock, surprised to see it was only two o'clock. "Well, do see him in, Jones," she responded, just then realizing the baron was probably there to see her brother and not her. "He is here to see Lord Everly, I suppose," she added as she nervously smoothed her skirts. Of all the eligible gentlemen in the *ton*, Jeffrey Althorpe was not a man she would expect to have calling on her, but one could always hope. His earlier missive had been such a surprise, she had immediately written a reply. "He only asked if your ladyship was in residence and apologizes for arriving earlier than his note indicated."

The thundering heartbeats nearly deafened her to Jones' last words—until she heard the part about an apology. Perhaps the earl had changed his mind and was withdrawing his offer of a ride in the park. "Do send him in, then. I shouldn't like to keep a baron waiting."

The butler took a breath and looked as if he was about to argue, but he must have seen the flush that colored Evangeline's face. "Right away, my lady," he replied, turning on his heels and leaving the parlor.

Evangeline took a deep breath in an attempt to compose herself. Lord Sommers was calling on her. Yes, he was one of her brother's friends, and yes, he probably spent far too much time playing cards at White's, and, yes, there was the hint from something her brother had said that Sommers had employed a mistress, but at that moment, none of those things mattered. Besides, if the man had a wife, he would no doubt spend more time at Sommers Place, his Mayfair mansion on Cavendish Square, and less time pretending to be a rake.

He wasn't really a rake, Evangeline considered just then. He couldn't be if he was a friend of her brother's. Everly would never consort with a rake, although he might if said rake was an explorer or adventurer or a member of the Royal Academy of Sciences. She had barely finished this last thought when she realized Lord Sommers was regarding her from the doorway. She struggled to withhold a gasp, for he was quite imposing, dressed for a ride in a smart, perfectly tailored scarlet jacket and buckskin breeches that hugged his muscular thighs. His black Hessians were polished to a high shine, and he held a riding crop in one black kid-gloved hand. She supposed she should have wondered why he hadn't given it to the butler when he gave up his hat, but it seemed to give him an air of superiority. A shiver shot through her when she imagined him wielding it. What awful deed might she commit that would have him threatening her with it? Her cheeks blushed a bright pink when she realized what she was imagining.

Blinking in an effort to pull her thoughts from those better left in a bedchamber, Evangeline forced herself to concentrate on Lord Sommers' other attributes.

Bowing deeply before saying a word of greeting, Lord Sommers' eyes seemed to caress her. "Lady Evangeline, please do pardon my interruption," he said, his voice almost a plea.

Evangeline, her lips slightly parted from her surprise at his appearance, afforded him a deep curtsy. Even before she had returned to a standing position, Sommers had moved into the room and reached for her hand, lifting it to his lips so that he could bestow a kiss on her knuckles. His lips didn't just brush over her skin as she expected they might, but rather took purchase and kissed her as she imagined he might kiss her lips. A tremor shook her body, the shock of his touch so unexpected and so pleasurable, she had to suppress another gasp. "Of course, Lord Sommers. You are most welcome at Rosemount whenever you should wish to call," she managed to get out, keeping a small smile in place. She felt almost giddy that Sommers would kiss the back of her hand as he'd done. Indeed, he hadn't yet let go of her hand. And, at the moment, she didn't really care if she ever got it back. As far as she was concerned, he could keep it.

Sommers seemed relieved to hear her response, his expression otherwise one of indecision. "My lady, I ..." He glanced back at the open door, wondering if the butler hovered somewhere beyond. "I know this may seem ... untoward," he struggled to get out, "But I was wondering if we might go for a ride in the park a bit earlier than I indicated in my note. I realize it's not the fashionable hour, but by that time this afternoon, I'm rather hoping I will have completed courting you and have an affirmative response to my request for your hand in marriage. So that I might find myself on the morrow at Doctor's Commons in pursuit of a special license so that we might marry in a few days." The words had come tumbling out, with no hint of embarrassment or self-doubt or regard for propriety.

Lady Evangeline stared at Lord Sommers for a moment, blinking before a brilliant smile appeared. "You're not being the least bit untoward, Lord Sommers," she replied with a slight shake of her head. *Marriage?* Lord Sommers intended to ask for her hand!

"Jeffrey," he stated, his hand moving to hold hers more tightly. "You should call me Jeffrey," he added, taking a step closer to her.

"And you should call me Evangeline. Or Eva, if you prefer," she countered, realizing her heart had settled into a rhythm that, although still entirely too fast, was at least quiet enough that she could hear her own words.

"Eva," Sommers breathed, his lips suddenly hovering over hers.

Evangeline closed her eyes as his lips settled over hers, as the hand that held the riding crop moved to the back of her shoulder to pull her body forward just a bit. She took a step forward so that her entire body collided with the front of his. Her free hand reached up to rest on his shoulder and then moved to the back of his neck as his lips opened against hers. She allowed her lips to follow suit, aware that the tip of his tongue was brushing over her teeth.

At some point, a moan or a mewl escaped her, which only encouraged Sommers to deepen the kiss. The hand that held hers released it and came to rest on the back of her waist, pulling her body harder against his. The bulge behind the fall of his breeches pressed into her soft belly through the fabric of her gown. He rather wished there was less fabric separating them. Far less. None, in fact, but there would be more appropriate places for that.

Evangeline thrilled at the realization that she had caused his arousal, not for a moment frightened by what could happen next. Lord Sommers was going to ask for her hand!

"Eva," he whispered, his lips pulling away from hers so they could leave soft kisses along her jawline.

"Jeffrey," she whispered back, her hand sliding through the waves of his silken brown hair. She was sure she felt a shiver pass through him as his lips moved to her earlobe. In a moment, his teeth were teasing the soft flesh, sending shivers through Evangeline unlike anything she had felt before. The hand behind her waist moved up and around so it rested on the side of one breast, the thumb caressing her suddenly hardening nipple. Evangeline couldn't stifle the small shriek that erupted from her throat.

Jeffrey's lips moved to cover hers, kissing her as he repeated the stroke over her nipple. "Marry me, Eva," he whispered, his lips moving to cover hers before she could reply.

Evangeline nodded against his lips. When he finally

pulled away to take a breath, she said simply, "Yes." She was aware of the hand next to her breast moving to somewhere inside his coat, so that he had to pull his body away from hers for a moment. Then her left hand was held in his and a ring was sliding onto her finger.

"It's not the real one, of course," he murmured, his forehead coming to rest on hers. "But I'll have one far better by tomorrow," he promised, his whisper urgent.

Evangeline dared a glance at her left hand, stunned when she realized his opal signet ring was wrapped around her middle finger.

"You have made me a very happy man, Eva," he whispered, his lips saying the words against hers.

"And you have made me a very happy woman, Jeffrey," she replied with a sigh. "Perhaps ... perhaps we could just skip the ride and continue this instead?" she wondered, her words coming out in little breaths. Had she taken a moment to consider what she had just said, she might have gasped and begged forgiveness for her impropriety. But the look on Jeffrey's face suggested he would be most disappointed if she did such a thing.

"As my lady wishes," he replied with an enthusiastic nod. "Although, I do believe I need to sit down. You have left me quite unable to stand of my own volition."

Eva giggled, leading him to a large wing chair. Even as he sat down, he pulled her atop him, settling her so her bottom rested on one of his thighs and her head settled against his shoulder. "My brother said nothing," she whispered, suddenly irate that Everly wouldn't share the good news of her impending betrothal to Lord Sommers.

Jeffrey let out a snort. "That's because I haven't yet asked his permission to court you," he replied, his arms wrapping around her body so his hands were clasped together as they rested on her hip.

"Oh," Evangeline replied, wondering if she should be disappointed that he hadn't followed protocol. "I do not think he'll object," she murmured, reaching out with her lips to kiss his jaw.

"He had better not, or the Earl of Torrington will have his hide," Jeffrey stated, his own lips moving to cover hers for a quick kiss.

Evangeline straightened on his lap, eliciting a slight gasp from Jeffrey as her hip pressed harder against his hardened manhood. "What does my godfather have to do with this?" she wondered, her brows furrowing together.

Jeffrey had to suppress a chuckle. "Your brother may be blind to love, my lady, but Grandby is not. He's a rather convincing matchmaker when he puts his mind to it."

Evangeline regarded Jeffrey for a moment. "You didn't ask for my hand because he *ordered* you to do so, did you?" she asked, suddenly doubtful of the baron's intentions.

Jeffrey tilted his head to one side. "No," he replied carefully. "Although I admit I am asking a bit sooner than I expected to be able to, only because he said he would see to your brother on my behalf."

His future baroness seemed satisfied with his answer, for she settled her head back onto his shoulder. "Would it be all right if we had a small, quiet wedding?" she whispered, her lashes resting on the tops of her cheekbones as if she might take a nap in a moment or two.

A chuckled erupted from Jeffrey just then. "I would prefer it, but I want you to have the wedding of your dreams," he murmured sleepily.

"Mmm," she purred, her eyes still closed.

In a moment, her even breathing indicated to Jeffrey that she had fallen asleep in his arms. He gave a sigh of his own as he closed his eyes and concentrated on the scent of honeysuckle that wafted around her blonde bun and ringlets. Not only had Lady Evangeline given him the kind of response he could only fantasize about, she had been everything Sommers had hoped in the woman he would one day marry. Even if that day was just a few days hence. Had he followed Grandby's instructions to the letter, he would be taking the lady for a ride in the park later that afternoon, perhaps choosing to detour on foot through the lesser-used walking paths among the trees. He would ask to court her before they left the park, and then he would ask for her hand when he was depositing her on the steps of Lord Everly's home with the promise of a ring the following day.

Instead, he had managed to accomplish an entire afternoon of courting in just a few moments. And an even greater miracle was that, despite the fact that the butler hovered just outside the parlor door, the man never once interrupted Lady Evangeline's nap to take issue with him over the impropriety of how he held her or how she was positioned rather suggestively against most of his body. He was just deciding he was going to enjoy being leg-shackled when the sound of a carriage turning into the drive caused Evangeline to give a start and suddenly open her eyes.

"Good afternoon, my beautiful," he whispered with a teasing grin.

There was a moment when Evangeline thought she had simply moved from one dream to the next, for to wake up in the arms of a man as handsome as Lord Sommers wasn't something she ever hoped to do. But the light press of his lips against her forehead brought her back to reality and she smiled. "Are you quite sure you can abide a wife who would fall asleep in the arms of her intended?" she whispered, her furrowing brows suggesting she was quite serious.

"Absolutely," Jeffrey replied with a nod. He kissed her then, most thoroughly, just as the sound of the front door closing reached his ears.

Evangeline was quite sure she had never moved so fast in her life, especially when it wasn't of her own doing. For one moment she was nestled against the front of her betrothed and the next she was sitting quite primly on the settee and Jeffrey was back in the wing chair with a cup of tea covering the bulge in his crotch, regarding her as if none of the previous thirty minutes had happened.

Her brother's entrance into the parlor might have been a

bit on the violent side, he no doubt having been briefed by Jones regarding the presence of Lord Sommers. But when he found his sister regarding him with an arched eyebrow and Sommers quite properly seated across from her, he relaxed. "Is it ...is it done then?" he asked, his attention going back and forth between the two.

Jeffrey Althorpe stood and gave Evangeline's brother a nod, wondering if Grandby had just spoken to the man. "I have asked for your sister's hand, and she has accepted," he replied with another nod. "And, as Lady Evangeline would prefer a small ceremony, I will see to a special license so that we might marry as early as ... next week?" He turned to confirm the arrangement with his fiancée.

"That would be lovely," she replied, giving her husband-to-be a brilliant smile.

Lord Everly shrugged and gave the two each a nod. "What a relief. I can get on with my next trip. I was beginning to think I'd be stuck in England for the rest of my life." Before either his sister or his future brother-in-law could respond, the explorer took his leave of the parlor.

"That went well," Evangeline commented lightly.

"Indeed," Jeffrey replied, the barest hint of disbelief in his voice.

Later that night at White's, when he sat at a card table with Lord Barrings, Sir Richard, and his future brother-in-law, Sommers couldn't help but notice the Earl of Torrington sitting in a wingback chair nearby. In a voice he intended Grandby to overhear, he mentioned having had a rather memorable thirtieth birthday. "I have asked for the hand of a woman I have wanted to marry for some time, and she has agreed to be my wife," he said proudly.

Two of the other gentlemen regarded him with looks of surprise. "You? *Married*?" Lord Barrings replied, his astonishment apparent in the way his eyebrows lifted.

"You sound as if you *want* to be leg-shackled," Sir Richard stated, his own bushy eyebrows raised in surprise.

"Indeed? It's too bad. I'd rather hoped you would

consider my sister, Lady Evangeline," Lord Everly stated sadly, his one eye winking in the baron's direction. He picked up his cards and studied them, unaware of Sommers' glare and the eyes he sent skyward.

"Who's the unlucky chit?" Lord Barrings asked as he raised a cheroot to his lips.

"Pray tell," Sir Richard encouraged.

Sommers sighed and shook his head. "Her identity, gentlemen, is known only to myself and Grandby, who will be informing the brother involved," he waved a hand toward the older earl, who acknowledged his comment with a nod, "Hopefully, tonight," he added, wondering at Lord Everly's claim to ignorance. "Oh, and the lady herself."

With that, he threw in his cards and left to pay a visit to Stedman and Vardon.

The Earl of Torrington smiled.

Chapter 24

DINNER AND A SHOW

Allowing Daniel to pull out her chair, Clarinda took her place at the end of the long table in Norwick Park's dining room, suddenly conscious of the fact that Daniel would be the only other diner that evening. In a surprising move that morning, Wallingham had no sooner arrived at Norwick Park before he whisked Dorothea off to Bognor, claiming he had business in Brighton and may as well escort her ladyship to her home on his way—never mind the twenty-five mile distance between the two locales.

Neither Clarinda nor Daniel expected the two would actually *make* it to Bognor.

Clarinda thought that her mother-in-law and Lord Wallingham made a rather happy couple, although she could agree with the new earl that his potential father-in-law was 'oily'. At least the viscount wasn't a habitual gambler. In fact, his only vice seemed to be his propensity to bed older women —at least six last Season, if the wags were to be believed. Since most of those wags were men who frequented White's, and since Wallingham was a member there, Clarinda thought there probably had been at least that many women who succumbed to his expert use of his ... family jewels.

"She probably won't marry him," Daniel said suddenly, as

if he could read Clarinda's thoughts. There was a tinge of hope in the comment, as if he was trying to convince himself as well as Clarinda.

Watching Daniel take his place at the other end of the table, a considerably shorter table now that several leaves had been removed, Clarinda considered his comment. "Are you ... relieved then?" she wondered, placing a napkin across her lap and doing a quick survey of the table and its settings. Although David might not have been a stickler for details when it came to a dining table at dinner, Clarinda didn't yet know Daniel's thoughts on the topic.

"Not yet," he replied, allowing a wan smile before he shrugged with one shoulder. "She was still wearing that blue rock when she left here this afternoon. Although, I must admit I am very relieved to know Wallingham didn't shoot David." He straightened as a footman came into the room and placed a bowl of soup in front of Clarinda.

Having just picked up her wine glass, Clarinda nearly dropped it. "Shoot him?" she repeated, her mouth opened in shock. "Oh. You refer to that misunderstanding that nearly led to a duel, then?" she clarified, bringing the glass to her lips and drinking a bit more than she intended.

Daniel's gaze drifted from the bowl of soup that the footman had just placed before him back up to Clarinda.

"Misunderstanding?" he repeated, wondering at her curious wording.

Clarinda nodded. "A couple of weeks ago, David was rather incensed at Lord Wallingham. Claimed the viscount had said something rather gauche about me. So David slapped him in the face with his gloves and challenged him to pistols at dawn." She paused to take a spoonful of soup. "And then he forgot all about it. But, since no seconds were chosen to make the arrangements as to place and time, the duel came to nothing. The two probably would have laughed about it except David ... David died two days later." She wondered why the thought didn't make her cry as it had just a week ago. She began eating her soup in earnest, feeling more hungry than she had in days.

Daniel regarded Clarinda for a very long time, his expression quizzical. "David told me that duel was about something gauche Wallingham said about our *mother*," he commented carefully. "And then Wallingham told me it was about David having impugned *his* honor. Odd, don't you think, that they had two completely different reasons for the duel?" He nearly stopped in the middle of his sentence, thinking it wasn't appropriate to be discussing duels with a lady. But Clarinda didn't seem to mind and, in fact, seemed quite interested. "So, if Wallingham didn't shoot David, then who did?"

Clarinda's eyes widened in horror. "Who said David was shot?" she managed to get out. "The constable said he broke his neck when he was thrown from his horse."

Daniel sighed, realizing just then that David's ghost hadn't told her about the hole in his head. "He claimed he was dead before he hit the ground. There is a hole in the back of his neck—I saw it with my own eyes. He was shot, Clare," he stated, his head cocking to one side. "Which means someone either murdered him or ... accidentally killed him."

Clare's brows furrowed so the little fold of skin appeared between them. "If you're referring to that hole in the nape of his neck, that's an old hole," she said in a matter-of-fact tone. "From when *you* shot him."

Daniel's bowl of soup nearly toppled over. "What?" *What could she mean?* "*I* didn't shoot David!" he countered, stunned she would accuse him of such a thing. And do so while calmly eating soup.

"You did, too," she countered. "You shot each other, if David's story is to believed," she claimed, taking another spoonful of soup and acting as if the hole in the back of David's head was supposed to be there. "You have a matching hole on your chest," she added, as if she'd seen it first hand.

Daniel stared at her for a very long time. He was about to ask how she knew about that hole between his two lower ribs and then remembered he had been in her bed that one time —although he couldn't recall one of her fingers finding the divot in his flesh. He had to finish that thought before he allowed it to progress too far. His pantaloons were too tight as it was. "From the slingshot," he remembered suddenly, his gaze directed somewhere beyond Clarinda. "A piece of gravel."

"Uh huh," Clarinda confirmed as she continued eating her soup. She watched as Daniel's face took on an expression of recalling something long forgotten, remembering how he had shot his brother with a piece of pea gravel, and while David howled in pain, his brother had shot him right back. And they'd declared a truce while they dug the offending shrapnel from their bodies and hurried off to have their nurse apply plasters to the holes.

Daniel shook his head, wondering if David had used the hole in his head as a ruse to gain sympathy, or if his brother truly thought he'd been shot with a bullet the day he died.

Finishing her soup, Clarinda considered Daniel's words. "When did you speak with David about the duel?" she wondered, suddenly straightening in her chair. Her mouth opened and shut very quickly, one gloved hand reaching up to cover her lips.

Shaking his head in resignation, Daniel sighed. "He ... He has seen fit to visit me quite frequently since ... my arrival," he stammered, not wanting to say, "Since his departure," which, although might have been more appropriate, certainly wasn't the case given David still hadn't actually *departed*. "His comments would lead me to believe you have suffered the same ... visitations far more often than I imagined."

Clarinda held her breath for a moment, stunned at Daniel's words. "'Suffered' is perhaps a rather harsh word to use to describe what I found to be rather comforting moments," she spoke in quiet tones, hoping the footman or another servant wasn't about to appear with the next course. "Although, some of his comments have been rather hard to

... abide." If Daniel really was hearing and seeing David like she had been, it meant she wasn't the only candidate for Bedlam.

"Like when he claimed you are having twins?" Daniel wondered, glad to hear her acknowledge David's visits again. At least he wasn't a candidate for Bedlam.

Or, if he was, then so was she. Perhaps they would be allowed to share a room. And a bed.

"I found that particular claim rather ... welcome, I suppose. According to him, I'm having twin girls, though, so you'll be relieved to know you truly are the earl," she said with a nod in his direction.

The words weren't spoken with any kind of spite or disappointment, Daniel was relieved to note. *Twin girls.* He gave the idea some thought, his lips curling up a bit at the edges. "They'll be beautiful, just like their mother. I'll bestow generous dowries on them and ensure they marry men who are at least viscounts in the peerage and who aren't notorious rakes or gamblers," he claimed, saying the words as if he'd practiced the vow for some time.

Clarinda's eyes widened in surprise. "Goodness. It will be a wonder they marry at all, then," she replied, her own lips curling up a bit. She sobered, though, and sighed. "Some of David's other assertions are a bit more difficult to comprehend," she spoke carefully, her eyes downcast.

"Oh?"

Clarinda blushed, hoping her reddening face wouldn't be so evident under the candles of the chandelier.

"You're blushing," Daniel murmured, the tone of his voice not necessarily sounding humored.

Dipping her head a moment and wishing a footman would appear to take the dishes, Clarinda sighed. "David believes I should marry you. And he claims I will bear you twin boys about two years from now."

From the tone of her voice, Daniel tried to determine if David's wish was hers as well. *Twin boys.* She couldn't despise him that much now, could she?

She would after she bore the twin boys, of course, but that was still two years from now.

Daniel stood up suddenly, startling Clarinda so her head snapped up. She watched him as he approached her, wondering if she should flee the room. His brown eyes were nearly black, his expression so fierce Clarinda thought he intended to ... well, she wasn't quite sure what he intended to do until he suddenly grabbed a pink rose from the vase on the sideboard and knelt next to her chair. He took one of her hands in his. "Pretend this room is an entire garden of pink roses," he whispered as he handed her the rose. She took it with her free hand, remembering the roses in Kensington Gardens. "And please, Clare, agree to be my wife."

Clarinda held her breath, shocked when he pulled a sapphire and diamond ring from his waistcoat pocket. It wasn't Dorothea's wedding ring—the sapphire was far too large, as were the series of white diamonds that surrounded the blue-violet stone. Clarinda gasped when she saw it. Daniel had it slipped onto her finger before she had a chance to speak.

"Daniel!" she breathed, throwing herself into his arms. Given his position on one knee, he toppled backwards, Clarinda following him down so she ended up atop him on the floor in a tangle of silk skirts and arms and legs. Her lips were on his, then, kissing him and breathless with her "Yes" and "Of course, I will marry you."

And, of course, the footman would choose that very moment to appear to remove their soup bowls. Although he let out a surprised gasp at finding them on the floor, he never once missed a step in his duty, pausing only to ask if they were ready for the main course.

Daniel held up a hand. "We are," he replied, allowing Clarinda to continue kissing his cheek. "We have been for four years, I believe," he murmured happily.

The footman bowed. "Very good, my lord. My lady," he replied before he hurried back through the door to the kitchens.

Chapter 25

A TRIP BACK TO LONDON

The last of Daniel's trunks were loaded onto the back of the Norwick coach while Clarinda's valise was placed on the roof with one of the grooms. Another coach, loaded with the dowager countess' remaining trunks, had departed only moments ago on its way to Bognor by way of Brighton. If anyone would have asked Daniel's opinion, he would have said the coach would make it to Brighton—he rather doubted his mother would be back in Bognor for some time, if ever again.

Inside Norwick Park's estate house, servants were lifting Holland cloths into the air and allowing them to drift down to cover all the furnishings. Daniel's valet, having just finished packing his master's clothing and personal items, would begin his retirement on the morrow. Daniel had bestowed him with the five-hundred pounds David had recommended for a settlement. He was especially pleased to see the old man's eyes widen in disbelief. The rest of the staff would remain in residence, their presence required when Daniel and Clarinda returned for the summer and then again for the Christmas holiday. By then, there would be babes in arms, girls—if David's claims could be believed.

Clarinda glanced toward the east edge of the property, to

where the gravestones were silhouetted in the light from the morning sun. She wondered if David would appear, and then felt a bit of relief when he didn't. He had all but dismissed her two nights ago when he told her to marry his brother; perhaps his dismissal was as much for him as it was for her.

"Are you ready?" Daniel wondered as he joined her where she stood on the edge of the cut lawn.

Her face suddenly displaying a look of fear, Clarinda glanced over at Daniel and swallowed. "I ... I don't know," she answered. She bit her lip, feeling an odd sensation she thought might be morning sickness. It passed as quickly as it had come, though, and she took a deep breath.

"We'll have the entire ride back to London. We can talk about everything. We can talk about the wedding. We can talk about the girls. Or, I can spend the trip courting you," he suggested, his brows wiggling in anticipation. He leaned over and kissed her temple. "Or kissing you." He watched her lids lower over her eyes and her mouth curl up. Her head settled into the small of his shoulder, and he wrapped an arm around her waist. "Or you can sleep in my arms," he offered, thinking they might be doing that as soon as the following night.

"Mmm," Clarinda responded, thinking that they would probably do a bit of everything he mentioned during the coach ride back to London. Her attention turned back toward the graveyard. "Do you suppose we'll ever see him again?" she wondered, her voice catching at the last word.

Daniel wondered the same thing. Truth be told, he *wanted* to see David one more time. He had questions for his brother, unresolved issues he wanted to deal with now rather than later, when he joined his brother in death many years from now. His brother had died for a reason, he was sure, and Daniel wanted to be sure it was so he could finally marry Clarinda and be her husband for the rest of his life. There might be another reason, but he wanted some kind of assurance his brother's death held some kind of meaning. "He had better show up at least one more time," Daniel replied, a bit more harshly than he intended. "I still have some questions for him. And I have that answer for him about his being shot," he added as his eyebrows lifted.

How could David have forgotten about being shot by a piece of pea gravel? he wondered, once they were in the coach and headed north toward London. Of course, given all the other wounds the two brothers had inflicted on one other over the years, perhaps a few were better left forgotten. He sighed as he wrapped his arms around Clarinda's shoulders and pulled her against him. For once, he actually enjoyed the long trip to Norwick House.

He would deal with David whenever his brother next appeared.

Chapter 26

GHOST TALK REDUX

"So, why now?" Daniel wondered before taking a long drag on his cheroot. He normally only indulged in smoking right after dinner while enjoying a glass of port, but given the eerie presence of his dead brother only a few hours after he and Clarinda arrived back at Norwick House, two hours after dinner seemed just as suitable a time.

David furrowed his brows and gave his brother a quelling glance. "Why now, what?" he responded.

Daniel watched as a tendril of smoke wafted up and around his brother, as if he was physically in the room. "Why did you ... die ... now?" he stammered. "Or last week, I suppose?"

David snorted. "Do you think I *chose* to die? *Now*, of all times?" he asked indignantly. "My wife is increasing with child ... with children," he amended, his pride adding to his indignation. "I was advancing important issues in Parliament. And I was finally beating Barrings at whist!"

Daniel stood up suddenly, his own ire increasing as he watched his brother. "Yes. Yes, I do think you *chose* to die. And I want to know *why*," he insisted. "And don't tell me because it's my turn to have your wife as my own."

Staring at Daniel for a very long time, David's fierce look softened. "I ... didn't *choose* to die. I ... was shot ..."

"You were not shot," Daniel countered. "I checked with the mortician. He found no evidence of a bullet hole in your body," he insisted, his own ire disappearing. "And when I asked if he had checked for a wound at the back of your neck, he assured me he had done so."

David's eyes widened. "And my," his hand moved to the back of his head, "My hole was there, right?"

Rolling his eyes, Daniel finally nodded. "Yes, he found the hole, although it was merely a ... a divot ... from an old wound," he said in exasperation, not wanting to admit that he had been the one to put the hole there with his precisely shot piece of pea gravel. He didn't have the time to consider it just then, though. "There was no bullet hole in the back of your neck."

David seemed shocked by the news. "I was sure ... I was sure I heard a *shot*."

Daniel cocked his head. "Were you in front of Jover and Son's shop, by chance?" he wondered, thinking that the gun shop might have been the source of a gun shot.

"No," David replied with a shake of his head. "I was in front of Thomas Simpson's shop. My horse ... he reared up, and I lost my hold. I am quite sure I was dead before I hit the cobbles."

Daniel sucked air through his front teeth as he imagined the circumstances of David's death in front of a goldsmith's shop in the middle of Oxford Street on a busy day. There would have been all manner of conveyances clogging the road—drays and carriages, barouches and carts, town coaches and horses. Perhaps there had even been the sound of a shot — anyone could have discharged a gun, and not necessarily for the purpose of shooting someone. And when the horse reared, David's head could have struck any number of blunt objects on its way down to the street. "Did your horse rear up at the sound of the shot? Or did something else cause him to panic?"

"Thunder never panics," David replied, his face quite severe, as if he'd just then been personally offended. "The beast has shown a remarkable affinity to life in the city as well as on the hunting grounds. A gunshot would *not* have caused him to rear," he claimed, perhaps a bit too firmly.

Returning to his chair behind the desk, Daniel shook his head. He was about to take another drag on the cheroot when he realized it had burned to a nub and was nearly out. He stubbed it into the crystal tray at the edge of the desk. "Then what happened to cause your unflappable horse to ... flap?" he asked. His patience was growing thin. He wasn't even sure why he brought up the topic of David's death except that it had seemed ... important, he supposed. Important to discover how the accident had happened—if it *had* been an accident. And, if not, then it was even more important to determine who killed David and why they would want the earl dead. Perhaps David would finally disappear for good once the truth of his death was revealed.

At the moment, Daniel realized he wanted David gone so that he could get on with his own life. Get on with a life that he was now sure would include Clarinda. He'd nearly convinced himself he hated her for choosing his brother over him all those years ago, but she really had been confused as to whom she was marrying. Yes, she had despised him over their argument, but now that she knew for herself he'd been telling the truth all along, she had come around. And now they would marry. Over time, she'd realize Daniel was the better husband—and father—once he'd had a chance to prove himself to her.

"Thunder didn't flap," David said with a shake of his head.

"You said he reared up ..."

"He did, but he did because ..." David paused, his expression indicating he was thinking back to the moment when his horse had suddenly reared up. "Because he was trotting along and ..."

Daniel stared at his brother, intrigued at the look of him

as he seemed to recall the details. Even his hands were posed as if they held the reins, his shoulders positioned square to the saddle, his head held up. For a moment, Daniel was sure he heard the sound of horse hooves clopping on cobbles.

"And?" Daniel encouraged, hoping his brother hadn't lost his train of thought.

"It was a child," David murmured, as if he was still deep in thought. "Curly red hair. Adorable, although rather filthy now that I think about it," he whispered. "She looked like I imagined one of my daughters would look. Like a small version of Clare with her blue-green eyes and soft skin." There was another pause as he continued to stare into the space just beyond the front of his face. Daniel watched him, mesmerized by his brother's recall of the events of the day he had bit the dust, so to speak. "She ran out in front of the horse, and I had to pull back on the reins." He did so in mime, his expression indicating instant anger at having to halt his horse so quickly to avoid trampling the moppet. "She'd been chasing a ball, and Thunder stepped on it ..."

Daniel's inhaled sharply. "The ball popped."

"Sounded just like a gunshot," David murmured. "And the girl's eyes turned angry and ... she cried out. She *yelled* at me! Just like Clare does when she's playing at being a volcano." Here, he stopped, his eyes indicating he must have felt more frightened by the girl's outburst than by the thought that he might have flattened her with his horse.

An understandable reaction, Daniel thought, having been the target of one of Clarinda's volcanic eruptions. *Besides, her ball had just had popped.*

"She pointed her finger up at me, accusing me ... And then I was seeing sky and clouds and the top of the dome above Lord Barrings' apartment, where he had the flag waving to indicate he was in residence. As if everyone in London cares whether or not Lord Barrings is in residence!"

Daniel had to stifle the urge to groan, knowing exactly what David meant by the comment but wanting him to get on with the story.

But David's voice had trailed off, as if the memory had done the same. When he didn't say anything for a moment or two, Daniel inhaled and slowly exhaled. "You must have hit your head on something on the way down, Davy. What was it?" he asked gently, not wanting his brother to lose his place in his recollection.

He watched as David began to contort his body, his head back, his spine arching as if he was falling backwards off his horse. And his brother turned himself around and stared into space behind where he'd been standing. "Lord Everly," he murmured.

"Lord Everly?" Daniel repeated.

"The name on the crate."

Daniel's eyebrows cocked up so they were very nearly into his hairline. "The *crate*?"

"Yes. The crate in the back of the cart that had just crossed at Berwick Street on its way south. It was right behind me," David murmured.

"Oh?"

"It had the words 'Live fish' stenciled on it." David's head turned sideways again, as if he was trying to read something upside down. "Cape Horn, Africa." He slowly straightened, his head shaking back and forth very slowly.

"You hit your head on a crate? On a crate containing Lord Everly's *tropical fish*?" Daniel half-questioned.

David suddenly seemed himself again, alert but solemn. "I always said those fish would be the death of me," he said with a bit too much bravado.

Daniel blinked. "You hit your head on a crate containing Lord Everly's tropical fish?" Daniel repeated, his own mouth doing a fine imitation of a goldfish's mouth.

David nodded, his shoulders slumping suddenly. "Indeed," he whispered, his head barely nodding. Then, as if nothing of import had just happened, he lifted his head and regarded his younger brother. "Well, I'm off. Take care of Clare and the girls, won't you, Danny?" he said quietly as he turned around. He disappeared before he made it out of the room.

Stunned, Daniel stared after his brother's ghost. "I will," he answered to the thin air.

Chapter 27

FISH TALES

Dressed entirely in black, Clarinda entered the vestibule of Norwick House followed by Lady Torrington. The older woman's moss green carriage gown and pelisse might hide the signs of her pregnancy for another month or two, but from where Daniel watched from the railing at the top of the stairs, the glow that surrounded Clarinda instantly gave away her condition. She was the epitome of impending motherhood. He felt a clenching in his chest at the sight of her, an immediate desire to descend the stairs by riding on the bannister as he had once done as a boy on the staircase at Norwick Park so that he might scoop her up into his arms and twirl her about the room. Thinking back to the morning she'd been sick, he quickly suppressed the thought and instead remained where he stood, watching and listening, not the least bit ashamed of eavesdropping on the two women.

"Thank you for talking me into the ride and the visit to the bookseller," Clarinda said as she removed her large-brimmed hat and veil. "It does me good to get air every day." She carried her reticule and a wrapped package—a book about the condition of expecting a baby—to the table just beyond the vestibule.

With Porter's help, Lady Torrington divested herself of her pelisse. "You're very welcome. I must say, the last person I expected to see in the book shop was Lord Everly."

Clarinda smiled. "And yet I would expect to find him in no other place. Well, except for his own library, I suppose," she countered with a grin.

Adele shook her head. "True. I meant that I thought he would be gone on his next expedition by now. I do believe this is the longest he's stayed in London since he reached his majority."

At the mention of Lord Everly, Daniel leaned his elbows on the railing and listened more closely.

Clarinda turned to regard Adele with a look of surprise. "I thought you would know why," she said, hinting there was a reason Everly was still in town.

"What makes you say that?" the earl's wife replied, her brows furrowing.

"Rumor has it he has to see to a marriage for his sister before he can leave on another trip or your husband will apparently cause him great bodily harm."

Adele rolled her eyes. "Oh. That's already taken care of. In fact, Lady Evangeline is set to become Lady Sommers," she murmured, shaking her head as she allowed a smile. "I was rather surprised she didn't mention it today, but in all the excitement with the fish ..." She allowed the statement to trail off as she gave a slight shrug.

"She's already betrothed?" Clarinda asked in surprise. *I've only been gone a few days.* The last she'd heard, the girl wasn't even being courted by anyone, although she remembered Adele saying something about Lord Sommers' interest in the chit.

"Can you imagine being her and having to rely on Everly to find a husband? I think I would prefer spinsterhood," Adele said with a shake of her head. "My husband—he's the girl's godfather—took care of it. Told Sommers to take her for a drive, ask to court her, ask for her hand, and acquire a ring. All in that one day. His thirtieth birthday. And the man did it!"

Astonished at this news, Clarinda blinked. "I take it Lord Everly ... *agreed* with the arrangements?" she wondered.

The air seemed to go out of Adele just then. "I don't think he was even aware of the situation until after his sister agreed to accept Lord Sommers' suit," she replied uncertainly.

"Lord Everly is an odd duck, but I cannot fault his enthusiasm," Clarinda said, moving from the vestibule toward the parlor door. "And I think Lord Sommers will make a fine match for her. I admit I was surprised when Everly mentioned him as his first choice for his sister, but it makes perfect sense. The man apparently said he wanted to marry whilst playing cards at White's. All his friends are leg-shackled."

Daniel moved along the railing so he could keep Clarinda in sight as long as possible. "I do wonder, though, who *he* will decide to marry when he must. Can you imagine having *him* as a husband?"

Adele Grandby's musical laughter drifted up the stairs. "I am sure there is a biddable bluestocking that will love him as much as he will tolerate her," she replied with a wave of her hand as she disappeared into the parlor. Daniel could imagine Clarinda ringing for tea. He descended the stairs, keeping his attention on the door to the parlor.

"A bluestocking would be *perfect* for him," Clarinda claimed, trying to decide if she knew any of the younger debutantes who found books more intriguing than fashion plates. "He'll require someone who loves those fish just as much as he does, though. I must admit, those large, white triangular ones he pointed out were rather beautiful. What did he call them?" she wondered, one eyebrow arched up as she tried to recall what the viscount had said.

"Angel fish," Adele replied, settling herself into a Chippendale chair and letting out a sigh. "He received them not even ten days ago." She held her breath for a moment when she realized the day the fish were delivered to Everly House was the same day as David's death. "They were quite taken with you, as well," she murmured, not wanting to remind Clarinda of David's passing. She hadn't seen her friend cry since her return from Sussex.

Clarinda giggled. "Because they nearly drowned me?" she wondered, taking a seat in the chair in front of the tea table. She spread out her skirts, apparently to determine if the bombazine fabric displayed any water stains. The wave of water that had crashed over the top edge of Lord Everly's fish tank had soaked one side of her gown, although the dampness hadn't seeped through her petticoats. "They did the same to David when he was last there. He claimed the water ruined his favorite russet riding coat." She recalled when she'd last seen him wearing that very topcoat—when he was riding that morning in Hyde Park while she and Adele were climbing into the carriage after their walk.

Clarinda's mention of David was made without a tinge of sadness, a fact Adele found intriguing and a bit of a relief. She gave the countess a grin in return. "Until today, I do not believe I have ever seen fish pay any notice while people were looking at them."

Giving a wan smile, Clarinda shrugged. "It was as if they knew me—swam right over and waved their fins." Clarinda lifted one hand above her head and another to one side, waving them in imitation of the angel fish's movements.

Adele laughed aloud just as Daniel made it to the side of the door. Peeking around the opening, he watched as Clarinda imitated the fish that had apparently waved at her. He smiled at her antics. *They were probably the fish that killed David,* he thought suddenly, remembering the words that David had said were stenciled on the crate his head hit on his way down to the cobbles. *Killed by angel fish,* he thought with a shake of his head.

At least they had the decency to pay their respects to Clarinda.

He was thinking of going in to greet the ladies but

noticed Rosie rolling the tea cart toward the parlor. He nodded in her direction as if he was merely passing by the room and then turned around, hoping to overhear more about Lord Everly's fish.

"I believe you were out of earshot when Lord Everly made mention that he's never seen his fish react as they did to you today," Adele said with a cocked eyebrow. "Made me wonder if he was thinking of *you* for the role of Lady Everly."

Daniel straightened himself against the hall wall outside the parlor, his breath held in disbelief, stunned at what he'd overheard. Had the women been to Everly's house just *today*?

"Adele!" Clarinda scolded as she saw to the tea service. "I do not believe I could abide being married to a man who spends most of his time in jungles when he's not in residence and then with his nose in a book when he is," she admonished her friend.

A sense of relief settled over Daniel as he heard Clarinda's words. Under no circumstances would he abide Clarinda ever marrying Lord Everly—or anyone else, for that matter. He crossed his arms over his chest as he continued to eavesdrop on the ladies, and suddenly started when Rosie came through the doorway on her way back to the kitchens.

"Good day," he murmured, acting as if he'd paused by the door to allow her an exit. At that point, he couldn't hide his presence from the women in the parlor. Clarinda was already glancing in his direction, looking as if she was about to stand up. "Please do not get up on my account, my lady," he said as he paused on the threshold. "Good afternoon, Lady Torrington," Daniel added as he moved into the room and afforded them both a deep bow.

Adele, still amused by her conversation with Clarinda, gave him a glance from head to foot. "Norwick, you are looking well, although a bit peaked, perhaps," she commented. "As if you've seen a ghost," she added, her head cocking to one side.

Daniel blinked, daring a quick glance in Clarinda's direction. She was holding the edge of her teacup to her bottom lip, her eyes suddenly wide. She gave him a quick shake of her head, as if to let him know she hadn't mentioned David's ghost to Adele Grandby.

"Probably because I have not yet resumed regular outdoor activities since my brother's death." *Nor started any of the indoor activities I plan to engage in now that he's dead*, he thought to himself, the color returning to his face in a flash.

"Do join us for tea, Daniel," Clarinda invited, motioning with her hand toward the chair David usually used when he was in the parlor.

Daniel nodded his acknowledgement of the invitation but took the chair adjacent to David's. "I could not help but overhear Lord Everly's name mentioned as I entered. Did you perchance pay a call on the explorer?" he wondered, accepting a cup of tea from Clarinda. Two ladies—one married and one widowed and neither one a relative—calling on an unmarried gentleman at his residence wasn't exactly a regular occurrence. Some might think it scandalous, in fact.

The two women exchanged knowing glances. They weren't about to allow Daniel to believe the worst of them. "His sister, Lady Evangeline, is in residence, poor girl," Adele replied with a shake of her head. "When Lord Everly saw us shopping for books in The Temple of the Muses, he asked us to pay her a call."

Daniel's eyebrows lifted in surprise. "Lady Evangeline? You mean, she isn't ..?" He was about to say 'married', but thought better of it when Clarinda shook her head ever so slightly.

"Her brother had been left to find her a suitable husband," Adele said with the kind of sigh in her voice that made the task sound as if it might never get done. "At three-and-twenty, some might consider her on the shelf."

Daniel's eyebrows furrowed. "I hardly think three-and-twenty makes for spinsterhood," he countered. "From what I remember, she was quite pretty and rather accomplished considering her age."

Clarinda felt a pang of jealousy at hearing his simple

words, wondering if he was considering more than Lady Evangeline's age. "Who do you know who would consider her biddable?" she wondered, hoping to get his mind on other gentleman wanting to marry the chit so that he would stop considering her. If, indeed, that was what he was doing.

Daniel shrugged, not sure how to respond. He hadn't been back in London long enough to know who, if anyone, was in the market for a wife. *Besides Wallingham,* although Daniel still couldn't believe his mother would be the man's wife— ever—even if the rake had given her a ring with a rock so large it probably caused his mother to walk with a limp when she wore it. "I understand Lord Sommers is interested," he said as if he had personal knowledge of the man's intentions. "He must be thirty by now and in need of an heir," he added, taking a good deal of satisfaction in seeing the delighted faces of the two women in the room. Apparently they, too, believed Lord Sommers was agreeable as a husband for Lady Evangeline.

"Grandby has already seen to it. Lord Sommers asked for Lady Evangeline's hand only a few days ago," Lady Torrington stated with a kind of pride one might exhibit when a son or daughter had done something wonderful. "Milton takes his godfather duties quite seriously."

Clarinda leaned forward. "And, not to be outdone, Lord Sommers acquired a special license and plans to make Lady Evangeline his wife in the next few days."

Daniel gave the countess a nod, thinking he would need to speak with Grandby about being a godfather for the twins Clarinda carried. "I suppose Lord Everly had his fish tank well stocked and on display?" he hinted, wanting to hear more about the killer fish. *Angel fish, indeed.*

Clarinda finished her tea and put the cup down on the saucer. "He did. His newest species are from the very southern most tip of Africa. He called them *angel fish,*" she explained in a manner suggesting she was rather interested in the sea creatures.

"But from how they splashed about when Clarinda went

to look at them up close, you would think they were demon fish," Adele interjected. "I do hope your gown isn't ruined."

Shaking her head, Clarinda held out the portion of her gown that had been splashed. "It's all dry now. It was just water," she said with a shrug. "And I never could understand why those fish had David so vexed," she added, moving to add more tea to her cup. "He always claimed those fish would be the death of him. Can you imagine?" She sighed as she lifted the cup to her lips.

His jaw suddenly slack, Daniel stared at Clarinda for a very long time.

He could imagine, indeed.

Chapter 28

IN THE MIDDLE OF THE NIGHT

A sob caught in her throat and she found she had to lift her head to take a breath. A handkerchief was suddenly filling one of her hands while a warm hand settled on her shoulder.

"Clare." Her name came from over her in a barely heard whisper as strong arms wrapped around her shoulders. Her head landed against the satin of Daniel's dressing robe, the scent of sandalwood and citrus filling her nostrils as she clung to his arms, as she wrapped one arm over his shoulder and raked her fingers through his dark, wavy hair. "Daniel!" she whispered as profound relief swept through her. "Oh, Daniel, I was just about to ..." She let a sob interrupt her when she realized how wanton her comment would sound if she told him she was about to visit him in his bedchamber. Her dreams had been filled with demonic angel fish and David.

"About to ... what?" Daniel whispered, one hand pushing her hair away from her face. He had one hip propped on the edge of the mattress as he held her, one bare foot planted on the carpet below to support his weight.

Clarinda used the handkerchief to wipe away some of the tears. She was mute for a long time, sobbing quietly. "Honestly, Daniel, until two nights ago, I did not believe you were ever ...

that you ever ... felt affection for me. I truly thought you were David. Even when you tried to convince me—that time a couple of years ago when you told me how you'd courted me and how you asked for my hand—I truly thought David had been the one who did those things. Back then, I couldn't tell you two apart. That's why I didn't believe you. That's why I slapped you when you made those claims." She buried her face in her hands just then. "Can you ever forgive me?" she whispered, new tears pricking the corners of her eyes.

Daniel sat very still for a long time, his arms still wrapped around her shoulders as he listened to Clarinda's admission and thought he had heard the same request for an apology before. He could claim he hated her for what she had done, feign indifference over her apology, even ignore her altogether. But, in the end, he could do none of those things. "So, how is it you know *now* that I was the one who courted you?" he asked, suspecting what her answer would be but wanting to hear it from her lips.

"David told me."

"And how do you know I was the one who asked for your hand in Kensington Gardens?"

"David told me."

Well, at least in death his brother was an honorable man. He had hoped that when they returned to London, David would stay behind at Norwick Park and leave them to their lives in Norwick House. Since his earlier visit and his disappearance after determining he'd died from a blow to the head by a crate of tropical fish, there had been no sign of the ghost of David. "I take it he just paid you a visit?" Daniel whispered, repositioning himself so his back was against the bed's headboard and Clarinda lay in his arms.

"The day we buried him, near his grave," she answered, one hand moving to cup his jaw. "He told me it really was you who courted me and asked for my hand in marriage that day in Kensington Park. I should have believed you. I'm so sorry, Daniel. Can you ever forgive me?"

Staring down at the woman he held, Daniel nodded. So, his brother had done right by him in the end, then, and set the record straight.

If he hadn't, Daniel had every intention of haunting David when he had the chance.

Assured by his older brother that he would live to a ripe, old age, Daniel closed his eyes and decided he could forgive his brother. It might take several years and a good deal of pleading, but he would eventually forgive the scoundrel. As for Clarinda ...

Daniel reopened his eyes to find the love of his life regarding him with her large, aquamarine eyes still limned with tears. Before he could give her an answer, she had reached up with her other hand and pulled his head down to hers, her lips taking purchase on his in a kiss that was as possessive as it was desperate. He returned the kiss in equal measure, surprised by her passion, humored by the mewling sounds she made as he nipped her lower lip and allowed her tongue to explore his mouth before his tongue tangled with hers. And then they were simply kissing, soft lips sliding over firm lips, little murmurs of pleasure escaping here and there.

When Clarinda finally pulled away, it was to hug him close and lay her head against the bare skin just above his robe's closure. At some point during the kiss, Daniel had lowered himself onto the bed, holding onto Clarinda as he stretched out his legs and settled her body atop his.

"I am happy I'm having twin girls," Clarinda murmured proudly.

Daniel let out a chuckle. "So am I," he replied, caressing her hair. "I, of course, will provide protection and act as a father to your daughters. They'll be my nieces, after all," he added when her face seemed to fall all of a sudden.

"Thank you," Clarinda replied, reaching up to kiss the corner of his mouth. "Will you love them as much as your twin boys?"

Daniel straightened his body on the bed and looked down to regard her. "Probably more," he said with a twinkle in his eye. "I was a twin, remember?"

Clarinda gave him a tentative smile. "I remember. But, if it's true—what David said about me having twin boys—you'll have an heir and a spare." The comment was made with just a hint of hope, as if Clarinda still wasn't sure of her future as Countess of Norwick.

Cocking his head to one side, Daniel considered his future as Earl of Norwick as per David Fitzwilliam. "Are you truly willing to be the mother of those twin boys?" he asked, his face displaying a rather harsh demeanor.

Clarinda allowed a gasp of surprise. Or indignation, perhaps. Daniel wasn't quite sure. "Well, of course," she replied, moving so she could see his eyes. She noted the gleam in his and realized he was teasing her. Her indignation disappeared, and she lowered her head back down against his shoulder. "If you still want me as your wife, and I won't blame you if you do not, I will happily marry you," Clarinda murmured into the small of his shoulder. She sniffled. "Tomorrow, if you've a special license that allows it," she added when Daniel didn't respond immediately. She waited a moment, expecting him to say something.

The silence stretched out for some time, prompting Clarinda to put voice to the sentiment she had come to realize a long time ago. "I love you," she said quietly before taking a breath that was interrupted by a sob. "My daughters will need a father, and your twin boys will need a mother," she continued, becoming concerned that Daniel hadn't made a sound in reply since she kissed him. "And you'll require a countess, of course, since you *are* the Earl of Norwick. And since I've been the Countess of Norwick for the past four years, I've quite a bit of experience," she murmured, thinking she was doing a good job of listing her qualifications for the position of being his wife. "I shan't embarrass you." She stilled herself, waiting for Daniel to say *something*. Her hand slid beneath his robe's fold and settled onto his chest. She felt the even beating of his heart, felt the steady rhythm of his breathing, found the small divot where David had shot him, and she sighed.

He fell asleep!

How could he *sleep*? She was making a confession of her love and adoration for him. She was finally agreeable to the idea of being married to the man—to the man to whom she should have been married all these years. He should be awake. He should be hanging on her every word and agreeing with everything she was saying! He should be kissing her and consoling her and promising his everlasting love and devotion! *Was he truly sound asleep*?

Clarinda was about to lift her head to check when her stomach rumbled, hunger pangs suddenly reminding her it had been several hours since her last meal.

A deep chuckle shook Daniel's chest as his hands slid down her back and over the swells of her bottom to cup them through her night rail.

Surprised he was awake, Clarinda gasped. "You *are* awake," she accused, wondering if he'd heard everything she'd said.

"Of course, I am. It's rather difficult to sleep when my beautiful betrothed sounds—and feels—like a little volcano," he countered, his voice filled with amusement. Besides, how could he sleep when he had the woman of his dreams lying atop him with barely a stitch of clothing separating their bodies? How could Clarinda not have noticed his raging cockstand pressing into her belly?

Despite her initial thought to pound on his chest with her fist, Clarinda suddenly giggled. "I cannot help it. I am hungry," she murmured, wondering if he would help her up from the bed and accompany her to the kitchen.

Then she realized what he had said and inhaled sharply. She lifted her head, placed her hands on either side of his chest and spread her knees so that her thighs straddled his hips. A curtain of brunette hair falling from over one shoulder, Clarinda stared down at Daniel. In the dim lamplight, she saw the humor leave his eyes as he regarded her. "Betrothed?" she repeated, her voice barely a whisper. She swallowed.

Daniel watched her throat work and then lifted a hand to cup her cheek. "You just said again you would marry me, didn't you?" he whispered, one eyebrow cocking with his question, much like David's would do under the same circumstance. "I suppose you've already forgotten you told me several times during dinner you would marry me," he accused. It was the middle of the night, though, and she had, no doubt, just awakened from a bad dream when he found her crying.

Clarinda nodded, giving him a tentative smile. Her stomach growled again. When she glanced down, she saw the evidence of Daniel's arousal poking up from between the folds of his robe, the wet tip hard against her belly. She turned her attention back to Daniel's face, saw the desire in his eyes, felt the heat that radiated from his chest and arms. Her own body, suddenly too warm in the night rail, begged to be bared. Her breasts, heavy with anticipation, made their presence evident when her nipples left their silhouettes in the thin fabric.

Before she was quite aware of what she was doing, the anticipation of what they should be doing at that moment suddenly pooled between her thighs. Lifting her arms above her head, she crossed them and grasped the folds of the billowing fabric. She pulled the night rail from her body as she also lifted her body onto her knees and then lowered herself so that she impaled herself on his turgid manhood.

Daniel recoiled in surprise at her sudden movements, at the feel of her tight sheath suddenly sliding over him and trapping him deep inside her, and the wash of cool air as she spread open the front edges of his robe, at the sensation of her tongue and lips covering one of his nipples. "Christ, Clare," he managed to get out before she'd lifted her hips so he was nearly outside of her. Then she pushed herself back down on him again. Her nipples brushed over the dark, curly hair that covered his chest, eliciting a gasp from her before her hips were back up.

With the initial shock having passed and grateful he hadn't allowed himself to climax from sheer surprise—the sight of Clare naked atop him would have been enough, he realized— Daniel matched her rhythm, meeting her downward motion with an upthrust that shocked her. She released one of his nipples to inhale sharply, only to trace her nose across his chest and latch onto the other with her teeth.

Daniel growled in response and managed to get a hand onto one of her breasts, his thumb brushing over and around her erect nipple until she was mewling. Moving both his hands to her hips, he grasped them and guided their movements as she continued to lift and lower herself.

When he moved one of his thumbs to the place just above where their bodies met and merged, she inhaled sharply. The slightest pressure there, the smallest movement of the pad of his thumb against the swollen nub of her womanhood, and ... Clarinda fractured. Her movements faltered, her lips took harder purchase on his chest to stifle her cries of pleasure, and Daniel allowed his own blessed release.

His groans of pleasure filled the bedchamber, stifled when her lips found his and captured the sounds until he could no longer make them and she felt the last of the tendrils of pleasure course through her body. Sated and limp from exhaustion, she settled her body atop his, her breasts resting against his chest as her head sank into the pillow next to his head.

His cock still quite hard inside Clarinda, Daniel took a deep breath and let it out slowly. Although he had imagined bedding this woman more times than he cared to admit, had pleasured himself countless times to the image of what she might look like with her hair down and her clothes removed, he had never imagined *this*. Never imagined she could be so wanton, so wicked, so soft and so warm. So explosive. He was reminded of her temper, how it could erupt like a volcano when provoked. But now, it was as if his manhood had been the wick, and once inside her liquid heat, her stoked fires had been lit. He had tapped that built up passion until she could no longer contain the steam and molten lava and she had simply exploded all around him, at once breaking apart and constricting around him so tightly he thought he might have become one with her. His body suddenly shivered again with the remembering of what she'd just done to him.

As if she could hear his words in his mind, Clarinda lifted her head and moved it onto his shoulder. "I apologize. I don't know what came over me just then," she whispered, her breaths still a bit short. One of her hands had ended up grasping his shoulder while the other smoothed down the side of his body, leaving a trail of heat in its wake.

Daniel imagined a burn scar would appear there before morning.

Apologize?! Daniel inhaled sharply in an attempt to stifle the laughter that nearly exploded from his chest. "Don't you dare," he whispered back, his lips finding her forehead to kiss her. "Don't ever apologize for having your way with me."

Clarinda sighed. "It was terribly wanton of me," she whispered. "Are you sure you didn't mind?"

Daniel's body shook with mirth, sleep tempting him almost as much as her luscious body still pressed against him. "I didn't mind a bit."

Sighing, Clarinda smiled and allowed herself to go limp atop him. Within moments, they were both sound asleep. When her stomach grumbled again, neither one of them heard it.

EPILOGUE

As Dorothea Norwick had predicted, Society practically ignored Clarinda's quick wedding to Daniel Norwick. The private affair, conducted by a bishop in the gardens behind Worthington House, was witnessed by the Earl and Countess Torrington and by the groom's mother and new stepfather. Although she wasn't sure, Clarinda thought she spotted David watching from behind a statue of Cupid, a wry smile lighting his face. Before she could confirm his presence, though, his visage disappeared. She hadn't seen him since the day of his burial and often wondered if he would ever return to visit her.

The Fitzwilliams enjoyed a brief wedding trip to Derbyshire before settling into married life at Norwick House, their social calendar clear given most of London had escaped to the country for the summer months. If any of those who remained in town objected to the idea of a widowed countess marrying before her year of mourning was complete, they didn't seem to voice their opinion. Indeed, Clarinda wondered if Dorothea had been right—most who saw her with Daniel simply addressed him as "Norwick" and continued to afford him the same courtesy they would if Daniel truly was the Earl of Norwick.

When she was nearly seven months pregnant, Clarinda realized Daniel's fortieth birthday would come before the twins were born. She thought of the paintings that still hung in his bedchamber. Would the artist who had rendered her so faithfully in those paintings be willing to paint her as a Madonna with child? With her left hand resting on her pronounced belly, Clarinda penned a missive to the artist, explaining she had little time before her daughters would be born.

Jean-Claude Lamorette responded to Clarinda's letter within the month, explaining he had taken up residence in England to do a portrait of Lady Sommers. Apparently, Evangeline's husband had commissioned him based on a recommendation made to him by a certain earl who claimed to enjoy the sight of the artist's paintings every time he was in his bedchamber. Clarinda nearly blushed when she read Monsieur Lamorette's correspondence, thinking perhaps her first husband had given Lord Sommers the man's name. But then she found herself wondering how many other aristocrats had the artist's work gracing their bedchambers. Certainly the artist was well known enough to have painted a variety of portraits over the years.

Perhaps David wasn't the first aristocrat to receive a Lamorette from his wife.

Jean-Claude agreed to paint Clarinda, arriving the following week with his box of paints and a large, white canvas he quickly erected in a guest bedroom. Gushing over Clarinda's beauty in her state of impending motherhood, he insisted she allow him to paint her as a nude Madonna. A translucent dressing gown was the only covering he would abide, he explained, adding that she had no need to feel embarrassed. Stunned, Clarinda nearly cancelled the sitting. In the end, Jean-Claude prevailed when he mentioned he had seen dozens of ladies of the *ton au natural.*

After six days of sittings, at times during which Daniel was otherwise occupied with estate issues, the artist declared he had seen enough of Clarinda to complete the work without her posing for him. He continued for three more days in the guest bedroom, his presence kept a secret from Daniel.

Clarinda ordered a frame to be constructed, one that matched those surrounding the other paintings Jean-Claude had completed, and arranged for the artist to complete the mounting. With only a day to spare, the Lamorette was draped with a Holland cloth and the artist took his leave of Norwick House.

Daniel regarded his very pregnant wife with an expression of doubt. The shape of the covered object suggested a painting was hidden beneath the fabric. But with Clarinda, he couldn't be sure. "May I?" he wondered as he motioned toward the top corner.

Clarinda's hands were suddenly clasped in front of her body, her wrists resting on the swollen evidence of her impending motherhood. "On one condition," she finally answered, dividing her attention between Daniel and the object in question.

"That being?" he countered, his brows furrowing so a fold of skin appeared between them. "You know I will be pleased simply because it is a gift from you," he reasoned with a carefree shrug.

Relaxing a bit, Clarinda tilted her head to one side. "I do not think you should display this where the servants can see," she whispered, her face coloring up to a soft pink.

Her suddenly coy manner had Daniel thinking of the manner in which he planned to pleasure her later that evening. If she was half as willing and as loud as she'd been the night before, he might have to find a secluded place in the park behind the house in which to try out his newest seduction. Thank the gods the French had been so thorough in documenting and illustrating sexual positions. And thank David, who had seen to it his library was well stocked with such literary fare.

Clarinda's words brought a wicked grin to Daniel's face. "For my eyes only, then?" he replied. He reached out to lift the fabric from the corner, but Clarinda's hand stopped his before he could do so.

"Allow me," she whispered, moving so she was between Daniel and the painting.

"All right," Daniel reluctantly agreed, stepping back a bit. He watched as Clarinda's flush deepened.

"You won't laugh?" she said with a slight shake of her head, the edge of the fabric pinched between two fingers.

"I will not laugh," Daniel agreed, his head shaking from side to side. "I may die of curiosity ..." He allowed the sentence to trail off as Clarinda slowly pulled the fabric from in front of the painting, exposing Jean Claude's familiar painting style as well as Clarinda's nude and obviously pregnant form draped in a sheer French negligée. Her hands were resting atop her swollen belly as she leaned against a wall next to a window, one knee bent slightly so most of that leg was uncovered by the filmy fabric. The lifted thigh hid the dark curls of her nether region, an effect far more titillating than if it had been shown. A cascade of brunette hair tumbled over one shoulder, hinting at the shape of the breast it hid while the other was readily apparent, its nipple poking against the sheer robe so it appeared as if there was nothing covering it. Light from the window illuminated her tilted face, giving her the look of a Greek goddess contemplating her future. The painting was perfect in every sense, Clarinda's likeness so well rendered Daniel was tempted to reach out and caress her.

Forcing himself to take a breath, Daniel regarded the painting for a very long time before turning his attention to its subject.

Clarinda's face was turned up, as if she was begging for forgiveness from some other being. "It's magnificent," he spoke in a reverent tone. "Amazing. I ... I find I am jealous that Jean Claude saw you like this," he whispered.

Clarinda lowered her gaze to meet his, her face still pink

with her embarrassment. "You're not laughing," she said quietly.

Daniel shook his head and returned his attention to the painting. "No. I couldn't laugh at this. I am awed, in fact. Awed, and rather touched that you would bestow such a perfect gift on me on the occasion of my fortieth birthday," he whispered. Before Clarinda could respond, he had her gathered in his arms and was kissing her with such possessiveness, Clarinda could do nothing more than return the kiss in equal measure.

When he finally ended the kiss, more because he had a need for air and found he could barely breathe, Daniel left his forehead pressed against Clarinda's.

"Happy birthday," Clarinda whispered before she winced.

Alarmed at her expression of pain, Daniel straightened. "What is it?" he wondered, his hands gripping the tops of her arms.

"My back has been aching all day, and my water broke a few moments ago and ..." She winced again, this time sucking air through her teeth as her hands moved to the sides of her swollen belly.

"Broke?" Daniel repeated, dumbfounded.

Clarinda waved a hand at the wet spot on the Aubusson carpet below. "Yes, and despite your mother's claim that I would be in labor for hours and hours, I do believe these girls are intent on being born on their uncle's birthday," she managed to get out before she nearly doubled-over in pain.

"Oh," Daniel replied as he stepped back. "*Oh!*" His eyes wide and full of fright, he glanced about. "What do I ... what do I *do?*" he wondered. Seeing Clarinda's pain, he lifted her into his arms.

"Have Anna send for the midwife. And for the physician. And ..." Clarinda struggled for breath. "Put me into that chaise over there ..." She pointed toward the chaise lounge in the corner of the room.

Daniel moved toward the chaise even before Clarinda

could finish her sentence. "Stay with me." This last was delivered in a desperate whisper that Daniel could not ignore.

"Of course," he answered, reaching over to pull the bell chord to summon a servant. "Isn't this a bit ... soon?" he wondered, trying to keep the worry from his voice.

Clarinda nodded and then shrugged with one shoulder. "Well, maybe," she agreed. "Maybe not," she added with a shrug of her other shoulder before a contraction caused her to gasp.

Daniel's valet appeared at the door, obviously surprised at the sight of his master's wife on the chaise as well as in the painting that was leaning against the far wall. "Shall I send for a physician?" he asked, tearing his attention away from the painting to find Daniel giving him a quelling look. "Yes. And the midwife. And make it fast!"

Once the valet had taken his leave of the room, Daniel pulled the counterpane from the bed and tossed it over the painting, not wanting any other servants or the physician to see his birthday gift. He hurried back to Clarinda's side, not sure what else to do.

Despite Clarinda's insistence that Daniel remain in his bedchamber with her, the midwife shoo'd him out before she'd even knelt next to the chaise, claiming it would be hours before a babe would be born.

Cursing the older woman in a voice that could probably be heard down the entire length of Park Lane, Clarinda threatened to dismiss the woman from her employ. In a matter of moments, a baby girl appeared, surprising the midwife and causing Daniel to reappear at Clarinda's side.

"I'm here," he whispered, his stomach roiling at the sight of the bloodied baby the midwife was working to clean up with a linen towel. Clarinda's hand gripped his, the strength of her fingers causing him to grimace. "I intended to use those fingers to tickle our children," he managed to get out before Clarinda grasped his meaning and relaxed her hold.

"Sorry," she whispered. She watched as the midwife stood and moved toward the door. "Where are you going? I'm not *done* yet," Clarinda wailed. The piercing scream she let out had the midwife hurrying out the door, as if the woman feared for her very life.

"Christ!" Daniel cursed, glancing at the departing midwife before returning his attention to Clarinda. "Are you truly having another?" he asked, his breaths coming in short gasps that perfectly matched his wife's.

"I am," she replied, her face scrunching into pain as her keening filled the room.

Daniel removed his coat and undid the cuff links at his wrists. He pushed his sleeves up his arms and positioned himself where he'd seen the midwife just moments before. "Oh, God," he murmured, surprised at the sight of dark hair where his cock had been only the night before. "Oh, Christ," he added, moving a hand to rest under the head of an emerging baby.

The sound of Clarinda's cry trailed off as the babe spilled into in his arms. Not sure what to do, he cradled its head in one hand and held the rest in his other hand, hugging the wet baby against the front of his shirt. "Oh, my," he whispered. Although the tiny girl squirmed against his chest, Daniel's attention was on Clarinda. Her look of pain had been replaced with awe, her arms reaching out to the babe he suddenly realized he had cradled against him. He offered it to her just as it began to cry. "Are you ... are you well?" he wondered as he moved closer to her side.

Tears were streaming down her face. Her hair had come loose from its pins, some of the curls plastered against her damp forehead. The gown she wore was wrinkled and probably ruined beyond repair. But at that moment, Daniel thought Clarinda looked more beautiful than she ever had.

"I think so," she said, positioning the baby in one arm as she used a finger to wipe its face.

At that moment, the midwife returned to the room, the baby she carried now cleaned and wrapped in a blanket. "Oh!"

she let out, startled to see Clarinda holding a baby.

"'Oh' is right," Daniel spoke with a good deal of authority. He strode to where the midwife stood and took the baby from her arms. "If you could see to the other?" he hinted as he settled the newborn against his shoulder.

The midwife gave him a nervous curtsy before hurrying to retrieve the other baby from Clarinda. "Bring her back as soon as you can," Clarinda said as she took the first-born from Daniel.

"Yes, my lady," the woman replied as she hurried out the bedchamber door, her burden letting out a wail that seemed to fade as the woman moved to the next room.

Clarinda kissed her baby's head, murmured quiet assurances, and let out a long sigh when the infant fell asleep. "She's perfect," she whispered as she caressed her cheek against the newborn's downy covered head.

"They both are," Daniel whispered in reply, sitting down on the edge of the chaise. He leaned over and kissed Clarinda. "The best birthday presents I have ever received, I think," he murmured before using the fingers of one hand to comb her hair away from her face. "Thank you," he whispered, his gaze one of adoration.

"You're welcome, my lord," Clarinda replied with a grin. "And now you truly are the Earl of Norwick."

At the moment, Daniel couldn't have cared less as to his status as an earl, preferring the title of 'father' or even 'uncle' to the just-born girls. *And I am both*, he realized with a grin as he took the second-born from the nervous mid-wife's hands. *So tiny, so perfect.*

Clarinda sighed again. "Well, before these two demand their first dinner, I suppose I should use the time to send a note to Adele."

Daniel shook his head, not surprised Clarinda would seem ready to resume normal life. "Or you could spend the time sleeping," he suggested. "You must be exhausted." He moved to place the other baby in her empty arm.

Clarinda's eyes opened wide. "Sleeping?" she repeated,

her voice loud enough to fill the bedchamber. "There will be time enough for that when I'm *dead*," she countered defensively, returning her attention to the baby girls in her arms.

Daniel grinned, lowering his forehead so it touched hers. "I couldn't agree more, my lady. I couldn't agree more."

EXCERPT

Read on for an excerpt from Linda Rae Sande's
Book 3 in "The Sons of the Aristocracy" series
My Fair Groom

"He is rather handsome," Lady Samantha commented, one hand pressed against the glass of Lady Julia's bedchamber window. "In a brutish, very *manly* sort of way."

The object of her attention was obviously down below, for if anyone was handsome and directly outside Lady Julia's bedchamber, they would have to have wings and be able to fly or be perched upon rather tall stilts. There was no tree or trellis to provide a climber a way to reach the bedchamber from below.

"Who is?" Julia wondered, moving to join her friend at the window. Afternoon sunlight filtered into the room as she drew back the heavy velvet drape with one hand. Glancing down, she could see one of the kitchen maids cutting herbs in the garden below. Just behind the garden's low rock wall lay the paved alley, and beyond that, the mansion's mews and carriage house.

After a moment, she realized to whom Samantha referred. A groom was brushing her father's favorite riding horse, Thunderbolt, at the edge of the pavement. When the young man's head lifted to draw the brush down the animal's neck, the brim of his cap no longer hid his features.

Julia's inhalation of breath made Samantha smile. "You agree then?" she murmured, obviously pleased with her assessment. Before Julia could respond, the groom had paused in his task, removed the cricket cap that hid most of his facial features from the young ladies, and used his forearm to push a lock of his dark hair from his face. For just a moment, his face was angled up, his eyes closed against the afternoon sun.

Julia sighed her appreciation. "He *is* handsome," she agreed, wondering if the groom in question had noticed the two of them spying on him. The young man certainly didn't look like a typical groom. He was rather tall and lean, although Julia realized his shoulders were quite broad—he wore a shirt, its sleeves rolled up to his elbows, and a waistcoat, but no topcoat. The exposed forearms displayed muscles that shifted beneath his bronzed skin as he continued brushing Thunderbolt. When he moved around the horse to brush the side facing them, she noted the look of his boots, the shape of his legs in the almost snug breeches he wore.

When had a groom ever looked ... not like a groom? she wondered.

And when had he joined the staff of Harrington House?

She had never had this particular groom as an escort when she took her afternoon rides in Hyde Park, nor did she recognize him as the one who usually saddled her chestnut bay—she would remember this particular groom!

Just as she was about to remark on this fact, the groom in question bent down, presumedly to check Thunderbolt's hooves.

"Oh!" It was Samantha's turn to put voice to her appreciation of the groom's physique. "Even his bottom is ..." She left off as a giggle erupted. She moved her hand to cover her mouth as Julia joined her in her amusement.

"Everything about him is ..." Julia broke off suddenly and stepped away from the window, a hand over her own mouth. Samantha followed suit, her eyes quite wide.

"I think he saw me," Samantha whispered, a hint of shock in the simple words.

"I am quite *sure* he saw me," Julia countered, her hand moving from her mouth down to her chest. She felt the pounding of her heart beneath the sprigged muslin gown she wore.

Had the groom really spied her spying on him? One moment he had Thunderbolt's hoof in one hand, his attention on the shoe, and the next, he was standing with his back to the horse and his attention directed toward her bedchamber window. And her! Did the man have especially sensitive hearing? Despite the unusual warmth of the afternoon, her window was closed. What had compelled him to look up?

Julia finally glanced over at Samantha, her look of surprise still in place. Samantha's face was a mirror of her own. As if on cue, the two began to giggle, their embarrassment at having been discovered causing their cheeks to redden. "I do not know what has come over me," Julia said as she dared another glance out the window. "But I am quite convinced that groom is much too handsome to be a groom."

Samantha settled herself on the edge of Julia's bed, her arms crossing in front of her. "What would you have him be?" she wondered as she watched Julia's careful observation of the stables below.

"Well, not a groom, certainly," Julia replied after a moment. The groom's attention was back on Thunderbolt, one of his hands gripping the bridle as he led the beast into the stable. When he disappeared from sight, Julia turned around to face her friend. "Not a servant of any sort, in fact."

From where she sat on the bed, Samantha regarded Julia with a raised eyebrow. "What then?" she countered. "A shopkeeper? A solicitor? A vicar?" She lifted her head as she considered her friend's implication. "Or a gentleman?" she added to her list. Her eyes widened. "You think he should be a gentleman just because he is ... handsome?" she spoke with a hint of disbelief. "Julia!"

But Julia was shaking her head. "Not just because he is handsome, Sam," she replied, glancing out the window from a safe distance away. "He holds himself as if he is a gentleman, as if he were born to it," she reasoned.

"However can you tell from this far away?" Samantha countered, her eyebrows raising in disbelief.

Julia gave a shrug and turned back toward the window. "I just can," she replied. "In fact, if I were to have my brother's valet dress him, I would wager he could walk down Bond Street, and everyone would think him a gentleman."

Samantha's mouth dropped open. "Wager?" she repeated in shock. "Julia," she spoke in a scolding voice. "Be careful what you say, or I shall be tempted to dare you to do such a thing." She paused, thinking of how those from the country sometimes sounded when they spoke. What if the man was from Wales? Or Scotland? Or any of the northern counties? "I rather think as soon as he opens his mouth to speak, anyone who hears him will know he is not a gentleman."

A smile appeared on Julia's face. "Indeed?" she replied, a mischievous expression appearing. "Then, I shall go one better. I believe he can be taught to speak like a gentleman," she boasted, suddenly wondering from where the groom hailed. She could only hope he wasn't from Wales or Scotland. Or any of the northern counties.

Rolling her eyes, Samantha grinned. "And perform a perfect bow?" She rather liked having fun at her friend's expense. "He cannot be a true gentleman unless he can dance at a ball," she teased.

Julia straightened when she realized what her best friend was doing. She was daring her to make a gentleman out of the groom! "He can be taught how to bow. And how to dance. I am sure of it," she claimed, the color in her face turning to a pinkish blush as she made her case.

Samantha uncrossed her arms and stood up. "All right, then. I *dare* you to do it," she stated, the edges of her mouth curled up to indicate she wasn't completely serious. How could Julia make such a claim? "I dare you to make a gentleman out of your groom."

Crossing her arms and angling her head to one side, Julia regarded her friend for perhaps a few seconds too long. For just as she was about to admit she was perhaps a bit too boastful and concede defeat, Samantha said the only words that could make Julia change her mind again.

"I don't just dare you," Samantha whispered, her eyes closing to almost slits. "I double dog dare you."

ABOUT THE AUTHOR

A self-described nerd and lover of science, Linda Rae spent many years as a published technical writer specializing in 3D graphics workstations, software and 3D animation (her movie credits include SHREK and SHREK 2). An interest in genealogy led to years of research on the Regency era and a desire to write fiction based in that time.

A fan of action-adventure movies, she can frequently be found at the local cinema. Although she no longer has any fish, she does follow the San Jose Sharks. She makes her home in Cody, Wyoming. See more information about her books on her website: www.lindaraesande.com.

For more information:
www.lindaraesande.com

Lightning Source UK Ltd.
Milton Keynes UK
UKHW011836220421
382456UK00001B/144

9 780989 397360